RED SHADOW AND OTHER STORIES

Novels published by Midnight Fire Media

Your Own Fate
Night on Earth
Dreams Belong to the Night
ShadowWalk
Alarums of Reality
Afterglow Dust
Black Dragon
Falling
Thunder road - Ice and Fire
Season of the Witch

The Janus Clan series:

The Defenseless
The Slaves
Birds Flying in the Dark
At the End of the Rainbow

Poetry:

Amos Keppler: Complete Poems 1989 – 2003
Secrets - Descriptions of what cannot be described

(A few of the) novels to be published:

Afterglow Rain
Lewis of Modern York
Fangs and Claws of the Earth
Forsaken
Resurrection Dreams

For a «complete» list of current and current future Amos Keppler and Midnight Fire Media projects see the back of the book and the Midnight Fire/Midnight Fire Media web pages.

Red Shadow and Other Stories

by

Amos Keppler

Midnight Fire Media
2018

Midnight Fire Media

http://midnight-fire.net/mfm
For more about Red Shadow and the other stories:
http://midnight-fire.net/rsaos

E-Mail:
Amos13@midnight-fire.net
manofhood@yahoo.com

Cover, text, design, premedia, art and photos Amos Keppler

ISBN 978-82-91693-23-1

main contents

and several short short stories

Red Shadow

«And the veil of all the years goes sinking from my eyes like a stone».
Nostradamus - Al Stewart

Chapter One

The harsh gales didn't batter him.

The wind brought a scent, one of rust and dawn.

He stood on dusty ground, looking at the dark red skies, and he dreamt of blood, and death and sacrifice.

The alarm on the night table woke him abruptly. He sat there, on the bed, staring at the dark red wall, soaked in sweat. The window drew him close. He looked down at the street far below. Mrs. Richards and several others left for work. He returned to the bed and picked up the alarm clock. This had been its second call. He hadn't woken up the first time and he was late.

Finally, he started moving, started speeding up his day. Lethargy, sleep stuck in him like dull claws. He remembered the shower. It woke him up, like always, at least from the daze where he had found himself before he stepped into the tight cabinet. He remembered eating, chewing the dry sandwiches at an accelerated speed.

Most of the day was a blur to him. Events faded away in his memory the moment he experienced them.

There was the city traffic, the Underground on his way to work, the slight scent of the office in his nostrils, one or two faces not delegated to forgetfulness.

The long, bright daylight faded away, as if it had never been there at all.

He left a busy building in the central parts of the city late in the afternoon. People flowed through the wide entrance. He stopped outside. The red western sky, with its elaborate cloud patterns was already turning dark, like the rest of the heavens above.

Something moved in his vision. His head turned, practically by itself.

He saw her stand outside the underground station. She looked at him with a steady, direct stare. There was no way of mistaking it. She didn't attempt to hide her… her interest at all. He didn't know her, had never seen her before in his life, but there was something strangely familiar about her he couldn't quite place.

She crossed the street on red, not even bothering with or bothered by the cars, and their loud horns, never taking her eyes off him. He wanted to look away, embarrassed by the attention, but something kept him from doing that. So, he kept looking at her. There was something about her, something that made it impossible for him to look away. Intrigued beyond words, caught in a grip of his own making he followed her the last few steps of her forward walk until she stopped in front of him, or almost in front of him, suddenly a

bit hesitant.
– Lawrence Watros? She asked, clearly puzzled.
– Larry, he replied, quite baffled. – It's Larry. Everyone calls me Larry.
– I'm Nelli, she said, reaching out a hand.
He took her hand, reeling at her uncannily strong grip.
– Nice to meet you, Nelli, he grinned.
She reddened. She was actually blushing right there in front of him, and he felt a little better, a little less aware his own shortcomings.
– Is there a place we can go? She asked strangely calm.
– I know a place, he said.
He took her hand boldly, surprising himself. She didn't object, but let herself be led down the street. He noticed the people around him, noticed them as hardly more than shadows, than hazy shapes not really there. The touch of the girl's smaller, strong hand burned his skin.
The bar had always opened early, for as long as he could remember. It was a place that had had many names. He had never really noticed any of them, and didn't now either.
They sat in the darkest corners of the room. She seemed to be more comfortable there than in the brighter spots of the place. He made himself look at her, stare into her downright weird eyes. She studied him, too. He realized that. But there was something uncanny about her interest or whatever it was.
He felt a sense of foreboding, of fear.
She was pale. After considering it for a while he would say she was unnaturally pale. It occurred to him like she had probably never been subjected to a second of sunlight in her entire life, as if someone had taken her to a dark cellar right after birth and held her there. Her eyes… they looked red. He was positive there was a red glimmer there, behind the close to colorless front. Her pale blonde hair had a reddish taint, but looked brown or like it didn't have any color at all.
The conversation was slow to start. He was afraid of scaring this wonderful creature off and she kept quiet, mostly responding to his small talk or its feeble attempt.
– Where do you come from, Nelli?
– I was told you would be different. She nodded to herself.
Enigmatic as well. He nodded to himself. A confused country girl on her first trip to town or a schemer out to have… have fun at his expense? His eyes narrowed slightly.
– You know, he joked, – I was certain that I imagined you looking at me and being on your way towards me when you crossed the street, and that

you would turn away and greet your boyfriend standing right behind me or something.

He had looked. There had been no one there. He re-experienced the moment, practically relived it.

– I was on my way to you, she stated softly.

She kept looking at him, hardly taking her eyes off him. He felt like blushing.

The drinks arrived. He grabbed one and pushed one over to her.

– Cheers, he said.

– Cheers, she echoed, taking the glass.

He drank. She drank. The strong liquor burned in his throat. He studied her, wondering if her breath turned a little more labored, looking for a deeper texture on her skin.

– It burns, she said.

– It does indeed, he acknowledged.

She looked confident, a citizen of the world.

She looked insecure, a country girl on her first trip to town.

He marveled at her clothes. They were… different, even in a city where clothing was an expression of self, of variety or at least a pretense of such.

– I don't understand, she said.

What exactly she didn't understand he wasn't quite clear on.

– I know what you mean. He nodded. – I've never really understood why people drink either.

She looked like, or resembled an albino, but he didn't understand that either. The red glare in the eyes was a kind of illusion, stemming from the lack of pigmentation in the corona. That fit. But he had seen albinos, and they didn't look anything like her. The way he understood it, there was no middle ground. You were either an albino, born without pigmentation, or you weren't. Ordinary redheads often had pale skin, but nothing like this.

– I was sent here, she stated, seemingly out of the blue.

Again.

– From where? Where are you from, Nelli?

He took her hands, sensing the burning heat of the alcohol spreading in his body and mind, a buzz slowly devouring him, like her close to non-pigmented eyes.

– Where? He prompted.

– Here, she replied in something very much resembling an automatic response. – I'm from here. I didn't walk long, not long at all.

She looked around her, wide-eyed, at the people in the room drinking and swearing and laughing.

But she also retained her calm, as if her surroundings didn't really faze her.

And he remained the focus of her attention.

Her eyes, her attention so different from that of all other women he had known, from anyone he had known.

There was no duplicity there, at least not in the ordinary way, the way he was used to. She studied him in a frank and even callous way, the way an observer might do from afar, not up close like this.

– So, do I measure up? He grinned.

She frowned again.

– A… joke? She frowned.

– A joke, he nodded, he shrugged.

He couldn't figure her out, and she seemed to have trouble figuring him out, too, and that was even weirder.

– So, you were sent here to meet me? He queried. – Has it got anything to do with the firm?

She tilted her head.

– No! She shook her head.

– But you knew my name, he said.

– Yes!

Nelli replied.

She hesitated.

– The… man sending me to you told me your name. I didn't know it before then, before that very moment.

– That sounds very puzzling to me, Larry said, shaking his head. – I don't understand.

– Neither do I, she stated.

She seemed to be thinking it through, considering something, before nodding to herself.

– He sent me to assist you, she said. – He said you would need it.

– In what way? He wouldn't, couldn't let up.

– You're in danger, Lawrence Watros, she said. – One of my many tasks here is to protect you.

He began sweating. The conversation was quickly spiraling out of control, becoming something completely different from what it had looked like a minute ago. He looked around him, suddenly very conscious of his surroundings. He looked for the candid camera crew, anything that would relieve the fear growing in his gut.

– That's ridiculous, he snorted. – Or at least not very plausible. No one is threatening me.

– I don't understand it either. She nodded, acknowledged. – But he insisted.

She rose, reaching out a hand.

– Come, she insisted, almost pleaded. – We must go. It's not safe here.

– Are you… are you from the intelligence or something.

– Yes, she replied. – I am from intelligence.

There was an accent there. He hadn't noticed it before, distracted by her obvious interest in him, but now he did. What he had taken for a local dialect was clearly a sign of a foreign influence.

I'm a nobody, he thought.

– Why would anyone want to harm me? I'm not threatening anyone. My job is hardly secretive or sensitive in any way, and…

My life sucks.

He followed her through the crowd, the crowds inside and outside. It was all a blur, suddenly, faint as a mirage. It didn't seem…

It didn't seem real.

– The way I understand it it's a matter of circumstances, more than a direct, obvious threat. She spoke fast, almost too fast for him to follow, while leading him away, down the street, and into totally unknown territory. – Seemingly unrelated events converging to strike you down.

– That sounds even worse, he cried.

She stopped, although her eyes, the entire her kept moving, almost on autopilot.

– It's Quantum Mechanics, Chaos Theory in practice, she said slowly, patiently, with a voice chemically free of irritation. – You just have to look for it, look for the pattern behind the veil, beneath the surface in a given population or society. Everything is in constant flux. All the elements are there, for things to begin moving, but nothing happens, because something crucial is missing. But suddenly, in what might be in a blink of an eye everything is turned upside down, transformed. A liquid surface may look peaceful, but throw a rock, a pebble in it, and everything changes.

He stood on a dusty surface and stared at an uneven, remote landscape, and he could almost make out what she was saying.

Insane music flowed from speakers in a building they passed. It resonated within him, and he didn't understand it.

He didn't understand.

She mumbled something.

He looked at her, and she turned her attention to him, as if she had known he would do that.

– This is all so… transitory, she said, – and superficial. The people here… they look more like specters than actual humans of flesh and blood.

There was something in her voice, in her eyes, in her words… It made him even more anxious.

He studied the passing people, attempting to tune in to whatever… channel she was tuned in on, doing so more or less openly, not casually, like a trained observer like she obviously was. He saw the carefree laughter of people celebrating, at least in modest ways a night out.

There was a kind of unrest below the surface, a kind of nervous flickering in everyone's eyes, but this was a big city. Stuff like that was practically mandatory in places like this.

And then it was her, her impassive mask, revealing nothing of what she was thinking or who she was. She seemed more like a mirror than any mirror he had ever faced, and he saw something, yet another flicker of something he couldn't fathom.

– They look happy, she said softly, – but they're really filled with sorrow and emptiness. What a sad bunch they are.

And Larry shook. Holding up his hand he could see it tremble. No matter how hard he attempted to hold it steady, he couldn't do it.

His heart hammered in his chest as they moved, as they moved like… like daggers through the modern city night. He attempted… In a hopeless attempt at being dangerous he emulated, somehow, her movements, but he was like a clumsy child compared to an adult samurai. She was trained in this, whatever it was, that much was certain.

He didn't see any weapons, not in her hands, and not on her body, not even blades. Her movements were very economical, measured. She moved in conjunction with the people on the street, with the street itself, fading in and out as she passed in and out of the shadows. He couldn't take his eyes off her. The truth slowly dawned on him: She was a weapon.

She returned his interest with slightly lowered eyes, seemingly… embarrassed? A shiver passed through her. She stopped, shaking her head in what had to be a kind of confusion.

– I'm sorry, she said. – I'm distracted.

– I've been known to have that impression on women, he joked again, deliberately adding candor to his voice to make that clear.

– But it makes me unfit! She cried, uncharacteristically emotional. – I can't do my job, the task I've been charged with.

– I'm positive you will perform excellently, if it comes to that, he said. – Sometimes the unexpected happens, that's all.

Another shiver passed through her, as she visibly pulled herself together, as the weapon was once more primed and ready.

– You are so wise, she said, with blatant admiration in her eyes.

He blinked. He hadn't seen wrong, had he? A girl he had just met had the hots for him?

– You sought me out, he stated. – Why?

She looked clearly uncomfortable again.

– I have already told you why. She frowned. – I was sent here.

She stepped closer to him, until their faces were close, breath to breath close.

– But I wanted to come, she whispered. – I embraced my mission.

He grabbed her shoulders, intending to pull her closer, close. Her lips parted, and her fresh breath invigorated him.

Something happened around them, distracting them. He noticed it only a moment or so after she did.

There were people here, and they weren't merely passing through.

The two of them found themselves in a closed-off square, a bit off the town's main walkabouts. He saw how distraught she was. He noticed that long before he noticed all the people surrounding them.

– What have we here?

There was a voice in the multitude of bodies. He heard it strangely clear. The other people, all of them, related to it, to the man moving forward towards Watros and Nelli. Watros noticed it in every little move the crowd made. Nelli looked distraught, more than a little, too. He sensed her anger, her calm, everything about her as she tensed, as her supple limbs turned even more so. She looked incredulous, not scared, both easily enough identifiable emotions.

– We have two loose birds in our neighborhood, and they shouldn't be here.

The large man stopped in front of the two, the two intruders. Watros realized it startled. They were strangers here, and not welcome.

– This is just a misunderstanding, Watros tried, without much hope of success. – We took the wrong turn somewhere…

– Ain't that the truth…

The stupid comment caused ripples of fake laughter to stir the gathering. Watros' fear was supplanted by just a tiny bit of anger, of resentment towards the people hounding them with their very presence.

– We will leave, now, Watros stated.

More laughter, more throaty sounds resembling cackling.

– We will leave, now, Nelli said. – If you stand in our way we will kill you.

The crowd fell silent. In fact, the silence dominated to such a degree that they could all easily hear the traffic several blocks away. Incredulity conquered their faces, but they didn't step aside or made any sign that they would. Nelli moved, and Watros moved in her slipstream. Two big bruisers tried blocking their path. Nobody saw exactly what happened. Watros certainly didn't. She moved, and the two lay on the ground with their throats cut open and bleeding freely. He saw that her hands… her hands had turned red.

A woman attempted to draw a weapon, a knife, a man a gun. They had joined their comrades on the ground before another heartbeat had been completed. Nelli nodded to herself, as she kept moving, as the slaughter began. They hardly saw more than a blur of motion as she moved among them, and slaughtered them like pigs. But she didn't truly move that fast, at least he didn't think she did. It was just that it was so effective, so beyond lethal that it made him shiver all over.

He saw how she gutted a man with the knife, and shot another in the head with a gun. She had merely picked the weapons up in stride from those she had recently killed, using them in inventive ways he had never seen before, not even on film.

Close to fifteen people lay dead on the ground. He didn't care to count them exactly.

She held the leader in her grip, her strong grip, pushing him at the brick wall. Larry marveled at how strong she was. She held him high. His feet didn't touch the ground. His eyes bulged so much that they threatened to jump from their sockets. She slit his throat, doing it with her hand, her nails again, her deadly hand, her sharp as claws fingers.

He studied her as she walked among the bodies, as she totally unmoved killed those still breathing.

– I brought us here, she said. – They must die, every single one of them. You would never have come here, if not for me.

Those words weren't exactly less cryptic compared to everything else she had said, in the short time, during the flashes, the moments, he had known her.

She turned towards him.

– Are you injured?

His voice sounded so weird. He was surprised to note that it didn't sound hoarse, not hoarse at all.

– No, she said calmly, smiling a little to him, – it isn't my blood.

They left. The running through dark alleys hardly tired him, hardly tired him at all. He was stunned to discover that he was hardly breathing harder when they stopped for a bit, and he studied her, saw how she was constantly on her guard, constantly listening.

They kept walking, kept removing themselves further from danger.

– You need to clean yourself, he told her.

She stopped, frowning.

– Of course, she nodded. – I forgot. How could I forget?

He grabbed a sheet from a nearby laundry hanging to dry, and wrapped around her.

– Thank you, she said… coquettishly? – Thank you… Larry.

He wiped the worst of the blood from her face, unable, of course, to do anything about her hair. But he suspected it would only look like auburn hair in the shadows and colorful lights of the dark, anyway. He rubbed it a bit, making it redder, a more even kind of red.

– You have never seen action before, she stated, nodding to herself. – Never seen death. And you still handle it in ways few others would.

– When I'm not wetting my pants, he grunted.

She giggled. He relived the fight in his mind. His good memory wouldn't let him forget, wouldn't even let the horror fade. He saw her sweet face superimposed by the carnage she had so casually and callously wrought.

Featherlight lips touched his, before she pulled back, shy as a bird, one confounding him further.

They kept walking, not entering the underground or any public transport, but kept walking until they had reached the opposite side of town, hours later, the visuals of the many streets his eyes at some point had caught, must have been caught dim in his memory. He remembered her shifting and unmoving face, every second of it, how she had constantly kept an eye or ten on their surroundings. Time had passed without him really noticing, without him even glancing at his watch.

His feet hurt. The shoes had been too tight after all, at least for such a prolonged, to him exhausting and seemingly endless walk. His legs had turned wobbly some time ago, even though he couldn't tell exactly when.

– Long office hours, he explained when she cast him a worried look.

It was uncanny how well they communicated, silent, without words, and how they still didn't understand each other at all.

– I'm not afraid of you, he stated, suddenly, out of thin air.

– I didn't think you would be, she replied.

– I mean, I should be, he continued, as if she hadn't spoken. – You killed those guys like… like a pro, hardly even breaking a sweat. You did so with impunity, without the slightest remorse, and yet I know you're no threat to me.

He sat down on a bench, one wet and cold after the night's rain, and he didn't care.

– I'm soaked, anyway…

He cackled, and hardly recognized his own voice.

She sat down beside him.

Eyes met again, and the sense of familiarity made him faint.

– You're disturbed by today's unexpected events, she said softly. – It would be strange if you weren't.

– Unexpected… He shook his head in bewilderment. – You sure got a way with words, lady…

– I studied and trained hard, she replied. – And I had excellent teachers.

Something was off, all the time. He just couldn't put his finger on what.

– You realized the dangers if the public discovered my blood-soaked body, she stated. – That's a very good thing. My guess is that most people in this city wouldn't have thought of that, no matter how obvious it is.

She still had the dark sheet wrapped around her body. It looked like quite the fashion thing, not really suspicious at all. It had indeed been a brilliant inspiration, improvisation, especially considering the circumstances.

– So, who's after me?

– As stated, I don't know, she replied. – I just know that the threat exists.

– And you were given license to kill anybody threatening me?

– They're not important, she said, boldly touching his cheek. – You are.

I should be cold, he thought. I'm not. I'm burning up.

He wouldn't be surprised if his clothes dried by themselves. His skin felt that hot, that burning hot, and he wasn't sick, even though he felt it as if he was running a fever.

Her eyes kept moving. They always did that. She noticed that he noticed and frowned.

– You don't scan the surroundings, she noted. – And you find it puzzling that I do.

There was a question mark there at the end.

– Of course, you do, she nodded.

She rose, swift and gracious like a cat.

– Come, she said, – we must keep moving. We should get you back, back home.

– But wouldn't that be… risky? Shouldn't we avoid familiar places, where people may be… looking for me?

– No! She shook her head. – That was what I did wrong earlier. I brought you to an unfamiliar place, outside your usual haunts. It will be easier to protect you in familiar surroundings, because you will more easily recognize things and people not belonging there.

She rushed ahead, and he followed her. He walked in front and she followed. And he was positive that she never let down her guard, not for a moment. But he also saw that she cast glances at him, now, clearly seeking his approval, and that was yet another thing that didn't make sense to him, didn't make sense at all.

– You know, I am puzzled by your level of awareness, he said, – but it would be very silly of me to wish otherwise… since you are here to protect me, and all.

And there was that strange mix of shame and gratitude in her eyes again.

– I am distracted, she said. – I'll do better.

And she became cold, distant, and businesslike again, a sharp blade walking the night. He almost felt hurt, abandoned.

He staggered. She was instantly there to keep him from falling.

– Christ! He laughed embarrassed. – I actually feel lightheaded. That almost never happens to me.

– You need sustenance, she said. – We haven't fed the entire night. Is there a place we can go, one you know well?

He nodded, while constantly attempting to keep up with her, her beyond sane paranoia. One moment he thought she was insane, and that he was, too, for following her, believing her. And the next there was no doubt in his mind that she was genuine. And that was probably the most insane of all.

His watch still worked. He looked at it, and at the clock in «Rostock» the combined grocery store and cafeteria they entered. It showed the same time. Twelve hours had passed since he had left work, and she had approached him outside the building.

– Hi, Larry, Sam, the man behind the counter greeted him, – burning the midnight, midnight oil, I see.

– Yeah, the «midnight» oil it is. Larry attempted to study him without studying him. – Nice meeting you, too…

He saw nothing, nothing out of the ordinary. It was just Sam standing there.

They sat down in a corner. He had read in crime novels that that was a smart thing to do. One got a good look at the room, and could observe everyone in it, everyone entering or leaving. She looked at him, attentive and eager.

– It's a good thing we came here, he said. – I had planned on dining out tonight. There are hardly crumbs left in my fridge.

She nodded, serious minded, clearly concentrating, even though he knew she hardly needed to concentrate. Every one of her moves was flow, grace and lethal economics. When she needed focus it just came to her, as easy as breathing. But sometimes, she seemed puzzled by the most mundane thing. He realized, if he hadn't realized it before that she was a walking contradiction.

He bought milk, juice, fruit and all he could think of that would give them quick sustenance. Then he found what he would usually buy, if he hadn't been told he was in mortal danger.

– Here, he said, giving her one of the apples, keeping one for himself, – this will be digested by your system in half an hour, and energize us faster than lightning.

She tilted her head, and studied him again.

– I read that somewhere, he confessed.

She took a bite of the apple, a big bite. He studied her. She looked astounded at him, as she stood there, frozen with the half-digested apple in her hand. He moved, and she moved, too. She took another bite. He realized that she studied him, to see how he ate his apple. She was clearly mimicking him, even though she struggled to conceal it. And he wondered if this was her first.

Her first ever.

She had another apple, and she devoured it like a hungry beast. Fingers like claws grabbed an orange, and wolfed that down, too.

– It is almost immediate, she acknowledged a while later. – It reminds me of…

Her claw-like hand grabbed his, grabbed it almost gently.

– You are a natural at this, she said. – I knew you would be.

She looked at him, but she looked at everyone else in the room, too, and he caught himself in doing the same.

He saw some unfamiliar faces, but they were just strangers. They belonged here, really, fit in, just as much as those he recognized, just a few more late-night stragglers and truck drivers passing by.

She studied him. He realized she did it to measure his response to the surroundings.

– Yes, I study you, to see if there is well-founded worry, she nodded, – whether or not you're… spooked. I'm trained as an observer as well as a combatant. It goes hand in hand, really.

– You are not the date I envisioned for tonight, he joked. – But you'll do.

– You know these haunts, Lawrence Watros, she said, leaning forward. – I don't. You must lead.

Her intensity scared him, but encouraged him, too.

And attracted him.

He had never met anyone like her.

– We should go home, he said. – Not make ourselves a target.

She accepted his words with a slight nod. And before he had had time to consider it further they were on their way. The somewhat chilly wind hit him the moment he stepped outside, but strangely enough it affected him only in minor ways. Something burned within, making a nuisance of a little wind.

Sirens faded in and out in his ears. He saw a flash of red light before it was gone, only red.

She noticed. He knew she did.

– There are always loud sounds here. She frowned. – Noise.

– One thing about any major city is that you can always hear sirens. He nodded.

– And see the red lights, she stated.

Someone screamed not far from there, a loud shriek stemming from pain and fear, a wail to chill anybody's blood, at least Larry's. She didn't react in any notable way.

– And suffering, she continued. – Everybody walks around with a dull knife in their hearts, but they don't take any action to pull it out.

She stopped and turned towards him, a flicker of uncertainty clearly showing in her eyes.

– I find that highly disturbing. She frowned (she frowned a lot). – And I don't know why. And that, too, disturbs me. Does that make sense?

– I think it makes a lot of sense, he assured her.

She flashed him a grateful smile again, and he didn't know why.

They encountered a few people walking down the street. Nelli x-rayed each and every one of them. Larry didn't doubt she was ready to act - and kill - at a moment's notice.

But it was just the last few stragglers heading home before dawn's early light hit them.

– My block is just around the corner, he said, – but I guess you know that already. You must have been briefed quite extensively about me.

She nodded, serious minded.

He looked around, scanning their surroundings, or at least trying to, before continuing.

– I can't believe we've done this, he said. – You've walked around with blood all over you for hours, and nobody has noticed. I can't believe I haven't totally freaked.

– It is as I said, she grinned. – You are a natural at this.

And in that eerie grin he saw everything worth seeing.

He sensed a wind, a hot one, blowing in his face, but when he looked at the branches on the trees and the girl's hair he saw no movement, no evidence that the breath of hot wind had any tangible existence.

She looked at him, penetrated him with her direct stare, smiling.

Two uniformed policemen walked towards them on the sidewalk. He studied her. She seemed totally calm, unafraid. The policemen passed them, and vanished in the dark behind them. Larry discovered he had practically been holding his breath, and that the heart hammered in his chest. He put on speed, walked markedly faster the final stretch to his block, while attempting to keep up the appearance of a casual return home.

Mrs. Richards cast them a glance, as she passed them on her way to work. It was that early, that late.

– Hello, Mrs. Richards, he greeted her, very good humored. – Nice meeting you this fine morning.

She mumbled something, hardly even acknowledging him.

Nelli didn't frown this time, but curiosity clearly manifested in her eyes.

– You were being ironic?

– I was indeed, he grinned.

She looked like she wanted to say something, but held back. He didn't push her about it. She made sure she walked inside first, as a precaution, holding up a hand to keep him two steps behind. When he pushed the button to make the lift door slide open she made him stand a bit to the side, tensing a bit before the room inside was revealed as empty.

– Home territory might be dangerous, she said. – A person feels safer, and can more easily be taken off-guard.

She stepped sideways into the elevator, while she kept looking in all directions at once. He followed her inside. The doors slid close, and they were on their way up.

The doors slid open, thirteen floors above ground. The city below revealed itself to them. He noticed that she stopped for a while, as if being dizzy, before her face once more turned impassive, closed again and her mind adopted to the circumstances. She walked ahead, and in a labyrinth of hallways and turns she chose the right direction, every time. He registered that without surprise.

He followed her, out of breath, strangely not because of the strenuous rush through the hallways, but because of the process of watching her move.

– You're Growing, she told him, as they stopped before the door to his apartment. – That is to be expected. That is good. You've caught a glimpse of the world, of how it truly is, Lawrence Watros, and you live to tell the tale.

His hand searched in his pocket for the key, but before it had found anything in his suddenly so very large pocket, she had opened the door. He blinked, unable to tell how it had actually happened.

The doors slid close behind them. She stood at the center of the floor in the living room, and watched him.

– We've reached Sanctuary, she said, – or at least its fairly close approximate. We can relax, for now. What do you want me to do, my…

She held back.

– What were you about to say? He wondered. – Tell me!

– Nothing, she mumbled, staring at the floor. – Nothing important.

– You should shower, he said. – Clean yourself. And we must get rid of your bloody clothes.

– At once. She straightened, as if saluting him, all of it, the works, except for being short of the actual salute.

She walked straight to the bathroom in the hallway. He saw her, as she turned the corner, heard her, as she opened and closed the door. A bit later he stood there, listening to the sound of the shower.

He stood by the window, staring into the darkness, the unknown. The approaching dawn still seemed far, far away. The sound, all the noises seemed extraordinary numerous, seemed infinite in number. He reached above his head, towards the high ceiling, and failed, as always to touch it. The rooms in the building, like with so many of the new condos in the area had previously been used as offices, creating a rather unique setting. He liked it. It didn't remind him of work at all.

It wouldn't be any work for him today, and he didn't mind, didn't mind at all.

He noticed the sounds from the street below. It had always puzzled him how they seemed louder up here than down there. He heard her, too, but way too late. Even if she hadn't been his physical superior, he would have been unable to stop her from… from killing him, or whatever she had wanted to do.

– I was testing you, she said sheepishly. – Sorry.

– Don't be. Thinking about it, it clearly seems to be a wise course of action.

He saw something in her eyes again, but didn't understand it, any more than he had done.

She had dressed herself in his clothes, his plain clothes. Her body filled them out in most places, being far more dense and muscular than his. She noticed his look, his obvious awkwardness. He noticed it easily by observing her.

– Yes, she nodded. – You've lived the life of the unaware, but that part of your life is over now.

There were cracks outside, sudden and shocking. Before he managed to react, she was on him, pushing him down, shielding him with her own body. A part of him kept calm, kept reasoning. It was amazing watching and studying her, see how her body and mind worked. There were no more cracks. She looked through the window, into the darkness, assessing the situation. And then she moved. It took him one moment, two before he realized she was heading for the balcony. He attempted to speak.

She opened the door.

– It's only fireworks, he cried.

She jumped from the balcony, and into the air. He wanted to cry out again, but there was no need. She had heard him the first time, but she had been so worked up that her reaction time had been delayed.

And then something incredible happened.

She froze in the air, standing still there, as if she was standing on something solid, and not air.

– Oops…

He saw her face, even though she stood, *levitated* with her back to him.

– You have a scar on your left shoulder, she said calmly, half turned away from him. – You got it when a stray bullet grazed you during your brief military service.

He finally realized it. She resembled a soldier.

– You broke your left foot when you were seven. Your father, disliking doctors didn't take you to a hospital. The fracture grew wrong, and you had to go to the hospital and reset it. You kissed your first girl the day you turned sixteen. It happened in her bedroom, with her parents doing it in the room next to hers.

He heard her dispassionate voice, as she told him more secrets, secrets he had never shared with anyone. There was no or little thought beyond stark disbelief.

She turned, turned in the air, free-floating back to him and the balcony, and the sense of unreality plaguing him the entire evening was finally hitting him like a blow.

– I come from the future, she said. – *You* sent me here.

Chapter Two

Nellie levitated back to the balcony, and closing the door behind them, they returned to the relative safety of the living room, of the quiet apartment.

He couldn't keep his eyes off her. She placed herself before him, displaying herself with a proud smile, and finally spoke.

– You told me to not tell you, until I exposed myself naturally. I wasn't sure what that meant, until it happened. You knew I would fail.

She showed him her hands for the first time, truly showed him. Her fingers didn't have nails, but claws. They were short, but sharp, at the very least as dangerously looking as any set of animal claws he had ever seen. This was what had cut the throats of the people in the alley. He shivered visibly, feeling strangely calm.

Every strange thought and notion he had entertained during the long day and night returned and hit him like a brick.

– You doubt? She nodded softly, looking at him with her pale eyes. – In spite of the wonders I've shown you? I guess it is to be expected.

– I don't doubt my own eyes, he said, his words sounding distant, as if he didn't truly speak them at all. – But it is still a stretch to… to compute your words.

– Most people, at least of this time, would doubt their senses, she said. – But you are not like them.

Her clothes began changing, changing back into her uniform. He saw no bloodstains.

– My clothes clean… themselves, she stated. – Even current forensic tests won't find a molecule of the blood.

She saw his expression, his incredulity, his slow, dawning acceptance, and nodded. The special smile lit her face, as she stood straight before him.

– Greetings, Red Shadow, she declared. – I've been sent here to safeguard you by your future self, during the difficult time of your Transition. He sends his regards and his curses.

Her voice had changed somehow, almost completely in inflection. She didn't act anymore. The night suddenly made some sort of sense to him.

– Red Shadow? He inquired, fearing his jaw had dropped to his chest.

– That was the name I knew you by, she replied, – my entire life, until you told me your birth name a cycle ago. You never told anyone else, as I am aware of, but you told me. That makes me very proud… Larry.

The way she said his name… he had never heard anyone say it quite like that before.

– And I'm yours to command, she stated, and he easily heard the pride in her voice, saw it in her stance and eyes.

– Is that wise? He wondered. – You're certainly more qualified than me to assess threats.

– You told me to obey you, in all things, she told him, encouraged him. – You know best.

– I must have turned insane on my older days, he joked. – It's funny. There have never been any signs of insanity in the family.

– I will advice you, and react to direct, explicit threats, she stated evenly. – But aside from that I will only act on your direct orders. I'm at your disposal in all things.

Her words echoed within him, pulled his guts in a thousand ways. The sound of her voice and the very sight of her churned in his mind forever. He noticed, absentmindedly the first rays of sunlight flow into the room, and noticed the tears twinkling on her cheeks.

– The light bothers you, doesn't it?

– Yes, she whispered. – The daystar is so bright.

He walked to the windows and pulled the dark curtains in front of them. The shadows once more dominated the room. He returned to her, and dried her tears. Her skin felt strange against his.

– I was born and raised in the ground, she said, – below the surface of the Earth. We hardly ever ventured up there, and almost never in daylight, and then we wore dark goggles.

She pulled something from her pockets, and there they were, the goggles. He could hardly see through them at all. Much more about her made sense. He nodded. She had adapted to a life underground.

Something about her, the way she looked at him, the way she stood. He realized startled that… that she was posing for him. And that he, from one moment to the next had grown a painful hard on.

The fabric melted off her body. In a matter of seconds, she stood completely nude before him. He stared astounded at her, as she looked at him with eyes filled with desire.

He couldn't avoid spotting the scars on her body, some old and some new, but they didn't seem in any way important compared to the sensual moves of the creature in front of him.

– You need to tie me up, she said.

– What? He blinked, replying in a daze.

– You need to tie me up, or I will kill you, rip you to shreds in my fervor.

He recalled the sight of her claws, and nodded, half calm, half beside himself. His feet moved, even while he remained in front of the naked girl.

He fetched the thick rubber ropes he used to hang clothes on from the balcony, and returned to the living room. She hadn't moved. He heard her breathe. His eyes caught her wet thighs, her hard nipples and swollen breath, her half open mouth.

– We're fierce lovers, she stated proudly. – I will please you, and please you immensely.

Her voice had turned hoarse, thick with expectation. She left the room, and walked through the hallway to his bedroom, and he, feeling like an idiot followed her there.

She lay down on the bed, on her back, stretching her arms and feet in four directions. He wondered, as he began tying her up, about the fact that he had found four ropes and not three or five. He wondered about his confidence.

– Leave a little slack, she instructed him humbly. – The ropes are thick and strong. They will hold.

He tied her right hand to the bedpost first, in hard, brutal moves, tightening the ropes. Then the left hand, and the right and left foot. He noticed the claws on the feet as well.

She lay there, writhing as much as the ropes allowed, looking at him in need and trust.

– I'm yours, she said. – You may do with me as you wish. I'm your helpless captive. You will do with me as you wish.

She sounded so sure, so confident. He shook his head in acceptance. She smiled.

He began undressing, but he experienced it as if his clothes melted off his body, just as hers had done, not really like undressing at all. His cock stood out like a sore thumb, and it felt like everything he was had gathered down below.

It was as if he beheld himself from outside himself, observing his potbelly and flabby body, and he knew, looking at her that she didn't see the image he saw, and that made him feel both ashamed and exhilarated. He crawled into the bed. She began shaking the ropes. But she couldn't really move much. She had been right. The ropes held.

He crawled on top of her. A hand touched her left thigh. It was soaking wet. She pushed her body against his, pushed her hips up. He kissed her lips. She responded instantly, naturally and beyond eagerly. He caught sight of the claws, of them flashing in the light of the distant lamps, and he felt himself turning hard. She noticed immediately, and her eyes turned misty. A loud, prolonged moan rose deep from her throat. He pushed himself at her, pushed himself deep within her, and he couldn't' believe how hard he had become.

She pulled the ropes. Pulled, pulled, pulled. They stretched, but held. Her claws raked at the rubber, but aside from a few scratches it didn't really impact the ropes very much.

He saw it all, noticed it all, in a series of flashes while he pounded on her body, while he pumped into her, while pleasure exploded all over his body and hers, and in both their minds, until they became for one, brief moment a single entity breathing together, and bathing in each other's juices there on the bed. They cried out, loud enough to shake the walls, and he didn't care. For that brief moment he didn't care at all, and nothing mattered, except the explosion spreading from deep within him and to every piece of skin on his body. He lay there, on top of her, kissing her, wildly, and she fiercely returned the kisses.

They slowly relaxed there on the bed, enjoying each other's close proximity. He untied her. It was a difficult task. The ropes had been pulled hard, and he had to use guile, not force to untangle them.

He held on to one of her arms, mumbling a stupid apology when he saw the bruises on her wrists.

– It's okay. She soothed him. – We learn to handle pain.

She curled up close to him, sighing happily with her head resting on his shoulder.

It was so peaceful, but at the same it was like a thousand ants crawled through his veins.

No, not ants…

– Fire, she said. – Fire, flowing like a molten river through your veins.

And it wasn't surprising, not surprising at all that she knew his thoughts.

She kissed him on the lips, still hungry, still needy. When he responded, she sighed content. She turned around and stuck her butt at his groin, wriggling it enticingly.

– It's all right. She mewed. – I'm mellow, now. Stick it in. Please!

He looked at himself, seeing himself grow large and hard again, feeling the irresistible urge rise again. He pushed himself into her. She was truly ready and eager. He knew that, beyond knowing. Her smell tore at his nostrils, and he forgot, forgot again about regret and self-incrimination and everything, except the sweet, writhing and irresistible creature in front of him.

They dozed off afterwards, fading inn and out of sleep as the day came and went. She spoke sleepily as she crouched in his arms, her voice clear and sharp as glass.

– The unrest, the total and irreversible breakdown of society, the fading of the world, as you know it, will begin not long from now. In a way it has already started. Its worst consequences just haven't manifested themselves yet. The thousand-year wind, the Twilight Storm, has already begun. It will grow to engulf the entire world and make it impossible to live on the surface. Eventually it will pick the land clean, suck off its moisture, leaving hardly more than a moonlike, barren landscape.

Her words created a stir within him, coming alive in his mind, turning into flashes, glimpses of incredibly vivid images.

– You will gather people, she said, – train them, and prepare them for their life. In their moment of despair and need you will be there to fan the flame of their power, and lead them to their destiny.

– That sounds like a fairy tale to me, he said.

– It isn't a fairy tale, she said, still smiling.

He saw her wonder, saw her think, saw her nod to herself, and he saw everything without her moving at all.

She disentangled sensually from him, and rose from the bed, and as she did her clothing reappeared and covered her body. Her smile turned serious, businesslike. She stood on the middle of the floor, facing him.

– There are things you need to know, she said. – I'm a lethal weapon and will be a great asset to you. Unchecked I can kill hundreds of people in a span of a few heartbeats. But when the bloodlust comes over me I cannot be stopped except by my pack leader, and now that is you. Your command will be obeyed instantly and without question. In a place filled with noise I may not hear your cry, though. That is why we have the hand signals. I will always *see* you, even in the darkest pit.

He watched her as she demonstrated, not feeling silly while lying nude on the bed. Her hands became a whirl of motion as they flickered before his eyes.

– I'm afraid my perception isn't good enough to catch more than a finger or two of that, he admitted.

– I was testing you, she grinned, and then lowering her eyes. – Sorry.

Mischief danced in the shadows of her face, her both sweet and brutal face, and he swallowed hard. He nodded, forcing himself into hardening himself, to become, at least in a tiny part what she expected him to be.

He saw, unmistakable the worship in her eyes, in the very manner she moved in his orbit. It wasn't unlike what he had observed in others, in reference to others in various times in his life.

She began showing him the signals anew, still fast, but not beyond his ability to catch them. For every signal she spoke, she hissed a word, a sound. It was more like throat-sounds than actual words. He realized that this was her language: that of the warrior and tunnel-rat in the future.

She began showing him the signs one by one, and she nodded

encouragingly to him.

«Now you», she said.

He repeated the sign and the sound, but he didn't get it right. It was not just a move with the hand, a sound from the larynx, but both, a movement and sound made with the entire body, the entire self, a language beyond words, beyond signs.

He concentrated, focused so hard that it made sweat flow from his exposed skin.

– Perhaps we should stop… She frowned.

– Continue! He snapped.

Her eyes widened. She nodded.

– Forgive me, Red Shadow, she whispered, as if she had just been chastised, and feared punishment.

He attempted to give her a smile, a way to soften the blow he felt on his face, the rock-hard place within himself.

She kept showing him the signs. He kept repeating them, attempting in vain to emulate them. She began showing him one sign and sound repeatedly.

– «Freeze», she said, making a follow up: – «Keep moving».

Then another string, slightly different.

– «Freeze and await instructions». And then yet another: – «Freeze and obey»

– What's the difference? He asked her.

– Subtle but crucial, she replied. – You'll know.

The lesson ended. He sensed it, even as he saw that her pose changed. She was so open. He knew her so well already.

She grabbed one of the shoulder pads of her uniform and casually ripped it off. He watched as it instantly regrew itself.

– This will hurt a bit. She admonished him. – Please steel yourself.

He tensed. She placed the piece of black fabric on his chest. The sharp pain cut through him. He gasped as the black mass, the sensation spread on his chest, from his chest and all over his body.

– It bonds with you, she said. – It learns to react to your thoughts, and eventually you can make it become whatever you want. Allow me to demonstrate…

She reached out with a hand, and something seemed to reach out with it, to extend her reach. The hand was far from the shelf it pointed to, but the shadowy and transparent something easily touched and picked up the small figure there.

– I could, as you know have done this with my mind as well, but both methods serve me well, in different circumstances. And the suit, by default protects us from almost anything, from cold, heat and deadly injury. Its capabilities are both defensive and offensive. Joined with it we become…

– Weapons, he stated.

She smiled.

He rose to his full height and the suit instantly became his everyday clothes.

– I can think of a few embarrassing situations that might arise from this, he grinned.

She looked puzzled at him. He had the impression that the word «embarrassing» had pretty much lost its meaning where she came from.

He visualized or attempted to visualize in his head and the dark uniform instantly returned. There was a flicker in the mirror, and that was it, practically instantaneous.

– It doesn't really look like a uniform, he said, – and could easily pass as ordinary clothes. Nothing is outrageous today.

Another word unfamiliar to her. He would guess she understood it technically, but not its finer, or lack of finer points.

– You adapt well, she said, glowing with pride on his behalf, – like I knew you would.

And he felt pride. It blushed inside him like a rose.

It was true. He didn't say it, but he knew quite a few people that would have run to the loony bin by now… and he hadn't even considered doing it, not even in the farthest reaches of his self. The thought hadn't even crossed his mind.

And he felt pride.

– We need supplies, he noted. – The little we fetched last night isn't any good the way you eat.

She knew he was kidding, understood irony, and she sent him a sensual grin.

He thought about dressing, about finding his shoes, but there was no need. A jacket completed what looked like his everyday clothes, and shoes grew around his feet as he walked. He found his wallet in his jacket. She put on her goggles, posing for him again.

– Nothing is outrageous today, she grinned.

She kissed him quickly on the lips, shyly, like a blushing teenage girl, and he realized again that she was, at least in his presence. He unlocked and opened the door, and they went out into the bright hallway. She walked ahead through the maze of corridors he had always found disconcerting, but now he knew why he didn't doubt her.

– Mr. Covington at the fourth floor is a potential dangerous nut, she said, – hiding firearms in his closet. Even his wife doesn't know about them. He isn't really a problem, but he could be, under the right or wrong circumstances.

– How did you know about that? I didn't know about that.

He wasn't really surprised, but old habits die hard.

– You didn't, but you knew when you told me. You made me memorize the schematics of the entire neighborhood, and its denizens.

– How on Earth did I manage that… that feat? Had I stored the information on a computer or something?

Now, he was incredulous again.

– You have or will have close to perfect recall, she said. – There was no need for a computer. You taught me everything from Memory, and I, being your passionate servant can do no less.

She pushed the button to the elevator. He looked down, at the city in daylight, so different from what it had been yesterday. At the very least his impression of it had changed dramatically.

The elevator doors slid close behind them, a slight pull, and they were on their way down. Everything seemed more detailed and… and real to him today.

She leaned on the wall.

– You related to me the most ridiculous secrets, at least ridiculous in the context you told them, compared to the life and hardship and lethal dangers we faced daily.

She cast him an enigmatic look, enjoying this, enjoying showing off for him.

– But you also imprinted on me the culture of this current society, about the necessary guile and subterfuge and hypocrisy, how secrets were important, how knowledge is power, and it's all ours, Larry.

He tried to not respond to that, tried to keep his face an impassive mask, but knew it was hopeless in her company. She knew him better than he knew himself.

– You told me you corrupted me, deliberately, to make me fit to live here. That's why I seem so normal to you. Even though I may seem out of place occasionally my pack mates would have been totally lost and confused, but I spent practically my entire adolescence in your presence, and you taught me what I needed to know.

They walked the streets, the short distance to the nearest grocery store.

– It's incredible. She shook her head in disgust. – People walk in the midst of poisons, and they don't react to it, don't protest its overwhelming presence.

He smelled the exhaust, too, today. It made his nostrils itch, and he found the sensation it created strangely comforting.

– Everything is poisoned, he taught her. – It's everywhere. In the air we breathe, in the food we eat and the water we drink, and there are places where the ground is so contaminated that people get sick and die if they come too close. We deal with it or rather avoid dealing with it, in order to not turn insane.

– I know. You told me. It's just so horrible that I had to voice my opinion. Your servant is sorry, My Lord.

– Don't be, he imprinted her. – You should speak your mind, also in my presence, especially in my presence.

– You're so wise, she breathed.

And he sighed and didn't attempt to hide it, because she would have picked up on it, no matter how hard he had tried to conceal it.

– You're right, My Lord, she nodded determined. – I still don't understand and have so much to learn. I will strive to better myself.

– Don't be sorry, he repeated. – One thing is to have something described to you. To experience it is another matter entirely.

– Of course, she mumbled.

She looked strangely at him then, strangely even for her, and this time he didn't understand.

They entered the local store, and all the familiar faces looked alien to him. He realized that he didn't know, didn't really know any of them.

He wondered if anyone truly knew anybody.

– It's so strange, she said. – All this. You know these people, but you don't really know them. In the pack we know each other, know our brothers and sisters inside out and trust them with our lives. We have to, in order to survive.

And he realized, suddenly what was «wrong» with her speech. She sounded like a cultivated foreigner that had learned the language through intensive schooling and supervision, not through living in the language's home country. No wonder he had entertained the thought, briefly that she was a foreign spy.

A man approached them with a huge grin on his face. Larry studied her just then. She didn't freeze, didn't in any way reveal that she was on alert, but he knew her; she was.

– Larry, MY MAN, the man exclaimed. – Nice seeing you. Who's the very cute lady by your side?

Christopher Randolph was a buffoon, but a nice buffoon.

– Nice seeing you, too, Chris, Larry replied. – Say hello to Nellie. She moved in with me yesterday.

– Hel-lo, the man said, suddenly a bit dizzy.
– Hello, she replied, greeting him with a smile.
She reached out a gloved hand. Randolph took it and shook it, overdoing it quite a bit.
– It's so nice to meet you, Nellie. I didn't know Larry had such a great taste in women, and I *love* your goggles.
– Thank you, Chris, she replied sweetly, – Larry has told me *so* much about you.
– He has, huh? The man's smile faltered a bit, but a second later it was back to its old glory. – That's old Larry for you.
They left Chris there at the entrance, a fact Larry felt very good about.
– I love my goggles, too, Nellie said, a little hurt in her voice. – I can't see without them.
She turned to Larry, exasperated.
– It's a weakness. It didn't matter where I lived before, since everybody had it, here it's different. They're hard to break, but not impossibly so.
– So, close your eyes if you lose them, Larry shrugged, deliberately. – You certainly oriented yourself through sound in the tunnels, anyway.
She brightened, looking at him with that puppy look again. He knew that even though he couldn't actually see her eyes.
– That's *so* smart, she said. – Why didn't I think of that?
A few moments passed, before she answered her own question.
– Because all creatures are ruled by habit, if they aren't careful, aren't constantly on their toes, she nodded, turning towards him yet again. – You taught me that. But I forgot. I will strive to do better. I must, or I can't serve you.
He wanted to speak, to assure her that she was being too harsh with herself, but realized that would only shame her further. His throat was too dry, anyway.
Then he realized he had a hard-on again.
The texture of her clothes began flowing again, reacting to her reacting to his state of mind.
She started mumbling something. He didn't understand the words, but realized it was a mantra of some kind. Her clothes fell to rest.
– «Control is an illusion», she quoted, – «but must still be strived for and achieved in critical circumstances».
He grinned. Perhaps she understood the finer points of the word «embarrassment», after all.
Then he realized he did want to fuck her, wanted it so badly that he could hardly breathe, and he wasn't sure which one of them was the most

uncivilized, and it left him sweaty and confused.

– You feel it already, My Lord, she noted, a little, just a little out of breath, – feel the Flow. You shouldn't be surprised that it comes naturally to you.

It makes sense, he thought. Damn it, it makes *sense*.

An old man stared at them, stared at them with… with *envy* in his eyes, and Larry understood, and he felt both weak and strong, both happy and sad.

– Life has passed him by, she stated solemnly, – and he looks back, and wish he had lived while he had the chance, while he was still young and strong. I assure you that you will never make that mistake, Larry.

They fetched and bought groceries, bought lots of it. The cart was filled over the top.

– Such is the curse of a double household, he said cheerfully to Mrs. Michaels at the cashier desk.

She did her best to stare him down, as usual, but it didn't take anymore, and he rejoiced. Nellie's carefree laughter thrilled and warmed him.

He handed Mrs. Michaels bills and she returned coins to him, looking to him like she gave him pure gold, and he grinned at her.

They carried six full plastic bags back to the apartment. She carried four of them, and still his arm felt like rubber after just a few steps. He had to take a break several times, make several stops on the way.

– I should probably quit my job, he gasped, he said to himself, to her. – I need to work full time on becoming… whatever I'll become.

– I believe that to be a wise course of action, Nellie nodded.

– It's just that we need a lot of money to survive in this damn world, he swore. – But I guess we can fix that, huh?

– We will get ourselves a lot of worthless paper, she half-joked.

– I will not quit immediately then. We need a cover, at least for a while, a way to at least partly explaining our good fortune. Guile and deceit must, for the time being be a part of our life.

The girl looked at him with glittering eyes, and he wondered yet again if it was truly Lawrence Watros walking here, walking these streets, saying these words, or some changeling that had inadvertently taken his place.

There was a dark glare in the horizon, he saw it. For a second, an eternity it burned through his eyes and into his open, his wide-open mind. Nellie saw him shudder, and nodded, nodded to herself, as if conforming yet another fact for herself.

They returned to Sanctuary, to their immediate neighborhood. Nellie caused quite a stir, of course, the more people that saw her, with her pale skin and hair (and dark goggles). She looked like a classic punk rocker or something. This was a fairly average region of the city, with quite the average citizens. Larry knew he should have felt embarrassed, but he wasn't. He knew he probably would have been, only yesterday.

She studied him, without studying him, like she always did, and he sensed how her spirits rose by each passing moment. She knew what he was going through.

That realization didn't surprise him anymore either.

People filled the elevator on the way up. They stared hard, while trying hard not to stare. He grinned, and it felt so good. They scurried away like flies when the doors slid open at their floor. Nellie ignored them in quite a patronizing manner, and he did, too. Only Mrs. Carmichael remained when Larry and Nellie left.

– They are very amusing, are they not? Nelli inquired.

– Yes, they are, he nodded. – And only yesterday I was one of them.

They reentered the twilight world of the apartment, and it truly felt like coming home. For the very first time, it did. The door closed behind them. She removed her goggles. The sight of her beautiful pale eyes was once more his to enjoy without distortion.

– I'm going to make dinner, he said.

She nodded eagerly, depositing the plastic bags on the kitchen table.

– I love your cooking, Larry.

He shook his head, bemused and unnerved.

They sat there, around the dinner table in the living room, sharing food and wine. The soft lights of the candles and the wine changed her skin tone into a darker hue. She toasted with him, bold and fierce, a big smile on her face

– You kept a lot of bottles of these, she said, indicating the red wine. – There weren't many left by the time of my departure, though.

The wine got to him, like it got to her. He felt it stronger, far more potent than he had earlier in his life. Her soft voice got to him.

– I was twelve, she said. – I was given the honor of being picked by you with eleven others. I had never been so scared and so excited before. You used to come and watch us occasionally, but the chosen was only few among many until that night. We knew we were Red, had known since our earliest memory, but from that moment on, we became Crimson, your Crimson Tide, your elite guard.

– Red? He inquired.

– Your home guard, your warriors, those born with extraordinary abilities, like you, with gifts beyond the many.

He didn't comment on that, but studied the shifting shadows of her face.

– The claws pointed to me early and I was loved. But my added gift of telekinesis didn't manifest until after my first Bleeding. I recall the moment perfectly. You watched me, as you made me perform beyond my very best. I crushed Robert, my fellow guard, in spite of him being older than me, and suddenly objects and people levitated everywhere. But you stayed firm, didn't flinch, didn't submit at all to the forces swaying everything and everyone else in the room.

He put the glasses, forks and plates at the dishwasher. Its hum haunted him as they returned to the living room.

– It's a good thing that you're… tipsy, she slurred. – You're weakened, and you have to strive, in order to function properly. It's a perfect occasion to begin, begin your education. I will be your teacher, like you were mine. It's perfect symmetry.

She sat down on the floor, crossing her legs and pulling them close to her body. She motioned for him to join her. He did, clumsily, and embarrassed beyond belief.

– You have your power of observation and your memory, she told him, frowning, clearly striving to comfort him, clearly ill-suited to that effect. – That's how it's done. Start with what you're good at and the rest will take care of itself later.

The thrill, the wonder in him, in her didn't go away.

– But you start… early, don't you?

– Yes, when we're three, she replied proudly.

Adding, catching herself.

– But even though you start late, rest assured that you will get there. When I first met you, as I have indicated, you were a mighty, fearsome creature of the Storm. We knew you weren't beyond the forces of nature, since no human can ever be, but we still felt it like you were. The ground shakes beneath your feet, and children and adults alike look at you with awe, terror and boundless love.

Her suddenly very intense eyes, even more intense than usual burned through him. The candles remained the only source of light in the room. They flickered and died, faded constantly out and in, and created vast shadows.

– Focus, she suggested softly, – go deep into the well that is your Self.

She repeated it, stressing without stressing every word. The candles flickered. She closed her eyes, but he knew they were still open. He closed his, and he could see the texture of her face with absolute clarity.

– You are three, she said. – It's four fifteen in the afternoon. It's three years exactly since you popped out of your mother's belly. What is happening?

He almost had it. It was amazing and frustrating and everything between. It slipped away.

– You are ten, she said. – How is the weather?
– Bright sunshine, he replied. – I look at the horizon, and I see two white clouds in the horizon. I shiver down my spine, and I can't tell why.
He shivered, and he knew why. The alcohol still partly paralyzed his tongue and lips, and he had trouble speaking properly, and he didn't give a damn.
– You are fifteen and a day, she chanted, speaking completely normal. – What is happening?
He hesitated.
– You are fifteen and a day, she hissed. – What is happening?
He rested on the hammock in the garden. It was such a warm, beautiful summer's day, and he enjoyed the sun's rays on his exposed skin.
– Our old, fat cat Absalom catches a bird, he said in a strange voice. – He moves fast, fast like lightning, like he did in his youth, catches its neck between his teeth. It's an amazing sight. I can't get it out of my head, and I have nightmares about it for years afterwards.
– You saw the Hunter, the predator, a primal force at work, and you never forgot it.
He laughed out loud.
– This is so weird. I haven't thought about this for *years.*
– You are three…
– I walk in the garden, he said. – Absalom fight with his brother, and I feel joy. I enjoy watching it, and I see the joy in Absalom and Alfred's eyes when they cut into each other, as the small kittens teach each other the skills they need to survive
She opened her eyes, and he did, too, at exactly the same moment. He sat there, sweating. In the course of a single second, his body had become soaked in sweat.
– There's no true malice there, he added like a sleepwalker, fresh like spring rain. – It only *is.*
– It's Life, she said. – No matter the context or the situation, our many-faced nature is with us always. In the tunnels it's beaten into us, but even here, in this society of sleep it's with us, always. To deny it doesn't make it go away, but merely serves to distort it, ruin its worth.
They sat there, in the silence for a long time, before he finally spoke.
– And this is what… what I taught you?
– Yes, she acknowledged. – You did so to me directly and indirectly, through my early teachers. This is the first lesson of the Red Shadow, the law of the jungle: kill or be killed.
His mind had, at some undetermined point cleared, and cleared completely. His lips and tongue were no longer numb.

– You remembered, she stated. – You remember everything that you've ever experienced. I didn't even have to prod very hard. And these weren't very important memories for you, not at this point at your life. All the facets of your past are an open book to you. I'm proud of you, Larry

She had torn a veil from his eyes, and he sat there shaken and trembling from toe to head. He rose, just as clumsily as he had been sitting down, following her smooth and relaxed moves. They stood there. She began moving, performing martial arts moves, doing so slowly and deliberately for his benefit.

– Now, remember. Move to my moves. Awaken your body, as well as your mind. You've been asleep your entire life, and awakening is bound to be rude and abrupt. It cannot be helped. You haven't the benefit of being born in the crèche.

And he knew that that word didn't exactly mean the same to her, as it did to him.

He imitated her moves, or attempted to, or attempted to attempt it, feeling completely ridiculous. She repeated the moves, nodding to him, solemn, focused and beyond determined. He began sweating almost immediately. Sweat poured into his eyes and made them burn, burn so hard that he couldn't see. He sat on the couch a while later, breathing so hard that he feared his lungs would burst.

– You will eventually know these moves in your dreams, she said curtly. – Then you will know them by heart, and then they, finally will be so integrated in your mind, body and shadow that they will feel no harder than breathing. And by then you will also be able to breathe properly, not the bad habit of an excuse you and your amusing neighbors have called breathing.

She reminded him of a drill sergeant, but while he had always seen those guys as buffoons she was nothing like that, nothing like that at all. She was lethal and inspiring and irritating and quiet confidence and all those things simultaneously.

He recalled her moves, almost in immaculate detail, but he couldn't reproduce them with his all too soft body and weak limbs.

– You've just been born, she told him. – You must learn to crawl before you can walk. Be patient and the rewards are great. The small trickle of the river will eventually transform into the waterfall of all waterfalls.

The twilight fell, followed by the evening and the night. The apartment, its walls, floor and ceiling became his entire world, in a way it never had before. She encouraged, goaded and drove him on without mercy, and suddenly he knew that she didn't really know the meaning of that word either. No matter what she had told him, there wasn't really any pretense in her, no deep-rooted hypocrisy. She chased her desire, her deepest nature, and made no apologies for it, and it pleased him to no end, no matter the exhaustion hammering his body.

The training ended eventually, or pausing, in a world without pause. They fed again, and like everything with her it was an event, a joyous occasion. She easily sensed his growing joy and blushed, and her clothes started eroding again, and this time, smiling the darkest of smiles, she did nothing to prevent it.

She writhed under him, pulling the ropes hard, later, in bed, crying out in her need, in her infinite pleasure, to the point he was certain the entire block heard her. He pounded at her, harder with every new thrust, forgetting how tired he was, forgetting everything except the growing pain transforming into the total and undeniable and blinding pleasure, fading into the most pleasant of shadows.

They rested close later, the ropes thrown away on the far floor like the garbage they were, slowly drifting into sleep, into Dream, caressing each other with hands, body and eyes.

He awoke abruptly, sometimes during the night, or believed he did. At first, he couldn't identify the sound he heard or the movement at his side. He turned and saw her twist and turn, her claws racing back and forth in the air, and he realized that she was dreaming, that she was having a nightmare, and that she was terrified. The wailing rising from her open mouth convinced him of that, if nothing else did. He studied her, both anxious and fascinated. The claws didn't really come close to him, as if she knew he was there, and somehow protected him from their lethal touch. He wasn't really afraid.

It didn't last long, a minute tops. Then she relaxed, sighed and laid still again, a smile resting on her lips. He lay awake for a while, all kinds of thoughts racing through his excited mind.

He fell asleep, and slept soundly, dreams racing through his mind like shadows, like shadow lightning a dim afternoon, and the dark shadow dancing at his side was his own, and somewhere in the horizon filling the sky he saw her smile.

Chapter Three

He was surprised, bordering on shock that his limbs, and especially his thighs, weren't stiff like felled trees the next morning. There was a certain stiffness, but he had learned to recognize that. It was negligible.

– You have exercised before, now and then, she explained, tutoring him. – Sufficient for your body to be ready for the next step, soon to be a giant leap. You, like many just needed a little push to become aware of that undeniable fact.

The office seemed even gloomier than usual, but oh, so different with her at his side. She was dressed pretty much like a young female executive, except for the goggles, of course, and she drew stares from everybody present.

It took Poulson, his superior exactly two minutes to come rushing into his office with his very nasty disposition, ready for the speech.

– What is the meaning of this, Watros? He barked.

– What? Larry grinned. – Can't I show my girl where I work without being hassled?

It was so very satisfying to have the idiot stare hard at him, and then pulling back, slamming the door behind him.

– There goes my promotion, Larry grinned.

She was clearly amused, too, though possibly for slightly different reasons.

– Two days ago, I would have cared, of course, being the more or less typical wage slave, but not anymore. I'm already past that. Amazing.

It was all so clear to him, now, at least compared to how muddled everything had been those two days ago. Even though he had felt secure with his place in this world he hadn't really.

He grabbed her and kissed her, kissed her hard. She instantly softened in his arms, and returned his affection tenfold.

The day passed like a puff of smoke. The eight hours didn't seem like such a long time, not like such a long time at all. She was there, with him all the time, observing the various insane deliberations, looking at everybody passing through his office with a patronizing glare in her pale red eyes. They grew nervous in her company, he sensed that, noted that with deep satisfaction. And he knew, with his newfound ability to see himself from the outside that his demeanor had changed dramatically, even though his overt behavior had not.

The two of them walked through Downtown in the evening. She seemed to be relaxing, but he knew she really wasn't. Her eyes moved without moving. When she tilted her head slightly, to cast him a lovesick glance she took stock of the entire street, and all the people walking up and down both sidewalks. It was a blurry, ever-shifting and confusing imagery to him, but not to her.

– I kind of like this, she noted, frowning again. – We're venturing into enemy territory, but there isn't an enemy in sight.

– Everything is shades of gray here, he told her gently, sharply, – blurring around the edges.

– I gathered as much, she nodded. – The danger is not necessarily instantly apparent, but just as real.

– You're a child, he stated, – learning about the world.

– Yes, Red Shadow, she said, bowing her head. – You told me that much.

– But so, he said, – am I.

Her eyes grew large, and puzzled by his cheerful voice and demeanor.

He spotted a tavern, a new place that hadn't been there before the moment they turned a corner, and the dark letters above the entrance in deliberate, seemingly written letters:

Shadow

– Look at the simplicity of that name, he said. – No ordinary shitty name like the Dragonet's Arms or something.

– The name is known to me, she said in her usual cryptic, non-cryptic manner.

He resisted the almost irresistible need to look at her, to probe her.

Except for the name and its very elaborate signpost the front of the building didn't look instantly different.

But there was something here, speaking to him and certainly to her. There was no need for him to study her in order to convince himself of that.

He noticed immediately that most people walked past it, that very few, even though some hesitated and slowed down ever so little, walked inside. The two of them did, without hesitating in any way. She knew, by watching him, watching his moves that he was headed inside, and she joined him before he had actually made a conscious decision about it, and for the thousandth time in the short time since they had met he marveled about her.

It was… murky inside, pretty much like he had expected, but the mood there, the mood within himself still surprised him. There was music, but not loud music. He noted that people by the tables enjoyed low-keyed, relaxed conversation.

The corner table was available. They sat down there. He signed for her to remain and walked to the bar. There was no queue. After buying two pints of Guinness he returned to the table. She looked at him with her large, curious eyes.

– Why did you choose this place? She wondered lightly.

He didn't have to think, to consider his words.

– Because people don't have to scream to be heard here.

He stopped in his «tracks», pondering his words and thoughts.

– But I couldn't tell from the outside, of course. There's no way I could have known that… is there?

She nodded, to him, to herself, grinning when he gave her the eye, smiling as she accepted the glass he handed her. He sat down, and they toasted quietly, with eyes glued to each other. They drank.

– It's funny. He shook his head in wonder. – This taste is better than I can ever remember.

– I understand what you mean, she whispered.

And incredible as it was… he heard her.

She looked at him, studied him, even when it wasn't obvious. It didn't bother him anymore.

– Yes, she stated, – your hearing, like all your senses will improve with time. The abilities you're born with will assert themselves, break through the haze muddling them.

Her words… her words sounded true.

A new song began. She cocked her head, stopping him from speaking by raising a hand. A smile broke on her face. She rose, hurrying to the dance floor, not looking at him, but he knew she was paying attention to him anyway, and knew it didn't have anything to do with any kind of inflated ego on his part, but was the indomitable fact.

Her dance began. It warmed him, merely by a glance. He realized that she knew the song. She had to, the way she danced to it. And then he heard her humming, her song, and it sounded eerily like the voice coming from the speakers. Seconds passed like eternities. The others present quickly noticed her. They didn't instantly, because she made no effort to draw attention to herself, but she did anyway. The dance wasn't really a dance, not what passed for one these days, wild, without wild, soft, but yet raw, untamed. It was a slow dance. Not really being played loud. Her movement seemed muted, but was passionate, aggressive and savage beyond words, beyond thoughts. He got a painful hard-on, and knew, beyond knowing that so did every fucking male in the room.

She climbed onto his lap afterwards, slipping into his embrace, hugging him, kissing him, before pulling back, returning to her chair, blushing deeply. He could still feel her claws on his neck, through the gloves, and he realized, upon searching his feelings… that he wasn't afraid.

He couldn't tell exactly the moment he had stopped being scared, just that he had. The world had seemed closed to him, locked away outside his box, but now it was open, ripe with possibilities.

The bartender brought two more beers. He could only vaguely recall making the order.

He raised his glass, and she raised hers.

– To the future, he said.

– To the future, she replied excitedly.

They had a toast. The sound of the two glasses meeting and parting rang in his ears.

– I danced for you for the first time three years ago, she revealed, – to the melody you had hummed to me since the night we first met face to face. This is the place where you first heard it, that will be yours eventually, the venue where you gather your first warriors.

He wasn't really startled, but her words still penetrated deep within him. She still surprised him, and always would, like a never empty well.

- I guess that's what, according to conventional space/time theory is seen as a paradox.

- I guess it is, she said.

She cocked her head again, as if attempting to pick something up from the very air.

– It is a strange song. She frowned. – The singer… he seems to be weeping. Why is that, you think?

It was a strange song, now, when he listened to it through her senses, her sensibilities.

He shook his head, having no answer for her.

– This is a good place, she declared, – well chosen. Only the special and the lost will come here, excellent warrior-material.

They drank a lot that night. Her sober or rather sober-like giggle rose above the sound of the music and the conversation. He saw that she was drunk. It wasn't apparent to others, but he noticed the small, revealing signs. Others looked at them, at her. The men looked at him and the women at her, with envious eyes.

The evening and the night passed, fast as a whirl, as he pondered new and to him unknown territory of the mind and existence as a whole. He got drunk, on one level, but on another it was as if the alcohol just vanished into a vast black hole somewhere inside of him.

His flesh or at least his skin turned numb. His spirit soared. Some parts of his mind turned themselves off. Other parts worked better or at least dissimilar to how they usually worked.

The song, their song was played again, and this time they danced together. She clung to him, giving him lingering kisses, and even stumbling a bit. Time passed, but he didn't notice its passing, except for the fact that everything seemed different, seemed strange and alien and wonderful with his new eyes. Somebody had taken the world and repainted it, to the point of it becoming unrecognizable.

Dizziness grabbed him, just as clarity overwhelmed him.

He had a sense of the room and the people there that went beyond anything he had previously experienced. Perhaps the world hadn't been repainted, hadn't changed at all, only his view of it. His eyes, or rather how they worked, had certainly changed dramatically.

The woman serving at the bar looked at him. He knew, beyond knowing. Nellie did, too, even if it was impossible for «outsiders» to see it.

– She has a hawk's eyes, Nellie stated calmly, conveying just enough of a warning for him to notice.

And now they began studying the woman behind the bar. He left it mostly to Nellie, but couldn't resist using his newly discovered stealth capabilities. It felt invigorating in an entirely new and unknown way.

She was tall and big, and her eyes, her eyes, like Nellie had related told her story. He knew she was on her guard, that she never quite relaxed behind that protective bar.

- Can you smell the stench of metal, Nelli asked him, - the gun she keeps under the desk?

He could, and more: he felt it in the woman herself, a distinct, lingering smell separating her from everybody else in the room.

Relaxation stayed in his system, but the anxiety never quite left him.

When they rose to leave Nellie was unsteady on her feet, once again enough for him to notice. Her balance was off with the slightest of marks. People watched them as they left. The woman behind the bar kept watching them, practically studying them. He sensed that, too, through his newly discovered eyes in the back of his neck.

The street was quiet, as if they were immersed in a bubble, a void closing them off from the people and the cars and the noise. Brief, muted roars reached them, there, far away, as they exchanged glances and long, lingering stares.

– I like it when you're staring at me, she said. – You used to stare at me, stare at me a lot, see right through me with those burning eyes of yours.

She kind of shuddered, and so did he.

– I wonder what person, what kind of person can inspire such loyalty from you, he said hesitatingly.

– I don't, she replied promptly, not really attempting to assure him, not really seeing the need for it, and that stunned him most of all.

They crossed the street and entered a square, a place filled with outdoor pubs and noisy spots. People sat in several clusters drinking their beers.

– Explain yourself! He said, sharper than intended, making it a command.

She froze, but the smile stayed in place.

– Every person or every person worth shit goes through an evolution of sorts throughout their life. I couldn't do a triple somersault before I was eight, and it bothered me, bothered me terribly…

He was about to point out the obvious when she once more got ahead of him.

– … and even though you are an adult that isn't really relevant here. The true Human Being keeps growing as long as it breathes, and you will get there. I *know*. You're a man inspiring respect, Larry Watros, and eventually everyone will know that.

She shrugged and gave him her best of smiles.

And there was a lot where that came from. The warm feeling inside of him intensified further.

– I want more beer, he said hoarsely. – Would you like one, too?

– Yes, Larry, she said, – I love beer.

He knew she wasn't stroking his ego, like so many of the girls he had dated inadvertently did, he just knew it. She just wasn't.

There was no… duplicity there, at least not the dishonest kind he was used to. Her dishonesty, if there was any was on a completely different level.

He shook his head and chuckled to himself, as he watched her sit down under the red lights in the legal smoking zone outside, as he made his way to the bar inside. No seats were available here, as expected. He returned to her with two glasses in his hands not too long afterwards. She sat there with a smug smile around her mouth.

– Has anything happened while I was gone?

– Nothing I couldn't handle, she grinned.

He spotted, easily a man sitting two tables away, rubbing his hand, and looking very, very hurt.

– I can't hide anything from you. She shook her head in bewilderment. – I never could. You know me so well.

It struck him that others might have had some trouble recognizing her smugness, the small, revealing signs of her state of mind that was there from time to time, and he didn't understand.

– Cheers, Larry, she raised her glass. – To the future.

– To the future, he replied automatically.

The sound of the two glasses meeting, briefly encountering each other cringed in his ears.

– Good beer, she nodded. – Whatever is wrong with people in this day and age they make good beer.

Those on the neighboring tables heard her, clearly, they did, and they glanced at her, at him.

This was a busy, noisy place. People had to speak loud because of shrieking music and vehicles constantly passing by, blowing their horns to boot.

– This place is angering you, she noted. – Do you want me to act on that?

The thought suddenly amused him to no end. He imagined her making mincemeat of guests and cars alike, and could hardly contain his laughter, and in this case, that seemed… proper.

– I wouldn't normally ask for permission in such a trivial and obvious matter, she enlightened him, – but these are different circumstances, so I found it… prudent.

– You did the right thing, he said, – and no, no matter how tempting it is I don't want you to act on it.

He grinned, and she looked puzzled at him.

– You were wise when you warned me that this time and place was different, she noted. – And in so many ways you could never properly prepare me for. I need to listen better to you, Larry, much better, or I might fail you.

– Listen…. He began.

And she saw that she did, that she froze and became very attentive, waiting for his message, and he hesitated.

– I think you're doing fine, he finally said, quite simply. – I felt awkward because I was thrown into totally alien circumstances, but that's nothing compared to how you must feel.

– You're so gentle, she whispered.

– Cheers! He lifted his glass. – To alien circumstances. To Change!

She worded it with her lips, without speaking it aloud.

This time the sound of glass meeting glass sounded beautiful in his ears. She drank deep and so did he.

They rose and left simultaneously. This place wasn't to their liking. And it felt so right to react simultaneously, so satisfying. Her smile warmed him, melting the ice covering something precious inside. She cast a look of contempt at the still sitting guests, and he did, too, with a stint of humor in his eyes. They, those among them catching it shifted uncomfortably and with a bit of fear in their chair.

Good, Larry thought.

And the girl looked approvingly at him.

– You will rule, in part through fear, she conveyed to him. – Everybody does.

They were about to leave the Square, its main parts already behind them. She moved her eyes, he saw that even though she walked ahead, attentive like a hawk. He looked at her back, studying the play of muscles there, the pattern he grew increasingly familiar with.

A man and a woman stepped out from the inside of the pub to the facilities outside designed to cater to smokers and their companions. Suddenly the entire scene changed, and changed dramatically. He made the sign just as she was about to charge forward, and she froze instantly.

She didn't move, not even the slightest, didn't even turn her head to look at him, even though he knew she was looking at him.

– Speak, he said, attempting to sound somewhat casual, even as his nerves rattled violently beneath his skin.

– They are red, she stated, as if that was sufficient to remove all doubt, to explain everything.

He looked at her, encouraging her to explain herself.

– Everyone red is your home guard. That's the law.

She frowned, her bewilderment fading, though not leaving her completely.

– But you made the law. You can break it at will.

He made the countersign. She relaxed, to a point, but it was still like a thousand wasps crawled through her veins.

– They are not red, anyway, he told her. – It's just the light from the heaters.

– They are, she insisted. – It is a different kind of red, clearly distinguishable from the artificial lighting. You should be able to see it easily…

She relented, bowing her head in shame.

– You can't see it yet. How silly of me.

A glass broke somewhere in the vicinity of his hearing. He couldn't tell where, only that it did.

– You shouldn't feel bad about it, he stated, as forcefully as he felt he could, without further undermining her suddenly so brittle confidence.

Her mind was working overtime. He saw that, how her reason and natural spirit fought to overcome her… her rigid teaching.

– Even though you keep confusing me with that half omnipotent demigod of yours.

He laughed himself silly, unable to stave off the awkward moment completely.

She turned to him completely, nodding.

– It is a bit confusing, she acknowledged. – You are him, and you are not. Not yet.

As they often did, her words sent a thrill through him.

He studied the man and woman sitting under the orange light. They seemed totally unremarkable. The man had a pot belly, and the woman quite a bit of excess fat around her waist, something Larry never would have noticed or would have bothered noticing just a little earlier in his life. He cast a glance at his own smaller, but clearly visible pot belly.

His hand sought the mobile phone in his pocket, almost by itself. Suddenly he stood there, staring at it. He turned off the flash, raised the phone to his eyes and snapped a photo of the two sitting there. They didn't notice anything. Neither did anybody else. Larry felt positively strange, but he was getting used to that, to the pleasant tingling beneath his skin.

– There's more than one way to catch a fish, he said.

To his astonishment she bowed her head in… in reverence, smiling in pure joy.

– You don't have to skin the prey to kill it, she whispered.

He heard her, heard her loud and clear.

Curiosity riddled him, and anxiety haunted him. He found himself walking to the table with the eager girl in tow.

– May we sit here? He inquired.

The man looked up, looking at Larry and Nelli, ogling the girl briefly, before casting a quick glance around at the other tables. This was the only table with available seats.

– Please do, he replied, visibly uncomfortable, as if he had swallowed a hard ball or something.

Larry sat down. Nelli did, too, light as a feather.

– I'm Larry, he said. – This is Nelli.

– Travis, the man coughed.

– And I am Chloe, the woman smiled, reaching out a hand to Larry.

He took it and squeezed it lightly. She suddenly breathed visibly faster.

Nelli smiled relaxed and patronizingly at the woman, seeing no threat in her. Larry suspected even the very concept of jealousy was alien to her. She rose relaxed, putting a light hand on Larry's shoulder.

– I will get us more beer.

She turned towards the two, looking at their nearly empty glasses.

– Do you want more, too?

Travis gave her an admiring smile.

– Don't mind if we do, he replied.

She ignored him and left the table, walking into the steamy insides of the building.

Larry studied the two without studying them. He let them talk, letting them give him all the information for free, revealing nothing of himself. And it felt so easy, like second nature. He focused on them, on his surroundings, on practically everyone around him, and it felt like the most mundane of trifles.

A woman had a drink, not beer three tables to the left. The strong liquor burned on her lips. It sent shivers down her spine and his. She rocked to the beat of an oversized disk-player close by. She wasn't talking, but was still communicating on so many levels, being unaware of most of them herself.

But not he. He was very much aware. He could still hardly believe how Aware he had become.

Nelli returned, balancing four pints of Guinness in her hands.

– That was *quick*, Travis stated, both admiringly and incredulous.

Larry imagined her slipping forward in the queue, making elegant mincemeat of everyone standing in her way, and he stifled a giggle.

She put the four glasses down on the table. Larry knew she hadn't spilled a drop, which was next to impossible. She raised her glass. The other three did as well.

– To the Red, she cheered.

They repeated her words and glasses met and parted, and they drank.

– The… Red? Chloe wondered, studying Nelli cautiously.

– The night, Nelli told her, – far beyond these artificial lights. When we look deep, deep into the night we see the fire.

She made a sweep with her hand, a wide sweep clearly encompassing far more than the tiny move of her hand.

And then, there it was, the night, so close, close enough to reach out and touch. Larry did it, the others, too, to a lesser degree. Nelli didn't have to.

– I think I actually understand what you mean, Chloe said awkward, clearly not believing or completely believing her own words. – It makes sense to me.

– Perhaps it does. Nelli nodded. – But not as much as it eventually will.

They laughed, Travis and Chloe clearly uncomfortable, scrutinized as they were by Nelli's penetrating eyes.

She's prepping them already, Larry thought, for their future life.

Other strange thoughts kept haunting him.

Strange chords reached him from the speakers, from the very night surrounding them, and he was not certain he heard exactly what the others heard. The evening, the night progressed, not in a daze, but in utmost clarity. All the beer didn't seem to matter. He remained sharp and focused, even though his drinking clearly masked his intentions in the other two's eyes.

They didn't see what he saw, the small things that others might miss, didn't notice the world through his newly wide-open eyes. Chloe raised her glass and cheered. He heard and noticed, beyond noticing how their glasses met and parted, how both the sound and the very event echoed through the air, no matter the loud noise and visible static of the place.

He frowned, suddenly sensing, almost actually feeling a shadow passing him, touching him. Travis and Chloe kept laughing, kept up their silly prattle, and ignoring their surroundings. But he saw them, the four of them, saw everything and everyone around them, as if it was the very first time. He looked at Nelli, and she looked, too, like she always did.

– Look at this, he heard himself say, – at all this.

They looked at him, listened to his hesitating, forceful voice.

– It is so damn static. Look at us, sitting here behind fences, believing we have a good time.

Everybody sat here, under the artificial red lights, framed by the ropes of an orderly existence.

Chloe and Travis looked at him, and he believed, imagined he saw a glimmer of understanding in their muddled eyes and mind.

He rose, turning slowly, and had a look around. The group he had noticed earlier sat four tables away, listening to the oversized portable disk-player with rather large speakers. They didn't play it very loud, just loud enough for them to hear, he gathered, and did not draw too much attention to themselves. He walked to them and stopped by their table. They ignored him.

– Excuse me, he said softly, but yet loud.

They looked rather annoyed at him, and at the shadow, at Nelli behind him.

– I wonder if I can borrow your player, he said, with mischief in his eyes, a glimmer they could not help but noticing. – It's so damn boring around here, isn't it? The need to make something happen is overwhelming, the way I see it. What about you?

They looked at each other. They looked back at him.

In one of the girls' eyes he saw mischief, carelessness and dawning joy. She drank down her whiskey and handed him the portable.

– It's mine, she declared, she pointed out the obvious truth, also to one of the others that looked like he might be voicing a protest.

Larry carried the portable to the middle of the street, turning it back at the would-be revelers bathing in the red and warm lights, and cranked the sound up to the max. It was a great piece of equipment and the music filled the street, with very little distortion. Nelli slipped into his arms, and they began dancing. He followed her tune, as her dance turned wilder and wilder and wilder. Others joined them, hesitatingly at first, and then to his great joy and triumph in ever more savage moves.

– So, what do you think of my little performance, he wondered, as they were dancing tight, but yet wild.

– It is… inspired… She nodded, considering it yet again, and nodded vigorously. – Yes, inspired.

– The police will be here eventually, of course, he grinned, – but by then it won't matter.

One of the dancers howled, howled loud enough to wake the dead, and Larry felt a jolt deep inside. Others, too reacted to the primal scream, and echoed it.

He glimpsed a couple of colleagues from work, saw them go apeshit in the heat of the moment, and he enjoyed himself.

BANG! A heavy drum-session resonated from the speakers. The dance turned savage.

In a brief, somber moment he touched Nelli's jaw, making her look attentive, even more attentive than usual at him.

– We may have to spend the night in a cell, he told his companion, a little worry tangible in his voice. – Can you handle that?

– It won't be a problem, she shrugged. – The magistrates hold no terrors for me.

The way she said that, both relaxed and with a snarl encouraged him further.

BANG! A long, wild guitar riff was fired from the player. It fired all of them up further. They began jumping up and down, and then, giving in completely to the moment they hammered the street with their feet, making the ground shake.

Drivers leaned on the horns as ever more cars lined up on both sides of the congestion. There were those that attempted to rush the dancing floor and turn off the music, among them the employees of the establishments at the square, but Nelli kept them at bay easily, with a look and a few threatening/non-threatening moves, without actually *doing* anything. They grew fearful and timid and couldn't say why.

The street party or celebration continued. Alcohol was consumed in far greater quantity outside the legal parameters than inside. So, the establishments in the area sold a lot more during that short time than during an entire ordinary night.

Larry noted pleased that Chloe and Travis eagerly joined in on the great and wild time. Perhaps, if they could have seen themselves the way Nelli and also he could see them, they would be more than a bit scared, but they didn't

and partied on.
Chloe jumped into Travis' arms and kissed his lips fiercely, and he met her with equal measure.
– It feels so great seeing them like that, Larry said to Nelli, – so unrestrained.
She nodded with huge eyes.
– They were dead, but now they are alive, the way all humans should be, and you woke them up, Larry, like fire from the sky.
He heard the tangible excitement and joy in her voice, unavoidable.
It turned sweaty and tight there on the square. Residents stood in their windows and shouted hateful words at the revelers, to no avail. The celebration, the wild abandon continued.
The sound of sirens grew in the distance, unnoticeable at first, but then loud and shrieking. The dancers kept it going for a little while longer, even after the numerous constables had arrived, but after that the activity slowly faded.
Only Larry and Nelli, and a few others kept dancing, until a policeman turned off the player and a whole lot of people, both uniformed and not surrounded them with pointed stares.
Larry grinned at them, a *very* silly grin. So did Nelli, of course and some of the others.
They were handcuffed. They were actually handcuffed. Not that he hadn't expected it, but it still made him shake his head, even as he fought to uphold his spirit.
– I've had some experience with this, he told the others in the Black Mary later. – Don't worry about it. Play dumb, at least to a point. Be calm and you will do fine.
They returned his grin and felt strangely uplifted.
– I could be out of these restraints in a second, Nelli told him calmly.
The others stared incredulous at her, at him.
He considered it, actually considered it, for half a second, before shaking his head.
– No, let's ride it out. Just be calm and centered when they come to bully you, and don't sign *anything*, no matter how insistent the nice man or woman is, and we will be released tomorrow.
It was an uncontrollable situation. He admitted that to himself, before brushing off his worry like a breeze.
They didn't put them in the holding cell immediately, but actually (again) brought them to an interrogation room, put them alone in a tiny, square room and left them there.

He waited it out patiently, closing his eyes briefly, listening to the calm breeze outside the walls. It spread from there, from the ugly building and to the city at large and even to the land surrounding it. In the brief time he closed his eyes an eternity passed.

The thought struck him suddenly, unpleasantly. He wondered if Nelli had papers, but ventured that she had made provisions, somehow.

The policeman was a cliché, a big bully with a big belly. Larry felt like laughing.

He didn't though.

The handcuffs squeezed his wrists. The other man just waited for him to ask to have them removed, and thus gain a sort of a perceived advantage, but Larry wouldn't.

Bully Belly sat down, in the chair, at the other side of the table, and consulted his papers, which was bullshit, of course. There was nothing there yet.

– Drunken disorder, disturbing the peace, antisocial behavior… this could be serious…

– I just wanted to dance, Larry said sheepishly.

Bully Belly stared at him, one eye a little bigger than the other.

– If I'm not very much mistaken, there is a dance hall two blocks from The Square…

– That place stinks, Larry pointed out. – Besides, it was a spur of the moment thing.

– I wouldn't be so upbeat, if I WERE YOU, Bully Belly said, foaming around the mouth. – This can have very serious consequences, you know, if you don't WISE UP.

He didn't really raise his voice, but he very much wanted to.

– You're not going to slap a terrorist charge on me, are you?

Larry shrugged, very deliberately.

The man's eyes started bulging.

The interview ended. They were thrown into holding cells for the night, a place stinking of piss and shit and bad breath.

– I'm quite okay, Nelli cried to him across the room before they closed the cell doors, – we just had a little philosophical discussion, and that was it.

Her grin was as wide as the world.

The heavy metal doors slammed shut, and everything turned unnaturally quiet. No sounds reached him from the outside, none at all. He rubbed his wrists. The handcuffs still hurt, even after they had been removed. There was no chair or bench or anything in the square room. There was a bucket. It was half full with vomit and human waste. Somebody had thrown the almost empty roll of toilet paper into the corner.

He sat down on the floor, closing his eyes, listening to the night-breeze outside.

Time stretched out like a dark and windy cloak, and it was a wondrous thing. The stench, the sparse, horrible green painting on the wall and the potent memory of tonight's events… it all served to lighten his mood.

Larry Watros spent the night behind bars, in a tiny, tiny cell, looking through the bar-covered window, at the night beyond the walls, and felt free as a bird.

Chapter Four

They walked through the forest, carrying huge backpacks. The forest seemed endless, even though he was fully aware that it wasn't, that it was dwindling, attacked on all fronts by human activity, even as they spoke. She looked around her, wide-eyed like a kid.

– This growth is phenomenal, Larry, she cried. – This is fairly… common?

And once again, he could confirm to himself that she wasn't from around here, from this day and age.

– Yes, but increasingly rare.

– We had… trees, a few here and there, but they looked nothing like these, and there was little or no… growth.

She was clearly spooked as well as excited, but not very much so, because of whom she was.

Her teaching had prepared her for this, for any eventuality she might encounter. He felt proud on her behalf.

She learned in minutes, seemingly. Not to the point that her footing on the treacherous forest bed was as firm as it had been in the city streets, but well enough. She didn't stumble in roots or hit her head on low branches. Her balance on steep and skewed trails was off for a while, but she learned to compensate for it, instinctively, as if she had been born to it.

But she hadn't, and it became apparent long before she had to give in to the unbearable terror of their surroundings. Her eyes flooded. After a while the smell, the stench of the growth simply grew too overwhelming on the senses for someone that had grown up in a world where nothing like this existed.

– It burns, she gasped. – I feel like I am on fire.

They stopped on a rise, where there were few trees and bushes, but it was no use. She was sweating profusely and kept gasping, as if not getting enough air, but she got too much, in an environment she had never before experienced, where oxygen was abundant.

She sat still on the rise, focusing, meditating, and attempting to regain a kind of equilibrium. He saw how she practically fought tooth and nail, and succeeded, at least partly, at pulling herself together.

– It's so fantastic, My Lord, she told him after a while. – I've never sensed its like. Nature was only a husk of its former glory by the time I was born. It's quite unnerving to experience it fully.

She… adapted, as always. He saw her do it, like a human chameleon. She rose with a happy, radiant and sexy smile on her face.

They headed deeper into the forest. He walked first, fairly well-versed in the art of walking on the soft, uneven ground. She trailed him, clumsy and inept. Even though she learned with each passing moment, she was clearly out of her bounds. This was his domain, a fact that further stressed the order between them.

It bothered him, but not her. Her attention was locked on him with the same unconditional admiration. He knew she took it in stride as yet another proof of his superiority, and it… bothered him.

He made a fire. It burned within minutes, and its light danced in her eyes.

– I was a boy scout, he said. – We all learned to light fires under impossible circumstances.

– We searched for dry wood, she said. – It practically lit itself.

Night fell. The dancing flames, of the fire itself and the illumination cast on the trees and branches were the only lights they could see, except in each other's eyes.

She snuggled in his arms, so content, so spent after they had made the ground shake, and he had convinced himself they had done so for hours.

– We always knew you were different from the rest of us, she said, looking up at him with her characteristic, direct stare. – You, coming from another world had experiences we could never have, never share with you.

He shrugged and said lightly:

– Why did you come here, to the past? To… change it?

– No. She shook her head, frowning. – Why should it be changed? It is as I said, to safeguard and support you through your difficult transition.

He didn't voice his comment on that, but he knew he did anyway, with his body language, and he knew she read him like she would a book.

– I guess it cannot be changed, he said. – It has started already, and nobody is doing anything to stop it.

– Even another cataclysmic event stopping the release of all pollution on the planet won't stop it, she said. – The warming that is already in the system will continue to increase the temperature for a thousand years.

He nodded slowly, not sure why he nodded, or certain if he actually noticed himself nodding.

They sat there, in the silence of the forest, warmed by the fire, not saying much, but still communicating on a level his former self had been unable to even imagine.

He got a lot of that lately.

Birds rose from the treetops, a sound he recognized immediately and that didn't alarm him in any way. But Nellie froze in combat mode, before noticing his calm and relenting instantly.

– It's just birds, he shrugged. – It could be a sign that something has scared them, but it isn't likely. That would have sounded different.
– In my time many birds are deadly predators, she said. – They, too, have to be, to survive.
So, they sat there, listening to the sounds of the forest, he with half closed eyes, she with hers wide open. A bird landed on a branch there in the darkness, and he saw that. He saw it turn its head back and forth, attempting to look in all directions at once.
He stared at the dancing flames, the bright fire, and saw the pale shadows. They didn't just dance in front of him, but also inside his bright burning mind.
She turned to him, studying him, and it felt remarkable how he was able to sense that, know that.
– You look at peace, My Lord, she said. – Are you happy? How do you feel?
She knew, but she still asked.
– I always feel at home out here, he said, after pausing a bit, considering his words. – Both the mind and the body work so much better. In the city, among the dead trees and dead people it's always inevitable to feel dead yourself, dead inside, like stone on the outside. But here, and especially now, with you… I feel… I feel strong again, and free.
He pulled her to him, and kissed her, kissed her hard on the lips, and she moaned in joy, giggling wildly and coquettishly when he released her.
She sat up, looking attentive at him, catching his attention.
– With your permission…
– Yes? He encouraged her, attempting not to reveal his tiny sting of irritation, knowing the attempt to be futile.
– Let the fire fade.
He nodded, feeling excitement, having some idea of what she had in mind.
The fire faded, until there were only embers left. It took time, but she was patient and so was he, enjoying the slow change in their surroundings, enjoying the sensation of not having to rebuild the fire every five minutes. The darkness came to them before it truly did, in the intersection between the embers and the night surrounding them. The shadows turned a deeper hue.
– We live in darkness, she said. – There's not a single ray of light where we live. We use fire, but only for making certain types of meals. There's no cold left, anywhere.
He envisioned it in his mind, based on her words, her intonation before he actually experienced it. The light from the last few embers faded to black,

and they sat there in the pitch-black darkness.
– We go up into the light. Wearing our goggles, to hunt and scavenge. But we usually do so at night. The stars are sharp points of ice pricking us in a thousand ways. We don't fear the light, but we prefer the cool and deep shadows.
Her words… At first, they were mere words, but as he sat there, listening to her voice they changed into images, into movement and life.
There was sand no matter where he turned, endless dunes from horizon to horizon. He smelled it, its stark scent. It flowed slowly into the tunnels through the large hole above. They climbed up and down through an intricate patched ladder system. He was one of those hunters and scavengers making their way across the dunes, was all of them. His feet moved through the wind, the hard grains whipping his protected body. He felt like one with the sand, with the wind, the ongoing storm. It grabbed hold of him and held on, digging deep, and he imagined he could actually control it, to a point, making it bend and shift to his will.
A hawk flew in from the east, crossing the sky. A vulture floated above, patient like time.
He blinked, sitting there face to face with the girl, seeing her clearly, and then his attention shifted once more, and he became one with his surroundings, with all the growth around him, with the entire forest, and he saw himself and the girl from a thousand different viewpoints, both close and far away.
She stopped, looking at him with awe in her pale, reddish eyes.
They rose simultaneously, gazing at each other in shared amazement.
– Come, she called, – let's run.
She ran and he followed her, remarkably easy. He didn't even have to look at her, to mimic her. The path was so clear to him, illuminated like traces of pale and invisible luminous paint. He couldn't see it, but he still saw it. They rushed through the forest in complete blackness, not stumbling in any roots sticking out and there were a few of them, even on the well used trail.
They reached an open space in the thick growth, and stopped there, stopped and looked, taking in everything before them. He felt it all, in every piece of his body, the tingle in the skin, the glow inside.
– Almost all of us in the crèche are born with the ability to sense in the dark, she said. – It stands to reason that you, the progenitor were also born with that gift.
He frowned, not quite getting it, something about what she said escaping him.
The two of them straightened there, in the darkness, and he… sensed it,

knew where the nearest tree was, even though he couldn't see it. He saw her, the glow in his mind pulsing and waning and burning like a star.

He heard her breathe, heard her grow excited, sensed her reacting to his presence, like he reacted to hers.

– That is amazing, he said, shaking his head. – That's just amazing.

– We seek the deepest darkness when the change comes over us, she said. – We seek it alone or with others, to go where we've never gone before. A given change can be big or small, but it will always be *tangible*. I *knew* going out here, in a place saturated with life would give you a push forward on your path to glory.

She clapped her hands excitedly, looking at him with that very telling look of admiration and awe.

– I've always been able to tell if I encounter kin, she said, – and now, so are you.

They lit the fire again. It burned incredibly bright in his far more sensitive eyes. She put on the goggles. They hid her eyes. He still imagined he could see them, somehow, large and luminous and open, open to him. She didn't speak and didn't need to. Her body language told him, both his conscious and subconscious self, everything he needed to know.

The fire faded once more, slowly. It was as if it had only burned for seconds, even though he knew it to be hours. The fire faded and the darkness ascended. The birds sang in the dark. He heard them, heard the hawk, the vulture and a thousand other voices. She removed her goggles, and held out her hands. He pulled the rubber ropes from his bag and began tying her up. She stood on all fours above a heavy fallen tree. He tied her hands to thick branches ahead of her and her feet to thick branches behind her. She smelled him, and he smelled her, too, and he felt the arousal hard and poignant.

He kept dreaming, as the night turned black, turned alive with vivid images and strong colors and sighs and growls and moans of longing and joy. They lay there later, side by side, slowly falling into sleep, into dream. He knew that, even though he was asleep.

The hole in the tunnel high above looked small, but he knew it to be huge. A building had fallen through there once. It was still fairly intact in the dry air and desert soil, very much like the ruins he had seen in Greece, the process of entropy slowed down to a crawl. Crossing the openness under the hole was like bathing in light, in a glow radiant like the sun. He moved with his brethren through wide and narrow tunnels, but that light stayed with them no matter where they moved.

She woke him not long after dawn. He knew after just a few moments, because of the way the light hit them and their immediate surroundings. To his surprise he sensed distress in her eyes and body.

– Today is September fourth?

She held up his watch for him to see.

– Yes! He nodded. – What's this about?

– I forgot, she said, nearly mumbled, both to him and herself. – We don't measure time the way you do.

He waited, somewhat calm, even though clearly influenced by her emotions.

– Your half brother, she said. – He will die today, at noon.

– Albert? He frowned. – I haven't seen him in *ages*.

– You have the same father, she said. – What makes you different, makes you *red,* you got through your biological father.

She ran and so did he, leaving behind their gear.

– We must make haste, she cried.

They ran and stumbled through the dense forest. He could sort of keep pace with her, because of her inexperience in moving on uneven and soft ground, but just barely. When she stumbled in roots and fell she was up again almost before she had hit the ground. Eventually he got tired, on the verge of exhaustion and they had to stop, for him to rest.

– Go! He told her. – Go alone.

– I don't know where your brother lives, she sighed. – Even if you tell me the address and describe the place to me there's no way I could find it in time. I'm so sorry, so sorry…

He stopped her, stopped her self-recrimination with a touch and a look. She gave him that grateful smile again.

She rose.

– This is a great opportunity, she noted. – A potentially great training exercise. We should make the best out of it. You can take hardship, take exhaustion and spitting blood, and you will be that much better for it.

They ran. He felt it, how he moved beyond hardship, beyond exhaustion and spitting blood, how he seemed to be floating outside himself, even as his feet touched the ground, hammered against the hard asphalt below.

It was hours later, he knew that much, when they sat gasping for air at the bus stop.

– We take a taxi, yes?

Her usually so melodic voice was hoarse and ragged. He nodded and pulled the phone from its soaking wet place in his pocket. Miraculously, it was still working.

It fizzed out and died just a few seconds after he had broken the connection to the taxi central.

They waited, ten fifteen, twenty minutes before the car screeched around the corner.

– I haven't spoken to him in ten years, he said. – I can't even be certain he still lives in the same place.

– He does, Larry, Nelli assured him. – He does!

The taxi driver really went into his role, and kept driving recklessly. He speeded up the moment they sat down and kept rising the stakes. Larry expected to hear sirens at any moment and could swear he smelled burned rubber. It was strangely exhilarating.

In spite of the speed, he saw clearly what passed by outside his window. Even the slightest shift in angle was stored as an image, as a moving image in his mind. He could recall it on a whim, as the simplest of tasks. A man stood still on a sidewalk. The light had turned green and the man in dark clothes didn't move, didn't cross the zebra stripes, but just stood there, staring straight ahead at nothing.

People around him didn't notice or didn't seem to be noticing anything, but Larry did.

The cab kept screeching as it turned corners, as it approached its destination, one only faintly familiar to Larry. It was a fairly typical worn-down suburb. Two abandoned, rusty car wrecks stood at the far end of the parking lot they passed. Parts of the driveway where the car screeched to a halt were overgrown.

They jumped out of the car. Larry threw some bills to the driver and was surprised by the fact that they actually reached the man's hands. The block of flats loomed over them, as they made their way to the entrance.

– He lives on the second floor, Larry said. – We'll be there…

He heard a scream, one sounding strangely loud in his ears, one of fear and helpless protest. Then he heard the sound of a gun being fired. He experienced it as if it had been fired close by, but when he looked up he realized the thunder originated high above him.

A body hit the driveway right in front of them. It cracked in countless bigger and smaller ways, even though it sounded more like a sack hitting the ground. He recognized Albert, recognized his brother through a tunnel vision of absolute clarity.

Nelli knelt down by his side, having rushed there fast as lightning. Nausea almost overwhelmed Larry where he stood frozen on the spot.

– Stay with him, he heard himself say. – I'll call for an ambulance.

He remembered, just before he looked incredulous at the ruined phone.

He looked at her, at the bloody face on the ground.

– Come close, she implored him. – Stand here.

He moved the necessary steps closer. The body down there was still breathing or attempting to. Two or three more seconds passed, and then the chest stopped heaving. Larry felt pain, non-localized, all over his body. It wasn't grief, he knew what that was like, but something new and unidentifiable. Nelli felt it, too, he knew that much, but it was muted in her, not so potent.

It passed quickly, fading like a dream.

– He was shot, he said, – and thrown from the roof. I heard him, heard him beg for his life. Then there was laughter, and they shot him.

– Yes, Nelli nodded. – I'm sorry.

– Not as sorry as they are going to be, he said with clenched teeth.

She saw him enraged for the first time, felt the burning glow grow within him.

– They'll probably leave through the opposite entrance, he told her. – If they do, you will follow them as far as you're able, identify them as best as you can without being noticed, but you will not engage them. If you're forced to engage them, you will not kill them, or harm them more than necessary, only subdue them. Do you understand?

– Yes, Red Shadow, she replied evenly.

– If they come through here, they will identify us, and we will engage them, subdue them, without harming them. Do not use your claws or your power.

– I understand, Red Shadow, she replied just as evenly.

People didn't exactly rush forward. A few of them walked, reluctantly towards the dead and the two standing by the body.

The elevator inside slid to a halt. He heard it, or sensed it, he wasn't sure what. Four men and two women exited it and departed through the opposite entrance.

– Call the police, he told Nelli.

Nelli rose and slid away. He knew she wouldn't call the police. She knew it to be a ruse, a part of the necessary caution he had chosen to spin around his life.

– I've called the police, a woman stated, ten, fifteen seconds later.

He looked, forced himself to look at the man, the broken, cooling body on the ground, analyzing himself, finding that the sight created very little emotion aside from the anger.

– Are you… the brother? The woman wondered. – You kinda look the part.

– I am, he confirmed.

– He spoke of you.

Larry noticed the nuances in her voice, the tiny variances telling him, somewhat, how she truly felt, what she was truly saying.

Conflicting emotions kept raging within him. He realized this was the first time in God knew how long he didn't have Nelli there by his side.

Sirens and blue lights finally reappeared in his ears and vision, after long minutes of waiting. Nelli was there, back by his side. He didn't need to see her in order to know she was there.

– All the phone booths were leveled, she reported.

They had seen them on their way here, victims of unofficial urban renewal.

His hair was still wet, but the suit kept his body dry, and warm, and his insides and his skin kept glowing, kept burning, a warm and strange feeling tickling all over.

Something had happened, something extraordinary, and upon contemplating it, he knew the exact moment it had.

The police interviews were routine this time. They told the detectives exactly what they had seen and left out all speculation, without being evasive.

He watched her, studied her without studying her, very much like she had always studied him. She was good at this, at the subterfuge and stuff, sucking up knowledge about this unknown world very much like a sponge. When he looked at her with his eyes, the way he would have looked at her only a few days ago he saw nothing but the distressed and sympathetic girlfriend of her boyfriend that had lost his brother under horrible circumstances.

The police let them go early. There was no suspicion there, nothing except the general distrust and spite any policeman exhibited towards anyone.

He walked through the unfamiliar surroundings of his brother's apartment. The police had been here, rummaged through it all and left, and released it to the deceased's closest living relative. The late day's sunrays cast its soft shadows on the wall. Everything turned deep, natural yellow, slowly turning red.

– The detectives were right. He shook his head. – There's nothing here, nothing explaining why he caught the *ire* of those people.

She studied him, not saying anything.

– It could be random, of course, a matter of casual, urban violence...

– But you do not believe that? She asked casually.

– No. He shook his head again. – They sought him out, even bothered to follow him to the roof or take him there. Random killings are either domestic *disputes* or a result of random street violence.

She was smiling behind her serene mask, and he felt the glow rise within himself.

– I didn't really know him, he said. – I don't even know what to feel about it all…about his death.

– You sent me after his killers, she pointed out. – You wanted to know who they were and where they lived. It wasn't hard finding out. They are local, at least most of them are. We can easily find out more, their names and everything, if you so desire.

He loved her punctuations, how she spoke, the inflections and innuendo in her words.

She raised a hand, clearly noticing something that was beyond his capabilities.

The bell rang. Both froze. In a moment she had moved between him and the apartment's hallway.

Stay here, she signaled, and moved silently, and like lightning towards the door.

One person, she signaled, when she stood by the wall by the door. Female. Upset. Calm.

And he knew she could tell by the sound of the other's breath through the wall, and he once again shook his head in wonder.

She opened the door. They both recognized the woman from the yard, she who had called the police. He approached her cautiously, with no outward display of anxiety.

– Yes? Nelli said.

– My name is Roberta Allen. May I come in?

– By all means, Larry nodded.

Nelli stepped back. Roberta stepped inside. Nelli closed the door behind her, not allowing it to close by itself.

– I'm sorry for your loss, Roberta began.

– Thank you, Larry said. – That's very kind.

– I knew Albert, knew Al…

Larry wanted to ask her to come with them into the living room, but realized that this dark hallway was the best place for clandestine activities.

They couldn't be seen through any window here.

He noticed that her eyes wavered, that they were constantly moving, like his own, even in this fairly safe haven.

– The trouble in our neighborhood began two months ago. It didn't look like much, just more of the usual urban unrest. Most people still think of it as such.

– But you don't? He heard himself say.

– I'm former army intelligence. I'm trained to see beyond appearances.

He understood more of where she was coming from, now, and so, evidently did Nelli. Understanding grew even more as he looked at his warrior, as he saw her take her alertness down a notch.

– Two of the original gang members are locals, have lived here for years, but the others have newly moved here, and there are others still. And, knowing what I know now, I notice things about even those two original locals, things that don't *fit.*

There was something… It was if the world shifted to him, as if he suddenly saw the woman in a light previously unknown to him. When he looked at the woman, he saw her, saw her shimmer in red.

He saw The Red for the very first time, and he marveled.

– Why are you telling us this?

She grinned darkly.

– Two reasons: One is the obvious: you are Al's brother, and I thought you would want to know, no matter how much you two had grown apart. The second is also self-evident to me: I watched the two of you, and noticed things about you as well…

– Your expensive military training at work, he nodded.

– Quite so, she conceded.

He found himself admiring her tall, curvy body, her compassionate smile. She stood there with slightly split displayed legs, and his dead brother became even more of a memory.

– That was all I wanted to say. Again: I'm sorry for your loss. I liked Al, and I hope the butchers doing this to him will get what's coming to them.

– Thank you, Larry said.

– Thank you, Nelli said.

Roberta left, with a final glance at the two of them.

– She said a lot without coming right out and say it, Nelli said dryly. – I like her.

He realized she was joking, joking.

After a brief hesitation he stepped close to her. He held her. They just stood there for a while, holding on to each other, and it felt so good, so very good.

Time passed, melted off the wall, until the clock on the wall faded away. Lawrence Watros once again searched through his brother's things, not really searching this time, but just looking, looking at a life both familiar and distant.

There was a card with a name, an address

Pingross Limited
Ebert Lane 534

and a phone number.

That was all.

He put it in his pocket, realizing he hadn't been certain there was a pocket there, until this very moment. What he wore, what was wrapped around his body wasn't fabric like he had learned to understand it, but he already wore it like the comfortable second skin it had become.

Stories he had read would give cause for concern in a case like this, but there was no sense of discomfort, no sign of any malady or wrongdoing taking place. He had tested it. It could be easily removed, de-attached from him without anything sinister happening.

He had done it with her watching, as he had long since realized the idiocy in attempting to keep secrets from her.

– It was only you and your brother, she said. – Now, there are only you. You have a female cousin on your mother's side, but she doesn't count, and you have no idea where she may live, whether or not she is alive or dead. You're the last of your line.

– No, he shook his head, – now, there are us.

She blushed and walked to him. Her lips were soft, the fingers, even her claws playing on his neck likewise, soft, enticing skin. Their extra skin faded simultaneously, and they stood there, fondling each other. He grabbed her and pulled her close. She yelped happily, as they were melting into each other's embrace. He noticed the sweet taste of her lips. The smell made him almost lose his mind. They went down on their knees right there. He felt himself harden, as he smelled her, smelled her scent, as she began moaning and writhing in his arms.

– Yes, she gasped, – I can hear the drums, feel them shake the Earth.

Her nipples stabbed him in the chest, and he felt them penetrate his skin, cut his heart. He held her arms, squeezed her in his grip. She stretched her arms above her head and leaned backwards. He lowered her to the floor, and stopped a moment to admire the beautiful animal, before mounting her. She screamed sharply. That startled him a bit. He realized that she was letting go and he had never really seen her do that before. It didn't stop him, but spurred him on. He heard deep growls and realized they were coming from him. They mated there on the floor, wild and with wild abandon. His friends and he, too, only a few days ago would have said she was a screamer, but it went far beyond that. She was a howler in the deepest night. He felt himself slide back and forth inside her, on her. The sounds erupting from her sounded like a harmonic discord he had never imagined existed, attuned to her body's movement in a totally uncanny way defying description. He felt her nails rake the skin of his back and he felt detached by the thought even the brief moment it crossed his mind. They kissed and mated and mixed, and when the explosion came it was like being pulled into a current of currents in a mighty river.

She sighed, exhaled in a thoroughly content expression, curling up by his side, glowing in pride and empowerment. When she grabbed his hand and kissed it and looked shyly at him under lowered eyelashes, he felt the heat of her pale eyes.

Somebody began hammering on the door, and screaming themselves hoarse.

– HEY, WHAT THE FUCK IS HAPPENING IN THERE?

He recalled it, now, the hard knocking both from the apartments below and above.

– Allow me, My Lord.

She rose like the cat she was. Her clothes flowed back on, transforming into a night dress, very daring and revealing. He shrugged, knowing she had the situation well in hand. She approached the door with caution, of course, but as expected it proved unnecessary. The tall, fat man shrank to a dwarf the moment she opened the door.

– May I help you? She smiled sweetly.

– No, not really, he said flustered. – We were merely wondering about what was going on in there, that's all.

– Yes, I guess it grew a little loud, she grinned. – Will you accept our most sincere apologies?

– Certainly, he said, turning tomato red in a second. – Sorry for disturbing your… your…

The last word was never actualized. He just stood there, unable to continue.

– Of course, she granted him generously, – have a nice evening, then.

– You, too, he gawked.

He sat in the chair when she returned to the living room. He wasn't surprised when he saw that she had dressed herself as well.

– I guess he didn't see the blood under your nails, then? He remarked.

– I guess he didn't, she acknowledged.

She lowered her eyes, awaiting his judgment.

– I completely forgot, he said amazed.

– Yes, My Lord, she acknowledged.

– But you didn't, did you, my little astute bitch.

– No, My Lord, she shook her head.

– My back itches like hell, but I'm still alive.

– Very much so, My Lord.

She blushed, still wary.

– So, how come? *Explain!*

She drew breath sharply.

– Your skin has turned hard, My Lord, hard enough to withstand the worst of my ardor. The reason for this is your influx in power. When your brother died, you and I, as his kin, standing close to him the moment he expired, absorbed his energies, sharing the spoils of his ashes.

He shook his head, incredulous.

– That's amazing.

That, too is amazing.

– You felt it, knew what happened, she stated. – You just needed time to acknowledge the fact of it.

She was right, of course. He recalled the strange sensation and he reminded himself of the red aura he had seen surrounding that girl, Roberta, something he had never seen before.

– Nothing goes to waste in our world, Larry, she stated solemnly. – Nothing.

He… liked that, in a way.

But the tumultuous thoughts didn't fade from his mind, his ever more overactive mind.

– Your powers have reached a critical level, now, she said softly. – They will continue to grow in leaps and bounds, even without… incentives, until you're powerful beyond belief.

Her words sent a shiver of delight and apprehension through him.

He pushed at his underwear that wasn't really underwear, and the clothes once more faded from his body, and hers did, too, at exactly the same moment. She went to him and climbed onto his lap.

– You enjoy your servant scaring the wits out of people, don't you, Larry, she teased him.

– I find it absolutely hysterical, he admitted.

She lowered herself right on him and without pause, with a directness still startling him began moving her hips up and down. He held back a little because he was watching her, how her face dissolved into a featureless mass of gratification.

Her palms pushed against his shoulders, moved over the skin, both gentle and brutal, squeezing lightly, at least for her.

– I can feel the increase of muscles, she mumbled. – The texture of thy skin plays my fingertips. I'm hammered by the rising of the red sea.

He began pushing harder back, and the already beyond excited female released beyond pleased a loud howl. She grabbed the chair and held on, her claws cutting the fabric to shreds. He saw it, more than he heard it, even though he had no way of seeing it.

Nelli smiled, an ecstatic smile sending waves of pleasure through him.

Saliva flowed from her mouth and in his eyes… in his eyes it turned to blood.

– It's happening, she mumbled. – It's happening.

He heard so much, the traffic outside, the couple speaking in hushed, excited, fearful and hateful voices in the apartment below, noticed so much, the tiniest detail in the room, the piece of velvet on the floor, cut by her claws, the miniscule pattern of the shadow on the wall.

The shadow on the wall moved and grinned to him, and smiled with its sharp fangs.

She cried out, one single cry before she slumped against him, before they both tensed, and everything blackened out for him, and he heard her beautiful discord echo in the emptiness engulfing him, and he saw nothing but red in the vast black sea.

Chapter Five

It was on the night Nelli started her training. She was not yet three, among the youngest of the children gathering in the larger tunnel. Nelli remembered that night clearly, one of her very first vivid memories, the reason for it not immediately manifesting itself. It was a special day, but not particularly so. The day a moon ago, when she had been given her first goggles had also been great, and when her younger brother had been born to the tribe.

She noticed, with her keen senses an unusual restlessness among their teachers, the older children. At first, she couldn't properly identify it, new and stark as it was to her, but then she noticed the quick glances the ten-year-olds sent each other. They were nervous. Something unnerved them to the point of them exposing themselves to those they viewed as lower than the worms in the ground.

The trainees stood there with their little wands in their hands, shaking under the onslaught of the older kids' contempt, but still excited because of the new turn their lives had taken.

A teacher, Adelaide stepped forward. They instantly fixed their attention on her.

– Do as I do! She told them. – Do it well and you will learn. Do it badly, and you will still learn, through kindness, hardship and pain, like all those before you.

She moved, and even though she obviously made sure she moved slowly, it looked fast as lightning to her students. Feeling awkward and clumsy, and on the verge of tears Nelli strived, like her fellow students to keep up and failing miserably.

– Again! Adelaide beat her wand at the ground. – *Again!*

And again and again and again, until muscles and limbs felt like lead, and the sweat burning in their eyes was a constant in their lives.

It was minutes, hours later, Nelli couldn't tell, when something changed, when the restlessness she had sensed in her teachers grew to stark terror and awe.

There was a hum, a chant, a single dark voice filling the tunnels.

Nelli saw *him* for the very first time. He appeared from the shadows, out of nowhere to take the place of the observer. The small children stared astounded at Adelaide and the others, how they faltered, and their eyes flickered.

They didn't dare look at the beyond imposing creature, but they saw it still.

It invaded them. One glimpse was enough to freeze them all in their tracks. Adelaide kept snapping at her charges, kept striving to appear casual and failing miserably.

Strangely enough it made Nelli feel better. When they were finally given rest and sat there, gasping for breath she studied the man across the room. She couldn't do so for long, but one glimpse was sufficient to sense him, to be totally overwhelmed by his mere presence.

His face stayed in shadow, even in the shifting light. There was a campfire burning in one of the other tunnels. She smelled the raw meat burn. The stench ripped open her nostrils like the sharpest of blades. It reminded her of how hungry she had become, but she knew she wouldn't be allowed to feed, not until the exercise had run its course.

Just like Adelaide and the other children she put more energy into the exercise. Everybody eventually did, spurred on by the presence in their midst.

The pain from the bruises and the beating made her cry herself to sleep that dreamtime. But in her pain, through the red haze of pain she saw the shadow, and she imagined she was able to see or at least glimpse its face, and she writhed and moaned in her sleep, in every place in the world dreamtime brought her.

He writhed and winced in his sleep, without really knowing why. The shadow didn't chase him, but held its distance, observing him with cruel humor forming his mouth, with cold and merciless eyes.

Larry woke up, covered in sweat. Nelli sat on her ass and with her legs crossed in front of her and looked steadily at him.

– I saw him, saw you for the first time that night, she stated. – You made one of your rare visits to the crèche, as you did infrequently as I grew older, until you came and fetched me to your court, bypassing every protocol and selection process, yet another act previously unheard of.

He heard the traffic from the streets outside and below unbelievably clear. The dream, no, the vision didn't make sense, and he couldn't make sense of it.

– You live through my memories, she stated. – It's not unheard of, among distant kin not having grown up with the tribe and joining it later in life. It's also yet another sign that your power is growing, both in strength and complexity.

She searched the city a bit for proper wands, searched long and hard, clearly frustrating herself, before she was somewhat pleased and found a type with the right balance and weight. Larry didn't mind following her around. He enjoyed studying her, both her physical and mental processes. It astonished him that he was able to actually do that, but the evidence was sensed and felt and pondered, undeniable in his mind. To study her was to study himself, what he had become, what he was fast becoming.

– These will suffice. She nodded to him, deferring to him, as she always did.

He knew the testing she did, moving and swinging with the two wands in her hands was slow compared to how fast she could move, if necessary, but it still made the people in the store gasp in awe.

– We'll have these, she told the girl behind the desk. – How many do you have?

– Ten, the girl breathed. – Ten in all.

– We'll have them all.

A boy stepped forward, bursting with excitement.

– Excuse me…

They both looked at him. He reddened, but in their eyes, he shimmered in red.

– Do you *teach?*

– We might, Larry replied, – but not quite yet.

Nelli looked at him with her strange smile. He knew that, without looking at her.

– Great, the kid said quickly, out of breath, – I can give you my contact information…

– It doesn't work like that. Larry shook his head. – You must find us on your own, devote yourself to that and to everything following.

– I… understand, the kid replied, after a brief hesitation.

Larry and Nelli carried the ten wands openly and left the store. The air, its smell and context outside had changed again. Larry drew his breath. It hadn't changed, only his perception of it.

– You're so good with them, My Lord, she bristled. – They will flock to you, eager and devoted.

They walked to the nearest underground station. It wasn't far, just a few blocks. Larry wanted to turn his head, take a peek behind them, but withstood the almost overwhelming temptation.

– They're not following us, she said casually. – They're convinced of our superiority. Right now, at this point in their development they're…

She frowned, clearly considering something.

– … sheep and not wolves.

He understood. There were no sheep or wolves in her time, in what had been her time. She translated her meaning to terms he could understand.

They returned to the apartment briefly, to leave eight of the wands, before seeking out an abandoned construction site not far from there. There was always one nearby, in his experience.

She turned the wand in her hand, while circling him, and he did the same, circling her.

– You're a novice, she stated sternly. – You've much to learn. You're a child in a man's body, catching up in a rush of fever and condensed empowerment. I envy you, My Lord.

She bowed. He stood still, tense, waiting for the sudden attack he knew would come. When she *moved* he still had trouble reacting in anything even resembling fast enough speed. He parted, awkward and slow her first blow, but the attack just continued, until he was crouching on the ground, bloody and bruised.

– The children are treated with brutality and scorn, she stated. – They're brutally introduced to a world quite different from the fairly soft life in the Crèche.

– Good, he said, with clenched teeth, through blood and swollen skin.

Her features softened briefly, before once again becoming the mask of rage and passion.

– We use the wand, she told him, – both because we may not rely on our powers in all situations and also because it can be used to better their use.

She played pure defense for a while. He struck her, and while she blocked most of his strikes with the wand, she also did so with the suit, with protrusions of it, reaching far beyond her body, and also with what seemed to be thin air.

– You've become *so* much faster, she marveled. – I must really work up a sweat to keep up.

He understood the subtext of her words perfectly. Her subtle criticism spurred him on further.

But… it didn't make him careless, like it would have just a week ago.

Just a week. He sat there with her, resting, dreaming unclear ideas of the past. His body hurt everywhere. His skin buzzed and bristled in what he once would have believed was in all the wrong ways. Now, he knew it was the sensation of his body healing itself. She laid in his arms later that night, retelling the stories he already imagined in his mind about her childhood in the Crèche.

– You appeared during our training sessions. No one knew why. You didn't favor any of us, but since you never watched other novices training it was clear you had a special interest in us, and we were given special attention by our teachers. By your very presence you posed a question, a riddle to them, unsolvable and mighty. In their zeal to impress you they brought down all their wrath on us.

– I'm sorry.

The moment he said it, he knew it to be wrong. And wasn't it stupid to apologize for actions he hadn't actually done or done… yet?

– No, no, My Lord, she said serious-minded. – We learned. We learned better than anyone else and were chosen for progress faster, not because you watched us, but because we proved ourselves, and others picked up on it, and everybody else improved as well, and yet again we marveled at your wisdom.

– You're just a little girl, he joked.

– Yes, My Lord.

She bowed her head in shame.

He could control her so easily, if he chose to do so.

Nelli turned nine that night. She had been made a junior teacher one full season before most others. Her training intensified, and she joined packs on her first tour upside, joining what would one day be her fellow warriors on their run across the vast dunes, bathing in the bright silver light of the night star.

They chased like specters around the main hunting party, acting as scouts, a position certainly not safe. They learned that the hard way, in blood and sand.

The two groups reached the abandoned ruins close to dawn, in the nick of time. It was further away from their home turf than most of them had ever traveled, one of the biggest ruins and subterranean lands not populated by human beings.

They sensed the emptiness long before they entered the large opening, and more so when they descended the stairs to the underground tunnels. There was no connection to this place from their home tunnels, but it looked and seemed and smelled eerily familiar. They removed their goggles. The light from behind flooded their senses. Shapes turned visible in the dark down there.

A sound reached them from far below, very strange and unfamiliar. They smelled it and the delight it created inevitably pulled and pushed them. It speeded up their descent. They found the water pond after circling and re-circling several times.

Several of the pack brightened and wanted to rush forward to fill their flasks. Ryx, the pack master stopped them with a small sign. They looked astonished at him.

– It's poisoned, he said. – Someone poisoned it long ago, and it's still unfit to drink and even touch.

The very thought felt alien to them, and those not privy to this knowledge earlier suspected it was part of the reason they had been brought here, to learn, to realize such an insane mindset existed.

– But who would do such a thing?

A small pebble loosened from the ceiling and hit the water, creating a ripple on the surface. Ryx didn't reply, and they suspected he never would.

They picked up a few things. This place was still fit to scavenge. They and their kin would return to this place many times, for what they would find here, and as a reminder.

Nelli remembered the run back the moonless night. They were all visibly upset, both the younger and the older, distracted, making mistakes, fearful of making more. The sound and sight of the pebble hitting the water haunted their collective memory, for some reason, and it always would.

They were assaulted, blindsided by a rivaling tribe, the Seths, a cruel and sadistic people. In just a few seconds many had fallen.

Nelli was close enough to dead close relatives to catch their life force. So were most others.

– When we die we still live, they breathed.

The influx empowered them, and did make them feel better. The words comforted them, empowered them further.

GO! Ryx shouted to the children and about half of the adults.

It was a wise move. He and the others staying behind would delay and decimate the enemy enough to save the rest, like the animals that would sacrifice a limb to save the body. The limb would grow back.

Nelli's arm was bleeding and the wound hurt, hurt a lot, but she didn't release a sound. She didn't shame her pack. They returned to their tunnels, and the wound was treated. She didn't get any praise for her perseverance. It was expected of her. She returned to her training in just a couple of days, while the wound still hurt. The young adults, the teenagers trained them to beyond exhaustion. She bit her lip and fought on. Her surroundings and the details of the fighting, the swinging staffs and her opponents seemed to have become so much clearer.

Larry sensed or believed he sensed the pressure wave from the wand a moment before it struck, and he pulled his head back, avoided being hit by a fraction of a second.

He sensed her excitement over his progress, simultaneously with her striving to uphold the mask of calm. In one swing he felled her, hit her on the head, making her go down, and he knew it was a lucky shot, one he wouldn't be able to repeat even faced with death.

The same contradictory emotions warred within her when he reached out a

hand and helped her up, pride and wounded pride.
– Christ! He said. – I thought we had it rough when growing up, but it's nothing compared to what you lived through.
– You, all of you living today live your life in a dream, she nodded somberly, – no matter how bad this time is, or how harsh you think it is.
They left the construction site after what he considered hours of hard, brutal exercise. She was hardly breaking a sweat. There were quite a few bruises on her face, though. But while he gritted his teeth every time he moved a muscle, she didn't flinch.
And he knew why, now, began to feel, beyond mere knowledge, information. She had trained her entire life for this life, a life of strife and constant struggle for survival.
– It's getting dark, he said puzzled.
He looked around. It was a cloudy day. The sky had been completely covered in gray the whole day. The sun wasn't visible in any obvious way.
– You can sense it. She nodded, before he nodded. – Feel it in the air around you.
Instead of taking off to the right and start on the run home, she chose left. He followed her with a curious look in his eyes. He always felt curious these days. It was a new, strange and exhilarating sensation to him.
He noticed, was very aware of the glances they drew from the crowds. Some of them stared at them. Others didn't want to look at them, but they all had that look in their weary faces.
It took a while, but he eventually realized that they were headed for his office building. He realized it well before the building appeared before them. She didn't cross the street, like she had done the day they met, but turned left and walked down the street to the underground station. It slowly dawned on him why she was doing it, but the incredulity didn't pass him by.
They walked inside, used their cards and headed downstairs, into the intricate maze of tunnels.
– This city, with its elevation is one of the few cities that will be spared the ravages of the rising sea, she told him, – but it will not be spared the thousand-year-wind and the subsequent drought. Nothing and no one will escape that.
She led on, downwards, glancing around, frowning, hesitating now and then, before moving on. They walked down a spiral staircase, a bit away from the trains.
– It is not like I remember it, she explained.
Larry knew that. There was no gaping whole in the ceiling, but the surroundings, superimposed on his fleeting «memories» still felt strangely

familiar to him.

The ground shook every time a train passed by, and that was what felt unfamiliar to him, not the eerie silence in the world of darkness he glimpsed in his surroundings.

They arrived at a closed and locked door. Nelli stopped briefly, listening to sounds from the inside, before opening the lock with her telekinetic power. It was basically a storage room, even though there wasn't much stuff stored there. She didn't turn on the light, before closing the door. He stopped startled. She stood close to him. He heard her silent breath. The details of the room slowly reappeared before his eyes. He stared around him in astonishment.

– Darkness is not your enemy, she said softly. – It is your friend and sister and brother and fellow warrior. You and your eyes are adapted to the night and everything in it.

He stood there, breathing, seemingly reaching out with his arms, and for each new breath the world seemed to grow brighter and more distinct before him.

– I noticed the signs in you, she said. – I notice them as they manifest, one by one. It is quite remarkable to witness how you're awakening, Larry, like a sleeping giant.

He turned and looked at her, seeing her in yet another light.

– You told me that story, she said. – It was one of my favorites.

She walked to the other door, at the other side of the room. It was locked, too, but presented no trouble for her. They appeared into what was evidently an abandoned tunnel. The rails were rusty and covered in dust. They crossed them to yet another door at the other side. The click when Nelli unlocked the door echoed painfully sharp in the eternal darkness.

They entered a much bigger room. If this was a storage room, it had to be where all storage rooms came to die. It was…

It was perfect.

Dust covered the entire floor. One set of footprints led from a central point and to the exit.

– This is where all Red gathers, she said in a hushed voice, – to be initiated into the tribe, its mysteries and joy.

He saw it, or at least glimpsed it, without the spider webs and mess, with its decay and vibrant life.

– There are entire safe houses down here, built to protect people from nuclear blasts, no longer in use by anybody, ready for our use. Some of them are even for sale, I believe.

She smiled as she stopped at that central point, a dreaming look very visible

in her face.
He noticed the circle of ash around her.
– You came «through» here?
– Yes, I faded out and in, at this exact spot. It was quite an experience, My Lord. – I saw the world and time in a thousand fractured glimpses. I learned even more of what I needed to learn.
He frowned a bit of her wording, but not more than he usually did.
With one glance he took in the place, and realized, or at least glimpsed the infinite possibilities.
This hall, the surrounding hallways, an intricate pattern making out what could become an entire world below the surface of concrete above.
He sensed that world, that society. It was practically born in his increasingly aware mind. One breath felt like a lifetime. He stood there breathing, sensing for minutes, seeing her smile.
They returned to the surface. The soft breeze struck them the moment they stepped outside. They realized it not long afterwards.
– The dry wind, she breathed, suddenly out of breath, excitement visible in her pale eyes.
He noticed it, too, the unmistakable change of quality in the air.
It wasn't instantly noticeable. When he studied people, it was pretty clear that they weren't really noticing anything. They were sweating easier. Some removed their jackets or took a break in their walk. It was just another hot day to them, no different from countless similar days of weather change.
– It is true, she cried excitedly. – Your rise to power coincides with the rides of the hot wind.
He could not help but share her inflated good mood and enthusiasm.
They headed back to the apartment, both filled with a renewed sense of urgency.
Confusion rattled further his already upset thoughts.
He couldn't stop musing over *details*. When the red light changed to green he didn't look at the light, but at the people before they crossed the zebra stripes. They didn't begin their crossing immediately, but had a delay in reaction time reaching seconds. He and Nelli had almost crossed half the distance across the street before most others took their first steps. Most others. There were those that were faster, and a few with flickering eyes, constantly supervising their surroundings, but no one keeping their eyes on him and Nelli, at least not right now. He knew that by studying her, too.
– There are warriors here, she confirmed, – or at least what you call soldiers. They have been taught war, taught strife, and the soft life doesn't make them forget, not completely, no matter how hard they try.

She shrugged.
– They're mostly damaged goods, of no use to you.
He grew even more astute as they approached home territory, catching himself in mapping familiar objects and people… and the patterns of complexity surrounding his block.
The girl, the owner of the stereo player from earlier in the week approached them. She was breathing hard and looked at them with a happy, bordering on ecstatic smile. But there was a caution, a purpose behind the smile making both Larry and Nelli look closer at her.
– I'm Patricia, she greeted them. – I'm Red.
– Yes, you are, Nelli nodded.
– I heard you two speak…
Nelli stepped close to her, as fast as lightning.
– Then you should know enough to bare your neck and bow before the Red Shadow, the pale girl said icily.
Patricia didn't hesitate, but bowed her head and curtseyed graciously, before going down on her knees, doing everything simultaneously, just to be on the safe side.
– Get up, he bid her. – Someone can see you.
But as he glanced around he knew no one would. She had made sure of that before she approached them.
The girl rose with a cautious smile. Nelli nodded approvingly to her.
– You will come with us. Nelli told her how it would be. – You will be interrogated and prodded and taken apart, taken beyond everything you know. Your old life is over. Do you understand, pack sister?
– I understand, she whispered with shivering lips. – I thought about it long and hard before I approached you. When I listened to you I knew you were for real. I'm ready.
– She's ready, My Lord, Nelli reported, – ready for the initial indoctrination into your service, ready to submit to your indomitable will.
He attempted to make his face impassive, to mask his feelings.
What was he thinking? She always knew his mind, even if he, himself didn't…
He walked away, like Red Shadow would do, without a word, and the two females followed him.
And then they joined the even stream back to the block commencing each afternoon. His neighbors noticed that he brought two women with him home, of course. He grinned widely to everyone he met.
Nelli and Patricia did, too.
Patricia looked at him with fever in her eyes, making him more than a little

uncomfortable.

They stepped inside and took the elevator to the top floor. Patricia snuggled against him. She gave him smothering wet kisses. He felt her hard nipples against his chest. She was beyond excited, almost beyond reason. Passion ruled her head to toe.

He noticed he was slipping, that his clothes began fading. He held back with an effort.

She walked ahead through the hallway, wriggling her butt lazily, non-demonstratively, naturally. He felt himself turn hard below, and then the pressure was gone in a heartbeat, and both he and Nelli were nude. When Patricia next turned her head, her eyes turned huge and misty. She pulled her top above her head and liberated her swollen breasts. They didn't encounter anyone on the remaining stretch to the apartment. In a hilarious moment Larry wished they had. Patricia kicked off her shoes and wriggled out of her pants. Nelli picked that up, too, like she had done with the top.

– You're Magick people, Patricia whispered. – I knew that the moment I saw you.

– So are you, pack sister, Nelli pointed not, not unkind. – You just haven't been able to realize your potential yet. From this moment on you will.

– Yes, Patricia whispered. – *Yes!*

Larry unlocked the door to the apartment. Patricia walked right through the open door to the bedroom. She crawled onto the bed and knelt on it, spreading her legs, grinning pleased over Larry's obvious interest. He was hard pressed to not focusing solely on her, and sighed in relief when he heard the door closing behind him, and noticed that Nelli's ever watchful eye was still very much operating. She quickly checked all the rooms, as was her want, and had returned before he had reached the bed.

Patricia began touching and fondling herself, half into a wild state already. Larry crawled onto the bed and grabbed her, and pulled her to him, and she released a happy moan. They knelt face to face and began tangling, caressing, squeezing and fondling.

– Won't you come and… join us? She asked Nelli with a slurry voice.

– Not if you want to survive the next few minutes I won't, Nelli grinned dangerously.

She stepped closer, revealing her claws. Patricia shuddered in delight. She twisted her body, rubbed her breasts, her hard nipples at Larry's chest.

– So, how do you… do it? She frowned.

– I used to tie her up, Larry replied, – but I don't have to do that anymore. My skin has turned hard and resilient.

He couldn't keep the grin off his face.

The pace of her breathing increased noticeably. She scratched him on the shoulder with her long nails, scratched him hard. There were no marks. Desire increased in her already misty eyes. She fell down on her back, and lay there, moving her entire body in a snake-like fashion, writhing on his behalf. He could smell her, in ways he had never smelled anyone before. When she pushed her groin at his he pushed back and found himself inside her.

He lowered himself, and they pushed and pulled at each other. When he touched her, he didn't just do it with his hands. Added wasn't only the organic, fluid clothing he wore, but also his mind doing whatever it was it was doing. Both released loud sounds guaranteed to raise hairs and stir things up elsewhere in the building. In a flash he realized how that pleased him, how the very thought pleased him immensely.

Smothering the female beneath him he pushed, pushed and pushed at her. They both screamed when they came, when they exchanged fluids, when final thought faded briefly, and moments afterwards returned in powerful and potent ways.

She snuggled in his embrace, sighing happily.

– That felt so good. I've never even been *close* to feeling something like that before.

Her voice and behavior stressed her words. She kissed him again and again and again.

Nelli joined them, slipping between them like the wind, giving them both wet kisses on the lips, studying Patricia with her lupine stare.

– Yes, she decided, – I think you will do. You will be our oldest little sibling to train and mold.

It was still strange to both the other two to hear her speak like that. Patricia was clearly the older of the two females.

But in truth it wasn't. There was no doubt who was the dominating personality, the most mature.

Nelli began making out with Larry, offering herself to him. It happened so casually, so naturally that it made Patricia gasp. Desire once more grew in her eyes while she watched the other two. Fascinated beyond words she kept her distance and studied them, moved with them, breathed with them.

Swaying, swaying on her knees, back and forth, leaning backwards, way beyond the balance point of her hips, but not falling. She felt it all, the kisses, the touch and the bodies sliding against each other. When Larry penetrated Nelli Patricia felt it, too. She shouted in savage joy and fell, fell on her back, lying side by side with Nelli, being fucked senselessly by Larry, moving like she did, choiring her sounds of need, of wild desire.

Nelli clutched Larry, digging in with her claws. Patricia saw them, sensed them, felt them, gasping in fear and awe, felt Larry, moved beneath him, moaned in his ear, screamed when he came in her, in them.

Larry and Nelli kissed and fondled each other in the aftermath of the fucking. Patricia caught their attention, like a slow-moving train.

– Come here, little empath, Nelli called softly.

Eyes lit up behind Patricia's happy smile. She pulled herself close to the other two, pushed herself at them, like a purring feline.

– I always believed there was something there, she said with a dreaming expression in her sweaty face, – but I had no way of knowing, no references in which to base my notion. Now, I understand so much that was hidden from me. Thank you, thank you.

She gave them wet, lingering kisses, projecting her chaotic emotions, her joy inevitably affecting them with her nascent power. Nelli allowed it to go on for a time before grabbing her with her claws, brutally putting a stop to it. Patricia yelped in pain, but the smile persisted.

– You have great power, one that, once you gain control over it will benefit the tribe greatly. Come, now, little sister, and I will take you the first steps on your long Journey.

Nelli kissed Larry on the lips, and Patricia, shyly, did, too, and they left the bed.

Larry lay there for a while, enjoying yet more of the pleasant sensation his new life brought him, recalling only faintly despair and boredom, so prevalent in his old life.

The heat of the fairly cold room and the presence of the two females washed over him in waves, bathing and surrounding him. Thoughts and passion grew from his center and returned to him. He sensed the heat of the other bodies, their presence and position without looking at them, as they moved through his air like flickering flames.

He rose, and walked to the window, a move so casual that it took his breath away.

The world outside flashed by, the streets below, the thick layers of pollution all the way up. He had noticed such things before, of course, through prevalent coughing while walking in the morning and afternoon traffic, but now he saw more.

Nelli put Patricia on her knees. She tied her hands behind her back with the rubber cord. It seemed excessive, but then he nodded to himself, realizing that was probably the point. Nelli made a mask with the material covering her body. She made it to cover Patricia's head, even the mouth. Patricia breathed in and out, snapping for air, like a fish out of water.

– You've placed yourself at my trust. You're a newborn, learning to walk.

Patricia shivered. For a while she shivered badly, making weak attempts at liberating herself from the ruthless grip, but every time Nelli shook her brutally back in place, striking her hard all over the body. Finally, Patricia sat still, with almost no visible breathing.

– Very good, Nelli whispered. – You relaxed on your own, conserving the sparse air by slowing down your breathing. I didn't have to tell you the obvious.

She shook the chain, shook it hard. Patricia winced, but only a bit, before turning calm again.

The living mask dissolved itself, pulling back to Nelli's body. Patricia remained on her knees, seemingly just as blind as she had been with the material covering her eyes.

– On your feet, warrior to be.

Patricia jumped on her feet, standing straight. Nelli nodded pleased, as she untied the rubber ropes.

– Do as I do.

Nelli began moving, striking air with her hands, moving light as feathers on the floor. The student attempted clumsily, to the best of her ability to copy her. Even if Nelli clearly moved deliberately slow, the other couldn't keep up. Nelli struck her often and cruel. Patricia cried out in pain and frustration and rage, but kept going.

It went on and on. Larry forced himself to watch. He began moving, too, seeing himself in Patricia, sharing her pain, frustration and rage, knowing beyond knowing that he was far beyond her.

He glimpsed himself in the dark window, his remarkable speed and cunning, drawn ever closer to the surface by the harsh training regime he, too, had endured.

He doubled, tripled his efforts. Sweat poured from every piece of skin on his body.

Patricia stood there, on shaky legs, finally totally exhausted, way past any chance of quick or even close recovery, while Larry felt exhilarated, empowered and powerful.

– On the table, Nelli told her ward.

The girl stretched out on the long living room table, groaning in pain and discomfort, biting her lip in determination. She shrunk under Nelli's stare.

– You show promise, Nelli finally said.

Patricia choked when she imagined she glimpsed kindness in the other's pale eyes.

Nelli began massaging her. It still hurt at first, but then to Patricia and Larry's amazement the pain subsided, slowly fading into the pleasant haze of exhaustion.

Patricia sat on the floor, with her legs crossed in front of her, her eyes open but not seeing this room, these surroundings.

– It's four fifteen in the afternoon, Nelli said, asking the same question over and over again. – It's three years exactly since you popped out of your mother's belly. What's happening?

– I…

I don't know, the ward wanted to say again, stopping in mid-sentence.

– M-mother is late for dinner. My older siblings have made dinner. Father has started eating. Mother is often late. Father never stops eating, focusing totally on the spoon, fork and knife, and the food he puts in his mouth.

They caught her emotions through her power, leaking through the reliving of her childhood memories. She was sad and angry, and they were, too, in spite of them being aware of how she was inadvertently affecting them.

– One day. mother didn't come home. She had thrown herself from the office where she worked, sick and tired of her job, her life and everything. Father started adding alcohol to his diet… and he never stopped. We found him in the bathtub a couple of years later. He had cut his wrists.

The girl, the child, the adult woman drew tears from her face in sad, angry bursts.

She looked at the other two, eventually, doing so with dry eyes.

– Thank you, she said with love in her thick voice. – Thank you for making me see this, see it again. I hadn't forgotten, but had still forgotten what it felt like, and I didn't want that, don't ever want to forget again.

– You connect, Nelli said, – connect with your heritage and with yourself, and knowledge and wisdom… and Power follows.

She rose in the air, until she levitated halfway between the floor and the ceiling. There wasn't really an expression of surprise in Patricia's face, only more of the awe and devotion directed at both of her companions.

– Do you trust us, child? Nelli asked.

The girl grinned and giggled a bit embarrassed.

– Yes, I…

– No, do you *trust* us?

Awe and devotion changed the girl's expression, her very features.

– I do!

She felt a pull, and both she and Larry rose to join Nelli in the air.

Then the door to the balcony blew open, and all three of them drifted outside, until they floated in the wind and open air, and Patricia looked down at the ground far below.

Nelli stared at her, with those pale eyes of hers.

Patricia strived to catch her breath. She heard the sound of the distant traffic, and music coming from an open window somewhere. Her breathing returned, slowing down again, as she found her center, found herself, and she looked around with profound excitement in her eyes.

They returned to the apartment. The door closed quietly behind them.

– You know, now our power, Nelli said.

– Yours is awesome! Patricia gasped.

– Yours is its equal in its own way, Nelli said. – It will serve us well in the hard times ahead.

Neither her somber words nor her praise affected Patricia's excitement.

– Do you think anyone… saw us?

– What if they did? Larry said.

And when she looked at him a different kind of excitement ravaged her.

She walked to him on unsteady feet, kissing him, smothering herself on his glowing body.

The trio returned to bed, touching each other affectionately, pulling together and grunting and stretching on the soft ground, dreaming potent dreams of yesterday and tomorrow.

Chapter Six

The hot wind was still blowing a week, seven days and nights later. They sensed no difference as they moved through the dark urban night. Larry looked pleased at the fleeting glimpses of himself and Patricia in storefront windows, recalling the seven more days and nights of hard and harsh training under Nelli's stern supervision. They both looked visibly leaner and meaner, and just the fact that he so easily was able to discern that was a major improvement.

His progress was considerably more prevalent, but she was getting there as well. The very manner in which they experienced reality had changed in this brief time since Nelli had entered their lives.

Cars and people passed them by, silent, like the ghosts they were. Movement itself ceased, until nothing but paintings or pieces of paintings surrounded the three wanderers in darkness. Lights blinked on and off, until they were all gone and the three of them grew masks covering their heads without witnesses. Nelli's eyes still looked enormous to him.

The trio stopped in a dark alley where no one else stopped. Larry looked bemused at Nelli. She reddened.

– I need to concentrate, concentrate hard for this, My Lord, she said with regret and shame, explaining her reasoning, her limitations to him. – Up is harder than sideways and I am not in fighting mode, now.

He nodded in acknowledgment. She closed her eyes. He sensed her rock-hard focus, how she reached out to her surroundings and how she pulled it back into her.

There was a slight tug, felt simultaneously all over the body, and then they were all levitating above the ground, floating upwards from the alley and until they stood on the roof. Patricia was practically speechless once more. Larry searched his own feelings, realizing that he felt calm, collected.

– I can feel… he said puzzled, not puzzled. – I can feel the wind.

There was no wind.

Nelli smiled, even as she kept focusing her main attention on their surroundings.

They stood on a roof of a fairly modern office building, not a tall skyscraper, but the less recent British three-storey kind.

– I studied the wall, Larry said. – There was no way for us to climb it.

– It was for me, Nelli said in her non-condescending, straightforward manner. – Not for the two of you, not yet.

There was an open hatch. There actually was an open hatch in the more shadowy part of the roof. He shook his head. She reached out again, this time, he suspected actually touching objects, surfaces with her power.

– There are no sneaky alarms, she reported.

And he found himself interpreting that statement again.

She opened the hatch wide. Then the three of them floated down in the room below. It was clearly an office of some kind and elegantly furnished.

– These guys clearly have some cash to burn, Patricia said encouraged. – It definitely looks like we've come to the right place.

The safe was placed completely in the open, by the wall lit by the moon. The image created a powerful stirring in Larry's deeper mind. And this time he recognized it as such, easily.

And that realization in itself brought more sensations.

And awakening kept haunting him.

He watched as Nelli advanced towards the safe, as if it was an enemy to be vanquished. She didn't linger, but went right for the kill. There was the first click. She stopped in front of the safe with her eyes more than half closed.

– You trained me for this, too, she mumbled.

There was another click. And only then she finally touched anything with her hands. She grabbed the handle and pulled the door open without visibly straining herself.

– This was easy prey, she said matter of fact.

There were two shelves inside. One contained stables of bills, of money, the other drawings, architectural drawings.

– We hit the jackpot! She added, the words sounding very strange coming from her.

It would be clear to everyone hearing her speak then that she was a foreigner.

They put the money in two bags, the building plans in the third.

– They will wonder about this forever, Nelli giggled.

Drawing a startled look from the other two.

– I'm becoming better at this, she stated proudly, – better at serving you.

Three bodies stood still and listened, listened hard for a while. There was no alarming sound, no sign of commotion anywhere.

Larry and Patricia felt a thug, or thugs in their bodies shortly before they once more rose into the air, up through the ceiling hatch. The open space of the roof welcomed them. They stood there, for seconds, minutes, savoring the sensation.

All three of them rushed through the night, the memory of the descent from that roof practically erased from their consciousness, the excited smile never leaving their faces.

They rested in a dark alley somewhere, not caring about their surroundings.
Patricia caught Larry's and thereby Nelli's attention.

– It isn't like this wasn't exciting and all, but why did we join in when she could have easily done everything alone?

She directed her question at Larry, of course. The smile didn't fade.

– Why do you think? He asked her.

She didn't have to think about it, at least not twice.

– Because we do everything together, she said.

The smile slowly transformed her face. A tremble passed through her. She walked to Nelli and bowed her head.

– Patricia is sorry for her denigrating thoughts and actions, pack sister. She will strive to improve herself.

– I know Patricia will, Nelli said softly, not angry or resentful at all. – I saw that she was worthy of the Red the moment I first spotted her.

They raced on through the night, Nellie leading on, hardly breaking a sweat, the other two sweating hard, feeling the rush of the moment, the thrill of success and not the least: the beyond pervasive heat.

There was more light, deep sleep, more haunting dreams. Larry sensed the two coddling on each side of him in bed. He slept and was awake. The sensation swept him up and he flowed down the red river. He had a hard time, even harder than usual distinguishing between dreams, the visions and sweeping consciousness.

They counted the money, studied the maps. Nellie nodded to herself, to them.

– The tunnels haven't really changed. The paths are the same.

Larry had to suppress a giggle while he watched the other two counting the money: Nellie virtually indifferent, Patricia with an eagerness she couldn't conceal.

– Is this… sufficient? Nellie frowned.

– It's a start, Patricia deliberately shrugged, – a nice start.

They laughed together, truly laughed *together*. Larry reached out his hands and the other two grabbed them. Patricia put away the last heap of bills without counting them, and both the females pushed themselves at him, snuggling and breathing in his sphere, and three smiles widened, turning into one.

When they woke up the next morning they did so together as well. Patricia stretched content. She rose from the bed in smooth, casual moves.

– I will make breakfast for Red Shadow and his mate, she declared.

She danced towards the kitchen, displaying herself to them both.

Nelli blushed deeply when Larry looked at her.

They sat nude by the dinner table, the three of them, feeding, drinking to their heart's content. The twilight created by the dark curtains cast a pale glow in the room.

– This is so great, Patricia marveled. – I feel like I can do anything. The three of us together surely can. The three of us made history, you say?

– We do, Nelli said. – The Red *is* history. Records are spotty, but our descendants remember us.

She frowned.

– What is it? Patricia wondered.

– It's nothing. Nelli shook her head. – Nothing important. Just something I don't understand, that's all. Red Shadow, the Red Shadow of my time, in his wisdom, being all-seeing withheld information from his dedicated servant before sending her back to aid him in his ascension and she doesn't quite understand. She…

She frowned again, raising a hand to her mouth.

Then she rose abruptly and rushed to the bathroom.

They heard her throw up and exchanged looks.

– Is everything alright out there? Larry called.

There were more sounds of her vomiting.

– I don't think there is any reason to be concerned, Patricia said quite relaxed.

Her grin puzzled him.

Then slowly, the obvious dawned on him.

Nelli returned to the living room. She looked pale, even paler than usual, as she wiped the vomit from her jaw. A big grin decorated her face.

Larry's voice failed him.

She knelt and put her head in his lap.

– This girl has bad news for you, My Lord, she whispered. – She fears she will be forced to take a leave of absence from your Crimson Guard in not so many months.

– Don't worry about it, he managed to reply, with a low, euphoric chuckle.

Her face cracked in a relieved, delirious smile. He saw and sensed that she was almost breaking into tears.

– This is great news, he stressed, – nothing but good news.

– Yes, My Lord, she sniffed.

She grabbed his hand and drowned it in kisses. Patricia went down on her knees too, and embraced her.

– Such an innocent, devoted creature, she marveled, a bit patronizing, – such a lethal weapon, and it's ours, ours to do with as we please.

– Yes, Nelli nodded, – Nelli is yours, forever.

Emotions kept bottling up inside her. Larry looked at her, unable to hide his concern.

– You're so kind, she mumbled in his lap, – but you need not worry. The tribe always celebrates the first evidence of conception with everything we are. We remain Red Shadow's devoted and dangerous creatures.

They walked outside just as the red started coloring the western sky. Nelli still wore her goggles. They walked through the streets, to the tavern Larry and Nelli had visited a night just before the air had turned desert dry and hot.

– I can feel the air on my skin, Patricia marveled. – I could never imagine that such sensitivity was possible.

The other two looked pleased at her.

It was still early. People had left the streets from work not that long ago and not quite returned yet.

Larry studied people, doing so effortlessly. His eyes hardly had to move in order to more or less probe them, gauge their reactions and intentions. Mostly all he got was a fuzzy nothing or close to that, but not always, and he was able to pick something from almost everybody catching his attention.

The meeting and parting of glasses had begun. He heard it, sensed his surroundings and also, easily the two females by his side.

It made him dizzy all of it, as if there was information overload or something to that effect.

He noticed Nelli's look, both tender and not. Red lights were lit outside some of the pubs and once again their glow gained a special meaning in his mind. They added to the heat both physically and mentally, creating yet another subtext to his experience of reality.

The name

Shadow

glowed darkly in the twilight of the early evening.

They walked inside, into the unusual silence of the pub. The room revealed itself to him, even more so than before. Its people, its space and its scent stood out to his senses.

– Three pints of Guiness, please, he told the bartender, the woman behind the counter.

He studied her fairly openly, making her blush. She took his money and returned his change.

– You've got yourself a nice place here, he remarked.

– Thank you, she whispered.

The three grabbed their pints and found a table in the corner, the same spot he and Nellie had chosen at their first visit here. They sat down.

– Cheers, he said, raising his glass. – To the Red.
– To the Red, the girls choired.
Glasses met and parted. They drank.
He looked at the other guests present, at the special and the lost.
– The people here, Patricia mused, – I can… they are weird.
– Look at them, novice, Nelli told her. – Look at them all. Reach out with your senses. *Feel* what they are about.
She did, automatically reacting to Nelli's bidding… and then she did it deliberately, focusing on it.
After one slow blink, two her eyes remained open and opaque.
– They are not Red, she said, – not by birth, but perhaps by inclination.
The boy rose first, followed by a girl and half a dozen others. They approached the three in the corner.
– Greetings, he said, as they all stopped in front of the table in the corner.
– Greetings, Nelli replied.
– We met two of you in the sports store the other day. We took your word to heart and followed your scent to this place, to this night. May we join you?
– You may, she shrugged.
They brought their glasses and themselves and gathered around the table in the corner.
– We bought our own wands, the girl with a pale, non-descriptive face and red-blonde hair said. – The store owner, no doubt expecting lots of upcoming business has stocked them extensively.
– I'm Larry, Larry said. – These two cute bitches are Nelli and Patricia.
– I'm Nora, the redhead said, her skin remaining pale.
– I'm Daryl, the boy said.
The others voiced their name.
– Cheers! Larry raised his glass.
– Cheers! Everybody choired excited.
They drank.
The conversation was strangely… casual from the beginning. It started up in earnest long before the alcohol made loose lips looser.
– It struck a chord in us, you know, Daryl said, swallowing lots of beer, – you guys procuring wands. There was something about the two of you standing out from others. I can't explain it…
Nelli looked overbearing at the bungling young boy.
– It's the weird weather, another said. – The very notion of that brought the point home to us, I believe. We might have played at training martial arts before, but now the very thought takes on a far more sinister meaning.
Larry studied Telford. He didn't hide it. The calmness within felt good,

felt like a tremendous, quiet boost. The boy's face and eyes darkened, as if a shadow had covered it.

There was a draft, a rush of wind outside. Larry noticed without trying. A branch bent on the nearest tree.

– There's a high tide tonight, Nora said. – I've heard it will be higher than any in recorded history.

– It will be far from here, Daryl stated with confidence or perceived confidence.

This city was far from the ocean. The others nodded.

It began raining. Everybody glanced at each other. Hard rain, in a gust of wind making the building shake suddenly struck the windows on the western side of the building. Daryl almost jumped out of his skin.

It was amazing. The weather had changed from fairly bright skies to a storm from one moment or at least one minute to the next.

– There was almost bound to be an… explosive change in the weather after such sizzling heat, one said.

The last arriving youths glanced at each other with flickering eyes.

Larry commanded their attention. He didn't really do anything, making no conscious move. Everybody heeded his command. Nelli and Patricia looked at him with what couldn't be interpreted as anything but devotion.

– We will enjoy ourselves tonight, he said. – That won't keep us from doing what needs to be done later, in the many days and nights to come.

He raised his glass in a quiet salute and everybody responded and joined him. They drank, drank deep of the beer and mood dancing between them.

– I can smell… can smell salt water, Patricia said stunned.

– It's coming for us, Nelli acknowledged. – We better be ready!

Others, guests or people seeking shelter from the storm rushed in from the outside, soaking wet in a matter of seconds. One held an umbrella, but it was twisted beyond recognition and totally useless. The place filled up quickly.

The barmaid, the owner of the establishment was on the phone calling for employees to get their asses here pronto. Larry heard the conversation, or imagined he did. She didn't have much luck.

– I need you to come here, *now*, she insisted.

Larry couldn't pick up the man's reply, but the general meaning was clear. She practically slammed the thumb down on the button when she broke the connection and threw the phone on the bar desk. It stopped perilously close to the edge.

– She's at her wit's end, My Lord, Patricia whispered in his ears.

Nelli heard her, of course and her eyes turned wide and shiny, and Larry nodded to himself.

– Will it be fair to say that everything is crashing down on her at once? He queried.

– That will be fair, Patricia nodded.

She looked eager at him.

– You have… a solution? He stated startled.

– I've been an accountant and I've been a barmaid, she stated proudly, modestly.

He had to strain himself in order to keep himself from grinning.

– By all means, he said. – Get on with it.

She jumped on her feet and then, pulling herself together walked casually towards the bar and struck up a conversation with the weary woman behind it.

– Everything is coming together, Nellie told him, almost unable to contain her excitement.

Their new friends didn't really notice much of what had happened. They noticed when Patricia walked behind the bar and started serving after a brief conversation with the owner, of course, but didn't make much of it.

– She has experience, doesn't she? Daryl ventured, studying her elegant moves.

– She has, Larry acknowledged.

The party continued. The deluge and the storm picked up, waned and picked up again. Sometimes it was hard to actually see through the windows because of the thick film of water covering them.

The girl with the pale skin and strange eyes danced and others joined her, even as they were drawn to her and to her companions, to the growing number of people sitting there by the corner table. If this had been a ship it would have capsized quickly.

– This is such a thrill, a girl marveled, – such an unbelievable kick.

There were those clustered at the other side of the room that wanted to leave, but there was nowhere to go. The incentive to stay was far stronger than to leave, to venture out into the raging storm.

The door opened by itself and hit the wall with a crack. Water instantly flooded the entrance area. They needed to lock the door to make it stay closed. It creaked and bent, but held.

Some more joined the girl with pale skin on the floor. Among them was Nora, the other girl with pale skin. Others rocked on their chairs. The celebration was both wild and subdued. It continued and added to itself, as the seconds and the long minutes passed.

Larry glimpsed the cold blue moon beyond the clouds and the storms again. More truths overt and subtle dawned on him. He and Nelli danced together. Eyes met eyes and glimpsed more concealed knowledge.

– This is so much fun, Larry, she whispered. – And so much destiny fulfilled.

She didn't sound that much different from the other girl earlier, but there was a subtext in her voice that he would have noticed even if he hadn't known what she was talking about.

– It's happening, she said. – Step by step, small and big we get closer to what is preordained.

He felt more than a little unsettled then, no matter how much he was swayed by her happiness and enthusiasm.

The night passed in a daze filled with clarity. It was as if he noticed everything, every single minor movement and change in people's expression. The alcohol did affect him, but only to a certain point.

Nelli danced at the top of a table, swaying elegantly, not even close to losing her balance. They watched her and clapped their hands, all of them rocking to the beat.

The owner looked at them all from her position behind the bar. Larry walked to her.

– Why don't you join us? He offered.

She hesitated only briefly before cracking a smile and taking him up on his offer.

– I'm Larry, he presented himself.

– Corinne, she said. – Corinne Marlowe.

He easily noticed her interest. Such emotions were obvious to him, now. He didn't have an emphatic power like Patricia, only his power of observation. It was enough.

When he kissed her later, he imagined he knew the taste of her lips before he touched them. He expected her to hesitate briefly and then turn soft in his arms, and she did.

The night kept flowing, half an hour or so, before he kissed Corinne, eager Corinne again. She clung to him, giving as good as she got.

They danced and each glance she sent him under the lowered eyelashes was filled with promise.

He pushed her at the wall, not quite in command of himself. Her sweaty, happy face revealed that she wasn't exactly put off.

She freed herself from his grasp with regret.

– I have to go to the bathroom, she said.

He followed her with his eyes, as she crossed the room and disappeared in the deeper settings of the room.

– Do I exert some kind of… influence over her? He asked, even as he knew the answer, when Nelli slipped close to him.

– You don't! She shrugged. – Your power doesn't work that way. She's just taken with you, that's all. It may not be obvious, but she acknowledges your power, your superiority. The simple truth is that she's yours to do with as you please.

The stir of excitement within him grew. He couldn't help it, help himself, even as he resisted the very thought of it.

There was confidence as he spotted Corinne the moment she reappeared in the room, as he returned to her and continued where they had left off.

– I thought about making her eat of his hand, he heard Patricia giggle somewhere, clearly speaking to Nelli, – but there's no need for that. She does already.

Larry heard and wanted to observe her, as she walked from person to person, as she probably used her power on them, heightening their passion, their growing need further.

The volatility outside grew, even as those inside did their best to match it. The entrance door creaked, loud enough for everybody to hear its banshee cry.

– Block it! Corinne shouted.

Nelli rushed to do so. The door cried out its pain again. Nelli used chairs and tables and everything at her disposal in her effort. She stepped back, giving the door an apprehensive look.

One window gave. It broke in a single burst of wind, as the storm gave itself one more crucial boost. In one swoop half the room and the people there were struck by a wall of water.

In that very moment electricity failed, all over the building and in every other in the street and probably across the city. Larry glimpsed it, glimpsed the streets, the streets of water and fire.

– Everybody into the other room, Corinne shouted even louder, loud enough to be heard in the roaring inferno filling the air.

There was shock, but also prevailing laughter. The latest event didn't really put a damper on the mood. They hesitated.

– We can't stay here, Corinne persisted. – You will have to be my guests for the duration. There's no other choice, really.

They followed her into her private quarters, a small but nice living room. They brought chairs from the outer room and everybody managed to find a place to sit, even though some chose to sit on the floor, on the soft carpet. The door stayed open while they brought a few more chairs and more beer.

– The wind is still hot, Nora said startled, – as if we're actually bathing in the rays of the afternoon sun. The draft isn't unpleasant, not unpleasant at all.

At that precise moment a chill trickled down Larry's spine.

– You're aware, Nelli stated, – aware through a haze, through the bond we share what the future will bring.

As he studied her an even more powerful enthusiasm and expectation flooded her being.

Someone closed the door, and the intimacy of the room turned very pronounced.

– Yes, this is it, Nelli stated, – the long day before the war.

The way she said that, the same way she said everything with a certainty bordering on acceptance made his certainty grow.

She walked to him, pushed herself at him, offering herself to him even more than she usually did. He knew all the present males and also some of the females stared at her. The two of them embraced and the dance began.

– We dance, she hummed in his ears, – dance to music only we are able to hear, that the others slowly will begin to notice and then heed.

The dance spread among the revelers. He sensed it more than he saw it. The sensing part wasn't even hard anymore, more a part of him than the clothes he wore steered by his thoughts and emotions.

He held back and couldn't fathom how he was able to do that. There was low-level arousal, but it didn't go further. Nelli followed his lead, like she did in everything.

The dance turned tight and hot. Others sought together and left the room, seeking distant parts of the house and a quiet bedroom.

He returned to Corinne after a time that felt both brief and long. She looked at him when he sat down beside her.

– How are you doing? He asked her casually.

– The insurance will cover some of my losses, but not all.

She shrugged, not fooling him, not even trying.

– As it happens I have some money stashed away, he said.

– You would do that for me? She wondered.

– It fits well with my own plans, he said.

She hesitated only for a few moments of doubt, before looking at him with stars in her eyes.

– It so happens that I've been looking for a partner…

She said coquettishly and very ambiguous, her face flushed, her healthy colors very pronounced.

– I've been looking for change without constants, or at least mundane constants, she said, her eyes dwelling on his. – Change is a constant in our lives, and if it isn't it should be.

– I agree, he stated, feeling his passion boiling beneath the surface. – Like virtually everyone else I was pulled in by the general deceit, but I'm not anymore.

– I love it when you speak like that, she declared.

– It's so true, Patricia cries not far away.

They look startled at her.

She jumps up on the dining table and suddenly everybody's attention is on her. Everybody still in the room stares at her and can't look away. She stands on the dining table. Her eyes are wild. She crouches there before them.

– Pain cuts the world, she whispers. They catch her words easily. – Pain so pervasive it makes ashes of us all. But the sorcerer stands on the corner, weaving his great Chaos. Strands of night and fire grow out of thin air. Lightning scorches the ground.

They hear her deep inside, where no sound can reach.

She's deep this woman, deeper than he knew. The realization startles him. He can hardly see or sense the end of her, but he still isn't drowning in her, only breaking the surface of his own self, diving far below what he has perceived as his own limits.

Nora, pale Nora stares at him with her disquieting reddish eyes. They all do to one degree or another, but not like she does.

The party raged on, both noisy and calm. A tree fell outside. They witnessed the event as it hit a building and made a huge dent in the wall. They heard the sound of it, but it seemed to come from everywhere but the most obvious direction. Nora clung to Larry, making him unmovable. Water leaked into the living room from under the door, creating a sea on the floor. People removed their shoes. Some used the furniture to walk around, while others didn't bother to keep their feet from getting wet. The storm raged on. It rose on the skewed tangent it had begun, creating a dissonance in flesh and ears both.

– I remember the first time you visited this place, Corinne said quietly to Larry, – you and Nelli.

– Only a week ago that would have surprised me, even stunned, me, he said stunned, – but not anymore.

Nelli stood up tall and proud.

– Red Shadow's tribe is finally gathered here, in its lair, she cried, she hummed her evocative song. – We dance and sing here, at the Red Shadow Inn. There is low, penetrating music…

They heard it, beyond the silence and the roaring storm.

– There are whispers haunting our ears.

It was later, much later, or so it seemed and felt. They raised their glasses and choired their song.

We sit here
Many of us
And many of us
Yet not here
Drowning our joy
In barrels of beer
There are whispers
Haunting our ears

We sit at our center table
Swinging our glasses
Singing our song
«I wanna drown my joy
In a barrel of beer»

Loud and defiant laughter filled ears and walls alike. It echoed their depths, burst their core. The song faded only slowly. At some point there was a notion, a suspicion strong as a conviction that it would never fade.

The wind blew through windows and flesh alike. The noise ended, and only quiet voices remained. They turned deaf in the onslaught the world had become, but still heard better than ever.

They fell asleep, one by one, group by group. Larry experienced how he slept and dreamed in a completely different lair. What was not flesh, perhaps not even matter rose from his physical form. Larry ran, ran through dry sand and across wet wastelands. He walked with the wand in his hand. Sometimes he fought, while other times he just carried the wand in his left or right hand.

He dreamed in a whirl of water and sand. He knew he was dreaming, even though he occasionally feared he wasn't, and he knew it made no difference.

Landmarks drowned in dust and rising sea. He lived through it all. They stayed in the shelter in the oldest parts of the underground where Nelli had once traveled back through time. He saw it as it happened. She looked at him, giving him a sense of himself, a stronger than ever awe she felt in his presence. He saw himself but no one else he knew, no one surrounding him and sleeping with him in the wet and moist living room. Even she wasn't the same, but changed, changed by facing his younger self, the child in the man. The puzzled look grew slowly on his face. Awareness didn't come easy, but was hammered into him like nails.

– I will honor you until death, Red Shadow, she cried, blown away by the white light.

He studied her as she trained in his presence, as she worked harder than hard to be worthy of his trust, of the decision he had made that no one in his tribe understood.

The tunnels were old. He couldn't believe how old they were. There was little or no familiarity there. They were covered by growth and mud and… He didn't truly see anything familiar, anything at all.

As if…

As if

And suddenly, as more pieces of the puzzle fell into place, the truth dawned on him.

He stood on the roof of the battered building of Shadow the next morning. To say that the area and the city looked like a disaster zone was a gross understatement. Trees and bricks and cars and windows and roofs and countless downright unidentifiable parts had spread and fallen across a vast distance.

Nelli came to him like she always did when he needed her.

– It is true, she stated.

He didn't move from his position, didn't even look at her.

– You have decades, centuries even, to catch up.

Catching his inevitable stare of disbelief.

– Yes, she confirmed, – you are immortal, or you will be. A thousand years on, except for being bigger, you basically look exactly the same physically as you do now.

He sat there, astounded.

– I thought you came from just a few decades into the future. He shook his head. – I thought you spoke of the Thousand Year Wind as something approaching, also for you.

– No, I was born a thousand years hence, she said. – I've never experienced a world without It. I, like many others of your tribe have been entertained by tales of Its conquests since the cradle.

He looked across the street. A man stood there, a man in dark clothes. He seemed very interested in this particular house.

– You were very enigmatic, secretive even, she related to him. – It was unheard of and downright eerie the way you behaved. It didn't, in any way reduce the respect we had for you, but it made us wonder. The elders were vexed, or would have been if it wasn't you. You were ageless, like a god living among his subjects. They were not. Only a few others shared your longevity. Many of those who had done so had been killed throughout the centuries.

– I had come to know you in the time since you had adopted me, since you had brought me to your court and inner circle, since you had made me Red, made me Crimson in fact as well as blood, or so I'd thought. But in the days and seconds before my departure you stumped me yet again. There was no evident reason for this. You were quite forthcoming and talked for hours and weeks and months, filling my mind and dreams with endless facts. But you also made a point of the fact that you didn't tell me everything. You said you would figure out the rest by yourself. I was ordered to tell you everything you told me, and what I knew of my world and its history.

– I didn't want you to tell me everything I knew, he grinned and shook his head. – I feel properly and positively schizophrenic…

She nodded somberly. She understood.

The wind was still blowing, albeit in a reduced, ridiculous capacity compared to the long night, but unchanged, undiminished in its true shape behind the veil they both sensed.

– I eventually learned what you wanted me to learn, what you wanted to impress upon me, I think…

She shook in his arms. He held her, held her hard.

– I taught you well.

She looked up at him, nodding slowly, solemnly.

– Yes, Red Shadow. You did.

Chapter Seven

They stood behind a curtain on the upper floor and studied the street scenery yet another hot and sizzling afternoon. The storm had briefly brought lots of water and slightly colder weather, but that hadn't lasted long and now everything had become as it had been in the days before the raging wind and flood.

The hammering and noise from the ongoing and extensive restoration work could be heard from all over the house.

The man in dark clothes or another man virtually identical in appearance or at least inclination watched the house from across the street.

– Does Red Shadow want his Crimson Guard to remove the interloper?

– No, that will only tell them more than we want them to know, he told her. – And they will probably send another, possibly several others. Fell free to keep assessing the situation, though, and to act if it changes in significant ways.

– Yes, Red Shadow.

He studied her. There had been a change, yet another change in her approach to him since the night of the storm.

She studied him as well, even more casually than she usually did. He noticed that easily. She stood there, patiently awaiting his acknowledgment, his renewed acknowledgement.

– You may speak, he said, with an irritation he could not quite conceal or hold back.

– Red Shadow is so wise, she stated. – He keeps his servant reined in, but still leaves her with room to roam.

He waited, equally patient, or so he hoped.

– Red Shadow doesn't care much for disobedience, even though he seems to have a fondness for rebellion as well. That always confused his servant greatly.

The chuckle worked its way up his throat. He noted how she loved that, relished that.

He heard the familiar steps rushing up the stairs. Patricia entered the room. She looked very cute and innocent in her overall and the spots of paint on her face.

– We need more supplies and more recruits, she reported. – The work is going slow, I'm afraid.

She emanated passion and dedication. He felt her heat.

There was no conscious attempt on her part to entice or seduce him. He would have known if there was. She just was like she appeared: very forward and sensual.

– That is an excellent suggestion, he heard himself say, felt himself grin.

And he couldn't say he didn't get off on the way the two of them looked at him.

Chloe and Travis lived in a typical red-brick neighborhood. Their home didn't deviate in any way from the others in that street or the entire neighborhood.

Larry and Nellie stopped just by the gate outside their house.

– They're both at home, Nellie reported.

– I know, he stated calmly and devoid of irritation.

The lights were lit in the living room, but he sensed the two of them as well, in ways he hadn't done just days ago.

He marveled at the very thought, taking his time savoring the pleasant sensation coursing through him.

Nellie grabbed his hand, smiling shyly at him. He petted her cheek affectionately.

Through what he experienced as real, he felt the thunder and its storm approach him.

They walked to the door. He knocked on it. Nelli kept an astute eye on their surroundings, the very image of the both relaxed and tight spring feather he had always known her to be.

Even as he knew that very few others would see much more than an ordinary girl, even with the goggles.

He heard Chloe and Travis having a low-volume, fearful conversation in the hall in the conviction that whoever knocked on the door couldn't hear them.

The door opened. He noticed easily how they instantly recognized their visitors and how suspicion ruled their being.

– Come inside, Travis hissed.

Larry and Nellie strolled inside.

– So, you've spotted the suspicious man across the street, Larry grinned. – Very good!

– How did you find us? Travis asked sullenly.

Larry looked at him, at a recent mirror of himself.

– You're Red, Nelli stated. – You're born to serve Red Shadow. Tonight, you will leave this house and never return.

– But this is our home? Travis protested weakly.

– This isn't your home, Nelli snapped. – Red Shadow and none other is your home.

Chloe stood straight, looking at Larry, practically displaying herself to him. She understood and revealed it in thousand big and small ways.

– You will come with us, right now! Larry said casually.

Travis straightened, too, no matter how ill-fitted he was to do so.

Nelli stepped forward, stopping right in front of them. She grabbed Travis' jaw.

– You're soft, she said patronizingly, – but we will get you into shape. You're Red. You're strong and fierce.

– Yes, we are! Chloe cried at Larry. – Thank you, thank you, Red Shadow.

Her nipples hardened visibly against the tight sweater.

She was a tall and big girl, very soft, flabby and unfit. Larry saw her as she would become, exactly as Nelli described her.

Larry and Nelli returned outside. The other two followed them. No one closed the door.

The man across the street spoke in his phone. Larry imagined that he was able to hear his excited voice.

– What is this? Travis said exasperated.

He received no reply.

Larry left him to ponder the answer to his own question, and saw that he did so. Larry found himself nodding pleased to himself.

Nelli took the lead as they left the place. Most people would only see a casual walk. Larry easily saw more, saw her tension and awareness glow in every movement she made. He could hardly believe how much he saw.

The man across the street, a fairly trained observer saw it, too. Larry saw her, saw them from his point of view, through his eyes, his perception. The entire street and its surrounding area moved to his touch. Nelli began breathing faster, and the slow smile widened the stretch of her lips.

– You see me, she breathed. – I'm so happy, Larry.

Then she frowned.

– He sees me, too, she frowned, slightly troubled, casting a brief, non-glance across the street. – He's good. It can't be helped.

– I know, Larry said. – Don't worry about it.

The man faded from their view, deliberately holding back, even fading from their immediate attention, in order to make his interest less obvious. Larry presumed others took his place. They passed by a few fairly good candidates, a woman with a baby stroller and even a baby, a man looking at them from an apartment and others.

– The threat is turning real, Nelli said to Larry, non-committal, unworried, but still with a poignant voice. – What was just a glimmer, a possibility becomes a certainty.

She spoke in a very low voice, one he could hardly hear. The others didn't hear her. Neither would any possible listening device of those spying on them. He realized she was in full combat mode.

It got easier to identify those in the shadows as they walked, and not only because he watched her and her reactions. They moved a certain way, in spite of their training, or rather because of their training, one they on a fundamental level could not hide. Their skill exposed them, so to speak.

Once more, he shook his head in amazement. He had lost count over how many times he had done so lately.

A man walked toward them, in the middle of the street. Nelli instantly readied herself. Larry gave her the signal to stand down. She looked astonished at him, even more so when she saw that he was smiling.

They wish to test us, he signed, easily making the correct movements, the speech flowing from his hands only slightly awkward. Let's not show them more than we have to.

She acknowledged his statement and did as she was told. He sensed more joy beneath her attractive frame.

The man walked straight in Larry's path, obviously on a collision course with him. Larry kept walking unconcerned forward. The man was big, both taller and bigger than Larry. Larry steeled himself, sensing his soles touch the sidewalk, his muscles softening and hardening as he inadvertently stretched them. The moment before the seemingly inevitable collision the man towered above Larry.

He stepped to the side, thereby avoiding Larry with a smidge. They brushed against each other shoulder to shoulder, and there was a hard knock. None of them was pushed much from their path.

The man walked on, turning a corner down the street.

Larry's companions all looked at him with inquiring eyes.

– He was playing dare, Larry shrugged.

– Dare? Travis blinked.

– Precisely, Larry nodded, the devil may care grin still feeling strange on his lips. – Luckily, we weren't driving or something.

They had slowed down, but not stopped, as they had turned their heads and seen the unknown man vanish around the corner.

– It was a test, Larry mused. – He was only one more information gatherer, slightly different from the rest, and he succeeded, though not as much as he set out to do.

The quartet returned to the house by the broken trees. A woman sat on the still muddy stairs. Larry recognized Roberta immediately.

She rose as they approached.

– I want to help out, she stated. – Al would have wanted me to do that, I think, and would have been here if he could. I used to be army intelligence. I can be very useful to you.

Nelli sniffed her out, circling her.

– I'm sure you can, Larry said.

– Do you submit to Red Shadow and swear to serve him in all things, even beyond death? Nelli snarled.

– No, Roberta said startled. – Of course not! You don't want blind obedience, do you?

– You're quite correct, Nelli grinned dangerously. – Red Shadow wants truly free beings at his command.

– Then I'm in, Roberta said, visibly relieved.

She picked up her bag and put the strap on her shoulder.

– This contains my only belongings. I had no real stake in the place I lived. I read somewhere that truly free human beings shouldn't own more than they can carry with them.

– Roberta is wise, Nelli acknowledged.

They went inside. Everybody met them there, and smothered the three newcomers in their embrace.

– Welcome, Patricia greeted them.

She pushed herself at them and kissed them on their lips. It made them all flustered and hot. Then she pulled back and called out with a loud and powerful voice.

– C'mon, slackers, there's work to be done.

She gave the three overalls and they joined everybody else in the slow and hard task of returning the place to its former glory.

Daryl and Telford assisted Corinne in the task of making dinner on the large, hot stove in the kitchen.

– You were absolutely correct. Daryl gritted his teeth to the chef. – There's a vast difference between making food to a few and to many…

Nora stuck her head in, grinning wickedly.

– I got that. I got it on tape.

No one was idle during the making of the dinner. Everybody took a break from the renovation of the house, and joined in on the making of the table, putting cutlery and finally food on the visibly soiled tablecloth.

They gathered around it all, doing so in working clothes and with spots of paint on their skin. Blushing cheeks and eyes touched with reverence greeted each other once again, clearly aware of the moment, knowing beyond knowing that this was different, was something they had never previously experienced.

Larry studied Roberta, or rather, he saw how Nelli studied her and kept studying her, from all possible angles, without being noticed. That alone was a fantastic experience. And his life was suddenly filled with fantastic experiences.

– It feels great, doesn't it… Larry? Nelli said.

– It does, he acknowledged.

She toasted shyly with him and they drank.

He rose. Everybody cast their attention at him with aware eyes.

– This is an alternative gathering, he said, not raising his voice. – I know a bit about that subject, though not very much. The time I've spent in squatted houses and such is short and easily measured. It isn't that I have anything against squatters. Most people look at them with dismay, but I wasn't one of them. It was rather that I felt that I was too busy with my career to participate.

Laughter, not unkind. He realized that they were listening to him. A part of him still found that an unlikely prospect.

– What I do know is that all kind of squatters and similar will eventually face various forms of pressure from the bigger society surrounding their four walls. It may take several shapes, both official and not. I would guess we have a slight advantage compared to other «squatters» because we own the building where we're residing, but that's by no means a certainty. Any alternative society with a certain success and longevity will sooner or later draw unwanted attention to itself. Nelli, Patricia and I have prepared for that in advance. There will be more about that later, when we have more news. But tonight is sort of our official initiation for this house, the house that Corinne has been generous enough to share with us, and we should focus on enjoying ourselves, enjoying ourselves without thought of tomorrow.

He sat back down. There was applause, low-keyed like his speech, but unmistakably applause.

– Come to think of it, it seems like I've paid attention after all…

Patricia and Nelli kissed him from each side. He enjoyed it, doing so far beyond the purely physical sensations.

– We're also better prepared than almost all other squatters, Roberta pointed out, reddening because of the added attention her speaking out brought her. – We train and exercise, preparing ourselves for the worst, even as we keep striving for the best.

– Roberta is very much correct, Nelli acknowledged. – She has glimpsed a crucial bigger truth.

– The training with wands in general is an underestimated activity in society as a whole, in my opinion, Daryl said excitedly. – It makes both the body and mind… wake up. I'm so glad that I've finally found people understanding that.

The meal… began. The consummation of food and experiences rose quickly to dominate their perception. The candles burned softly in their eyes. The special mood grew and multiplied.

Nelli called everybody's attention to herself. There were no grand gestures, only tiny moves making them look at her and listen to her.

– The tales are clear, she began. – They all tell pretty much the same story. What we have experienced recently is nothing compared to what's in store.

Half of those present looked at her with the usual interest and curiosity, the other half with a frown added to their features, a frown stemming from a thought, a notion or suspicion they couldn't quite catch.

– Oh, yes, Nelli said with a conviction making them all shake, – the thousand-year wind will blow, and we, like everyone else will be swept up in its smallest draft. Its power will transcend by far any worst-case scenario presented by official information channels.

There was no outright information in her words causing a kind of uncertainty to rise in their minds, but the wording and her unique conduct still made them wonder and made their minds go down uncharted paths.

– We will prepare ourselves for it, she stated. – We already do.

They sat in the confines of the tiny, pleasant space and enjoyed each other's company, dreaming in both good and bad ways about the outside world.

– Everything will become an enormous waste, she related to them, – one with little or no life. Only in the shade below the ground will we find shelter, find belonging. There we will survive and thrive.

Silence greeted her as she stopped speaking. They couldn't take their eyes off her.

– You're such a great storyteller, Nelli, Roberta beamed. – I can practically experience your tale as you are telling it. It's almost like you have actually experienced it.

Some of those present glanced uneasily at each other.

– Thank you, Roberta, Nelli said solemnly. – That's good to hear.

Most of those present shifted their attention to Larry before he started speaking. He noticed easily, how attentive they had already become, how Nelli nodded pleased to herself, and studied him with even stronger than usual looks of affection.

– Those in charge won't really do anything in order to prevent what's coming, he said, knowing beyond knowing that they were listening to him. – No matter how much they want to keep up the pretence and deception, they are neither able nor willing to truly stop or even stall the process quickly becoming irreversible. So, it's up to each and every person or group of persons to prepare for the inevitable.

The knowledge, no, certainty that they were listening to him wasn't self-conscious at all. It was there, just as the storm had been and the solid floor he touched.

– Most people just don't *get it,* Corinne pointed out. – They listen to the lies and deception and have little or no awareness of themselves or their situation, of themselves and their place in the world. They buy the illusion of a safe life with little or no thought of the consequences. You're absolutely correct, Red Shadow: what has never worked won't miraculous suddenly start working. We're on our own.

He noticed the impact on the others the moment she used his taken name for the first time. There had been no statement or proclamation on his part. They had heard Nelli use it.

– The three of us, Nelli, Red Shadow and I have already taken the initial steps, Patricia said sweetly, immensely pleased with herself.

– What are you talking about? Travis blinked.

Patricia was about to answer when Nelli seemed to stumble, doing so with the drink in her hand, spilling her drink all over Patricia.

Patricia looked astonished first, but then she evidently got it, and a very enigmatic smile supplanted the previous.

– Oh, you know, putting our heads together long before there was a crowd and all that.

She put a hand on his thigh, touching his naked arm, and he got a hard on almost instantly, practically forgetting the question or even that he had asked one.

Larry watched her, how she began focusing on her talent, her power, and how it affected those closest to her. She rose and walked to the stereo and turned on the music, and began swaying, dancing.

– Yes, she cried, – we need to prepare, to become wild, ferocious and clever.

She didn't even have to try, in order to affect all the males, and even the females in the room. It was low-key in a way, but unmistakable. He found himself affected. It didn't grow sufficiently powerful to achieve anything even approaching control, though. It dawned on him that she wasn't trying to control anyone, that she projected… the opposite of control, a wild, fierce abandon.

Her words stirred him and the rest, just as much as her enhanced sensuality.

He was dancing with her. They all were, but he was dancing with her even when they weren't physically close. He realized that she was a political animal. She had always had that about her, at least since they had first crossed paths, her analytical mind, the ability to see beyond the present, to gauge what was coming.

– Patricia speaks truth, Nelli said. – The thousand-year wind will spell death for almost everyone. The hot wind is blowing, and the birds won't fly south for the winter. There's no winter anymore.

Her presence was different, but equally potent. They always listened when she spoke.

– But it will not spell death for us, she continued. – We will thrive!

A rush of wind and emotion seemed to roam their space. They felt it, almost like something tangible, solid. Her words both stirred them and worried them.

There was still food and drink left on the table. They chuckled and enjoyed themselves in the further anticipation of what the evening and night would bring. Whatever chill there was grew distant in their increasingly excited minds. There was no hurry, not even the implication of it in lazy movements, only the calm and excited certainty of what would follow.

They melted into each other's embrace, moving and stretching like one entity, one beast on the floor, on the carpets, couches and beds. Their clothes didn't have to be removed, but just faded away without effort. All of them stayed in the dining room or close to it. A plate broke as it fell from the table and hit the floor. No one reacted visibly to it. Several of them glanced awkward at each other.

– This feels so…. Nora frowned, – feels so *right*.

She crawled on top of a male with slow, determined moves and began riding him, rocking up and down.

Larry watched the others, watched them without watching them. She was the first, she and Daryl under her. The moment he penetrated her… a wave spread from that hot point and to everyone present. The heat shivering in the air, shaking flesh rose several notches in an instant.

Larry looked for Roberta, but he didn't need to. He found her right in front of him. She was kind of shy, avoiding looking into his eyes, but whatever reluctance there might be vanished completely the moment he grabbed her. She pushed herself at him and kissed him hard on the lips, her nails burrowing into the skin of his back.

She clung to him as he lifted her up a little, sufficient to make her hips adjacent to his. He held around her hips and pushed into her.

Two mouths close by gasped and stayed open, breathing each other's air. He heard a sound from somewhere, from every angle possible. Something new and previously unrevealed entered his conscious being. He was half aware of Patricia tying up Nelli, tying her wrists hard to the lower staircase pole with the rubber cord, how both smiled enticingly to Telford and Travis before something else overwhelmed him completely.

The other half of him had the attention fully focused on Roberta, on her sweet and beyond desirable form, a face dissolved in passion, but then, suddenly, there was an impossible third half, something he couldn't quite grab hold of, but couldn't deny. He was distracted when he grabbed her, distracted when he pulled her close and distracted when he penetrated her and pushed and pulled inside of her.

Clouds raced across the sky. They were red, they were all red. Fluid flowed from the girl's mouth and he couldn't decide if it was saliva or blood. She released a moan that could just as well be a death rattle. He kissed her, kissed her hard. She shouted in pleasure and pain.

The glowing heat from his surroundings warmed him, burned him. Nelli shook her restraints. She was taken from behind. She never took her eyes off him. The smile never left her face. Red, he was surrounded by mist, glowing in red.

The others noticed. At least some of them did. Everyone noticed something, something making them pause, something exciting most of them, making fear fill the rest.

Roberta's eyes turned wide, but her surprise did in no way impede on her building ecstasy. On the contrary, it seemed to add to it. She began shouting, even screaming. Her hard nipples stabbed his chest. She began pushing her hips so hard at him that he imagined it actually hurt, hurt a lot, but ecstasy built up in him as well. Both exploded in orgasm. He kept moving within her with several thrusts long after he had emptied himself in the warm and wet hole. She pushed herself tight to his body, flooding him in kisses.

– So good, she mumbled in his ear, – so good, so good, so good…

Her hair was in complete disarray, covering half her face and glued to her skin. She made no effort to brush it away, but just stretched lazily in his arms.

Chloe had been riding a male and slipped off him with a content smile on her face. She displayed herself to Red Shadow in a thousand big and small ways. He knew he would fuck her at one time or another tonight. She began breathing faster almost instantly.

He felt her, felt almost all of them and could tell their exact position in the room. It was… intoxicating, a powerful, unimaginable sensation. Nelli studied him. He watched himself through her eyes. It was easy, no more than a shift of focus. He saw how he stretched and flexed his muscles. It seemed like they were actually growing on the spot.

Wonder warred with lust in everyone's eyes, until there was war no more.

Awareness kept soaring as the wild, intense mating kept going, kept going, kept going. Nelli was released from her bonds. She had become calmer, less dangerous and could control herself better. She still scratched vulnerable skin during her most passionate moments. The others glanced curiously and startled at her, at the marks the cord had made on her wrists and the blood on her hands, but most of them still didn't quite get it, no matter their ongoing, growing awareness of the true nature of the world.

Sleep and rest, the haze of red mist danced in open and closed eyes. The experience of long, dark tunnels and vast sand dunes in the moonlight charged through aware and dazed minds both.

He stood before a mirror, as the first rays of dawn hit the hall. He didn't see anything special then and wondered if that was because he was in a state of low burn after all the fucking or because there was nothing there to see.

Feet carried him to the roof in swift, light moves. He stood on his spot, looking at the neighborhood, the near parts of the city, imagining he spotted red dust in the air.

She came to him after a timeless time on that spot. He saw her without seeing her, with his back turned. His olfactory sense, his ears and whatever other senses there might be, told him everything he needed to know.

– You love standing here in the morning, don't you?

It was not a question. She quite simply stated, in her typical way an indomitable truth.

Patricia embraced him from behind, caressing him gently on sore skin.

– You're so hard, so soft…

He turned to face her, giving her his steady, penetrating stare, and it worked. It worked instantly. She reddened, a deep, improbable red impossible to mistake.

– Have I ever thanked you, thanked you for bringing me into your fold, removing me from a dull, lifeless existence?

– You brought yourself, he pointed out.

Her smile, filled with gratitude further brightened his morning.

– That may be true, but you awakened my power, my very self. I, similar to what everyone else will be, have become a goddess in your pantheon. I can raise everyone's desire, now, whether they want to or not.

She was soaring, and he soared with her, like he knew she was soaring with him.

– Don't misunderstand. I don't want anyone's submission, just to be a perfect partner for you and Nelli. I want to support you in any way I can and help my brothers and sisters achieve their full potential.

She chuckled.

– Most of the others are still in for a rude awakening. They keep thinking that she's into bondage or something, and can't see the forest for the trees, but they will, won't they, Red Shadow. Their eyes will widen to such a degree that they will never be able to close them again.

– Yes, he heard himself give a hoarse reply.

They stood there nude. People walked in all directions in the fairly busy streets and crossroad below, and there were stares and pointed fingers and other evidence that people saw them, but he didn't care, and he knew she didn't either, that she, on the contrary enjoyed the ruckus they created, and pondering the issue, he acknowledged to himself that he did, too.

– You will be leader of a tribe that will thrive for a thousand years. I'm Red. I'm yours!

He read absolute sincerity in her misty eyes.

– The fact that you believe it makes it real for me as well, he said, – perhaps for the first time.

A feather-light kiss and she was gone.

A timeless time later Nora approached him, and for a moment he imagined that it was Nelli instead.

He watched as she appeared through the hatch.

It dawned on him that Nora was physically similar to Nelli. The moment the thought struck him he started studying her closer, and the similarity became obvious. The eyes resembled each other, the curve of the jaw and the way they moved. She grinned to him, giving him the sweetest of smiles, one filled with both mischief and humor.

– You never thought you would get a touch of the good life, did you?

She was different from Nelli in one important aspect: There was none of her inherent cruelty. This was a young girl that had yet to experience the harder and harsher part of life.

He pondered her statement, nodded before he was consciously aware of doing so.

– This, all this, he said slowly, indicating the house and everything below them, – in spite of the inherent dangers… seems too good to be true, too much like… wish-fulfillment. I fear I will wake up one day and that it will be nothing but a dream.

– Many things may be uncertain in our lives from now on, she said, – but I can *promise* you that this is real.

The passion in her voice pleased him, pleased him immensely.

The training picked up again right after breakfast, with an added urgency and eagerness and incentive shared by them all.

The dreamy smiles didn't leave their faces, at least not until they had been struck down several times. They looked at the girl that had become a center in their lives, doing so with anger and hurt and desire and admiration constantly changing the shadows casting their features.

– Pain is a good teacher, Nelli instructed them. – We will keep enjoying pleasures, but we will not let it distract us out there in the big bad world.

She gave them their creed, their rules to live by, and they listened, listened with increasing astuteness. They gritted their teeth, biting bloody lips and went at it with all their passion and growing ingenuity.

They moved on the roof with their wands, both during various exercises and during fighting one on one.

– I will never learn, Travis gasped in despair.

– If we had recorded this, and you could have seen yourself a week ago, you wouldn't have uttered such a silly statement, Nelli both chastised and praised him.

His big belly remained, but they could actually watch his progress from hour to hour.

– You will learn a lot during initial training, Larry said, – like a newborn soaking up information. After a while the lack of further visible progress will frustrate you and you have to step up your game in earnest.

They ran through the forest, walked a little and kept running.

– This is slow, Patricia teased them. – This is nothing. Just you *wait.* In six months this will feel like a Sunday stroll in comparison. You will be able to cover vast distances on foot, and you will never even consider riding the bus or using a car anymore.

It was raining, an even, endless downpour in air so hot and moist making it almost impossible to breathe. They were back on the roof. The rain didn't let up. They imagined that it had been falling forever. Nelli struck down Nora, struck her down hard.

– You haven't grasped this yet, Nelli scolded her, – but I assure you that you will. You will know the difference between life and death, the line to cross from slave to a truly independent human being.

They hated her, they loved her.

She still wore her goggles during the day, one more thing serving to separate her from the rest. There were other, far less obvious signs of her otherness.

Nora fought herself back on her feet, drying blood from her lips and jaw.

– Thank you, teacher, she cried, – for your precious gifts. I will savor and treasure them forever.

Many of the others nodded, knowing without knowing that those words would linger and become part of their gospel in the months and years to come.

Larry saw it, practically experienced it, watching it unfold with open eyes.

They were all showering, using all the available guestroom showers, making themselves ready for a quick meal before going to bed. There still weren't enough showers. Men and women showered together, like they had done all week. It just wasn't a big deal anymore.

Everyone gathered in the dining room, drying themselves without being shy about it. Nelli had, among a thousand small and big things picked off their shyness.

It did help that they were tired, physically exhausted beyond belief.

– I'm beat, Daryl declared. – I can guarantee that I will sleep for days.

– If not for the fact that Nelli, sweet Nelli will drag us from our beds before first light tomorrow, Chloe moaned.

Roberta smiled, as she pulled the sweater, the last piece of clothing down her head.

– You look insufferably great, Corinne said, visibly envious, – like you haven't really exerted yourself *at all.*

– I was in the military, in the Special Forces, Roberta grinned. – That more than prepared me for Nelli's cruel machinations.

Everyone present looked at her in awe and envy.

– I have to say that this is a great refresher, though, and Nelli does beat my old drill sergeant soundly in terms of zeal and brutality.

Laughter echoed through the room.

– We laugh so much, Travis said with wonder in his voice. – I didn't think it was possible to laugh so much.

Chloe rubbed his cheek, kissing him softly.

They retreated to the living room, chuckling and enjoying life together.

The pleasant sound echoed between them.

Everyone froze when they entered the living room. Larry and Nelli and several of the others stood by a bag with a very solemn expression in their eyes. Everyone recognized Roberta's red and green bag.

Nelli held up a very small electronic device.

– We found this transmitter very well hidden in a closed off compartment in your purse, Nelli said calmly.

– You looked through my stuff? Roberta blinked.

– Of course, we looked through your stuff, Nelli said, just as calm.

She walked slowly to the entrance, blocking the only easy way out.

– It's not on, Roberta blurted. – I turned it off days ago.

– We know, Patricia said. – That speaks in your favor, of course… to a

point.
Roberta lowered her eyes and sought towards the exit. Nelli blocked her way.
– Explain yourself, Nelli said harshly, the volume of her voice rising slightly.
– I will leave, now, Roberta said
– You will never leave, Nelli stated calmly.
Roberta attempted to walk past her.
Nelli moved, fast as lightning. She attacked Roberta hard and fast. Roberta could defend herself, and it became clear that she had held back, hidden herself the entire time this week, and that she wasn't rusty at all. They saw that, that she was trained by the way she moved, a way they had become intimately familiar with, though not seen fully utilized, but she was still totally outmatched by her current opponent. She managed to deflect the first two strikes, but then she was overrun completely and incapacitated in a manner of seconds. A hand to the jaw, making blood flood from the mouth, a strike in the abdomen and another blow to the head took care of her resistance. Nelli struck her down in the blinding flash of moments. She hit the floor and lay unconscious and still.
The recruits stared at their instructor in awe.
– She shows some limited skill, Nelli told Larry. – She may be useful, eventually, depending on whether or not she is who she says she is.
She began undressing the other woman, ripping off her clothes so easily that it looked like she was skinning her alive. A clawed hand grabbed her hair and dragged her to the wall, and knelt down by her side, and waited patiently. Larry found himself staring fascinated beyond fascinated at the display.
The others did as well, noticing, fearing that the claws on her hands were real.
Roberta stirred. She moaned a bit as she opened her eyes. Her eyes widened in fear and apprehension as she looked at the creature hovering before her.
– You're Red, Nelli told her. – I'm your pack master, and you will tell me everything you know. You're a child standing straight, coming clean before an adult, inferior and eager to learn the secrets.
– Lieutenant Roberta Allan, she responded automatically, – serial number…
Nelli held up the clawed hand, displaying it in all its glory, turning it around for all to behold, and if anyone in the room had been in denial about that small fact concerning her nature earlier, they could be so no longer. Roberta's blood froze to ice in her veins. Everybody else froze and gasped in

awe. The woman in front of them didn't hide anymore.
– You're not former army intelligence, Larry told Roberta.
She looked at him, a drowning woman looking for a lifeline.
– No, I…
She held back. Nelli patted her cheek gently.
– There's no return to the life you knew, pack sister, Nelli stated calmly. – There are only two choices confronting you, no middle ground.
Roberta froze, bowing her head in capitulation, submitting to the superior woman.
– I'm a part of a secret military program, she replied, her voice turning drowsy, her eyes glazing over. – I was sent to observe, because we suspected a private enterprise had similar objectives. Those objectives are to spot and capture and study… parahumans, both in a controlled environment and through field studies.
She broke into tears.
– My immediate superior is Captain Colin Thornton. I report directly to him. We don't know much. I didn't know much. The entire project is… a long shot, with allocated funding. We're interested because we listened to the conversation of the aforementioned interested party and their… social experiment. They move into various urban areas and heighten the tension, in an effort to draw out… interesting subjects. I was drawn to Al from the first time I saw him, and I came to l-love him.
– You felt kinship with him, Nelli nodded. – He was Red.
The creature rose.
– She's telling the truth, My Lord, she reported. – At least how she sees it.
Roberta shifted her attention from the girl to the man, instinctively sensing who was in charge, who the dominant personality was.
– What happens n-now?
– You've undergone trials, child, Nelli told her. – You've just been born. Now, your indoctrination, your training begins in earnest.
– Stand straight, Larry commanded casually.
Roberta rose and stood straight before him, reddening under both his and her direct stare. Her breasts swelled, and her nipples hardened. She turned wet between the thighs.
Her head hurt, and coagulated blood on her cheek made it hard to move her head. He knew she wanted to clean her wounds and probe her possible injuries, but she kept staying at attention.
– Speak! He bid her.
– I… disown my past, she said, looking straight ahead. – I embrace my new life, my life with the Red, with my pack and tribe. I will help it to the very

best of my ability, no matter how much it might harm my former associates. They no longer matter. I'm Red. That's the only life I know.

He nodded pleased. She understood.

Nelli kissed her on the cheek. A tremendous relief and joy charged through her. Larry felt it, unmistakable, almost visible in the air. The others stepped forward, embracing her, welcoming the new and reborn Roberta and gathered around the shivering form. They all joined, through her, most of them very much aware of this as a watershed moment.

She collapsed in Nelli's arms. Tears filled her eyes.

– Thank you, she sniffed. – Thank you so much!

She surrendered herself to her new life, the old fading into unimportance. Waves of acceptance hit her from all sides. It felt so good. She shook like a little girl in her tribe's fawn, while tears of joy kept flooding her cheeks.

Chapter Eight

Roberta spilled all her secrets, confessed to her heart's content. They could hardly shut her up and just had to, now and then, to ask a question or clear something up.

– It doesn't matter that much that the transmitter is turned off, she told them. – They told me in the briefing that I would probably do that from time to time, for various reasons, mostly of convenience. It will be easy to keep up the game with them, to keep them from suspecting anything, and if they do suspect, it will be easy to alleviate that suspicion. We do need to be on our guard, though, more than ever.

Larry nodded, two major forces stood against them, gathered around them, posed to take them down, one way or another.

The entire tribe moved through the streets late in the evening. And as always lately, when they were out walking a considerable amount of shadows tailed them.

– That, Roberta mumbled, – is the private enterprise and not any I was affiliated with.

They were out in force tonight, when all inhabitants of the tavern headed outside simultaneously. It served the reds well that they didn't react to Roberta's words or looked visibly at their shadows, but left that to Roberta and Nelli.

– Please, Red Shadow, Roberta implored him, – allow me to take care of them, of them all. Between me and Nelli they wouldn't stand a chance.

She had become loyal and dedicated, awaiting his words with a zeal that sometimes felt like too much of a good thing.

– Not yet, he said, – not out in the open like this. When you do, I want it to happen in the true shadows, where nothing is seen or heard.

She nodded in acknowledgment, smiling, proud that he trusted her and relied on her.

He yet again wondered about the calm he felt. It was as if the potential dangerous situation where they constantly found themselves hardly affected him. Patterns, analysis and decisions flowed constantly through his head like slow lightning.

Six, Nelli signaled.

And with that, he spotted the sixth he had failed to notice earlier.

They kept walking towards the underground station, not making haste in any way. It looked like they were strolling to any untrained eye watching them. The six observers easily saw their anxiety. Larry sensed their excitement and gathering joy over their discoveries.

– They're a fairly large group, Roberta told him, – about two dozen in this city alone. They're privately funded, with far better resources than «my» army group to draw on.

She no longer saw herself as part of that group. He was well aware of her eagerness to prove herself as a member of the tribe. She had indeed made a break with her past and embraced her new life.

We must act decisively, Nelli signaled him. The tribe isn't ready for a full-fledged confrontation yet.

He signaled his consent to her.

They walked into the underground station. There weren't that many people either entering or leaving at this hour. They took their time buying tickets. None of the six followed them inside. Only two other people entered after them, an old lady and a young teenaged boy.

Roberta led on down the escalator. The first part of their descent remained uneventful. After that Nelli took over. She led them away from the trains and down the spiral staircase. It was marked as an emergency exit path. They didn't encounter anyone.

More narrow corridors appeared to them. They imagined that they walked for a long time.

– Won't they see us on the CCTV? Corinne wondered.

– There's no… CCTV here, Nelli replied. – I would have known if there was. We passed that point minutes ago.

– They watched us through the cameras, Larry frowned. – They can't anymore. They're… coming.

The awe in everyone's eyes added to itself.

He and Nelli speeded up and the others matched that with an urgency burning in them.

This was clearly an unused, virtually abandoned area of the underground system. Dust and rubble were more common than a somewhat clean spot.

They arrived at the first closed and locked door. Nelli opened it just as easy as the last time. No locked doors could keep her out. The door closed behind them. The world turned dimmer in Larry's eyes, but he still saw well enough, in what he knew to be stark darkness to most others.

– Some of you already see fairly well or at least glimpse shapes in spite of the total blackness, Nelli said. – In time your sight will improve further. The rest of you will also learn to move through places such as these without the slightest effort, learn to move without the use of your eyes. The darkness is and will be our friend.

There was a bolt on the door. She used it and then rushed to the other door, the abandoned tunnel, where the rails were covered in rust, and then the other room. Those that could see or glimpse their surroundings led those that couldn't. Nora's eyes lit up when she stepped into the much bigger space.

– I can… see it, she brightened, – practically see what it will become.

They moved around a bit, exploring, stretching their senses. Larry felt them, actually felt them as if they were tendrils moving in his brain. They were all more or less circling him, in various elliptical orbits. Nellie was as well, but she had her focus more on them than on him.

– Listen, his ghostly voice told them. – Sense your surroundings.

Everyone stopped and stood still.

Larry sensed what they sensed when they both deliberately and not reached out in an effort to grab what couldn't be physically grabbed. It was there, just beyond the tip of their fingers.

– Sit down!

They did.

The red and their extended tribe sat on the floor, with their legs crossed in front of them, their eyes open but not seeing this room, these surroundings.

The both alien and familiar voice began speaking, and they paid attention to it.

– It's four fifteen in the afternoon, Nelli said, asking the same question over and over again. – It's approximately three years exactly since you popped out of your mother's belly. What is happening?

They sat there, listening to her voice, seeing her without seeing her. She repeated her words and repeated them again and again and again.

The voice droned on in their mind, even when it on rare occasion paused and demanded their response.

– Stop listening to me. Listen to that tiny voice within you. Make it grow. Fan its flame. Listen to my voice. Let it fill your being completely, until nothing is there, except that, and your own burning thoughts.

Fan its flame fan its flame fan its flame

Her soft, intense voice entered them all. It was as if it changed, turning into something it wasn't, something it couldn't be. It filled them up and even as it filled them, it faded from their surface consciousness.

She is good at this, a remote stray thought told Nora's conscious self. So very…

Time passed, an immensely long time, there in the darkness, in the warm, warm surroundings filled with a presence that couldn't be denied.

Roberta shook. Larry saw it easily.

– I'm in the garden outside our summer house, she said with what seemed very much like a normal voice.

It didn't disturb their trance-like state at all.

She… hypnotized us.

The thought brought strangely little turmoil. It didn't fade away, but lingered, and she surmised that Nelli wanted them to remember.

Remember.

Reach back in time, Nelli told them, kept telling them, even in her silence, and find all the little pieces of yourself.

They sat there and breathed in the dark, each breath filling them up further. A distant voice in their head feared they were gonna pop.

They spoke up one by one.

– I walked in the garden, Roberta said, – straying from the safe haven of my parents. A vicious dog charged me, and I froze, unable to move, as the vicious predator rushed at me.

He had forgotten that he was a dog and remembered that he was a wolf. She saw everything in his crazed eyes.

– Nothing much happened that day, Travis said, – but two days later I ran into the road, right in front of a big, bad car.

More voices added themselves to theirs, stories upon stories of startling and mundane memories.

– I saw it come at me, and jumped away just in time. It graced my leg, but even though it hurt for days, I wasn't really injured.

The others smiled at the wonder and apprehension in his voice.

Roberta rose. Nelli moved. They both presented themselves to Larry.

– Take out the six intruders, he ordered them. – Make a spectacle of it. Nail them to the wall or something. Be creative.

Roberta shook once, twice before calming, before finally turning into the deadly creature she was. Nelli acknowledged his orders with her usual quiet enthusiasm.

They moved away like the shadows they were.

There was a hardly noticeable glimmer of light when one of the doors was opened and closed, that was all.

He saw them move through the twilight and shadows and darkness, Roberta a little awkward at first, but quickly getting the hang of it, emulating Nelli moving in front of her. What started as vague glimpses grew distinct and clear in his mind.

The nascent tribe rose like one being, newfound awareness added to everything else they had learned recently. He noticed that Nora and Patricia also sensed the movements of the hunters, Nora like she actually walked by their side, Patricia more their emotions and fleeting thoughts.

Travis experienced it all as if he was actually there, levitating like a ghost through the abandoned parts of the Underground system. Larry shared that and the sudden breakthrough with him, blinking and gasping with him.

The six communicated through a special, elaborate communication system. They spoke with hardly audible whispers. Roberta and Nelli, splitting up, very much aware of each other in the space of the underground heard them, heard the Whisperers.

Nelli broke the first neck. The man never saw her coming. She didn't change expression at all. Her movements stayed economical, deadly, a predator's flow throughout the act. She moved on without breaking the stride.

Roberta strangled a woman from behind. The woman's eyes grew aware of the lethal human being just a moment before it struck, but she was helpless in its ruthless grip.

All the six intruders entered the tribe's territory and all of them died brutal deaths there. Nelli didn't use her claws at all. There was hardly a mark on any of them, except small lacerations on the neck and damaged skin.

The two hunters found ropes and strung them up like butchered meat. It was done quickly and efficiently.

Roberta returned with one man alive. She had dislocated both his shoulders and his arms hung down, completely useless. She dumped him at Larry's feet like a trophy.

– For interrogation, she said. – He's ready and eager to talk, to spill all his secrets. He will live long enough.

He was, looking around him with pain and haze and terror in his eyes.

Pride lit Roberta's eyes. Something had turned in her, something irreversible. She had evolved far more than the others.

– He had a microphone attached to his throat, she reported. – That's how they communicate. Quite the elaborate setup, really.

She was calm, relaxed, triumphant.

He had lots and lots of marks on him, and blood and cuts and wounds.

Nelli lit a lighter. Everybody saw him clearly. All of it became real to them. They could no longer hide behind the pretense of normality.

The man talked and talked and talked.

He spilled his guts in tears, between chokes and whimpers.

They recorded every minute of it. It was way too detailed to merely recall. They still remembered bits and pieces, chunks and stretches, their visual and listening senses working overtime, long after he had choked on his own blood.

– He carried a gun, Roberta said. – They all did.

She carried three of them, Nelli the other three.
The tribe left its territory, temporarily leaving it to wind and rain and dust. Roberta carried the dead man. She nailed him to a wood wall of an electricity substation, while they were still moving in the shadows.
– She's in need of clothes covering her up, Nelli pointed out.
Dylan gave her his jacket with a hood. That did the trick.
They emerged back into the light, the pale, dirty light of dust-covered lanterns concealed and walls and ceilings. Nelli and Roberta kept scouting, moving a bit ahead of the others. The walk up, on stairs and escalators proved eventless. They walked through the broad exit and into the neon-lit night.
Roberta slowed down, until she walked on Larry's left side.
He looked at her, acknowledged her.
– I foolishly thought I had put the killing and strife behind me, she said humbly. – Thank you, Red Shadow, for proving me wrong.
She still appeared calm, cool and collected, even though he did sense turmoil beneath her surface.
– I found my calling, she insisted. – I've been half asleep since I returned from the war. This is what I'm born to do, I know that now.
He didn't know what to say, so he didn't say anything.
– We need guns and we need to be good at using them, she stated. – There's no way of avoiding that.
He found himself nodding. It was self-evident, really.
– I'm a little rusty with guns as well, she continued, – but that, too, will return to me, I know that, and I can teach you all, to use them for as long as we can, until bullets become obsolete.
Nelli slowed down, until she walked by Larry's side as well. He made an effort to keep himself from sighing.
– She has become eager, dedicated and dangerous, Nelli said, nodding towards Roberta, – the perfect tool, different enough from Nelli to be equally valuable to Red Shadow and his reign.
«Until bullets become obsolete», he thought, while having his attention on Roberta. She had said it like she truly believed it. If she didn't, she would have to be a far better actor than she had shown so far. It dawned on him, dawned on him again what she was actually saying.
Nelli nodded, once again correctly gauging his reaction.
They kept their eyes on the terrain as they walked on, constantly scouting for their enemies. There were none they could discern. Larry certainly didn't spot any, and the two sentries clearly didn't either.
The two of them spread out again, becoming one with their surroundings,

practically turning invisible. Even with everything that had happened, that still impressed him and astounded him. They covered the rear and front and most other positions so effectively that it seemed like they were everywhere simultaneously.

Nora was the next one up. She did her best to mimic the other two, slinking back until she walked on his left.

– Hi, she said shyly.

She wasn't shy, he knew that much.

– You have… a job, don't you, Larry? Nora blushed. – How do you deal with that?

– I had a job, he grinned. – I told my former boss I was sick and wouldn't appear for a while. He grudgingly accepted that. Since then I quite simply haven't communicated with him at all. He still pays my salary, but I suspect that won't last much longer.

– Of course, she nodded.

A smile of clarity slowly broke on her face.

They reached the tavern. Nelli gave the clear signal and they approached the building feeling fairly safe, still moving as if they weren't. It pleased him.

– I do understand, Nora insisted, she assured him. – What your former boss, whatever society and other people may think of you no longer matters. In truth it never mattered. You were only, as you said taken in by the general deception.

It pleased him.

– Everything has become so clear, she marveled.

He realized startled that her thoughts echoed his own.

– I try to think back, to the time before I encountered Nelli, he said. – I find it increasingly difficult.

She nodded solemnly, excitedly because he gave her a piece of his mind, because he shared his increasing honesty with her, with them all. There were few secrets between them, and less so for each new day.

Machinegun fire thundered through the woods.

– Short bursts, Roberta shouted like a drill sergeant. – Short bursts, dammit!

She had, with the tribe's assistance procured the automatic weapons on the black market. It had been easy, ridiculously easy.

She also trained a selected group as sharpshooters.

The stench of the forest imposed itself on Larry, on them all. The harsh imposition of the guns mixed with that, creating something new and dangerous within everyone.

They occupied a large part of the area, with sentries guarding its parameters, ready for trouble.

The parking lot at the edge of the forest remained empty.

Nelli sat in the top of a tree at the highest vantage point, surveying most of the forest. There was no suspicious movement.

– It's so… hard moving through nature compared to flat city ground. Dylan spoke with difficulties during one of Roberta's most brutal exercises. – So much better!

Most of the others cracked a smile, but didn't have the energy needed to actually laugh.

The bow and arrow training commenced. It wasn't really that different from using the other guns, except for the silence, the deadly silence, the absence of the roaring thunder.

– I love this, Telford said content. – I just love it! And this isn't temporary, like the guns, but something we'll teach our children.

Those words, in turn created a long line of thought and sensations within them all.

They sat around the campfire at night. Larry breathed everyone's scent and felt like he could actually smell each and every one of them, their emotions and reactions. Every face he watched looked like it was glowing, and independently of the glow from the dancing flames.

Larry took more and more part in the instructing. It felt more and more right to him. He no longer felt awkward and insecure faced with the others' admiration, their awe.

It was the next day or the day after that or the one after that. He chased Nora up a steep rise. She did her best to shake him off, even though they both knew she had no chance of doing that.

She stood facing him at the top of the rise on shaking legs.

He slapped her on the cheek. She tried to strike back at him, attack him. He slapped her again.

– Get angry! He told her. – You're improving greatly, but the final, crucial piece is missing.

– You said that before, she gasped. – I *am* angry!

– No, you're not *angry*. You don't feel it burning within you like a storm incarnated.

He struck her down. She jumped back on her feet in an instant and struck out at him. Her fist hit his jaw and he felt blood flow in his mouth. There was hardly any pain, but he staggered backwards. She froze in astonishment. A smile broke on both their faces.

– I felt it, she gasped astonished, – felt the burning.

Her smile turned triumphant, showing the type of exhilaration he had come to know well.

– I do as well, Dylan said from a distance. – It's such an accurate analogy. My flesh feels like it's actually on fire. It hurts, but feels increasingly good.

– The Red is transforming you, Nelli told him, told them. – It will become a natural part of you. You will hardly remember how it felt without it.

They stood there, pondering her words, taking them to heart.

Time changed into flashes, glimpses of what Larry's life had become, each lasting a lifetime.

He stood alone on the rise, lost in thought. Nelli caught his attention, stepped into his immediate sphere. He read undiminished pride in her eyes and stance.

– Their initial testing is complete, Red Shadow, she reported. – Everyone is healthy and has no injuries to speak of. They're ready, ready for their true training to begin.

– Very well, he said, – you make the final preparations and I will be with you shortly.

– Yes, My Lord, she said promptly.

She remained, clearly unresolved. He studied her. She was blushing. Another smile threatened to break her solemn expression. She straightened. Then she curtseyed and went on her way.

He had sensed it, how she had imagined herself to be back in the tunnels, the tunnels where she had grown up, when she had grown up. She had seen him as bigger, as he had been then, not as he was now, and in just the smallest of flashes he had as well.

Anxiety and expectation continued to war within him and there was no winner.

He walked down into the valley, into the hollow ground forming a natural bowl. Two sets of to him similar visuals and audio stereo revealed themselves to him. He walked through a place of naked, dead trees and forlorn buildings. He walked down the rise into a particularly vibrant spot in the forest. Both felt equally real.

Nelli met him halfway down. She carried a number of torches tied to poles in her arms.

– I recognize this place, she cried. – Even though its appearance is very different from what I remember I did so almost the moment I first visited it with you, with Lawrence Watros. They will build an entire «industrial park» here, desecrating it, not knowing what it will eventually become. It is or will be the place of final testing of your Guard. You, Red Shadow brought me here the very first time the day I turned fourteen.

He watched her as she lit one torch and ran away with it, with them all.

She put the pole in the ground, lit another and stuck that in the ground a considerable distance away from the first. He watched her as she formed a wide circle, one that could only be seen from above, from his vantage point. The circle formed in his head well before she completed it physically.

She completed her task. He continued on his way down the rise, reaching the spot at the bowl's center where everyone anxiously awaited his return.

They all looked attentive at him. He nodded curtly. They straightened, their features settling in a determined, very determined expression. Later he would marvel at how easy everything revealed itself to be.

– Those moving outside the circle are forfeit! He told them. – They will live, but only as a pale imitation of themselves, not truly living at all.

They nodded eagerly, not like dogs pulling their chain at all, but like unfettered and unchained beings seething with fire flowing through their veins.

Begin! He told them. They heard the growling hiss wherever they walked.

They spread out, setting out into the forest. Larry, Nelli and Roberta remained.

The three of them stood there waiting. Larry heard the ticking of the clock. He didn't need to look at his watch. The ever harder beating of his heart did the counting.

– You don't need to lead anymore, he told Nelli casually, relaxed. – I know what to do.

– Yes, Red Shadow, she acknowledged with a joyous whisper.

Her heat warmed him, thawing the dull chill in his bones, like it had done from the beginning. They ran. His muscles and awareness seemed to operate on an entirely different level than he could recall. Nellie remained the fastest and most versatile, but he caught himself in being able to follow her, to catch her shadow and make it solid, tangible. Pride and cunning coursed through him.

Nelli recalled her own initiation ceremony, and he experienced it with her. It wasn't hard, a little shift of focus, that was all. He remained in the present, even as a small part of him rode her memories.

Red Shadow stood at the top of the sand dune with his two chosen hunters. Nelli looked at him from below, fighting not to become distracted, spreading out with her fellow initiates.

This was one of the places always giving her the willies, filled with ghosts of trees and derelict structures. Everything turned black and gray, except the dry sand whirling in the weak draft. She sensed no wind. This was a carefully picked Hollow; one of the sacred ceremonial grounds used by Red Shadow and his people for centuries. She and her fellow initiates rushed into the hideout, where they could actually hide without being instantly spotted from far away. The daystar blinded them, the goggles not being sufficient protection against its supreme radiance. She heard Nastu mutter to himself, heard him pray. Her lips curled in contempt. He prayed to Red Shadow. How stupid was that? If God heard him, Nastu would do nothing but reveal himself, shame himself and his pack.

Sweat filled the inside of the goggles, filled her eyes, making it even more difficult to see. They couldn't remove the goggles. It would blind them, cripple them for life. She shivered in the violent heat.

Her lips moved silently. She muttered to herself her exercises of meditation, of the Moving Silence, focusing on her hearing, sense, smell and taste. She had been bred and born in the tunnels. That was her life, her strength. She returned there in her mind and perception. Eyes, though occasionally useful were the distraction, the little death, potentially worse. She heard feet touch the sand, smelled and tasted sweat and blood, fear and terror, moving according to that, turning silent and invisible in a terrain where any wrong move could expose her at any given moment.

The stark scent of the forest ripped into his nostrils, into hers. Spittle flooded her mouth and flowed between her lips. The hunt excited her. Exhilaration flowed through her veins. She slid into his slipstream, she and Roberta running side by side. Nelli recognized Roberta's moves. They were slightly different from those of Red Shadow and her own, but still very much part of her training and cellular memory. The three hunters moved as one, fangs and claws extended far beyond their body of flesh and bone.

They will catch us, the girl running between the dunes and skeleton trees and structures thought. It's only a matter of how.

She was bright and deadly, she knew that. Every pair of eyes and flesh-and-bone body looking at her told her that, conveyed that truth to her, feared her. She knew this was not the case with the sand beasts chasing her, chasing them all. They were beyond such concerns. She strived constantly with her anxiety, with shelving her panic and sense of inferiority, choking in distress.

Nora, Travis, Patricia, Corinne and the rest rushed through the forest the fastest they were able, expending way too much energy, burning out fast. They spread out, running alone through moors and dry forest beds, desperately avoiding dry and dangerous branches sticking out. They were stunned by the way they saw themselves in the terrain, its three and four-dimensional space. In a fluttering panic they couldn't quite discard, they still felt that amazement.

Red Shadow felt what they felt. They, at least in part felt what he did. The force of the interaction rocked him, and Larry, in the deepest recesses of his awareness knew this was just its modest beginning.

Red Shadow and the sand beasts moved light on their feet on treacherous ground. Dust and grains of sand danced in the air around them.

The girl watched the clumsy moves of her fellow initiates. She quelled the flare of contempt at its conception and focused on herself and her own prowess. Eyes moved fast and furious back and forth, and had already started hurting by the strain. She looked for shade. There was none. She scouted for hiding places. She spotted none.

Her feet moved faster. Her eyes flickered even more from side to side.

The three hunters charged through the old ruins. Red Shadow brought crimson darkness in the middle of the day. The girl was nowhere to be seen. Red Shadow smiled.

She came at him from an angle almost no one would suspect. He allowed her to strike him, even though he saw the strike coming, having seen it, having felt the pain, the blood flowing from his mouth a thousand times in his dreams.

He grabbed her and pushed her at the ground, stunning her, paralyzing her with an additional strike at her abdomen. She still had fight left in her, but no way of utilizing it, utilizing her deadly body.

– You tried to take out the biggest threat. I salute you!

She looked at him through the haze of worship and gratitude.

– Tell us, young pup, he prompted her, – about your reasoning.

Her shame was tinted with inevitable pride.

– I figured Red Shadow and his hunters knew the area. They've done this many times. There's no place to hide here.

He turned to the other hunters, the smile almost visible in his face. They bowed their head and acknowledged his wisdom.

The others were caught in a jiff, and they looked strangely displeased. The young girl sensed that, and more pride coursed through her, even as she fought to contain it, to not give in to its traitorous dangers.

He turned towards her and all the air left her lungs and her knees turned weak, and she couldn't help herself.

– You must start using your claws in earnest, he instructed her, – stop holding back, or you will never be the warrior you need to be.

– Yes, Red Shadow, she cried out her allegiance to him, attempting to quell the sudden shame and embarrassment overwhelming her.

– Why? He asked her.

She got confused for a moment, before regaining her wits.

– «Anyone I battle is my enemy», she quoted, she attempted to convey with her own voice, not his. – My enemy should be given no quarter.

The dry desert gave way to the wet forest, and it was the same, all the same. Larry and his hunters charged through the thick underbrush slowing them down.

It felt to him like it wasn't there at all.

Nora came at him at an impossible angle, just like he suspected she would do. He wanted to avoid her kick, but was unable to do so. Blood flooded his mouth. He grabbed her and slammed her at the ground. The ground was soft, but the collision still emptied her lungs of air.

– You tried to take out the biggest threat, Nellie said pleased. – I salute you!

And he echoed her words in his mind.

The ruthless hunt continued. They rushed across the soft ground with renewed vigor and what seemed like ever more strength. They caught up with Travis quickly, and slammed brutally into him. He crouched and gasped on the forest bed.

– Your old life is over, Larry snarled, making himself hard. – If you don't realize that, you have no place here.

He felt it, felt the power of his rage, his contempt and the certainty of his power. This was different. This was…

He had believed he had felt anger and everything else before, but it felt faint, like nothing compared to what he felt now.

– This is the Red Shadow I know, Nelli said softly somewhere from behind. – This is the man I learned to fear.

Travis fought himself on his feet. His legs shook, but he remained standing. A stubborn streak remained in his totally exhausted physical body. Larry nodded to himself, both aware and not of doing so.

They caught the others easily. They were like fish on land confronted with the mighty wave catching up with them. It was like it cost him no effort at all, as if his expenditure of power stemmed from an endless supply. He watched them all, watched himself. Roberta was marked by the hard run. Nelli wasn't. He saw the shimmering red shape through Nelli's eyes, an amazing sight threatening to take his breath away.

– Nora grasped the rules of the game, its true objective, he said. – She knew there was no escape from the hunters, and that the only chance of winning and surviving is to go for the throat. If the game had been anything even approaching fair and truly about survival, she would have been the only one with a chance, a slim change of surviving. The rest of you behaved like prey, and fled, and kept fleeing without thought or contemplation. You will earn, learn to kill countless enemies, your fangs and claws will become equal to the sharpest of blades.

His words slammed their mind as hard as his body had done their flesh.

They turned back, returning to the edge of the forest, the three in front walking in fast, fluid movements, the rest limping and gasping in their slipstream.

They returned to their current brief-home, to the small, pleasant cottage in the wretched city far into the night. There was no one there, except the few guards he had left behind. He fought against what he knew to be treacherous confidence.

– There's no one here, Nelli assured him. – There are no scents that don't belong.

They got the all clear sign, saw familiar faces in one window. He still couldn't relax and that felt strangely reassuring, and made him grin pleased.

Nelli still walked inside first. She confirmed the all clear no more than a breath later.

They all felt the exhaustion. He did as well. Even Nelli was sort of drained, at least mentally. Sleep entered them, long before they actually closed their eyes.

He woke up the next day, just early enough to see the sunset. He rose from bed, disentangling himself from still sleeping Nora and Patricia, and walked nude up on the roof. Roberta and Nelli, and Dylan and Travis stood in each corner behind the recently added fortifications and scanned the immediate area, guarding the fort, armored and armed. They waved both excitedly and serious-minded to him. He returned the wave.

Nelli moved before him in the tunnels. She was training with the other young warriors. She noticed him. He sensed it, as he watched her turn and face him, falling to her knees with the rest of them.

It was clear to all, when he walked towards those kneeling and stopped, who he was focusing on.

– You will come with me, he told her briskly.

He walked off without looking back. She looked astounded at him. Everyone else stared at her.

She remained frozen, kneeling, until she finally caught herself and made herself rise and follow him.

He brought her with him, to places deep into the tunnels where she had never ventured, spaces she had never imagined existed, and her eyes were opened to so many things.

– You will serve me directly from now on.

– Y-yes, My Lord, she stuttered.

– And I expect you to eventually rid yourself of that undignified girlish behavior and start acting like a woman and warrior worthy of the Crimson Guard.

– Yes, My Lord.

She was blushing, but straightened and exhibited a stubborn expression. Boundless curiosity and determination burned in her features.

He began tutoring her, filling her with tales and acts from his razor-sharp memory. The coaching stretched into weeks and months and bridging a gap of centuries vaster than an abyss.

Larry watched her standing on the roof with a rifle in her hands. She handled it beyond casually, as if the metal had become an integrated part of her. The rays of the sunset in her hair and on her skin mixed with his visions, intermingling, becoming one, singular impression. The horizon spread out in and behind his eyes.

He stood there and watched Forever with a catching in his throat and a growing sense of unease, of having forgotten something, something very, very important, wondering what he couldn't perceive.

Chapter Nine

The night rose in the east and spread across the sky, slowly becoming dominant.

– This is our time, Travis stated with pride.

The others found very little doubt and insecurity in his voice, in him as a whole and marveled at the change they witnessed in him.

The pack spotted no external activity as they moved in on one of the safe-houses of the Others. They stayed cautious, but that didn't keep them from advancing.

Travis was practically two places simultaneously; both in his flesh and in the invisible spirit form somewhere ahead. His inevitable wonder warred with his concentration, the strain exposed by the sweat on his brow.

The scents still lingered in this house, but they were faint, distant. It remained amazing to Larry how Nelli's sense of smell actually drew a picture in her mind, one not any less than what her eyes did.

– The birds have fled the nest, she snarled in contempt. – They are hardly worthy of being prey.

She… let go, hiding less and less, revealing her feral nature to the tribe, like she had done to him long ago. It had become visible in every move she made. Every change in her position resembled the flashing of a blade.

They entered the building physically. Their impression did change. They were able to study the chaos left behind, the incomplete cleaning up of the house.

– They were in a hurry, Roberta noted, clearly feeling almost embarrassed for pointing it out.

– I guess our decisive handle of their scouts made an impression on them, Patricia snarled in triumph.

She was beyond pleased, to the point of being sexually aroused. They had no trouble catching that either.

– My guess would be that all the local forts have been abandoned, Roberta said. – They would know that their man was tortured, and that he cracked. He was on the need to know part of the organization, but he still knew a lot about the operation and their modus operandi.

– But not that you've been a part of a team that has tracked them for years, right? Larry said casually.

– That *is* a fairly safe assumption, she replied. – Nothing I've seen suggests that!

He watched her, watched her ponder it further. A huge and wicked smile broke slowly on her face.

– They are the enemies we must face on our desert walk, Nelli stated firmly.

A load of impressions accompanied her words in Larry's increasingly feverish mind.

He sort-of understood, even as understanding eluded him.

They moved through the city, wearing wide coats, riding the Underground without causing undue suspicion.

– Look at people, Travis said. – They're nervous wrecks.

His growing awareness served him well. Larry nodded to himself. People looked with suspicion at everybody these days.

– You're correct, Patricia nodded pleased to him. – And we aren't causing it either. I remember noticing the heightened tension months ago. I couldn't see it for what it truly was then, but I did notice it.

– Modern human society has always been insane, Larry shrugged, – always been an unacceptable place to live. It has merely woken up abruptly to that fact lately. We were all like most others. None of us saw it, not until our eyes were forced wide open and our illusions were irrevocably wrested from us.

– Our paltry illusions, Patricia snorted. – If destiny called us, it had it easy with us. We embraced it!

They all found themselves both frowning and nodding in wonder.

The train pulled to a stop. They left it and rushed up the escalators in a fairly relaxed manner.

The human beings in motion pushed into the street like a solid wind. The pages of the magazines on the stalls in the newsstand flipped and the paper even came unbound from gravity for a moment. A van drove up by their side. They had been aware of it and recognized it, and Corinne, behind the wheel. The backdoor opened. More familiar faces appeared, and they jumped inside. The roaring machine rolled like lightning the last short, long stretch to their destination.

The car became their world, their reach, even as they more than ever stayed aware of what happened outside, of the people on the sidewalk and those crossing the road, off and on the zebra stripes.

They stopped well before their destination, leaving the car behind and advancing on foot, carefully, from corner to corner. One moved, followed by three, and then the rest of the scouting party. The area was beyond the tighter populated parts of the suburbs, close to the countryside. It was just a few blocks. They moved through the shadows of the twilight, as if they were born to it, marveling at their prowess.

Nelli moved ahead. The others watched her, watched her scan the terrain without anyone ignorant being the wiser. She spotted no enemy. They didn't need the decisive sign with her finger to know that anymore.

She reached the fence blocking the path to the industrial park. The others had already crossed the street halfway in her wake. A bit of sweat covered their brow, as inevitable anxiety made them look in as many directions they possibly could simultaneously.

A large sign said:

Pingross Limited
Ebert Lane 534

Larry's increasingly acute memory visualized the card he had found in Albert's apartment.

They reached the fence. There were a few trees blocking part of their visual access, but also providing them with cover. There was hectic activity in the storage facility across the parking lot. Well over a dozen people dressed in a distinct uniform carried boxes from the building and into the waiting trucks.

– They're moving, retreating, Patricia whispered. – *Fleeing!*

– More like a strategic retreat, Roberta said, hardly audible. – My guess is that they will be back, better prepared to deal with unknown, unexpected elements straining their dedicated long-term strategy.

– They do move like a military unit, don't they? Larry nodded to her, to himself. – They've invested too much time and energy to just pack up and go home.

He cast a glance at Nelli.

– They *are* our eternal enemies, she confirmed, – one of those we'll face time and time again in the vast sands of the ages.

Indecision rode him. He watched the action and couldn't decide upon a course of action and knew that doing nothing was also a choice. Flashes of Nelli's memories haunted him, as they always did, without that making him any wiser.

– They're in quite a few cities and areas, he finally decided. – Even if we were successful in eradicating everyone in this particular unit, we would only bring all their resources and manpower down on us.

– I believe that to be more than a correct assessment, Roberta agreed.

– We will wait for them to come to us, he said, – and be ready to give them the warmest possible welcome.

Nelli looked at him with unqualified pride in those pale eyes.

They watched them pack up and leave, even as they stayed alert, battle ready. Now, when the decision had been made, he could enjoy it more, savoring the process and his own fairly calm reactions and tactical evaluations. His mind remained a seething cauldron of thought.

– Do you guys think they know we're here? Corinne wondered. – Or that they have people posted in the general area?

– Nothing says that's the case, Nelli replied, – though we should always keep that thought in mind.

She had been joking, at least in part, and that made everyone smile.

They pulled back, even as the last of the uniformed people drove through the gate and the building across the divide turned dark and cold.

The fairly small group filled the van, and they drove off. Nelli called home. Chloe responded. There was nothing wrong. Nelli broke the connection.

They return to the small, nice house in the quiet street and are hugged by the members of the tribe that had been staying at home.

– I love this place! Roberta said, suddenly very emotional.

She was practically bursting with joy. They chuckled with her, not of her. She grabbed Larry's hands and met his eyes with even more enthusiasm and dedication.

– I realize now that my time with your brother was only a preparation for this, for all this.

He looked at her with an unease he couldn't quite conceal. She didn't seem to notice.

– You're so much more than he ever was, she whispered, not bothering to contain herself.

The experienced, mature woman looked at him with growing excitement and worship.

There was just no way he could be mistaken about that.

They had dinner. Everyone gathered, as usual around the long table with eager and easy smiles on their lips. The sentries stayed on their posts, as always and those around the table stayed alert, but they clearly enjoyed the simple and relaxing experience of the meal.

– We've come so far, Chloe declared, her voice and being overflowing with passion. – We won't allow anyone to *ruin* it for us.

Everyone nodded to themselves and to the others. There was a fierce mood among them, a kind of elation, not fear. Nelli looked at Larry with distinct pride in her eyes.

– There is indeed a good reason to be pleased with out charges, Red Shadow, she stated. – We've succeeded in the first step of our teaching. Your guard and tribe members have become true, independent beings. They've indeed come far.

They heard her words and bristled, the pride briefly filling them to the brim. Their appetite, already quite pronounced after all the hard and harsh exercise lately grew further.

– Your words stir my blood, My Lady, Daryl said. – It encourages me to do better!

– You must! You will!

He nodded, they all nodded, doing so beyond eagerness, beyond passion.

– Your training will now begin in earnest. You will learn to achieve deep sleep even in times of strife, and still sleep light, be able to wake up on a moment's notice if need be. You will become hardship, become joy and everything in-between and beyond.

Her words and teaching filled them.

Their experience of the dining and the table faded, and the stark reality of the training returned to the forefront of their consciousness. The abandoned construction sites, the deep and dark and shadowy tunnels supplanted the joy around the table and the fierce and pleasant mating.

Corinne stood at attention before Nelli, focusing through eyes filled with sweat and exhaustion.

They stood at the top of a tall building, looking at the vast city below.

– You have a hawk's eyes, the Crimson Guard whispered in her ear.

– I have, she acknowledged. – I used to study my customers and occasionally imagined that I would see straight through them, deep into their soul.

– Now, you must do far better, study people nearby, and the pattern in their movements, gauging their deepest secrets.

Dizziness warred with the growing awareness, as her vision cleared, and she once again took Nelli's words and teaching to heart… and she began seeing beyond appearances of everything and everyone below. She would have fallen if Nelli hadn't held her, but her eyes turned sharp as a hawk.

– It feels so strange, she mused, – as if I'm outside myself.

Suddenly, she seemed to be descending like a hawk, a bird of prey, and she found herself down there, among the afternoon commuters, both drivers and pedestrians. She studied them from above, from close up, both hovering above them and walking among them.

She stared straight into their eyes, and they didn't notice.

– This, she mumbled, – is far more than mere eyesight.

– It is indeed, Nelli confirmed. – It's a weapon far more valuable than a rifle or anything like that. You have the ability to spot enemies from far away and will be an asset beyond measure to your tribe.

Corinne shook as the unfamiliar, feverish sensation charged through her body, burning her mind.

– This is it, warrior! Nelli said excited. – This is your transformation!

Corinne felt it then, like a stab in the heart, like arousal. Larry felt it, felt her Rise.

They were all rising, all the Red, rising with and without him, Corinne, Patricia, Nora, Chloe, Roberta, Travis…

It didn't stop either, but continued relentlessly in the days and years following this one.

Larry and Nelli taught their charges the hand signals, the secret body language. They had done so for a while, but now they began teaching them their deeper, multi-layered significance. It was yet another grateful task.

He made the sign and the sound, and knew he got it almost completely synchronized, knew he got it right. It was not just a move with the hand, a sound from the larynx, but both, a movement and sound made with the entire body, the entire self, a language beyond words, beyond signs.

They repeated it with increasing confidence. It became second nature to them, like it had to him.

The hot wind kept blowing and showed no sign of receding.

Nelli performed for him. During what was supposed to be early autumn, but still felt like in the midst of a raving summer, she danced on the roof in his honor, doing so to their song, the music they had first heard in the bar below in what felt like ages ago.

It warmed him, making him burn with joy and desire, even though he couldn't help but noticing the frown on her brow. Even when she danced with half closed eyes and kissed Larry softly on the lips the frown was there.

– I can't help but worrying, Larry, she whispered, clearly ashamed and confused. – Don't worry about it!

He did, and he didn't, sharing her confusion and underlying fear, unable to break through it and find illumination.

Roberta appeared in the doorway. They turned towards her before she opened her mouth and cried out to them.

– Breakfast is ready, she cried to them with a joy-filled smile.

They returned downstairs and were greeted by the gang, the tribe with all the usual enthusiasm, with lots of fiery hugs and contact and loud laughter. He swallowed hard, and so did, he noted did Nelli.

The meal was just as happy an event as it had been most of the time since the tribe had first gathered. They acted as if they hadn't seen each other in a long time, as if they had never been apart. Glasses met and parted.

– These are really great glasses, Patricia mused.

– How so? Dylan wondered.

– They sound like a tuning fork when they meet. Most glasses today sound more like wood or even broken glass than actual glass. Good quality glass adds an extra dimension to a good toast, you know.

– It does, Corinne nodded. – I searched all over town before I found the right supplier, and paid extra for them, twice the amount I would have for ordinary glass, but they're worth it.

– They are! Patricia stated empathically.

The chuckle sounded soft and pleasant and great in everyone's ears.

It kept echoing in their ears in the days and weeks to come. Time's river ran down the delta in a calm, pleasant flow. Travis and Chloe, the last of the early recruits to retain a flabby body grew mean and lean. Their growth and Change became something visible, tangible.

Everyone, except a few disgruntled, disappointed guards gathered in Larry's old apartment. There was no furniture left there, nothing but dust and memories.

He raised a glass. Everyone present did the same.

– We gather here, he declared, – on this last day of my ownership of this unimportant place… in order to leave the past behind, doing so forever and ever, and embrace our new life.

He didn't say or cry «cheers». Theirs were silent cheers, except for the startling sound of the meeting and parting of glasses.

Nelli kissed him. Hungry lips met and held on. When they pulled back Nelli bristled in happiness.

Her belly had begun showing, becoming noticeable even with baggy clothing.

The occasional frown crossed her face less and less.

Therefore, he was beyond startled a few minutes later to spot tears in the corners of the pale red eyes.

Everyone stood by the window and looked at the city below.

She turned her face away from him, knowing fully well the futility of it, and that told him more.

He turned her back and touched her lightly under the jaw.

– I'm becoming useless to you, she mumbled.

– Never think that! He stated, insisted.

– I am! She said empathically. – It isn't the inevitable physical clumsiness, the ruining of balance and such in itself. Clan females stay active the entire time we carry children. I'm changing. My edge of the mind is undermined. My claws are being pulled. I'm turning soft and *useless*.

Everybody present looked awkward at her.

– Every single trainee suffering under your command would disagree, Roberta said lightly, not quite joking.

Nelli burst into laughter, a full and loud laughter almost shocking the others.

She turned towards Larry.

– You never prepared me for this, Red Shadow, she said quietly, – but it is something I must and will handle, like everything else.

She walked to Roberta and kissed her on the cheek.

– Thank you!

They left the apartment, left the tall building at dusk.

One more event faded, never fading from Larry's immediate memory.

Nelli threw herself into the training of the recruits as never before, to the point of appearing reckless.

But she never was. Larry saw that easily. She never strained herself beyond her capacity, only made use of the knowledge beaten into her while growing up in the crèche in an even deeper, more fundamental manner.

– Ever more of our females carry children, she said. – We are fierce, and will prevail, but our effectiveness is inevitably declining. We must all be even more on our guard, be even better in what we do.

She got her point through. She made certain they got it.

Several of those in her class practically stumbled from the training ground.

– You're overcompensating, Roberta told her in a quiet moment in the showers later.

– Thank you, sister, Nelli said. – I shall keep that in mind.

– It isn't such a big deal, Roberta joked. – You will still risk breaking bones and necks of the poor initiates…

Nelli giggled, not attempting to hide it.

– You have become a staunch sister, a fierce warrior, like I suspected you would be.

– Thank you, sister, Roberta whispered.

And broke into tears.

Nelli held around her, comforting her.

– I've become so emotional lately, she sniffed. – I don't know what's wrong with me…

Suddenly, she raised her hand to her mouth and rushed to the bathroom. She knelt down before the toilet bowl and puked into it, not quite getting her head deeper into the bowl before it happened, making the edge of the vomit flow reach the floor as well.

Nelli walked after her, standing over her, as Roberta turned her head and looked at her with swollen eyes.

– I think it's pretty obvious what's right with you, sister. Congratulations!

Roberta managed a weak grin, before turning back to the bowl and puking again.

The two of them returned to the living room, to the others. One by one they all hugged Roberta.

She sniffed and looked at them with boundless devotion in her eyes.
– You're my brothers and sisters, she swore. – You are and will always be a part of me, like I am and will always be a part of you, for as long as we live and beyond.
– *Beyond,* some of them whispered.
– If we die, we will still live, she breathed.
– *Live!*
She smiled, drying her eyes, doing so carefully, in an attempt to not rub them so hard that it would make the skin swollen.
The self-control she displayed impressed them. She was one of those the others looked to, her dubious and treacherous past delegated to the back of their memory.
Nelli smiled to her, smiled to Larry. He nodded slowly.
He heard it be repeated in the murky parts of his mind somewhere in the tunnels, in that future world where Nelli had grown up, heard it echo through the decades and centuries until it had become a mantra, a sacred saying, a reality everyone knew to be true.
– You can see it, can't you? Nora breathed to him.
– I can, he confirmed.
She and several others brightened even more.
– Red Shadow sees and will see many things not necessarily accessible to the rest of us, Nelli taught them. – That's one of several reasons he is what he is.
They nodded with wet eyes. He frowned, and she noticed, but didn't reveal it in any way to the tribe.
– I and Nelli will take a trip today, he informed them. – It's an excursion more than anything else, really, and won't be dangerous. We will leave now and be back before you know it.
– So *exciting!* Kelly blurted out, catching herself when she realized that her tongue was practically hanging out.
Nelli, unfathomable like a sphinx didn't say anything or revealed anything of her thoughts and notions, no matter all the curious glances directed at her.
She walked to Larry, immersing herself in his shadow and looked at him with eyes filled with trust. He grabbed her hand. They left with a brief nod to their fellow tribe members.
Just like that, like ghosts, or a breath of wind, they were gone.
She followed him quietly through busy streets, not really expecting an explanation, but still waiting for one. He fought to stay serious-minded and failed gloriously, and she lightened up as well.

– It is a hunting trip, he enlightened her, turning serious-minded again, and she did as well. – You need to stay sharp, and in order to do that, you will need to exercise your abilities without restraint.

He heard his own words, as if he spoke through a veil or a curtain or a filter.

She brightened, as if a heavy load fell from her shoulders.

– Red Shadow is so wise.

He nodded curtly, and she bowed her head in submission.

They walked around in the beyond hot day without sweating that much, on a day where most people dried their brow every second step. The heatwave, or what had seemed like an ordinary heatwave at first, showed no signs of relenting, but grew hotter and hotter as what was supposed to be autumn approached.

– The young ones idolize Red Shadow, she remarked when they had walked a while in silence, – perhaps a bit too much.

He acknowledged her words, her point with the slight move of his head, one no one but she would have caught.

– Red Shadow should not be concerned, though. They will learn!

They walked and kept walking, street through street through street, having long since left their territory and immediate area. She was frowning, a frown only he would catch, but it was there. She looked for the smile in the corner of his mouth, but didn't spot it, and the first signs of worry appeared beneath her mask.

– May Nelli ask Red Shadow where…

– She may not!

He gave her the sign as well, and she couldn't speak. She studied him and saw how determined, driven he was and stopped trying.

They stopped on a low hill a long time later. She shivered visibly in the hot afternoon sunshine.

– You're now far from the comfort of the tribe, he said. – You have only yourself and your skills to draw on if you wish to return to the tribe.

– Red Shadow did this to Nelli once before, she whispered. – Nelli had almost forgotten. Nelli is sorry.

He saw it. Red Shadow had let her go in the desert, left her to fend for herself, without giving her a clear path home. She had been frantic, terrified, but had persevered. It remained an unpleasant memory to her.

– You remember, remember this! She said startled.

They stood in the shadowy part of the entrance to a backyard. Those within didn't notice them. The two of them watched as a group of policemen beat up on a black kid.

– I want you to kill them, he commanded her, – but not with your claws. I want you to pummel them slowly to death, want them to feel it as it happens.

Her face cracked in an eager smile.

The kid remained conscious. They, with their wicked skill made sure he didn't lose consciousness. He choked and sobbed helplessly.

The coppers didn't notice Nelli until she was right there, in their midst, until she had grabbed one and pushed him hard at a wall, breaking all his ribs. He was conscious, but still practically dead as he slid down the wall and they stared incredulous at her and the amazing sight.

A flat hand broke a jaw. Blood flowed from the broken mouth. One attempted to attack, to grab and strike her. He grabbed and struck only air. She grabbed his head, grabbed two heads and smashed them at each other. It slowly became clear to the constables still alive that she dragged it out, that she was in control, not them. Those on the ground, unable to move or move much started whimpering in a paralyzing fear.

She worked her way through them in a deliberate and methodical way scaring the shit out of them. They realized what was happening. Some of them added to their efforts with grim determination and desperation, while others fled the fastest they were able.

She caught up with the last category fast, breaking their legs fast and efficient. Each jump she made covered several meters, covering the distance between them and her easily.

One raised his hand in surrender and opened his mouth to plead his case. He was deadly wounded before the first syllable was uttered.

Larry stood ready to intervene, if the need arose, if anyone succeeded in fleeing from her.

The need didn't arise. She wasn't even close to losing control of the situation, and somehow, he, or at least Red Shadow, had known that she wouldn't.

A big bruiser struck at the back of her head. The versatile body armor met the fist and cushioned the blow.

– What are you? He gasped. – What in the seven hells are you?

She grabbed his arm and broke it on several places in one powerful pull. It hung down. She kicked his leg and broke that just as easily. He fell and hardly moved after that.

The boy stared stunned and beyond fascinated on the display. He couldn't take his eyes off it.

Everyone had been taken care of. Those still breathing crouched on the ground or were otherwise unable to move, or move well enough to escape. Nelli cracked one man's ribs. He bled out on his back. Bright red blood flowed from his mouth. She struck one woman in the belly, practically penetrating the shivering body. The woman died slowly.

She did as she had been told, dragging it out, letting them feel it, walking relaxed now, from body to body. A glimpse of understanding was lit in the boy's eyes. The last remaining fear faded from his eyes, even as fear accompanied and dominated the coppers' final minutes.

She broke bones on all the men and women still breathing, casually but still very deliberate. Some of them breathed their last, while others kept holding on to life. Larry had seen this part of her before, but never so pronounced.

The last one was dead. The boy stood there, not taking his eyes off them, worried, but still strangely unworried.

– No one will bother you again, Larry told him. – You are free to hook up with us, or to strike out on your own.

– Perhaps I will! The boy said, striving to sound casual. – But I will always be grateful. They have terrorized us for years. Thank you so much for what you did for me and this community. We will take some heat for this, but they will still fear the consequences of excessive action.

He pulled back and walked, as calm as possible beyond the nearest corner.

– He will join us, she remarked, nodding to herself, to Larry. – Both his words and posturing say he will.

She had blood all over her. As he watched, her armor took care of it, absorbing it, until it was no longer visible, not even on her head and hands. It was an amazing cleaning process.

They left the place. No one had cried out and no one cried out.

– You don't need to worry, you know, he said offhand. – I rather thought that would be the case, but both I and you needed to be sure.

– Thank you, Red Shadow, she said and bowed her head.

They walked on, easily focusing on both themselves and their surroundings. They noticed no threat.

– I'm so proud of you, Larry.

She touched his cheek. He felt her claws. It was impossible not to. They felt good against his skin.

A bit of blood smeared his cheek. He smelled it, noticing its overwhelming stench without trying. His own soft armor took care of it in seconds.

They didn't turn their heads, even though they noticed they were being followed, but kept walking casually, as if nothing special had happened. Nelli gave him a row of blinding smiles. She was nothing but that blinding smile.

– Thank you for putting your servant back on track, Red Shadow, she said respectfully. – I'm yours, now, more than ever before, and thanks to you I've regained my edge. I will never lose it again!

They walked the long stretch back to their territory. They weren't in a hurry, but enjoyed the walk, and each other's company. She cast him long, admiring and unashamed glances. She seemed totally occupied with him, but he had no trouble seeing that she also kept her eyes on the surroundings. She had no trouble multitasking. She was indeed back on track, and he had put her there. Pride coursed through him.

– This is our desert, she stated, – the area we must sometimes venture in order to survive. It will be the young ones' place of trial and initiation.

He noticed the subtle change, the way the city had changed lately and kept changing. The various sections of it had always been slightly different from each other, but now, with each new day that difference grew more pronounced. He spotted more than one guard hidden on rooftops, people with guns in their hands.

The demarcation line to their territory was blurry, but equally noticeable. Larry imagined he felt a pressure give in the air he breathed the moment they crossed it. The tribal influence reached out from the house and in all directions. People still living in the other houses had started acknowledging that. He recognized that in the looks they sent them, in their behavior.

The two of them turned a corner, and they saw their home down the street.

He turned his head and cried out good-humored.

– You can show yourself now!

The boy did, flustered, but stubborn. He caught up with them and stubbornly met their eyes. They smiled, acknowledging him.

– You helped me, he said, – but you did more than that. You liberated the entire neighborhood. I wish to learn from you everything I possibly can.

They received a warm welcome, as if they had been away a very long time. The tribe members rushed to meet them outside and hugged them, hugged them fiercely.

– Red Shadow, in his wisdom deemed it necessary to teach me a lesson, Nelli said and smiled. – I feel great again and am once again fit to serve the tribe to the best of my abilities.

They understood. Nelli saw it in their eyes.

Everyone turned as one towards the boy.

– We found a wanderer, one restless soul in the desert, Red Shadow said.

– My name is Jackson, the boy said. – These two helped me when no one else would.

– They do stuff like that, Roberta said softly.

He wanted to say more, but hesitated.

– Go on, Red Shadow prompted him. – We have no secrets here.

His words flowed like a flood.

– She killed them, he breathed, – killed them all slowly, making them pay.

The ambiguous emotions were engraved in his features and body language.

– Yes, we do stuff like that, too, Roberta said.

They retreated into the house, into their den, their cave. It felt increasingly like that.

– Red Shadow taught me a lesson, Nelli stressed. – He reminded me who I am, and my usefulness to the tribe has returned.

They understood and nodded, solemnly and good humored.

– It never went away, Patricia said softly.

Nelli swallowed hard.

The rest of the day and evening passed quickly. The next morning and day arrived and passed equally fast, and the next after that again and those following.

Nelli wore her smile with growing ease as time passed, as her belly grew.

Patricia and others began experimenting with hydroponics in the basement and also down in the tunnels. They made selected plants grow without sunlight, and proudly displayed their work to Larry and Nelli and the rest.

The area changed and kept changing, both because of them and outside, less evident forces.

The sweltering heat didn't let up, not for a moment. They got used to sleeping with all the windows open at night, but even that wasn't enough. Only deep down in the tunnels, on the places they had picked as their own, they could find anything even resembling cold.

They sat in the living room in their small house, without any lights, not candles, not anything. Their features still appeared very distinct to them all, not only to those born with an ability to see in the dark. The darkness brought respite from the heat as well. They imagined that a chill touched them in the draft from the open doors and windows. The occasional light reaching them from the outside when a car passed by filled the room with brightness. It blinded them, and it could take minutes until their night vision returned. They spent most of the daylight in the tunnels, bringing down various stuff in order to recreate their surroundings, making it more like a home.

And they brought tech and computers and the first parts of production equipment, everything that would eventually sustain their community and a technologically advanced society far into the future.

Even if no one interfered, they remained on guard, kept moving their eyes and senses in their sphere, studying and assessing the realm where they lived and moved. More started wearing goggles. They began posting guards down in the tunnels. One changing set of sentinels was always present. Their territory grew better defined.

They sat in the small living room and laughed together. The laughter and its rhythm, its sense of community sounded and seemed completely different to anything they had experienced earlier. A warm, pleasant wave touched them and empowered them. The nights and days passed like that, like one uninterrupted flow of changing and pleasant emotion.

They had a feast, one more in a long row. It took off effortlessly, it usually did. Corinne whipped up one of her tasty meals. They sat there and wet their parched throats with both water and wine and put them on fire with strong spices. The burning exploded slowly and pleasantly in their stomachs, in expanding minds.

Most of them stayed together, as the night progressed, while others sought a little privacy in other parts of the house. They still felt it like they stayed together, like they breathed and moved as one. The darkness in the tunnels smothered them. It was there, surrounding them, no matter where they walked and breathed.

Peace descended on the building and its surroundings. Nothing noticeable stirred. Only the occasional squeaking of birds broke the silence.

Roberta moved with stealth, glancing left and right as she walked through the backdoor, as she left the house. She crossed the street at a fast pace, quickly vanishing between the houses.

She chased through dark streets. The electricity had failed for several blocks on her walk. Even though she stayed calm, centered, she kept glancing around her with wavering eyes. No one followed her or threatened her directly. When she, after quite the long walk approached her destination, she grew even more alert. She circled the area for several minutes before committing to it.

The red phone booths, one of the few sets remaining in the city pointed to themselves across the street. She chose the second from the right. Her hand brought a one-pound coin from her pocket, and put it at the mechanism at the top of the phone. She dialed a number. It rang several times before someone answered.

– Letterman Brooks and associates, the casual voice replied.

– It's about the business proposition, Roberta said. – I may have confirmation.

– You may have? The female voice said. – After all this time?

– Yes! Roberta stated firmly. – I'm sorry for the delay, but I've been busy.

Another click and more ringing. Another reply, and a far more familiar male voice.

– Letterman Brooks and associates, how may I help you?
– There has been some activity, she said. – I'm looking into it.
She heard him draw breath. That was the correct code, and also the extended code signifying good news.
– Go on, he said cautiously.
– I had to ditch the device. They grew suspicious. Fortunately, I got rid of it well before they searched my bag.
– But they did search your bag?
– That and other unpleasant things, she confirmed, – but it has been a long time. They trust me, now.
– Are you okay? He asked concerned.
– I am, but I'm still not certain or have final confirmation. What I saw could have been a con.
There was a pause. She held her breath.
– Maybe you should come in, he suggested.
She exhaled in relief.
– I don't know, she said. – Do you think that's wise?
– It's time, anyway, he insisted, – perhaps even overdue. You've been in the field for so long.
– I guess you're right, she said. – When?
– Any time you can safely leave, he said. – Everything will be ready for you.
– I'll let you know, she said.
Both hung up. Silence reigned in the already quiet street.

Chapter Ten

He saw a whirl of motion and people outside, like in a movie.

The sun brightened the hall of the shopping mall. The front, being one single, giant window filled the place with light.

They had bought lots of rechargeable batteries and other purely useful stuff. Almost all of them carried two full bags of equipment and groceries. They invaded a cafeteria on the upper floor, bringing lots of inevitable attention to themselves.

– This is a good start of procuring stuff on our long shopping list, Patricia enlightened him. – The large freezer should be high on our list of priorities.

– How to get it down in the tunnels should also be up there, Corinne joked.

– That's easy. Patricia blew her off. – We bring down parts and assemble them down there.

– Don't worry, Nelli said. – We will get there, get everything we need right where we need it to be.

A big smile lit up her face again.

– If only you could see it like I can, she said with dreaming eyes.

Larry could, too, through her. And she had seen it in its infancy through him, through Red Shadow, growing from a makeshift arrangement to a fairly advanced system able to sustain itself for centuries.

He reflected on it all, for the thousandth time, and could still find no crack in the rationale behind the events that had come to dominate his life, even though the doubt, the frown on his brow, the fear that something was not quite right remained.

Nelli and Patricia, both able to sense his anxiety squeezed his hands.

He could hear the sound of the water flowing below the ground, the rivers and waterfalls trickling below the desert sand, the countless grains of sand rubbing against each other and sounding like the whispering of a thousand souls.

He looked outside, without a conscious thought behind his action. He took in the entire scene in an instant. There was a man speeding up, as he charged another man. Larry noticed before anyone else. He knew he did, since he didn't just observe the two men, but everyone both outside and inside.

The man pulled a knife, just as he stepped close to the other man. The blade cut into human flesh, into the beating heart. The stabbed man gasped and fell to the ground.

Panic broke out outside and anxiety picked up significantly inside. A man pushing a cart of milk bottles pushed it much faster. A distraught woman wearing glasses and a green scarf rushed across the plaza, constantly casting long, scared glances around her. Whoever she feared seemed to be everywhere. Two police officers with drawn weapons rushed through the open doorway. The man with the knife was nowhere to be seen. In the chaos out there, he was impossible to locate, at least for most people, but Larry saw him, or at least sensed him, as he walked with fast steps around the nearest corner.

Larry could taste a certain spice in the air. The wind brought that, and thousand other things besides. A man stood by the information desk, speaking clearly excited, angry to the woman behind it. Three young women walked down the escalator. They seemed to be moving in slow motion to Larry.

Everything did!

The clock was ticking, but so very slowly. He could follow it all casually, catching every single movement in his vision.

The tribe sat there and finished their meal, sharing a calm they only found in a few others within sight. The situation sort of normalized itself, but only slowly, very, very slowly.

– This is a sign of the times, Travis said, and then he shook his head. – Such an event would be highly unlikely only a few months ago.

– He actually did it completely in the open, Daryl mused, – with security cameras recording everything.

He and several others cast a glance at the security cameras on the wall moving back and forth, back and forth.

They left the mall, walking to the left of the police officers gathering around the dead guy outside. The tribe walked down a busy street, where people buzzed back and forth and sideways like bees.

A girl set to cross the street looked both ways. She did so several times, hesitating, stopping herself just as she was about to step out in the road.

She finally did it. A car speeded up and struck her down just as she turned and opened her mouth to scream. The car didn't slow down for a moment, but kept racing forward on whining tires. The broken body hit the ground. The girl's neck had broken. She stared at the world with empty eyes.

One woman screamed. The others present didn't react much, one way or another.

A man drummed on an old, rusty metal plate and managed, somehow to make it sound like something other than a man drumming on an old, rusty metal plate. The sound of each strike echoed within Larry.

An old man sat on the one bench in the park and fed the birds crumbs from a meal he hadn't completed. One release of crumbs from his hands brought loads of excited movement and eager consummation from the birds. Sometimes the old man didn't bother with tearing the piece of bread or food into crumbs before throwing it away. Once he threw an entire pancake into the shifting mass of wings. One big seagull grabbed it all with its beak and devoured it whole, in one single move. It didn't seem to make it any less hungry.

– Birds, like humans will learn to be far more aggressive in order to survive, Nelli said. – There are far more birds of prey in the future desert sands.

Her companions nodded, nodded to themselves. Her words made sense, made so very much sense.

The thought made them tense one moment, relax the next.

The birds kept picking their crumbs as the tribe made its way down the street towards their home turf. A man standing on a corner stared at everyone. His gazing eyes never wavered significantly from their chosen direction, even though Larry imagined he noticed everything happening inside and outside his vision.

– He's telling us that he's here, Patricia mused, – doing so in an effort to distract us from what's truly happening.

The others nodded and glanced around them, studying all the nearby rooftops and corners. They spotted no one, nothing significant anywhere.

They walked down their street, entering the invisible line marking their territory. Most of them spotted easily the sentries, their fellow tribe members on the roofs on both sides of the street. From up there, they could easily keep an eye on a vast area in all directions.

The house grew out of the ground, the concrete jungle surrounding them. One moment they imagined it wasn't there, and the next it was.

One moment everything grew fluid in Larry's vision, the next it turned solid as a rock. People kept moving back and forth around him, both fast and slow.

The inside of the house, of their home looked like the outside. Except for the obvious distinction of furniture, he found no distinct differences between the two. He did notice the walls, but they didn't seem significant, in any way.

The tribe gathered around him. Those not tribe passed by a little farther away.

– Those on the edge will also be drawn to you, Nelli stated, – drawn into your sphere like moths to the flame, and they will burn. We all will, but some of us will become fire ourselves!

He saw it, saw them all, as the streets changed around them, as the buildings withered and crumbled into ruins.

People were drawn into his circle. Others turned back at its outer boundaries. Those joining and staying were trained in his ways, taught his code. The outside world grew increasingly distant. The tribe created its world on and beneath the ground. They made room for themselves above and filled the empty spaces below.

Some of them began sleeping below as well, sleeping on shifts. They changed the guard at uneven intervals. No one entered their domain down there.

– No one has come to this place in a long time, have they? Corinne mused. – Not after we started showing interest or even a long time before that?

– There were no footprints in the dust when Nelli and I first paid it a visit, Larry said.

Except for Nelli's, he thought.

– I feel so safe here, Corinne said with a catching in her voice. – I close my eyes, and everything… upworld slips away.

He sensed how everyone else present nodded their agreement.

They had their dinner there, in the darkness, and it felt like the most natural thing in the world. Those not able to see or glimpse in the dark still managed to move and use fork and spoon and knife.

The world below unfolded slowly, as they added items and constructed the necessary and unnecessary structures. They transformed the place, the vast array of unused tunnels, making it theirs. Larry observed it as it happened, past, present and future, even as specific details kept eluding him.

They sat in the garden in the backyard a hot, sunny day, unable to keep out the noise from the passing cars. The sight of them wearing goggles might startle anyone not part of the tribe, but none of the older members found it the slightest bit odd anymore.

– It's all truly coming together, isn't it? Dylan exclaimed abruptly, unprompted, stunned.

Everyone present looked good humored at him.

– It is! Corinne insisted.

– A lot is still incomplete, a work in progress, Nora remarked, – but the framework is very much there, if a true need should ever arise. I feel something, a key component is still missing, but that might easily slip into place with near future events. There is certainly no lack of incentives, even now.

Her words echoed in Larry's head and suddenly seemed so very important. He couldn't explain it, but there it was, playing and replaying in his thoughts.

He turned his head and Roberta appeared in the doorway.

– Two constables are headed our way, she said.

She, Larry and Corinne walked through the living room and into the bar. They observed the two through the window. There was little doubt that they were heading this way, no matter how seemingly inconspicuous their stroll down the street looked like.

Corinne joined Patricia behind the desk. The others left. There weren't many customers this early. They didn't look alarmed or even seemed to notice when the two uniformed police constables entered the premises.

The woman and the man walked to the desk in a very casual, deliberate manner. Patricia smiled to them, and they both turned more than a bit hot under the collar.

– Good afternoon, constables, she greeted them. – Is there anything I can get you?

– We just want to have word with Corinne, the woman said officious, but somewhat polite.

Corinne didn't say anything. She just looked at them with inquiring eyes.

– I'm sorry to say that we've received some complaints about this place lately, the man stated.

– I can't imagine why, Corinne shrugged. – I've always had and have an excellent relationship with the neighbors.

– Well, some of them clearly disagree with that statement, the woman contradicted her.

– There will always be some disgruntled people everywhere… won't there?

Patricia smiled sweetly to them.

– I guess that is a fair statement, the man said, suddenly visibly filled with uncertainty.

The woman nodded in agreement.

– There is no rule saying you can't have a pint on the job, is there? Patricia suggested.

Suggested strongly.

– No, the two constables choired with long and deep frowns.

– Let's sit down and enjoy ourselves then.

They drowned in Patricia sweet, sweet smile.

She filled three glasses with Guiness and brought the two to the deep corner table. Larry and Nelli and the others present enjoyed the spectacle immensely from the other room.

– Cheers!

– Cheers! The other two choired riddled with confusion.

They drank.

– You guys are so sweet for coming here and informing us of this problem,

Patricia declared. – You have our eternal gratitude.

She clearly enjoyed herself, excelling in her power, her ability to reduce the two bullies to sniveling sheep, making them eat of her hand.

Nelli giggled and cast a happy glance at Larry. A sudden catching in his throat made it hard for him to breathe.

The woman was sweating, clearly uncomfortable. She moved in the chair, turning red with embarrassment. The man didn't seem to notice. He was frowning and kept glancing out of the window. Patricia frowned, too, as she grew aware of what had become his obvious unrest.

Anxiety flooded Larry in a moment of utmost clarity.

– What do you fear? Patricia asked the man curtly, focusing her entire attention on him.

– We can't stay here, he said with a hollow voice, his fear not quite breaking through the fog of Patricia's emotional manipulation.

The two-way radio shook in Larry's hand.

– They're coming, Roberta shouted from the roof. – THEY'RE COMING!

Suddenly he imagined that he was outside in the streets, as if he saw through them far and wide.

– We're only scouts, the constable said offhand, in a sort of calm, eerie panic. – We were supposed to check out your defenses and leave well before the attack began. We need to get out of here.

– We need to get out of here, the woman said, – out of here, out of here, out of here…

She droned on.

Everyone was moving, grabbing their weapons, swords, assault rifles and all, even as they heard the distant sound of the approaching plane. They reached out and grabbed cold steel right by their side, and rushed outside. Roberta climbed down from the roof, sliding more than climbing down the water drain, landing softly on her feet.

They fled from the house, even as another sound, something resembling a whistle grew louder in their ears. A rocket headed directly for the house. It hit the front wall, and the building dissolved in an explosive inferno heating up the entire street. Some of them fell due to the air pressure, but got back on their feet fast and kept running, seeking shelter in and outside various buildings across the streets.

– Nelli could have taken care of that, if she had been here, Patricia cried. – Fuck!

The ground troops began their attack. The sound of machinegun fire grew as the noise of the explosion faded. Another rocket was fired from the plane, even as Roberta fired a rocket from the bazooka. The plane and what remained of their home exploded simultaneously. The plane crashed in the middle of the street and took out many noncombatants fleeing for their lives.

The tribe members posted on the nearby roofs began firing at the attack force. Larry and the others did as well. The fight began in earnest.

– I sent the signal, Nora gasped in happiness. – They're coming!

Larry saw, in his mind the others run from the darkness and up towards daylight, the daylight darkened by thick, black smoke and fire.

The entire area turned dark like night.

People dressed in what was clearly a paramilitary uniform charged them from all sides. Roberta fired her assault rifle first. Her fellow tribe members didn't hesitate either and pulled the trigger only a few moments later. Larry fired as he ran, and saw how enemies fell like dominos. They rushed into nearby buildings, gaining a momentary shelter and respite from the barrage.

Larry and Nora and others by his side smashed windows and began firing at the enemy combatants still out there. More moving flesh fell. Blood mixed with dust and the smoke and the fire. The streets and the surrounding buildings quickly turned into one single giant combat zone. Larry fired through the window, ducked, sticking his head up again and firing once more. Thought faded. He kept moving, firing, killing.

Moving flesh fell like targets on a shooting range. Pride coursed through him.

The fighting kept escalating by the second. When the reinforcements arrived, and started mowing down the assault force from behind, that didn't really add that much to the ongoing war that had erupted in these once so peaceful streets. Their support was felt by the tribe and brought instant relief, but Larry imagined that whatever remained of bystanders wouldn't notice much of a difference.

Nora was hit. Blood flowed from her left arm. She stumbled a bit, but kept firing. A bullet hit Larry's armor. He felt a slight impact, but nothing more. The armor deflected almost all the energy. He saw through Nelli's eyes from the others side of the street. She stood practically in the open for a few moments and took down a row of enemies, but had to stop because she encouraged her fellow warriors to do the same. She ordered them to take cover, and joined them in a rush of motion.

He spotted Roberta. She took down several enemy combatants in just a few seconds, picking them off like flowers as they exposed themselves to her ruthless aim. Then she was gone again, but he imagined that he could sense her, feel her as well, as she moved through rooms and houses and buildings like a hurricane. These guys didn't have anything even approaching her training. That was pretty much a given when he saw in glimpses how easy she took them down.

– They have numbers on their side, but not much more than that, Nora said with a feisty snarl.

She, like virtually the entire tribe had undergone a transformation the moment the fighting began.

The sun turned red. In spite of its position high in the sky, the sight reminded him of sunset or sunrise filled with light clouds and mist.

Travis attempted to make use of his spirit form, but he clearly had trouble focusing. One or two times he almost had it, but then another loud sound of thunder distracted him. He gave it up and rejoined the fight.

Nelli stayed with her group, instructing them, in part insulating them from what was happening, spitting harsh commands of encouragement and spite.

Wind and smoke and fire hammered Larry's skin as he moved, and kept moving.

He and Nora ran through a backyard. There were dead bodies there, but no active fighting. It seemed like a silent oasis in the crescendo of war. Then, as they reached the next house, machineguns played up close to them. Pieces of wood were shaken loose by bullets, as they just in time hid behind a corner.

She grinned at him with excitement written all over her face. She didn't seem frightened at all.

– I've taken to the teaching well, don't you think?

– You've excelled in it! He acknowledged.

Nodding to himself, pondering all of it further.

She filled a woman exposing herself with lead.

He knew tribe members was falling and dying, sensing it like tiny stings on the mind, unable to tell who it was. Rage filled him. He stood up and started spreading hot lead across the room. Enemies fell in more large numbers. He felt the bullets, but they didn't harm him. Nora joined him. They killed off all the wounded on the floor.

– Nelli brought me the protective suit, he told her, – but she couldn't make more.

– I… understand, she said softly.

The dying began in earnest. Telford fell. He saw it. Dylan was hit by a hail of bullets. He felt it. It hurt him far more than being hit would have done.

Eliza writhed on the ground, more dead than alive, gasping her final breaths.

He rushed to the window. Nelli rushed to the window across the street. For one moment, two they stood there, frozen like amber in time.

His hand flashed the signal, the kill signal. His larynx simultaneously echoed it. Nelli froze. She removed her boots, exposing the claws on her toes. She dropped the assault rifle, and rushed off. One concerned tribe member entered her path, saying something. She brushed him off like she would a fly, hardly even acknowledging his presence. The indistinct figure she had become faded away into the smoke and mist.

Then, a second, thirty later the adverse dying began.

Screams of pain and terror overwhelmed the noise and sound of battle.

He glimpsed her big belly and the twisted features in her face in the haze of blood seemingly covering the human storm taking on the first quadrant of enemies. The sound of weapons being fired virtually ceased from that angle of his surrounding area. She was in their midst. They couldn't fire at her without the risk of hitting each other. Crimson claws flashed in the bad light, the shadows submerging the fast-moving human form.

Everyone knew something was happening. Larry had to push those around him to act. Nora and the others looked at him with wide eyes.

Enemies fled from the slaughter. They were taken in crossfire the moment they exposed themselves to the tribe. People practically frozen in terror and indecision were hit and died. The entire dynamics of the battle had changed. She cut the throat of everyone close to her with swift strokes of either her hands or feet. Her true dance unfolded.

The screams unnerved their foes far more than it did them. Larry saw it, sensed it. The tribe gained even more confidence and bloodthirst. They grew more aggressive as the enemy wavered and hesitated.

– She's magnificent, Nora shouted. – MAGNIFICENT!

Shouts of agreement echoed across the battlefield.

Roberta made mincemeat of the enemies frequenting another segment of the battlefield. She was different from Nelli, but just as deadly. They glimpsed her now and then covered in blood.

Everyone in the tribe grew inspired, letting go of inhibitions, embracing the killer within. While there initially had been hesitation, there was now undiluted bloodthirst.

Larry began moving as well, increasingly ignoring those in his slipstream. He spotted the growing anxiety in the enemy's eyes, as panic caught more and more of them in its unbreakable grip, and they fled without thought, and were shot from behind. No one made it to safety. He saw that without trying.

The opponents were fairly capable fighters, but theirs were mostly a technical skill. They lacked the savagery of the tribe, and couldn't withstand the ruthless wave rolling over them.

The sound of the drums struck their ears like the sound of the gun, and just as loud. Larry felt pride and a dark, transcendent joy. Someone threw a hand grenade at Nelli, but she avoided it easily, was far away from where it landed. It hit closer than home, usually exploding in their own midst. They stopped doing that quickly. Then the grenades began exploding on people's bodies without them having touched them at all, and the panic grew to terror.

They hit their comrades in arms more often than they hit those they wanted to hit. The guns wriggled in their hands, more and more difficult to handle as the battle kept raging. Nelli's cruel grin widened to the point of showing outside her face, as her skill and understanding of current warfare grew to an uncanny degree. To Larry it did.

They focused the fire at her, forcing her to seek cover, to be sneakier. Larry saw a bullet penetrate her shield and her foot. He saw her limp, still fast, but not with the same effectiveness as before.

He gave her the countersignal, the order to stand down and return to more conventional fighting. She got it. There was no need for him to freeze her on her spot.

He rushed forward, assaulting those that had put a stop to her advances in the back. They fell like dominoes. He felt a pain in his stomach. A high projectile bullet had gone straight through his armor and him. It was a shock to his entire system, but it handled it. Nora and the others nearby cast him anxious glances. He ignored them and pushed on. His eyesight and reflexes and senses in general had improved further. When he fired the gun, when he directed it at another human being, that truth revealed itself to a degree that couldn't be denied.

Eternity passed and passed again every time he drew breath, fired a bullet and saw one more enemy go down. Fear touched him briefly, but drowned in the general noise and boiling of blood.

He faced a man in an alley. Neither of them had their guns pointed forward, at the enemy. He raised it much faster and shot the man way before the man had even raised his weapon halfway.

A salvo was fired from the opposite building, pinning them down. The enemy combatants singled out him and his group, like they had singled out Roberta and Nelli, and it was just as unsuccessful. It merely gave the others more room to roam.

– Are you okay? Travis asked anxiously.

– I am! Larry assured him and the rest.

He did feel the wound, but it didn't slow him down, didn't really keep him from doing anything. Nelli's wound certainly didn't keep her from exploding more of the hand grenades the enemy had discarded.

Roberta, pretty much unharmed kept cutting swaths through the opposing forces.

– They are our enemy, aren't they? Travis said, uncertain at first, then stressing it. – I mean, truly and unequivocally our Enemy?

– I would say that is a certainty at this point, Nora stated. – They are everything Nelli spoke about. They won't negotiate, won't stop - ever, not until either they or we are *gone!*

Larry frowned, and he didn't know why. Something, a crucial piece was still missing from the picture. That slowed him down, until he compensated for it and discarded it and focused on what was close and tangible, the blood and stench and immediate danger.

The assailants pulled back, out of sight. Nelli could no longer easily locate them.

There was a breath of silence. Then someone fired a gun at Larry from a deeper part of the building. Nelli grinned viciously and started up her tennis again.

Every time they fired their guns she sent a grenade at them and blew them to pieces. They tried in their desperation to shoot down the floating grenades, with scant success. Their effectiveness evaporated like dew in the morning sun. There was no more gunfire.

The noise faded slowly, the silence only broken by cries of pain and terror from those caught in the battle. Dark smoke and fire from burning vehicles kept dominating the streets.

– They're still here, Larry stated. – We must do a sweep, building by building, until we know for sure that every room and spot is clear.

His people nodded, eager and determined.

Nelli levitated to the top of the tallest building. Others covered her. No shots were fired. She could see movement across a considerable area. There was none.

Travis traveled in spirit-form into the buildings. Corinne cast her long, sharp eyes across the vast divides of the street. He signed the moment he encountered the enemy. They fired at him. The bullets went straight through his misty form. A hand grenade floated through the air and exploded close to the three people. They dived for cover, but it didn't help them. More blood covered the walls.

– I can do it, now, Travis said with his ghostly voice. – I couldn't focus during the battle.

– Some day, soon, you will! Chloe stated hotly.

Panicked voices shouted into portable radios. Larry heard it, heard the buzz, unable to understand the voices.

– It isn't over, he cried. – Never believe it is!

His tribe heard him, he knew they did, saw it by the way they moved their bodies, sensed it by the way they breathed. They all held back while Travis, Corinne and Nelli did their thing.

One more building was cleared, two, three…

Relief and anxiety kept warring among the tribe members. A few of them began smiling.

Then the distant look faded in Travis's eyes, and he froze.

– They have placed bombs, he gasped. – Big bombs!

The building to their left and several others, including the tall one where Nelli stood exploded in one single, close to simultaneous crack breaking their eardrums. A white light blinded Larry. It was if the hot wind hit him and he was pushed backwards. He glimpsed her as she fell, in a golden light softening her pale skin. A long, long moment he seemed to float in a nowhere state, until he finally felt the ground against his back.

He never truly lost the use of his vision, but it changed to a terrifying focus as he slowly rose, and all his senses returned in full.

– They blew up themselves, Travis said stunned, – did it on purpose.

He was unharmed. Dust covered his face. Others emerged with blood on their faces, but basically okay. There was more blood-red dust in the air and on the ground.

The buildings most affected were more or less gone, flattened. Only scattered ruins were left. Pieces of bricks covered the streets.

– Grab your weapons, Larry shouted. – Hold on to them, *no matter what!*

They obeyed. Weak hands clutched warm metal. He looked at the ruins of the tallest building. It had turned into a heap of bricks and scrap metal. He rushed across the street. Someone cried his name. It sounded like Nelli, but he knew it wasn't her.

He climbed the treacherous ground of bricks and metal, not generating a single thought concerning his own safety. The wound didn't bother him. He was aware of it on some level, but hardly felt it.

A horrible stench he couldn't identify at first ripped into his nostrils. It didn't keep him from moving, as he kept searching with a frantic, scary anxiety.

He spotted her from the top of one heap. A metal pole penetrated her body. As impossible as that seemed, she was still breathing. He rushed to her. His feet had no trouble moving on the treacherous ground.

She strived to speak, to look at him with eyes clouded by pain. Her amazing power of will shook him.

– It happened to fast, she said. – I tried to get away, but I couldn't.

Blood flowed from a wound on her head. She had to be dizzy, close to unconsciousness. She held on.

– I understand, now, she gasped. – I understand everything.

He grabbed the pole and tried to move it, making a supreme effort. It didn't budge. It was stuck, stuck in her and between two heaps.

Their eyes met and held.

– I'm the pebble. She smiled. – That's all I ever was.

– No, he wept his dry tears. – No!

– Be strong, My Lord, she breathed.

She shook; her face and body turning rigid, as it went into shock, into the final stages of life.

Nelli Watros and the growing lump of cells within her died at exactly the same moment. He knew, undeniable, as easily as he would a drop of rain, or a sharp, painful sting. One second passed, moments of failed heartbeats passed, as Lawrence Watros held his breath.

And then he felt it, felt the impact, as a current of a million needles coursed through his body, and the power of a thousand suns rose within him.

He screamed, and remaining windows for several blocks around him slowly broke and fell to the ground, and the ground beneath him shook a million miles wide.

The shaking body slowly straightened and stopped shaking.

People noticed. He saw them, sensed them, somehow, in his mind, as they shivered, deep down knowing that their comforting illusion of a safe, secure life was done and gone.

The noise faded, slowly, painfully, as the tall man stood there, attempting to catch his breath, desperate to pull air, any air into his straining lungs.

His crimson guard stood behind him. He heard a choke rise from Nora's throat. Another attempting to speak had trouble doing so, but finally managed.

– There are still wounded enemies around, Roberta said.

– Kill them, he said casually, without turning. – Make certain they're dead! Leave those wounded the least alive. Make sure they don't kill themselves.

She pulled back. He saw her, saw every step she made.

He heard the sound of machinegun fire, several short bursts, until silence fell once more.

Roberta returned. She didn't say anything. There was no need. She spoke anyway.

He recalled her leaving the phone booth and meet up with him in a dark port-room not long after her recent call.

– It's done, she stated, standing before him, a study in pride and determination.

– You know what is demanded of you, what you must do?

– I do, Red Shadow, she stressed, conveying her eagerness with her face and entire stance. – I'm ready!

He saw Roberta return to the military facility, visualized her reporting back calmly and dedicated, starting the executions when the time was right. She killed every single one of her former colleagues, anyone with even a remote knowledge of her and her original mission. When it was done she set the place on fire and left a smoldering ruin in her wake.

He stood on another roof, looking at the city below.

Red Shadow looked down at his hands, his fingers, where his nails had turned into claws.

The air crackled and burned around him.

He stood on dusty ground, looking at the dark red skies, and he dreamt of blood, and death and sacrifice.

The wind brought a scent, one of rust and dawn.

The harsh gales didn't batter him.

Author's word

Red Shadow was supposed to be a short story, but it quickly dawned on me that I couldn't give the story justice that way. The expansion from that point turned self-evident, as events added themselves. Even a prolonged short story would have been only one fourth of the necessary length I eventually ended up with.

I saw a girl sit outside a tavern, bathing in the red light from a heater…

That was all it took to get my muses going. The story grew from that very second in complexity and length.

I tested out various scenarios in my head, to see if there was material enough for a novel. There wasn't. I could have expanded upon Nelli and Roberta's stories, but not within the confines of the story about Larry and Nelli. If anyone should ever make a TV-series with lots of episodes, they would have to introduce a new element and thus ruin the cohesion and integrity completely.

So, this is a novella, a story too short to be a novel, and too long to be a short story. The story is done, is told and there is no point in continuing it. We know everything we need to know. There is no way there can be a sequel.

Which is kind of neat.

2016-10-14

Hidden World

I am terrified by this dark thing
That sleeps in me;
All day I feel its soft, feathery turnings,
its malignity.

-Sylvia Plath, Elm

Chapter One

A torn curtain hung from a branch, blowing in the wind. There were no houses, no buildings anywhere, only wilderness as far as the eye could see.

Almost half the roof was gone from the ravaged, old house. The white paint was gone from most of the walls. A tree was growing at the top of the stairs. Torn curtains were blowing in the wind, through broken windows. Doors were open. Inside furniture and carpets were wet and dirty.

A hand panned against a stone wall, back and forth, back and forth. Waves beat against the shore. Clouds raced across the sky. There was an aerial view of the city, of cars in line, line, line, slowing down to a crawl. Wrecks lined the highway, in streets, of humans, of machines. Spilled poison, a visible red and stinking fluid ran down river, destroying Life. Images showed a world out of whack.

There were two straight trees in the forest making out what looked very much like a gate.

Freya sat on her ass on the stage close to the audience, crossing her legs in front of her. Torches were lit close to her, lit far from her. Mist lingered behind her, in front of her. Her face danced in light, in shadow.

She gave her audience a smile, her eyes huge, wide and weird.

– Picture Reality as a wall, she stated, speaking in a low, steady voice. – Reach out your hands to both sides, as *far* as you can, and you might, you just might touch it. And the wall may crumble.

She sat there, with a look of immense concentration painted on her face.

And she reached out with her hands.

Five people walked on a path through the forest, a foggy path covered by mist and smoke from a fire.

A larger group of people moved through the forest, bare feet and legs touching the forest bed. Torches burned and flickered in the twilight.

Five people stood by the two trees in the forest, doing so on a clear, bright day.

A group of people, carrying torches, moved up a slope, towards a height under a small rock. Thick smoke rose in the night air. Fires were lit and flames licked naked skin.

The sun was still rising, slightly covered by clouds, on the clear, bright, cloudy day.

They sweat hard, breathed hard, as they walked up a steep slope.

Burt gasped for breath.

– How much farther?

Lisbeth breathed almost just as hard, shouting in joy.
– It's *far!* Isn't that the point, Burt?
The five of them walked and stumbled, ran and fell, crawled and climbed up the steep slope.
The other girl in the group shook her head.
– The sweat just keeps coming, Freya said, – through the headband and all. I thought we were supposed to sweat less as the journey progressed?
Ted fell in front of Burt. Burt stumbled into him, and they both hit the ground.
John ran ahead, turning around, mocking them.
– This is it, my fellow savages. Just one more steep slope, a bit of climbing and we're there.
They stumbled down the hilltop, slowly regaining strength after the strenuous climb.
They saw the height and the mountain plateau, where there were even more trees, another forest, at the other side of the valley. The fog didn't let up, not even in the middle of the day. The moist air made them sweat even harder.
The five climbed. They rushed the final steps to the mountain wall. Sweat kept flooding their eyes, and made it that much harder to climb, to find uneven spots in the rock where they could put feet and hands. Lisbeth reached for the edge, missed and was about to fall when Ted grabbed her. She sent him a grateful look.
John stood in front of the two straight trees forming a gate. He spoke loud and with a dramatic voice.
– Ladies and Gentlemen, I give you the Maelstrom of Madness, the Gate to Freedom.
Laughter. Strained. Four pairs of eyes burned at their friend.
– A place so ordinary, John, the boastful one, Lisbeth mocked him. – You make us walk for hours, to exhaust ourselves for the Goddess' sake, to watch a pair of geriatric trees grow a few more millimeters.
– But isn't madness truly the road to Freedom? He insisted. – And you should know that both my grandparents and others their age get a strange look in their eyes when telling the stories. After all, trees have been worshipped since time immemorial.
Ted formed an open hand, a closed fist. He repeated the movement time and time again.
Ted and Lisbeth stood on the mountaintop close by a while later. They observed the small campfire down below in the forest.
– Does this meaningless act really have any significance, beyond humanity's

perceived view of existence as a duality?

Lisbeth didn't say anything. She wasn't really paying attention, but stood there, preoccupied, staring at the air.

– Isn't the ordinary really the true road to madness? Ted pondered.

They returned to the height, the fire.

– Darkness is about to fall, Ted said. – This is my favorite time of the day.

He looked down at the valley. A strange mist covered it. Something… shifted before his eyes.

– Hey, did you see…

He turned and looked at the girl and froze. She looked like the same girl he had just looked at, but was dressed different. There was something about her that didn't feel… right. She looked different… but the same. He shook his head in bewilderment. A chill passed through him.

– So weird, language, Lisbeth, that other Lisbeth mused. – Darkness doesn't fall, it... grows, grows out of thin air.

She looked at him, a look giving him the willies. The moment seemed to stretch on forever.

He blinked, and everything had returned to… to what it had been.

– Did you say something? He heard himself say with a voice sounding strangely normal.

– No, nothing.

She shook her head.

– But someone did say something... didn't they?

– I didn't hear anything, she shrugged unconcerned.

He frowned. She didn't notice his distress. She had evidently not noticed anything out of the ordinary. The other three below seemed totally calm as well. The bewilderment held on to him, not letting go.

The smoke rose to the treetops, where darkness slowly fell. The thousand images of the shifting fire danced on the trees surrounding them. Freya hugged a tree. She cried out to the two above.

– Embrace the tree. Feel the sap boiling in its veins.

And they heard her wild, carefree laughter.

A forest path led to two trees, growing a step apart. Beyond was mist, just concentrations of wet smoke in white and gray, floating in the strange air, pulling toward each other. There was a gathering of people with strange hairdos clad in skins.

– I can feel it, the mists of Time and Shadow, Abkasha said. – There is a gate here, to the Shadow World.

A voice spoke in an empty bedroom at dawn:

– I don't know how to explain it. I'm in bed, on my back, with my eyes half closed, observing more than participating. Room seems to disappear... no, *dissolve* around me. I stand rigid, before a thin veil. I can't tell its size, its fabric, nothing more, in fact, than that it's *there!* My hands, or not, something that's me, are fumbling at it. A part of it is cast aside and I can see beyond it. But there's nothing there. I try to walk, but no matter how much I struggle I can't go any further.

In a living room in the evening there was a table, a round, five-leg table. There was Ted's face. Aside from that there was only the brown, indistinct darkness.

– It's the same dream I had, Ted said excited, calm, indifferent? – I had that dream last night. Or... once, whenever it was.

Sparks flew from the fireplace. The Fire sparked in the fireplace.

The four of them sat around the table, talking, not really eating and not really talking.

A television set, a studio debate sounded from the other room. A clearly disturbed man wearing a shabby suit and a skewed tie spoke:

– People say it's just the weather, just the weather acting up a little, but that isn't it. It isn't just the weather. The weather is just a symptom of something else, something deeper we can't quite grasp.

The four stood out, somehow in the hectic mood of the room at the restaurant.

– Nothing really happened on that trip, did it? Oh, it was fun, as long as it lasted, or it could have been, I guess...

Burt shook his head.

– If not for that creepy forest ranger guy, boy was he *creep - y!*

Lisbeth shook her head disgusted.

A Flash, a gust of dark blinded them, and they were back in the forest that night.

– You can't have a fire, the forest ranger told them. – Don't you kids know it's illegal to make fires here?

They sat at the trader restaurant on the corner and had a work-related conversation.

– ... and the quarter figures aren't in yet, Lisbeth conveyed, – but they say it will be our best term yet.

– Congratulations, skilled Lisbeth, Burt praised her. – You've worked so hard and long for this. I guess the older guys on the board have stopped pinching your butt, too, at this point, eh?

– Yeah, sometimes I despair and wonder if it is all *worth* it, she joked, – you know what I mean... But that is one, tangible perk, isn't it...

– Not here, please, Burt said, hardly audible, – it's like swearing in church.

– Yeah, your esteemed colleagues may not enjoy being served the truth, Ted said, his voice dripping sarcasm. – Not even once.

Lisbeth pushed her body tight to his, rubbing her cheek at his.

– I know it's bullshit, okay. I just need to pretend it makes sense once in a while. We all do, don't we.

He nodded, even if he wasn't sure.

– I'm sorry, he said with regret, – you don't need my recriminations on top of everything else.

– It's okay... okay, she whispered in his ear.

A guy from the neighbor table leaned on his chair, leaning in their direction.

– Wasn't that crazy chick friend of yours supposed to meet you here? He said cheerful. – It's been months since we all last saw her, and we sort of *miss* her, you know.

– I'm sure you do...

Ted said.

– What was that, I didn't quite hear you...

– I'm sure you do, Ted repeated.

There was something in Ted's eyes, or something, somewhere making the man at the neighboring table turn pale and retracting his position.

They saw Freya walk towards them on the street outside and waved to her. She didn't wave back, her movements stiff, robot-like, not the way they knew her at all.

Then she entered the room, and stopped right by the entrance. They, all four of them knew something was wrong, knew it in their hearts, immediately.

She spoke in a loud, monotone, slow voice cutting through the noise of voices filling the room.

– I SAW THE END AND I SAW THE BEGINNING AND IT'S ALL THE SAME

Another voice responded to hers, and no one could identify the speaker. It was as if it came from everywhere and nowhere.

– The people and circumstances may vary, but it all stays the same.

Freya glanced around her, before walking to the table, to her concerned and bewildered friends.

– They call it the Rot Race. The question is, as ever, who'll sink and who will swim... and it's foul beyond imagining.

– The *Rat* Race, Lisbeth responded automatically. – Say, Freya, are you okay, honey?

– Yes, yes, Freya replied visibly irritated, – it's all about success or not, and nothing more. I'm Abkasha and I *know*

– What happened, Freya?

Ted wondered.

She looked at him, not looking at him, with blank eyes deep in her skull, pulled by pale skin.

– Damn it, *Abkasha,* what happened.

She heard him, now. Abkasha heard him.

She hardly even resembled Freya anymore, as she spoke in a shaky, dreamy voice.

– I stood on a tall mountain and I saw the world crumble to dust before my eyes, saw all Life rotting on the vine. I SAW THE END AND I SAW THE BEGINNING AND IT'S ALL THE SAME

Two uniformed cops entered the restaurant. Ted, so immersed in Freya/ Abkasha and her immense presence hardly even noticed them at first.

The two cops walked straight to their table. Ted and the others frowned, shaking their heads in distrust and suspicion.

– Is she okay? She doesn't look quite *alright,* if you know what I mean... Shall I call the hospital?

– NO hospital, Ted replied in a sharp voice. – She'll be okay. It will be okay, just give her room to breathe, okay?

He looked closer at the two men. One of them seemed eerily familiar.

They find themselves back in the forest, facing the leering, obviously deranged forest ranger.

– You can't have a fire. Don't you kids know it's ILL - EG - AL to make a fire here... Yes, good kids shouldn't make aaaany fires if you ask me. Do ya get my drift, ya tiny, tiny PUNKS?

It felt unreal and very, very real simultaneously, both in the forest and days later when they encountered the two suspiciously acting police officers. It brought them both fear and amazement.

– You... hate the forest? Freya said with a thin, thin voice.

– What did ya say? The forest ranger scowled at her.

– You... hate the forest, don't you... you w-want to burn it, you want it to burn down?

They were back at the restaurant, the unpleasant experience in the forest still lingering beneath sore skin.

Ted stared at the two men, shaken between doubt and certainty.

– You're the forest ranger, aren't you, you're all the same?

The room changed, without changing. It stayed the same, but *Changed* in inexplicable ways.

– I don't know what you're *talking* about, the cop resembling the forest ranger spat. – You're not gonna weird out on me, all of ya, are ya? Let me tell ya something. I would get that chick of yours here under some sort of *control,* if I were ya, before someone else does it for ya. Proper TREAT - MENT may be the only recourse for people like her.

The voice from nowhere and everywhere returned.

– AND WHAT DO YOU MEAN BY USING A PHRASE LIKE «PEOPLE LIKE HER»? ARE YOU REALLY AS STUPID AS YOU LOOK, YOU DAMN PIG?

There was no reaction. Ted looked around, with thick sweat suddenly tingling his brows. And something dawned on him. Nobody had heard anything, the yelling being audible only in his mind.

He froze, feeling Lisbeth's hand in his, slowly melting, crumbling, slowly «pulling himself together».

The cops left. Everyone breathed easier, not just Freya's friends, but also those sitting nearby, close enough to have witnessed the event firsthand.

Freya sat down. Her eyes kept flickering. The five around the table glanced at each other with equally flickering eyes.

– We can't ignore this, all the weirdness anymore, John said. – We just can't. It isn't just us. It is as if the entire world has gone bonkers, truly bonkers.

He glanced at Freya, as if to apologize. She shook her head, dismissing it, the very need for it.

A fire hydrant broke outside. A geyser of water reached for the sky. People fled in panic. The street seemed to be flooding from one moment to the next.

And now they all did look at each other, unable to look away, filled with apprehension.

– We're not exactly without resources of our own, Lisbeth said good-humored. – There *is* something we can do, isn't there, an effort we can make, to seek and perhaps to find... an answer of sorts? We all want answers, right? Haven't we waited long enough?

– Perhaps there is, Freya said subdued. – I used to do stuff like that, used to *dabble,* but I stopped. It... scared me.

Lisbeth rubbed her back, comforting her.

– But you're still dabbling, without really wanting to. Whether it's... real or whether it's only you, you need to confront it, don't let it rule you.

– Yes, yes, you're right, Freya acknowledged.

– We all need to do it, Ted stated, – whatever it is. Like you point out, we're not clueless. Most people might be, but we aren't!

They kept looking at each other, looking and looking again with flickering eyes.

Whatever remained of their meal was digested quietly. Conversation faded to brief sentences and comments. They ignored the stares from the nearby tables as they sat there, as they rose and left.

– Everything changed after that forest trip, didn't it? Lisbeth mused. – It didn't begin then, but everything changed then.

– But nothing happened! Burt insisted. – Nothing distinguished this trip from all the other forest trips we've ever done.

They looked good humored at him, not commenting on his comment.

The five of them stepped out on the flooded street. They got wet on their feet the moment they put their feet on the sidewalk.

People ran back and forth in a completely useless attempt at avoiding getting wet. The five of them walked somewhat dignified, drawing more than a few ugly stares from those with panicked distress in their eyes.

2

Lisbeth said goodbye to the others with lots of hugging. She kissed Ted on the lips. They looked startled at each other.

She waved goodbye and went on her way.

– See you guys tonight, she called with hope in her voice and eyes.

Her destination wasn't that far off, just a few blocks. The water slowly returned to the sewers. Every person she encountered within the first block still walked around with soaked shoes and pants. It felt strange when that scenario slowly shifted and changed, until she eventually became the only one in her surroundings with wet lower pants.

She visited the nearest mall and stores selling pants and shoes (and socks). They stared at her when she asked for a towel. She didn't care. It felt good to dry herself and dress herself in dry clothes again. She walked out of there with her old pants and shoes (and socks) in the bag and continued on her way.

Melanie's Place was an alternative community house on fifth and Roxie. It was basically an old building that had been refurbished by the new owner. Everyone could walk right in during visiting hours. Lisbeth followed the uneven stream of people inside.

It was a popular place. Everyone could see that with half an eye. She couldn't help noticing the subdued mood, though, so pale compared to the impatience and unrest raging within her.

A girl waved to her from one of several couches in the reception hall. Lisbeth returned the wave. Dawn rose and met her halfway. They hugged.

– It's so good to see you again, Dawn said softly. – Are you here to see

Melanie?

– Yes, I realize that Mel is busy these days, but… yes.

– Melanie isn't here right now, but she will be back shortly. I'm certain she has time for you. Come and say hello to the guys.

Time for me, Lisbeth thought.

«The guys» were a bunch of newbies, of mostly young girls in their middle to late teens.

– Guys, this is Lisbeth, Dawn presented her. – She has been away for a while, but used to be a mainstay here, quite *merited* a while back.

They had heard about her. Lisbeth saw that with one glance. Dawn's excited voice didn't exactly improve matters. They looked at her with wide eyes.

– Your reputation p-precedes you, she heard Freya stutter.

She knew no one else present heard it.

– You walked away from *this?* A girl said incredulous with big eyes, making it seem like the silliest act in the world.

Lisbeth didn't take offence. She smiled.

– I was… frustrated after a while here without notable progress, she frowned, – and I left, and gave up the… arts altogether, but lately things have happened to me and my friends without us actively trying, more than encouraging us… to return to this life, even prompting us to take it all a step further than Melanie and I used to do, and we think all you guys should be a part of that.

– That sounds great! One of the boys cried eagerly.

Visible doubt crossed Dawn's face before she joined in, painting an insincere smile on her face. Lisbeth fought to keep herself on an even keel, to hide a frustration she had both expected and dreaded. It took a lot of effort.

They were mostly young and open to new thoughts, but she felt the wall between her and them, keeping her from reaching them properly.

– It's hard to tell, of course, what brought on this improvement, whether it was a result of our previous efforts or if it just happened by itself, but we will explore it, and I'm confident that we will gain both understanding and wisdom.

She felt awkward, feeling like she spoke with flowers, form without content. They caught her glancing at the entrance and nodded to themselves. She shook her head in further frustration.

– Melanie was my mentor as well as she's yours, she attempted to explain her position. – She taught me a lot, and that's certainly one reason why I returned here.

They nodded, smiling, relieved, less tense, but perhaps more condescending. She kept herself from shaking her head.

She easily noticed Melanie's approach well before she entered the building by the notable excitement charging through the room. Those spotting her communicated something to those not doing so. It was hard to tell exactly what that was. Lisbeth noticed brightening faces and elevated breathing.

Melanie entered the hall. Two aides accompanied her. Lisbeth didn't watch her, but her followers. A sigh of awe surged through the gathering.

Lisbeth rose and Melanie noticed her. The smile grew on Melanie's face after a brief hesitation. Melanie walked to her. They hugged each other.

– It's so good to see you, Melanie cried.

She grabbed the other woman in the arm and led her away.

– Let's go to my office, she offered. – We've got a lot to talk about.

– We have, Lisbeth agreed.

The two of them walked to the room at the end of the hall. They stepped inside. The two aides stopped outside the door. They turned and faced the others in the hall, like sentries.

Melanie closed the door. The constant buzz faded to silence. Lisbeth found herself appreciating that, and experienced an instant sense of shame.

– It's so good to have you back, Melanie said passionately.

– It's good to be back, Lisbeth said.

– You are back, then? Melanie said with a sore touch in her voice and eyes.

– Yes, Melanie, Lisbeth assured her. – In more ways than one I feel like I've never left, you know.

– Good, very good. Melanie seemed to be filled with energy all of a sudden. – I have so many plans you and I can carry out together.

– We would all love to hear about them, Lisbeth said eagerly, – when you guys come to our gathering tonight. We could compare notes. So much has happened with our circle lately, too much for it to be a result of false hope or our imagination.

She noticed Melanie's stark lack of excitement before she had finished speaking and trailed off.

– I'm afraid we have to postpone that, Melanie said with regret. – We have our own gathering tonight.

– Can't you postpone your thing? Lisbeth frowned. – I realize this is sudden and all, but we… we would love your input and participation.

– We have planned our ceremony for quite some time, Melanie reproached her.

Lisbeth's frown grew deeper.

– I'm not in a hurry, she stated, seemingly unprompted. – I can stay a while.

Melanie walked to her and kissed her on the brow, a reward for good behavior. Lisbeth's thoughts roamed and kept roaming unpleasant paths.

They returned to the hall. Melanie led her to a specific group close to the center of the full tables. Lisbeth realized suddenly that less than half of the seats were taken, that all the rest were vacant and cold. Clarity on the matter practically assaulted her.

She got occasional shivers as she sat down and hid it behind excessive movement, pretending to scratch her back. It ceased after a minute or so, leaving her in peace somewhat.

– So, what happened? A girl wondered, clearly curious, not just making a conversation.

The others looked at the girl first, as if blaming her for something.

Then, they directed their attention at Lisbeth. She felt it, the curiosity they couldn't deny, no matter how awkward they experienced it. A warm shake passed through her.

– It's hard to tell, she frowned. – I can't really put my finger on it. I feel like I'm being watched, like he or she is close. I feel the presence behind me, but when I turn and look, there's no one there. I even feel it when I look straight ahead sometimes. There's a… a buzz in my frontal lobe, and the world seems to shift in front of me. There's nothing my eyes can see, but I still perceive… something. There is something there. It is more potent when we, the guys and I are together. We have a shared experience of… menace. Freya is clearly haunted by it. She has dabbled for years. She didn't stop when the rest of us did, but kept pursuing it relentlessly. We've started having vision of ourselves as other people, us, but not us, but strikingly similar, living vastly different lives.

She felt drained, as if talking without pause, without thought had tired her, physically tired her.

– We walked through the Gate of Madness recently…

– You did? That's quite a walk. Most people drive there, at least the part of the trip you can drive.

– It felt like the right thing to do, Lisbeth said, frowning some more. – It felt more and more right the deeper we penetrated the forest. We found the way easily enough. In fact, we had no trouble with directions at all. We didn't really get that tired, but felt more vigorous the longer we walked. We practically ran some stretches, and *then* we got tired. The Gate of Madness isn't that special, nothing but two trees making something resembling a gate, but the weirdness began the moment we started out, even before we started out, and we realized that it had been there, with us for a very long time.

Silence greeted the end of her prolonged speech. Everyone kept looking at her. She still felt awkward when she rose, but determination and conviction triumphed it by far. She looked at the others with a steady stare.

– You're all welcome to participate tonight.

Melanie looked like she wanted to say something, but she didn't, and then she did anyway.

It was as if Lisbeth looked into a mirror, a twisted mirror, a feeling not exactly unfamiliar to her.

– I just don't think our beliefs need demonstration, that's all, Melanie said. – And, I might add, I'm looking out for you. I don't think those people, Ted and Freya especially, are good for you.

– They are good for me, Lisbeth said quietly.

She straightened, before continuing.

– Perhaps it needs curiosity?

There was no response from Melanie. She just stared intensively at Lisbeth, making her uncomfortable again.

– What about you? Are you going?

She spoke as if Lisbeth hadn't spoken or responded to her at all.

There was no response from Lisbeth. She looked into the mirror, into Melanie's eyes, seeing herself, studying her plain clothes, touching the sleeves of her jacket. An uncomfortable silence descended in the yard.

3

Ted waited, pacing back and forth in the living room, in his house by the forest. Tammy, the cat paced around his legs, seemingly just as nervous, clearly attempting to get his attention, finally succeeding. Ted crouched slightly, scratching the back of her ears. She instantly started purring.

– What a devious young cat you are, Tammy, he mumbled.

He sighed, looking for the tenth time out the window, up the road towards the garage and the small parking lot there. His pacing slowed down, about to stop when the lights from a car illuminated his vision. He saw them stop up there, and leave the car.

They walked down the road. Lisbeth waved to him. He returned the wave and walked to the entrance.

He opened the door just as the four of them stopped on the porch, bowing eloquently.

– Enter of your free will, he declared, using his put-on voice. – May I take your coats, sirs, yours, madams?

Freya giggled, kissing him lightly on the cheek.

Lisbeth kissed him on the lips. He returned her affection, feeling her, all of her, or so it felt.

She bent down with a huge smile on her face.

– Hi, Tammy!

Tammy knocked her head against the outstretched hand, matching the woman's happy greeting.

He felt happiness… swell within him, an emotion echoed within the others, in their smiles and eyes. They removed their jackets and shoes in a somewhat controlled rush, and walked into the living room, to the round table with five legs.

– I love it every time I see this table, Freya giggled solemnly. – It's such a simple, ingenious design.

Five people gathered around the table.

– We're all ready, poised, Lisbeth said hoarsely, distinctly different compared to what they had learned to know as her baseline personality. – Let's get started!

They lit candles, candles placed all over the room. It created a warm, pleasant and eerie glow.

Five people sat down around the table. They grabbed hands and held on in a grip both firm and loose. Everyone closed their eyes.

Breathing and heart-rhythm slowed down, as they relaxed, as they sat there making the final preparations, listening for the silence of the mind needed for the ritual. It was working. Impressions, sensations faded, except the feeling of skin touching skin. That grew more pronounced, not less. In the silence of the room, they hardly heard their own breathing, their own heartbeats, as if neither was there at all, as if they, themselves weren't there.

The candles flickered, and so did the electrical lights. Ted felt a pressure behind the eyelids, the familiar tingling in the frontal lobe. Anxiety touched him, as he felt the presence in front of him. The fear filled him, threatening to grow wild and terrible. He wanted to both open his eyes and give in to the powerful need to go deeper, but ended up doing neither.

– It feels... awkward, doesn't it? Lisbeth's voice was tinged with despair. – I didn't know it would be this difficult. At least I hoped it wouldn't be.

– Concentrate, Abkasha admonished them, – *focus,* give in to yourself. Reject the fear of what's hiding beyond the veil.

Freya's voice was slightly different when she spoke as Abkasha, her demeanor subtly changed.

They sat there, with their eyes closed, holding hands. Bodies turned rigid, tense, even more so than before. All five shook their heads and opened their eyes, relenting, letting go of the hands. They looked at each other, disappointment very distinct in the open eyes.

– Let's take a break, John suggested, – before making another attempt. If we need to push, we've already failed.

Everyone nodded. They knew his words to be true. Experience told them that, at least.

Ted walked to the kitchen and filled five glasses with water. He returned with them. Everyone drank, drank them empty. They remained thirsty. Their throat felt just as parched.

Freya shook, as she spoke.

– I was on my way to the restaurant, meeting you. Walking down the street, when... when the colors shifted, shifted to green, and then to gray, and then the visions c-came. I've hardly had any while awake before and certainly not that intense.

– I feel the fear, too, Burt said. – It's lurking below the surface, you know, waiting for the moment to s-strike.

They nodded as they looked at him, his stuttering not surprising to them. Bodies stayed rigid, tense. He didn't tell them anything they didn't know.

– It's kinda strange, John said good-humored. – After a while I do get this undeniable urge to open my eyes... to see if there is someone *there,* or if you all have turned into demons or something...

The laughter masked the fear, no matter how hearty, and they all knew that.

– This isn't really leading to anything, you know, he said, visibly down. – Can we put out the lights or something?

Freya shrunk on her spot, unable to keep it from happening, from wearing her inside on the outside.

– I don't know...

At that moment, with the fluttering in her voice, she was both Freya and Abkasha.

Behind eyelids they imagined to be closed waited what was right in front of them.

Lisbeth jumped on her feet. She stared determined at the others,

– Let's DO it! She practically shouted

She rushed around the house, turning off all the electrical lights, one by one. First in the other rooms, then in the living room. Pausing a bit, giving them a flashing, demonic smile, before «hitting» the last «switch».

And it turned Dark. Not pitch-black, but dark, as if the candles made the room darker, not brighter. She fumbled her way back to her seat, even as they knew she had to, had to see well enough.

– It is as if I can't see, she told them, as she fumbled and sat back down in her chair.

Then it fell quiet, and they could hear each other breathe. And they could feel the hands they held. And they imagined, in just the smallest bit of time, that they couldn't see them, see anything around them, except in the occasional flash of gray.

Those flashes, their quality changed, into something resembling daylight, there one moment, gone the next.

Seconds stretched slooowly into minutes.

– This is stupid, Burt cried, doing so with a voice in desperate need of an outlet. – At least that would be what most people would say, if they saw us now, a completely meaningless act, wasting time.

– If they «saw» us...

John snickered.

– It is dark, Ted stated. – There is no light anywhere, only the fire leading us into darkness.

His words did something to them, encouraged them to move on.

Eyes closed. The frontal lobe buzzed again, and this time they stubbornly ignored the fear that an invisible hideous creature lurked right in front of them, studying them, its eyes at the level of their eyes, staring at their closed eyelids.

– Take in the dark, Ted said with noticeable intensity in the voice, – breathe it in, breathe out what's inside.

– The Shaman, the Witch speaks, Burt said ironically.

– Hush, Lisbeth cautioned him, – sssjjj

She nodded to herself, looking at them with her closed eyes, her stare burning them all.

– As the ceremonial master I command you all... to empty your minds, to feel the Night, to discard the day and its horrible gray and lukewarm light.

Her words echoed within them. They took them to heart, heeded them and felt how they worked on them.

Minutes passed by as they sat there waiting without waiting.

– SPIRITS OF EARTH AND SKY, I COMMAND THEE TO APPEAR!

Silence persisted, like a day of endless rain.

Freya broke the silence, breaking out in a wholesale, irrational laughter fooling no one. They sat there, watching her, with open eyes and free hands. She stopped after a while, rising and switching on a lamp, looking as if she wanted to cry.

– It won't work for us tonight, Ted said, said stubbornly.

– Not tonight, Lisbeth agreed, understanding his subtle wording.

She kissed him on the lips, and he returned it. The night faded around them.

Ted tossed and turned on the bed.

A woman stood on a road in bright daylight, staring at him, glaring at him. Her wicked eyes burned holes in him. Ted moaned in distress.

He returned to the Gate of Madness. A portal opened between the two trees, but he couldn't see through to the other side. He imagined he could see eyes, though, wicked, wicked eyes in the thick, thick mist. The portal opened. There was nothing there, nothing at all, in spite of the horrible, growing pressure behind his eyelids, and the conviction that a creature with a sharp, sharp knife and a wicked, wicked grin stood by his bed and looked at him.

Ted woke up with a start, sitting upright in bed, sweaty and shaken.

Chapter Two

Dawn broke. They all woke up early, shaken and drenched in sweat, casting weary glances around the bedroom or living room.

Lisbeth made herself a sandwich, no butter, no fat, only vegetables, tomatoes, onions, and such. John looked at it all with disdain visible in his entire expression.

– Yeah, just keep looking at me, that way. You wouldn't if you had to worry about keeping your hard-won shape every second of the day.

Ted intervened before things could get ugly.

– Guys, what about last night? He asked, more than slightly off. – Any thoughts?

Freya tried speaking up, but couldn't do it. She made repeated attempts, shrinking from any comforting touch they extended to her.

– I blew it, she finally said, – I *know* that. I'm the one, of all of us, who should be most interested in succeeding with this, of at least making something of it. And there are times when I do feel there is something to it. And then I seem to reach an impasse, a block, and it all falls apart. I laugh at myself, at us, at our pathetic attempt to make sense of an insane reality.

They shrunk under her despair, her snarling contempt.

– For what's it worth, I don't think you «blew it» more than any one of us, or all of us together, Ted said, doing his very best at lacing his words with confidence. – There seem to be some constants in the doing of... of Magick, some necessities needed to bring about whatever result desired. Focus... or letting go of focus is clearly one, but that is mostly incidental. Our problem is first and foremost that we don't believe in it, believe that we can get it done. We should stop dabbling, and get on with it, but we're just a bunch of ridiculous dabblers...

No one commented on his outburst. They continued with their breakfast, staying quiet and sullen, unable to help themselves rising from the pervasive mire of consciousness that had caught them in its maw.

Lisbeth devoured the sandwich, doing so with empty eyes. The others ended up watching her, obsessing over her without really being consciously aware of their own feeding habit. They experienced the kitchen as a dark and foreboding place.

– Dreamtime? Burt said abruptly.

They looked incredulous at him, stunned that he was the one speaking up and saying what he was saying.

Ted looked closer at him.

– Aborigines in Australia and some other primitives do believe we're participating in Dreamtime, Burt pressed on, obviously on a roll, – drifting through an insane world, where nothing ever matters and nothing of consequence ever happens.

– I've read about that, Lisbeth acknowledged. – Every night, every time they sleep, they visit this Dream World of theirs, acting upon any desire, any whim they may have, they may get. It's supposed to be very... liberating.

Burt leaned eagerly forward. He sounded and appeared unusually and even eerily enthusiastic.

– That's one interpretation, but there's another. According to that one, we're living in the Dream World right now, and the other world, the one we're «visiting» when we're «asleep», *that's the real world.*

– Or both views are probably wrong, Abkasha said. – After all, we humans are, fortunately doomed to always have a fallible view on existence.

It was Abkasha, cocky, dangerous, confident, odd, shrugging, a Freya turned completely around from just a short while ago. The others studied her closely, as they often did, seeking common denominators between her and her Other, struggling to do so, as was often the case. They imagined they saw her by a frothing river, imagined they saw themselves join her there.

She pulled herself back into herself, and the others pulled back as well, in an effort to benefit her they knew to be in vain.

Their meal eventually ended, the silence and inaction adding to the uncomfortable mood.

As was often the case with these occasions, they would discontinue prematurely, unsatisfactory. They rose and the four guests in the house prepared to leave. Ted walked his friends, his confidantes, his... siblings to the hall.

They hugged, both group hugs and two and two. It worked, to a degree to lessen their frustration and ongoing dissatisfaction.

– I've participated in parties where everything has been *very* close to... to *taking off*, Ted said, – but didn't. This was, even if not much happened, closer than most, I think. Perhaps not because of what happened or didn't happen in itself, but because the attempt in itself is «worth» something.

Freya giggled, appearing very young and vulnerable.

– It didn't really... amount to anything, but it was fun anyway. I felt outside myself, and I... heard myself talking, if you know what I mean... I still do!

– You've always been extremely fond of hearing your own voice, Burt joked.

The joke didn't really catch on. No one laughed or smiled. Freya looked hurt and bewildered at him.

And that could've been it, as Freya kept struggling with the hurt and sense of betrayal.

Reality... paused, holding its breath, like the air before the storm.

Lisbeth lifted and lowered her hand, a poised finger, in order to get their attention. It was an eerie, stunning and successful move. They lent her their ears, looking at her, mildly interested, baffled by the sudden, fiery intensity in her eyes.

– Why don't we have a... party, you know, a *Witchnight?* We've talked about it often enough, haven't we? Without talking about it, that is... Invite lots of people and hope beyond hope that a considerable number will actually show. We've got nothing to lose and everything to win.

The word «everything» sounded different when she spoke it right then, for some reason, like an echo in an empty room or another effect they couldn't quite determine.

– «A night for Witches, for potential, proverbial Witches...

Ted declaimed.

– I like it!

– It's different, bold compared to our previous attempts, John said. – Perhaps we've... approached our quandary from the completely wrong end. Perhaps we need to *create* the Magick before we can use it.

They imagined that his words echoed in the void. Particularly the word «magick» sounded distinct in their ears, standing out from all others.

Freya kissed him on the lips, with dark lights in her eyes.

– We do need this, all of us! We know that!

– Lisbeth is correct, Freya stated stubbornly. – Once again, the success is the attempt.

– It's well over a month until April 30th, the traditional Beltane Night, Ted said. – For some reason, I've always pictured this as a starting point for something like this.

– It *is* an ancient Night, Freya nodded.

– I remember reading about it, John said. – I can remember how tempting it was to leave my room at midnight and run into the dark. It was always too cold, too wet, too scary, too anything. I stayed a chicken. I don't want to be a chicken anymore!

They all looked good humored at him, seeing themselves in him.

Everyone hugged once more, this time kissing each other, doing so several times, even on the lips, feeling the heat of the skin and the act.

They parted, to meet again.

Ted saw them drive off. He combed his hair with his hands, walking back into the artificially lit living room, a solitary creature of the night.

Except for the eyes he searched for and found in the corners and shadows every time he turned and looked around him.

2

Ted had a shower. The sensation of water on the skin, the entire experience of it felt uncanny, strange. A shower in the morning always made the cobwebs of sleep fade, but today, when he stepped onto the bathroom floor, he felt even more refreshed than he usually did.

It just boiled beneath the surface, a tangible, undeniable and ongoing surge of energy. The smile never quite left his face.

He dressed for the day, a suit, tie and shirt, unable to hide his distaste for himself in the mirror. His expression told him everything he needed to know. He loosened the tie a bit, more than a bit, already feeling like he couldn't breathe.

The casual glance at his watch told him that he wasn't in a hurry, that he could in fact have watched a movie before leaving for town. He sat down by the kitchen table, pondering whether or not he should have more food. Another glance at his watch made him wonder if the hands moved at all. He jumped on his feet and left the house on a whim, unable to stay there for a minute longer.

The garage seemed to be bathing in twilight. The early morning reached him through two dirty windows, one on each side. He sat down in the car and started the engine. The carport opened. He drove off. The carport closed behind him. He rushed through the neighborhood and reached the highway. It felt good to speed up, to see the world go indistinct on both sides of the car.

The highway had already become crowded. It would become even more so later in the morning, when most commuters wanted to arrive at work simultaneously. It didn't look too bad, now. There was no congestion. The cars could easily cruise at top legal speed. He could drive this beyond familiar road with half closed eyes and fought to keep his focus on the driving. His thoughts kept drifting off. They brought him in all possible directions, pulling him apart.

The cars heading for town slowed down before the intersection. He found himself close to the car ahead of him on the road and managed to slow down in time, to concentrate on the driving. The car in front of him, a rusty van entered the roundabout, successfully integrating itself in its traffic flow. Ted was next. Suddenly, he needed to keep his eyes on numerous situations simultaneously. He reached the flow without trouble. Everything looked okay. He glanced to the right. There was no one coming from that road, no one close enough to spot. He kept turning.

There was a loud screech. He looked to the right again and caught only a flash of the car before it rammed into him. The surprise and the sudden pain made him cry out. He found himself flowing upside down, floating through the air for what felt like minutes, before the car landed, landed hard on its roof. It slid across the roundabout faster than on an ice-skate and pulled to an abrupt halt in the midsection.

He hung in the seatbelt, shaking his head, fighting to breathe, still stunned, choke-full of adrenalin. Darkness claimed him. How long he couldn't quite tell. There were more people, far more people and activity outside when he opened his eyes. Someone, a fireman pulled in the driver's door. He finally managed to pull it open.

– Are you alright, sir? The man asked. – How do you feel?

– I feel fine, Ted replied, still caught in the silence of his own head.

The noise slowly imposed itself on him. His eyes caught the ruckus, the constant movement outside the car.

They cut the seatbelt and pulled him out, carrying him to an ambulance only ten steps away. There were wreckage and bodies everywhere, a considerable amount covered in blood, in glowing, glowing red. He saw himself in the window mirror. Blood trickled from a small wound on his forehead. It didn't seem too bad. He remained lightheaded. The ambulance drove off with him in it. They started examining him, using a flashlight to probe his eyes. He answered their questions as best as he could. They cleaned his wound and put a band aid on it.

– You seem to be okay, sir, one of the paramedics said. – We can find no serious injury. If you can give us your insurance number we can have a cat scan and stuff done just to be on the safe side.

He obliged. They didn't kick him out of the ambulance, but drove on to Central City Hospital. They turned off the sirens and that made him feel better, calmer at least. He closed his eyes. Bang! The flash of the other car revisited itself in his memory. The car appeared from nowhere, it crashed into him.

They held him down. He was sweating, no longer anything even resembling calm. They dried his forehead, but they couldn't keep the acid from his eyes. Some considerable time had clearly passed since… since he lost consciousness, but he couldn't tell how much.

– What happened?

His voice sounded like rusty metal plates gracing each other.

– The police are looking into it as we speak, sir.

– The car came from nowhere, Ted stated distraught. – Its speed must have been… been insane.

They exchanged glances. They probably believed he didn't see that, but he did.

He had regained his calm, somewhat when they reached the hospital. Several other ambulances arrived, unloading people with far worse injuries than he had. He walked to the designated area where the more fortunate victims of the accident waited for their turn to come. Time passed slowly, as people were called to the doctor's office. He didn't truly care, but sat unmoving in his chair without a single discernible thought in his head.

When the time came, and he was called in for the checkup, he couldn't tell how long time had passed. He spent more timeless time hooked up to machines, answering incomprehensible questions.

– We will contact you with the results, the chief examiner told him upon shaking his hand, – but you shouldn't worry too much. I would say that at this point.

He stepped outside, straight into the busy sidewalk, walking on a busy street with countless other morning commuters. Cars, buildings, queues, smoke and poison, hungry mouths of four-wheeled coffins big and small were all present in the late morning cityscape.

A man stood still on the sidewalk, staring straight ahead at nothing. A woman touched his shoulder and shook him, first lightly to no effect, then harder, to no effect.

A loud, piercing scream from further down the street shook everyone nearby. They stood there frozen, glancing at each other, fearing there would be more, more terrifying events.

Nothing more happened. People kept glancing uneasily at those closest to them.

Ted arrived at work, wearing a suit, shirt and tie, his distaste for it and general discomfort obvious. He stepped out of the elevator and into a typical modern office landscape. The woman and man behind the counter greeted him and he returned the greeting. They smiled and said hi, and he smiled and said hi in return, walking down the hallway to his office, the second door on the left.

He stepped inside and closed the door behind him. His hand reached for the tie and loosened it, almost on reflex. It did make it a little easier to breathe.

A colleague, Frank, entered the room. His attire, his being, was impeccable from head to foot.

– A bit late today, are we, my good, idle Ted?

– No, *we* are not late, Frank, Ted replied with an edge in his voice and stance, – not late at all.

– Hey, don't pick on me, Frank said and literally pulled back, – I just don't think your repeated lack of performance will get you any favors with the brass, that's all. Say... what happened to you anyway?

He noticed, actually noticed the band aid on the other's forehead.

Ted could still see it, see the accident before his inner eye. He had always been good at that, at visualization.

– I had a crash.

– That's... horrible.

– I never saw the driver, Ted added with half-closed eyes. – The car seemed to come out of nowhere.

– It's just a fluke that you caught a glimpse of it at all, Frank shrugged. – You quite simply looked that way by sheer coincidence.

Ted looked good humored at him. It felt impossible to not do it. Ted didn't say anything, but waited, waited patiently.

– No matter, Frank shrugged again, ignoring the pointed stare, – that's modern traffic for you, a driver can never relax for a moment.

He sniffed in the air, catching himself the moment he did so, looking very guilty.

Ted waited patiently.

Frank hesitated.

– You didn't have one of your... parties, last night, did you?

Ted chuckled unashamed, grinning with infinite patience.

– Yes, Frank, we did, and it was a feast of the ages.

Frank brightened, looking stubbornly at his colleague.

– Then it's not strange that your concentration was... off. Not strange at all I'd say. What will you do if our superiors find out? They will, soooooner or later, you know.

Ted's stare grows even more pointed. This time Frank looked downright uncomfortable.

– Frank?

– Yes?

Frank said.

– That you choose to limit yourselves to a completely boring, ordinary *existence* isn't really my problem. Some of us are a bit brighter than that!

Ted spat each syllable at him as if it was a foul taste in his mouth… and it was.

Five seconds, ten later, Frank had gone away, vanished into thin air, as if he had never been there at all. An extremely satisfying moment. So satisfying, so futile.

The office phone rang. Ted walked to the desk and answered it.

– Cartland.

– Edward Cartland? The pleasant voice at the other end of the phone said.

– Speaking.

– My name is Nelson, sir. I'm from the insurance company. We have the car ready for you. You may pick it up at our field office or we can bring it to you at your convenience.

It was the rental he would be able to use, until he bought himself a new car for the insurance money, or his old car was returned from the repair.

The latter sounded even more unlikely and ridiculous by the second thought.

– I will be more than happy to pick it up at the field office, he said generously.

It was only a few minutes' walk from here.

– Thank you, sir, I'll be sure to inform the attendant in question. You have a good day, now.

Ted sighed in relief when the man ended the conversation.

He walked to the restroom, stumbling the last few steps before reaching it and practically falling through the door.

– Restroom… what a completely ridiculous name.

The entire sentence sounded more like a snarl than actual speech.

Ted stared at himself in the mirror. He stood there, deliberately working himself up.

The restroom looked… different. He recalled with sudden, perfect clarity how it usually looked… ordinary, boring, a place one didn't give even a second glance. He noticed it the moment he stepped inside, doing so for what seemed like a second time. The colors of the lights shifted, shifted into green, into blue, into green. It settled into what resembled moonlight, as if there were no walls and ceiling, and the day had turned to night outside. He imagined the tap and the sink had turned into a spring. He heard its sound, very distinct in his ears. Trees and the sounds of nature surrounded him. He felt good about it, felt great.

He stood in front of the mirror, staring into it, at himself, his own face and features. The eyes dominated the imagery, somehow, as if he could read all kinds of things in them. Determination filled him. He rolled both hands into fists.

– Touching Reality…

Even his voice didn't sound like his own. It had a distinct, alien quality he couldn't identify.

He reached out, stretching his hands, his fists to both sides of his tense body. Sweat formed on his brow and he started mumbling, practically swearing.

– Down to my knees in pain

An alien voice echoed the words coming from his sore throat.

– Down to my knees in pain.

The room changed completely, no longer having any resemblance to what he remembered. Even the mirror faded away. There were people everywhere around him, all of them casting long shadows. Lights seemed to be cast from every angle, but that didn't affect the shadows. They remained, even in this place filled with light. There were ever shadows.

He dropped to his knees in despair, but raised his fist above his head and shouted defiant.

– I, *I,* swear by me, *by the entirety of my being,* to never change, to always continue to change, to never adapt, to always adapt, to never allow any man, nor any creature there may be, to be my Master.

– Down to my knees in pain, the alien voice echoed.

He walked the streets aimlessly the entire day, almost like a penance.

The scene shifted, and shifted again, turning green, turning gray.

It turned dark.

He spoke to people randomly passing by.

– Can't you see the complete falsehood of it all?

They hurried on, looking at him with a deep frown of worry on their forehead.

The neon lights had been lit everywhere by the time he picked up the car and drove home.

He sat in a room, a dark room, not completely dark. There was the mist, the shadow in gray. He called out to the darkness.

– There's no one here, but I am talking to somebody, at least I think I am.

He reached for something in the dark. His hand returned with a cup of smoking fluid.

– I don't know if I got home or how I got home… if I did. I was supposedly driving back, even if I wasn't certain the car was in the garage until I actually walked back and looked… I see it with my own eyes, the next morning I do.

He walked into the computer room, pushing the button making it live and breathe. The low hum filled the room.

The alien voice spoke. He heard it as well as his own.

– He has always felt strange, a strange ambiguity, using a computer. It's a tool, certainly, like all technology, but also a sort of dream machine, where one might project one's fears, one's hopes, one's desire.

He sat down and started opening the various programs. It had become an easy, instinctive process. He chose a phone number from a list and pushed return.

The sound of ringing hit him from the speakers. It rang once, twice and he began fearing that no one would reply. Then he heard the click and Lisbeth's musical voice filled his excited mind.

– Hello, you, she said sweetly, making him swallow hard.

– Hello, he said.

– So, what's on your mind, tall, dark and mysterious stranger, she said brightly.

He visualized her, sitting there, in her apartment, the apartment he had visited quite a few times lately.

– I've given our… project some further thought, he began.

– I like the sound of that, she said, – please elaborate.

He visualized her grin, her open, expectant smile.

– It's just growing in my mind the more I ponder it, he said eagerly, unable to keep himself from revealing his eagerness. – It's more like a compulsion than anything else at this point, something I feel we have to do. I've got this crazy idea of turning advertising on its head, making it work for us, instead of those we… we despise. I feel confident that if we establish the witchnight in the public consciousness, we will receive very negative feedback, and the attention will grow, and it will gain even more attention. It will be like grabbing a tiger by the tail, but the… the potential reward is great.

– I love the way you think, she chuckled.

A warm, warm feeling filled him, warmed both his bones and his mind.

– I bought the smoke machine, he said eagerly. – If nothing else, we can use it during photoshoots or something. We should all gather and have a brainstorm about it, make a list of what we want to do.

– We should hold an initial ceremony, a sort-of preparation for the bigger, later celebration, if you like, Lisbeth said, – just the five of us, by the full moon?

– That's a great idea, he replied instantly.

The obvious eagerness she displayed, the casual conversation made him even more eager and excited.

– We do need it, you know, she said, – need to work on our game. I feel like we need to learn to walk all over again, and we hardly did anything but dabbling when we made the first attempt years ago.

– We do, he said, – in order to better walk and fly.

She kissed the microphone on her phone. He got an instant hard-on.
– Just keep pondering the issue and court your wonderful inspiration, she said. – I'll contact the others, organize our first, modest get-together.
Her voice, her so very musical voice kept echoing in his mind long after the conversation had ended.

3

It… began. They kept making private invitations, and put up the first public announcements, through mail, putting posters on telephone poles and church doors, and on the Internet.
They sat around a table in Lisbeth's apartment in the city. John had made and served dinner and they sat there enjoying the food and drink. The sounds from the street outside sounded far away, more like distant echoes than actual sounds.
– Great dinner, John, Ted said, – my sincere compliments. You should be a chef somewhere.
– Thank you… I think, John said lightly.
They had a toast, one more of thousands.
– We agree then? Lisbeth said.
The other four nodded.
– We won't give away any names, phone numbers or home addresses, she clarified, – just the time and place of the pickup. It will cause trouble, be certain of that, but this way they'll have no one to point their finger at, nothing but ghosts.
Freya smiled.
– You're correct, it will cause quite a... stir. I've participated in such fun before, and we found out a lot of useful things afterwards then, valuable to us in advance, certainly valuable now. The law may easily stop a public gathering, and it will be a public gathering if we do not issue private invitations to all our... guests.
– It will be so fucking enjoyable, Ted chuckled.
– It feels strange, doesn't it? Burt said apprehensive, – like we're planning sedition or something?
They hardly bothered to scorn his predictable, cautious approach. It made them, on the contrary even more enthusiastic.
– Perhaps we are! Ted said with a demonic glee, not really caring about the other man's sensibilities.
Lisbeth walked alone through the streets. She paid a visit to a store hidden away in a narrow alley, more than a bit outside the high street area.

The discreet and simple sign said.

PAGAN SUPPLIES

The alley stayed empty throughout her walk through it. She opened the door and walked inside the store.

There were no customers. A lone woman stood behind the desk.

– Good evening, Lisbeth said brightly.

– Good evening, the woman replied cautiously.

– I need five simple costumes with a hood and robe and cloak. We're five people who have been designing ourselves different tasks for a party, a pagan party, where we look the part and also hope to act the part.

The woman behind the counter looked at her with a worried look on her face, as if she wasn't quite used to this type of customer, after all.

– What size do you need?

– We're three big boys and two big women, Lisbeth said casually. – The other female is my size. Will there be a problem? My impression is that these clothes are the one type fit all type, somewhat.

– That is true, at least to a point, the woman acknowledged. – Excuse me, I'll be right back.

She walked into the storage room. Lisbeth heard her roam in there, but didn't see her. She looked around, at the store. It offered many things she found interesting, even stuff she could hardly stop herself from buying. Suddenly, coming here felt like an excellent idea.

The saleswoman returned with five boxes.

– These are xx-large for the men and x-large for the women, she said. – If one or more doesn't fit, just return it, and we will find another.

Suddenly, she appeared far friendlier, making Lisbeth reassess her initial impression of her.

Lisbeth looked at the photos of the clothes and nodded to herself. She saw no need to check them out further.

– These are fine, simple and non-expensive. Just what we were looking for. Thank you.

The woman behind the counter said nothing further. Lisbeth paid cash. She was given a receipt. Lisbeth left.

The five visited the local grocery store together. They bought supplies to last the entire weekend. The woman at the cashier looked at them with suspicion. People kept studying them anxiously when they appeared from the store and crossed the road to the gas station. They filled two ten liter cans with kerosene.

– It's a beautiful night, isn't it? Ted cried to the other customers when he entered the place to pay.

He didn't receive a verbal reply. Instead he got the one he expected. The other two people present hurried out of the store, away from him.

He returned outside, to his four friends. The man or the woman had already started their car and they quickly drove off.

– What did you do to them? Burt wondered.

Ted granted him his wolfish grin.

– I shared my happiness with them.

They sat down in the car. It was a bit tight between the three in the backseat. John started the car and they drove off. It was just a few minutes' drive to the house in the forest. He parked the car on the lot outside Ted's garage.

They walked from there and directly into the garden, the wild garden, the short walk, into the Night. There was a nice-cut lawn, but the forest was close by. The moon's silver rays cast shadows through the trees, on the black clad people. There was no obvious preparation beyond the absolutely practical. They brought their hot dogs, their wine and themselves, and a lot of dry logs and twigs.

Ted carried one extra bag. He emptied the contents on the ground and picked it up.

– VOILA, one homemade pentacle maker.

It was basically two twigs, connected by a rope. He started unveiling it.

– The rope is four meters. That should make a Pentacle with a diameter of eight meters. Observe.

He pushed one of the twigs into the ground, walking a few steps to stretch the rope, bowed down, and started rotating around the created center, drawing the circle on the ground. Then he pushed five more twigs into the ground on various places on the circumference of the circle, about the same distance from each other. He tied a string around one of them and stretched it from twig to twig, until the string had formed a pentagram, a five-point star, within the circle, together forming a pentacle. The kerosene was poured on the string, on the circle surrounding it. One last line was established to the heap of logs and twigs and sticks at the other end of the lawn.

The five of them pulled back, removing (with a wicked, devil may care smile) the empty cans. And then they placed themselves within the circle, within the pentagon at the center of the pentacle. Freya sat down and crossed her legs at its very center. The other placed themselves around her, like her facing the darkness surrounding them.

– We're consecrating this place, giving it a soul, Lisbeth cried out aloud, – giving it ours. This is our Place of Power, our Aerie, where we'll make our Magick, where we'll start our Journey on the Winding Road, towards knowledge, towards Understanding. Towards Magick, towards… Life.

Ted lit a torch and waited patiently as it caught fire and until it burned with a steady flame, before throwing it at the kerosene-stained geometric shape around them. And the flames rose, and the fire ignited the night air, and they felt the heat surrounding them. And they feared that the center where they had placed themselves was too small.

That fear waned, though, as nothing happened, as they realized with a growing confidence that the flames wouldn't reach them. They stretched out their arms to the side and they were not burned. And they saw again the line of fire run to the awaiting heap of branches and logs, suddenly, seemingly so far away.

The potential was realized and fire stretched into the night, and seemed to burn the very sky.

The fire making out the pentacle burned them, making them sweat. It reached for them, and they once again feared it would touch them at any given moment. They felt like it did. Sweat poured from their skin.

Freya began humming, chanting. It stretched into the night and touched them, like the flames.

– We become fire, become shadow, Ted cried, – stretching into darkness. We become mind, become flesh, like it was always meant to be. We're witches, magickal creatures roaming and filling out the night.

… filling out the night, a choir of whispers seemed to echo his words.

Freya turned and turned and turned, rotating on her spot of soil, her voice cast like echoes across the void, the void they could all sense and touch.

– Witchnight is coming. The thirtieth of April, as it is currently measured on Earth, according to western, Christian timeframe.

The choir of voices, sounding like far more than four cried out:

– WITCHNIGHT IS COMING. THE NIGHT OF THE WITCH, THE NIGHT OF CHANGE. I LOOK SO MUCH FORWARD TO IT. I LOOK FORWARD TO IT *SO*. LET IT COME, LET IT *BE*.

The fire kept burning around them, roasting them slowly, as if there was no limit to the kerosene they had generously applied on the interconnecting lines and circle making out the pentacle. It faded only slowly, until there were only embers left, and they rose, and retreated to the still blazing bonfire nearby.

They grilled hot dogs and drank red wine. Ecstasy was still there in their eyes, but mellowed, laidback. And they danced and they burned, the burning being visible in their eyes, their every move.

– This is some night, some event, alright, John marveled. – It even makes hot dogs taste good.

All the food and drink had that delicious taste, and they devoured it like beasts and felt deep regret when there wasn't more to devour. They danced, danced to Freya's humming, to the rhythm she made beating a stick on the stem of the nearest trees. It sounded like a drum, a deep bass drum in their ears, in their limbs and bones.

The night seemed never-ending, even as it is ended, even as the line of dawn appeared in the east, and twilight supplanted the night, and that seemed never-ending as well, and they finally fell asleep, and lived never ending dreams.

4

Two weeks passed in a slow-burning flash. They went through the motions, feeling like they weren't quite present in their daily existence. It touched them only briefly. The night touched them constantly, like an integrated part of them, their skin and bones and seething mind.

They went to work, going through the motions of a mundane existence, focusing on the… the life awaiting them in the dark and murky part looming so pleasantly ahead.

Flashes of illusion danced before their eyes. They saw the clouds. They danced, and they saw. Time... flew. Clouds soared the sky. Waves crushed the fragile shore. The river reached the sea. Suddenly the time grew nigh, suddenly the night was there. Here... with them.

It rained the entire week before the event. Large droplets, heavy droplets, heavy showers. Almost torrential rain. Flooding the land.

Early afternoon on the day before the night, the clouds parted, and a hot sun started baking the ground and air and the beasts walking on it and through it.

Chapter Three

John and Lisbeth waited on the bus stop, clad in their hoods and cloaks, carrying torches.

People *stared* at them. Both the other passengers at the bus and the prospective guests they had come here to gather stared. «Ordinary» passengers, leaving the bus at the stop, hurried on their way. Some cast angry glances at them. Some just rushed on.

The guests gathered silently, in apprehension and anticipation.

– Welcome! John greeted them in a low-pitched, put-on voice. – We've come here to gather you, to lead you on your first, hesitant steps into the Other World.

And the two of them started walking, with a trail of oozing smoke behind them. And the others followed, with eagerness, accompanied by a nervous snickering.

– Did any of you good people have any problems finding this hallowed Crossroads? Lisbeth asked them good humored with a light, formal, slightly ironic speech.

– Not really, a girl replied slightly euphoric, – it was a real riot asking the people behind the information desk at the bus station for directions, though. They looked *real* funny...

The ice did not break, not completely, but that first, initial conversation did volumes for their sense of... belonging. They did seek closer to each other, overcoming the initial shyness and reluctance.

A car roared in the distance, in the north. Lisbeth and John glanced at each other. They spotted four people walking towards them from the south. John stopped, holding up a hand, signaling for the others to stop.

– There's a bit of trouble ahead, John said, perfectly calm, but still conveying a certain urgency. – Don't worry, we're handling it.

Lisbeth started handing out small pieces of paper, neatly folded, in sharp controlled motions.

A police patrol car stopped right behind them. The four in the car joined the group of uniformed cops approaching them. Blinding flashlights were directed at the small group of night people.

Lisbeth took one step forward, making them stop in their tracks.

– What is your purpose of being here, she challenged them, – of disturbing us like this?

One of the cops responded, speaking in a rough, cruel voice.

– What are you talking about? We're just passing by and we don't need no stiiinking reason anyway.

– We have reason to believe you've planned an illegal, public gathering in this vicinity, another cop said officious.

John smiled under the hood.

– You're wrong on both counts, sheriff... This is a party depending on *invitation* only, held on *private* land.

He proceeded to hand the nearest cop one of his remaining notes.

The cop looked at it, using his flashlight.

THE CHILDREN OF THE MIDNIGHT FIRE
INVITE YOU
TO
WITCHNIGHT
ON THE PROPERTY OF TED CARTLAND
ON THE EVENING OF APRIL 30TH
NO ONE WITHOUT AN INVITATION
WILL BE ACCEPTED ON THE PREMISES

– Yeah, that includes you... Lisbeth said, with a voice filled with sarcasm and venom. – You're not welcome. If you should attempt to enter the premises, there will be filed charges. You better be damn sure of yourself, to disturb our peace.

There was a brief silence. The cops exchanged glances, looking very vexed.

– Okay, guys, we're leaving, one of them said.

They kept looking at the gathering with malice on their mind. The gathering felt braver the longer they did. The cops' usual tactics of intimidation just didn't work.

The cops left. One by one, withdrawing as a group, backing off with silent snarls and looks filled with hatred.

The car drove off with the tires screeching against the road. The four on foot disappeared around a curve 50 steps ahead. A car started and the sound of its engine was slowly fading, as they drove south.

– Is it me, or do you guys have a feeling that this isn't the end of if? John mused.

– It's you, Lisbeth said.

– Thank you, I feel so much better now.

Rewards of laughter echoed from the Gathering.

– It's never the end, Lisbeth said, – but I think we're rid of them for the time being, perhaps even for the remainder of the Night.

– They have no business being here at all, one of the new arrivals said, more than a little aggravated.

– No, they haven't, Lisbeth agreed passionately.

– Okay, people, John said and clapped his hands, – let's continue on the path we had set out on, before we were so rudely interrupted.

The mood brightened a bit, just a bit.

They took off from the main road. No more tarmac, no more road lights. They walked down a slope of a road. Up again, passing a few houses, meeting a few people. John, obviously knowing some of them, greeted them cheerfully. Some actually returned the greeting, somewhat somber.

The mood turned into one strange and cheerful and eerie, as they approached their destination. John and Lisbeth glanced at each other, as they studied the others, at how the shimmer in the air and dancing shadows in the twilight affected them, changed their perception and their eyes darkened in wonder, and the two of them felt how that, in turn changed their own mood and experience of it all. Lisbeth felt how her breath and the pace of her heart quickened.

One right turn, two left turns and they discovered the house at the end of a long stretch, by the edge of the forest. At first, they couldn't quite make out what they saw in one of its windows, but after a few more steps, a few hundred, they started to get the idea.

An entity, clad in cloak and hood, observed them from a window. They could see «it» clearly in the skillfully arranged light. A skull was placed on something they couldn't see on the right. Torches burned both outside and inside the illuminating light. They could see a demonic face, free of human traits and they could feel their skin crawl. And the crawling skin was visible in their entire demeanor.

Suddenly he stood at the top of the concrete stairs, greeting them, a masked human being, removing his mask. They were not sure if that made him less or more demonic.

– Welcome, fair beings, the hooded man cried, – to this night of travails and pleasures, of petrifaction and phenomenon. We'll do our best for you to enjoy yourself. You will do your best.

A cat greeted them, too, either by rubbing itself against their feet or being visible, a silhouette against a light, a torch. Oozing torches illuminated the place, shadowing it. The shadows stretched long, deep.

People started arriving in numbers. Some were gathered from the bus stop. Others, knowing the way, arrived in cars. A buzz, a choir growing louder accompanied the growing number of people present.

One car, though, never drove through the green metal gate, but was parked outside. No one got out and no one inside was ever seen.

– They are creepy, a girl said.
– They're probably using that mountain to spy on us, too, a boy said.
– They are! Ted insisted. – I saw them earlier. Don't worry about it. They will not be able to see what we're doing, behind all the trees.

The last group to arrive was greeted by Ted in the door. He didn't wear his mask and the hood was pulled back. Melanie arrived, leading a strangely clothed bunch of entities.

– Welcome, good people, may I take thy coat, Madame?

She gasped in amazement, as he gave her a predatory kiss on the side of the neck.

There wasn't a single electric light lit in the entire house. The food, an entire pig and assortments was being roasted and prepared over fires in the garden.

The house was virtually empty, no tables, no chairs, no furniture to speak of. Everybody was standing, in their costumes and their masks. Even the windows had been... removed.

– Yes, I plan to redecorate...

Ted took a bow, showing off with his over-the-top attitude.

They could see straight into the garden. Sometimes they imagined there was glass in the windows, sometimes not. The fireplace glowed with a strange luminance. Smoke covered significant parts of the room, but they had no trouble breathing. On the contrary. They smelled the incense in the air and it revitalized them in strange ways they couldn't even begin to describe. Already. It worked itself up from there.

A female Witch approached them from the garden, seemingly growing out of the Night, illuminating the air around her. She wore her cloak and hood. The hood was pulled back. They imagined they glimpsed her nude body under the embracing cloak, but they couldn't be sure. Her hair was pulled back, and her face painted white. She had black and red stripes, markings on her face. She stopped under the window. It was as if she was very close, very far away.

– Hello, I am a Witch, she cried. – You know me, you know me not. I'm Freya, but I'm also Abkasha. She's my Shadow, the other part of me, speaking to me from the darkness between the stars.

She lit two torches. They seemed to catch without her doing anything, anything visible at all.

– It's Midnight, Abkasha stated, – we've entered the Hour of The Dead. It's time to feast! On food and wine and Blood.

A wave with her hand, an arm in Shadow. The long table suddenly appeared from nowhere. The deep part of the garden was lit, in color and fire of all shades. Another table appeared a bit to the left.

They walked out the door, out the window, floating to the feast below and couldn't help but noticing how they, about thirty people moved according to each other, how they flowed effortlessly forward, without struggle or resistance. It was difficult to gauge the exact figure, since everything seemed to shift once in a while, making it hard on the obsessive observer.

While people walked around, looking for chairs Abkasha approached a boy, interchangeable with the rest, perhaps noticing the slight look to the left, the nervous glance at his chest.

– What is thy name, boy?

– Clay, the boy replied.

She grabbed his shirt like a predator, tearing it apart, pulling out the microphone and gear inside, throwing it into the closest fire. In a dust of smoke, it was Gone!

– HEY, that's expensive stuff...

Abkasha stared hard at him.

– I do not doubt that. You guys spare no expenses, right?

He tensed, expecting everybody to jump him, reading condemnation and disgust in every face.

Nothing happened.

– Come, Clay, join us, enjoy thy Life.

Abkasha said softly.

And after a short hesitation, he sat down, keeping his ears and eyes open, all the senses normally so much use to him... totally useless in this horrible, shifting reality.

The hot night, much too hot to be April 30th at this latitude smoldered them. The ground had dried well under the hot sunlight, during the day. The clouds covered most of the sky now, but they were light clouds, with no chance of rain.

– *A perfect night.*

Lisbeth thought, speaking aloud, bringing her thoughts to life.

Ted echoed her statement, doing so almost simultaneously, synching his voice to hers.

– A perfect night!

Everyone repeated it. The guests glanced curiously and nervously at the hosts, at their eyes filled with mischief. Everyone cast glances around them, turning in an attempt to keep up with the garden's swirling mists and lights… and shadows.

Freya procured pieces of cloths from a bag, holding it up, offering it to the assembly. Some guests accepted it, others didn't. Lisbeth grabbed one, a hood, a tight hood, bringing it to Melanie.

– You should try it on, Lisbeth said eagerly, – and see if it works for you. It's really something, such a beauty in symmetry. You sit there. Everything is pitch black. All your other senses are working overtime, and then suddenly… VOILA, everything works better than ever before.

– I don't know…

Melanie looked at it with doubt and reluctance in her eyes.

Lisbeth put the hood on her, pulled it down her head. Melanie stiffened in her seat, then she went limp.

– Can you feel it? Lisbeth asked. – Can you hear the whispers in the Night?

– It's a bit tight, Abkasha said, – but don't worry about it. It may make you squirm at first, but then I guarantee you'll feel your pounding pulse, your beating heart, and the very ghosts and spirits in the air. Can one see such things? I don't know, but I know it can be sensed, and thus have a quantifiable existence.

Food and wine were placed on the table. People tried hard to catch a glimpse, the tiniest glimpse of those placing it there, in vain. They could all hear it, those sitting there with the tight hood pulled over their head. The fabric was thick, not letting any light through. There was a slight opening for the mouth, that was all. Otherwise everything had turned pitch black. Everyone could hear their own rapid breath.

– Taste flesh, wine like blood, a voice bid them.

Creating a murmur audible among them all.

Lisbeth gave Melanie to drink. Her old friend shook as the fluid flowed down her throat.

Ted stood up straight. They could all hear him do so, imagining they could actually see it as well.

– Picture a path, leading into a forest. The dark is thickening with every step you take.

A voice called out from the forest.

– FEEL THE ILLUMINATION OF THE PATH

They ate, and they drank, and pictured the path in their mind.

– The taste is enhanced, somehow... isn't it? Burt suggested.

– It's the best I've ever tasted, Melanie chuckled incredulous.

Taking a HUGE bite.

A piano, somewhere, and a guitar, and a drum began playing. Direction was hard, close to impossible to pinpoint.

– It feels weird, a girl giggled solemnly. – I hear drums, seemingly rising from the *Earth* itself. Electronic music, too. Perhaps electronic, but it sounds «natural». And it seems to be changing, doesn't it, as if we are imagining it, as if each chord is one of potentially thousands.

Dinner, food and wine, were devoured, had been devoured, the night was yet young. The Night began.

Lisbeth called their attention.

– I'm going to tell you about Witchnight now...

She pulled back, she stood still, saying nothing, waiting a bit, until everybody's attention stayed focused on her.

– This is an ancient night. A dangerous night, where we're drifting away from everything we've known. Older than the church, older than Christianity, than all the present, known religions and views. The more modern names are Beltane or *Valpurgis Nacht,* one of the four great annual witch sabbaths. According to legend it's a night where borders between the known and unknown world are weakened and sometimes erased. There is a Shadow World close to the day world we know. A mirror image, mystical, wonderful, exciting and terrifying. Yes, we know this world intimately.

Hoods were pulled off heads. Images once more flooded eyes.

– Everything has changed, hasn't it? Clay said weakly. – It didn't really look like this… before… did it?

The girl giggled.

– I do believe the trees are closer, or that there are more of them. Everything seems so much… I don't know… bigger… closer. You didn't have anything in our food, did you?

Ted stood before them with the skull, the very distinctive skull in his hand. His voice turned ghostly, eerie, hardly recognizable from how they recalled it.

– Hello, I am a Witch. You know me, you know me not. I'm Ted, but I'm also Anubis. He is my Shadow, the other part of me, my eternal Self, speaking to me from the darkness between the stars.

He turned, rotated one single time. Everybody gasped out loud as they discovered that his face had turned into a skull.

– Welcome, I am your host. I am Anubis... The Mystery of Death. And I am Mysteriam, The Secret of Life.

He held the skull in his flat hand, stretched above his head.

– Is this what you fear? This trifle, this sleep before dawn? Is it any wonder we wander through the day as ghosts of a Human Being? Man shuffles through this landscape of oppression, despair and humiliation, a pale, broken figure, into the twilight.

They saw that broken figure, glimpsed it in mist and shadow, and each one of them saw their own face on its shoulders.

– You've come here, seeking Life. And you've found it, rising deep within your own well. Lie down now... and *listen!*

And they did, closing their eyes. The ground felt soft and dry, warming them, like the fires did. Blankets embraced their bodies.

– Were the blankets there a second ago? John asked them, offered them a riddle. – Are they here now, or are you just imagining them, imagining all of this? Is any of this happening? Has anything, anything at all truly happened to you, before this moment? Are you born now, into Life?

– I, your Guide will not be accompanying you on your Journey, Ted said, speaking softly, low-keyed. – I will be Guiding you, pushing you forward, bringing you back. Between that, it is up to you. The ground warms you. It won't burn you. The burning comes from within, from your own heated furnaces. We are creatures of passion. Picture a path, leading into a forest. The dark thickens with every step you take. The path goes down, into a dark hole of nothing. Picture an opening closed. Imagine it opening. Light it with your Fire, walk through it, the Gate of Fire. Go back, go forward, through Mists of Time and Shadow. I'm counting to fifteen and you're going on your Journey, traveling to far lands. One, two, three...

– My mask, Melanie cried out. – Did you remove my mask?

They were all twisting and turning, before resting their body on the soft ground, the green blanket. All while low music played somewhere in the dark.

– ... thirteen, fourteen, fifteen.

Except for the music, there was only silence for a long time. But Ted turned and looked around him all the time. He didn't speak, but he moved his lips and uttered words, words like curses, like spells.

A voice sounded in the night, the dark voice between the fires.

– I can feel you...

– I can feel it, Freya whispered. – I can feel the Other World, what is Hidden!

– Me, too, me, too, Melanie moaned.

John chuckled, his laughter the echo of thunder.

– I can see the Dance, the Maelstrom of Madness.

There was silence, everlasting. Ted stood there, while the others rested on the ground, unmovable. He moved occasionally, silently, careful not to disturb the peace. He looked around, a bit apprehensive, more than exited at the surrounding darkness. There was a draft, a silent choir of whispers in the air. Everybody was accounted for, there on the ground. He could yet see shadows move among the trees, and even close to him. He stood there, a lone figure in the night. Everyone on the ground had vanished. They were visible, but Gone. He saw glimpses of them among the trees, and also in places far away. Lisbeth smiled to him. He saw Abkasha in a primitive outfit by the Gate of Madness. She spoke. He saw her mouth move, but he couldn't hear what she was saying.

The night, the mist, the shadow split, and everyone entered it, rushed into it. Silent feet touched the path appearing in front of them. They caught glimpses of shapes and creatures left and right and above, but every time they attempted to focus on anything, anyone, it slipped away from them, returning to night, mist and shadow.

He saw them, able to follow them, share their experience to a point, even though he couldn't join them. Everyone experienced the journey differently, but basically it felt as if a door or a portal opened up in the very air, and they floated or walked or rushed through it.

A path revealed itself in front of them. They walked or moved on it. Impressions and sensations bombarded them from all sides, all angles. Then, between one moment and the next… they were… elsewhere. Lisbeth recognized the field at the other side of the forest, the almost faded pentacle by the ruin, the long, long stretch by the mountains, even though it didn't look quite like it. Minor details were different, and everything seemed to be moving around her. She was alone. She was surrounded by people, both known and unknown, both by people at the party and not.

Both statements, all statements were true.

Suddenly she found herself on the mountain. Ted walked by her side. She smiled to him. His fixed expression didn't change. Her smile faded. She looked hurt at him. She realized the obvious, that he wasn't here, wherever here might be.

The mountain plain stretched on as well, with no visible end in sight. Suddenly, slowly, or at least noticeable, she found herself in the air, high up, looking down on the tiny bump that had been the mountain. She looked ahead, fixed her stare at a given point, zoning in on it, and it changed before her eyes.

It turned into a forest, and before she registered it, she was there, between the trees, and between the trees, she spotted tiny spots of light, of fire, and she realized startled that they were bonfires in the night, that they were stars. Giggling in delight, she reached out for one and held it in her hand. It warmed her, warmed so pleasantly in the palm of her hand

The light, the heat spread up her arm, to her entire body, and her entire shape turned to shadow, and she looked at the world, at the Universe with dark eyes.

She grew larger, and the crowd of stars was a sea below her, and then she stood there and looked at a Galaxy. More figures gathered around that sizzling gathering of stellar fire. They stood there and faced each other, and it felt so beyond fabulous.

– We are… travelers? One of them gave voice to a thought.

No one moved any lips, as far as she could tell, not even her.

– We are those filling the empty spaces, a dark shape cast its voice across the void between the creatures breathing fire.

– Yesterday feels like eons ago, the creature dimly remembering itself as Lisbeth gave voice to its thought. – One second like an eternity. I change with each moment, turning into something completely different from how I remembered myself then.

– It's confusing, for one tiny part of a moment or so, a male breathed, and doing that, casting stardust across the void. – Illumination, constant and eternal is ours to enjoy.

Reality shifted and shifted again, thousand times in a moment. One universe was a breath, and nothing more. They found themselves outside…. outside everything, and realized instantly, many yesterdays ago, that that was a foolish notion. We are somewhere, Lisbeth heard a voice, and that means we're inside everything. There was no space, nothing but nothing around them, not even the absence of something. They were lost, Lisbeth feared, as she faced a million versions of herself every time she changed her focus. She enjoyed her own company, and nothing besides, and she was a choir of multitudes making up everything for as long as she could sense, in all «directions».

She recognized no scale, no familiar references, and then she was back in the endless forest, and the journey began anew, again and again and again, and it consistently remained different every time. The spin grew in intensity. She had not been aware of the spin earlier, but now she couldn't avoid noticing it. She became the spin, like she became everything else, even though she imagined others, she couldn't be certain it wasn't her own twisted mirror image.

Ted prepared, prepared for the process of bringing them, bringing the travelers back. He started humming, in a low, atonal voice, dancing around them, turning and turning, until he slowly stopped.

– It is time. I, your Guide bring you back, back from the shadowlands. I bid you to return from your Journey. Fifteen, fourteen, thirteen…

He glimpsed their plight, their constant renewal, rebirth, how they didn't recognize themselves, how they did so better than ever.

And for a long time, nothing happened. Then, finally they started moving. Eyelids slid open.

They rose on their feet. Clay held up his hands. Eyes were huge.

– It's like taking a cold shower, he marveled, – but I'm not wet.

Everybody moved around, independently of each other, contemplating without pause and second-guessing their Journey.

Chuckles, incredulous laughter echoed between the trees, the breathing tree. The forest breathed. Ted felt it with the others, even though he imagined it was nothing compared to what they were feeling, experiencing.

Everyone started speaking, communicating simultaneously, but everyone still heard everything that was being said.

– I'm Awake! Lisbeth breathed stardust. – Far more now, than ever before.

– This is just the beginning Freya stated. – This is just the newborn's hesitant first fucking *steps*.

– I saw a floating skull, Burt gasped amazed, as he pointed, – there, right by the plumb tree.

– I breathe with the tree, John marveled. – I become the tree, the forest, the glen, the plains, the mountains, the…

He just trailed off. They all did.

Silence descended on the gathering. They just stood there for years without number and enjoyed the moment and each other's company, and the breathing, living night everywhere they cast their attention.

The Party, the Celebration moved on, hesitant at first, but slowly gaining momentum on its own.

Music flowed from the trees, from the near and distant forest. «The End» by The Doors reached their ears, their so very attentive senses.

John stood there grinning, almost stupefied.

– It's almost obligatory. We'll probably keep playing it on all the upcoming witchnights....

The Dance, the Dance of Life began, began once again, again and again and again. Faces faded in and out of their attention. Confusing imagery appeared and disappeared. Everything stayed, lingered in their consciousness. Nothing was ever lost.

They couldn't quite get a grip on their surroundings, as if they kept slipping through their fingers, even as they caught many of them, while they before this moment couldn't recall catching a single one.

They did enjoy alcohol, there is heavy drinking, but it hardly felt relevant.

– It's burning up inside of me. I've always felt ridiculous saying that before. Now, it feels right.

John sat down, enjoying the sight of the empty glass, studying it without studying it, seeing it from all possible angles, and that was how he experienced its taste as well.

– *We* are burning! Freya stated. – The biggest intoxication, wildness comes from within. COME

She stood above him, holding out her hand, grabbing his hand, dragging him off, pulling him into the Dance.

And it was at this point they started losing touch, truly started losing touch with the surroundings. Memory was lost, Time was lost. Life was gained. They kissed. Lips touched, bodies touched. People ran off left and right. The music stopped. Silence returned to the wild garden. The forest hummed.

Abkasha spoke, placing herself a bit away from the others, all the others, at equal angles from everyone, everything. Everyone heard her. They had no trouble hearing her *at all.*

– Stretch your arms, stretch your mind, and stretch *yourself.*

And they did.

They could hear the silence and the humming. They could. There was no doubt in their burning mind.

The skull spoke, with its hoarse voice. Everyone recognized it, even though they had never heard it speak before.

– And the blood gave up its secrets.

And the night and its countless dreams swallowed them all.

2

Ted woke up in his bed. He opened his eyes. There was no confusion in them, only the steady stare.

Was it in the bedroom or in the garden? He stood in the garden with other early bloomers, while still sleeping in his bed, while still celebrating Life in the night.

– That was FANTASTIC! He said, excited beyond words. – I don't think I slept more than two hours, perhaps hardly that, and I feel better than I've EVER done in my entire Life. Everything is whirling in my head, but there's no confusion.

He saw easily how contagious his excitement was, how it affected the others, how it changed whatever perception they might have entertained about a prosaic morning.

The excitement lingered, and even boiled over several more times during the next minutes. Every sensation, wherever he directed his attention felt like a burst of energy, one not fading the slightest as the minutes and hours passed by.

Everything looked normal now, even prosaic, in the light of day. It didn't matter. The tables were clearly visible all the time (or almost all the time).

Chairs had been tossed across the lawn.

It didn't matter. The memory of Night was still vivid in the mind.

He reexperienced the dancing, the dancing, firelit shadows still visible in the light of day, doing so almost before he closed his eyes and after he reopened them.

Most people had already left. But those remaining were staying and helped cleaning everything up, carrying the four parts of the long table back to the basement, the garden chairs back to the garage, and returned the cleaned-up chairs and table to the living room. Several people took care of the enormous heap of dish washing.

People left, waving bye-bye.

– They'll never forget *this,* Ted stated. – It has changed their lives forever.

– True! John agreed. – But will they wish to remember?

– I will! Ted almost shouted. – I will remember *forever!*

And he stretched his arms above his head, far up, into the air and mist the world had become.

3

The Storm raged outside. They rose with it, into the distant clouds, the heavens of mist and shadow.

Ted sat inside the house, while Nature howled outside, while wind ravaged mankind and nature alike.

He talked in his cell phone.

– No, there's No Way I can possibly come to work, unless we could send a chopper for me... We can't? No chopper can fly in this weather? Oh, that's too bad a chopper can't even move outside in this weather. Well, you see, that's true for everything. Has anyone else shown up? Not even Frank, eh... Well, there you have it. No one else lives in the building you see...

The man at the other end finally got the beyond caustic sarcasm. It was he that broke the connection, not Ted.

Ted put the phone down. He looked out at the bending trees. The howl of the wind filled his ears, his very mind and self. He walked outside. He had trouble standing still, as the wind, the storm assaulted him. Memories of the celebration, still fresh in his mind mixed with the wind, the rain, the storm.

Red lights flashed on bridges. No cars could cross them, any of them. Somewhere in the forest, trees broke like dry twigs. In the city, bricks flew through the air, hitting cars, houses and windows. People inside screamed hysterically as they ran from the room, while it was reduced to rubble behind them.

Traffic signs and thick poles were twisted into unrecognizable «art». Entire streets flooded and turned into seabed. White wisps of seawater washed walls normally five, six meters above normal sea level. Roads on the coastline were washed away.

The Storm lasted for quite some time, much longer than most violent storms ever do. But eventually it was quieting. The sea retreated, and a semblance of normality returned to the stricken area. Cars slowly, painfully refilled the wet, sand-covered streets. Electricity was turned back on.

Lisbeth was packing. Melanie looked apprehensive at her.

– You're certain everything is alright? Melanie asked, repeating or paraphrasing the question she had asked at least once before.

– Everything is okay, Lisbeth assured her. – The carpenters did their work on my place last week. Everything else was done yesterday. I could have moved back last night.

Melanie looked tentatively at her.

– And Ted and the others, will you return to them, too?

Lisbeth looked at her genuinely surprised.

– I've never left them, why do you ask such a ridiculous question?

– We've missed you at the meetings lately, Melanie grumbled. – We expected you to show up, you know. Why do you persist on going to *their* coven instead of ours?

– Well, I didn't realize that there was a competition, but... when you mention it, our meetings, as they were, still felt, in perspective, quite boring compared to Witchnight. It was so exciting, wasn't it? I can hardly wait until next time!

She couldn't hide her excitement, her seething passion.

– It was like the Storm, all-consuming... and dangerous.

Melanie said timidly. Her friend imagined she spotted shaking as well.

– Now that you mention it... Lisbeth just grew more enthusiastic. – There really are similarities. Even if the Storm was frightening, it was in a way... exciting, too.

– What about your work? You used to love it.

Lisbeth shook her head.

– It just doesn't seem all that exciting anymore...

She walked to the door.

– Thank you for letting me stay. I appreciate it.

She opened the door with one hand, turned and walked away.

Ted waited for her outside. They embraced, kissing each other on the lips, kissing hard and long. The handle of the bag slid from her grip. She let go of it. And she didn't hear the sound when the bag hit the hard ground.

They kept standing tight, while looking into each other's eyes.

They pulled back, just a bit, grinning at each other, enjoying the closeness of the other, the pleasant heat.

– The word «WOW» is on my lips just now, Lisbeth chuckled, – but it doesn't seem quite... sufficient.

– It doesn't, does it? Ted marveled.

– I feel everything that much stronger now, Lisbeth breathed.

The wild smile on Ted's lips felt so good, so very, very right.

– Yes, even the word «strong» isn't anywhere sufficient anymore.

They sat by a table, in a restaurant, waiting to be served the food. Everything seemed… different, a completely different scenery compared to their previous experience of the place.

– I just had the... strangest conversation with Melanie. It didn't occur to me at the time, but she sounded like she… like she *resented* the whole experience on the 30. When I think about it, it's obvious that she did, that she does. I find that absolutely bizarre. She was the one who brought me into her Coven.

– I think «her» is the key word here...

Lisbeth took his hand and squeezed it affectionately.

– I think you're right, but it would never have occurred to me before. There in the apartment, it was as if I saw straight through her, saw what she was truly about, for the first time. Everything is turned upside down, or rather downside up. I can see people and situations much more clearly. Even work isn't really interesting anymore. I'm just going through the motions. There was a time not long ago, when I enjoyed every second of it. Or thought I did.

– With me it's slightly different, Ted said. – I've never enjoyed my steady employment. I've always felt it was something I was sliding into, with no free will included, and I've hated every second of it. And now… I hate it even more…

They ate, occasionally slow, deliberate.

– Food... She breathed, – such an underestimated pastime... I can feel it, you know. Or at least I imagine that I do. Every grain of salt, every natural flavor adding to my pleasure, every added chemical of pollution decreasing it.

– All our senses, all the millions of them, are awakening, he said.

– *We* are awakening, she stated empathically.

They bent over the table, towards the other, kissing, embracing, unbalancing the table. Dishes, forks, knives, food and drinks were gloriously decorating the carpet, and they didn't notice any of it.

They walked the city streets. It was a wonder that they didn't bump into anything or was run down by a car. Or by busy city people hurrying from place to place.

Lisbeth looked at her watch and smiled.

– We're late, are we not...

– We definitely are! Ted said. – Don't worry about it!

– I'm not, she solemnly declared. – I don't worry about it at all!

He echoed her playful smile.

They rang the bell outside John's flat somewhat late. There was no replay.

– Not that late. Definitely not!

Just the first few seconds had passed of their sudden impatience, when they observed John, Freya and Burt cross the street just a short distance away.

– Sorry, good people, John shouted, – we got a bit carried away.

They thought he shouted more than a bit loud, but it only added to the excessive mood.

– That's okay, Lisbeth shouted back happily, – so were we.

John unlocked the door, and they stepped inside.

They walked to the living room. The apartment had an open solution to the kitchen, giving them the impression, the illusion of extensive space.

Images struck Lisbeth like soft waves in the air. She frowned.

– We met Clay earlier this evening, right? I didn't imagine that, did I?

The evening had been a jumble of sensations and memories hard to keep separated.

– Yes! Ted nodded. – At least... I think we did.

They reexperienced it, sharing it eye to eye.

Lisbeth and Ted had a conversation with Clay.

– I'm no longer with the Intelligence, Clay told them.

– That's great, Clay! Lisbeth brightened. – I'm happy for you!

The image of Clay froze in their mind, his face turning into a mask, into unmoving features.

And just like that the brief, indistinct glimpse ended. They returned to John's apartment and knew they had never left.

– Everything has changed, hasn't it? Freya mused. – Everything is different, isn't it?

– Yes! The others choired.

There was a break while they took in the mood, the excitement they still felt.

– Usually, I return to the boring ordinary existence a few days or even only a few hours after a positive experience, Lisbeth mused, – but this time I haven't. The joy just keeps bouncing around in my mind, in what feels like every cell in my body.

They shared that with her, that as well. She sensed it, sensed it beyond doubt.

John walked to the cabinet in the corner, retrieving a bottle and glasses, pouring glasses of wine, giving one to each of them.

– To us! He stated solemnly.

– TO US! The others choired.

– We are the few, the proud, he stated in the same, stubborn manner.

The others did understand, could sort of get the piece of his mind he wanted to convey to them.

– What do you mean? Burt still asked.

John had notable eye-contact with them all. They got that, got the urgency in his eyes.

– Have you noticed something peculiar about how most of the participants of Witchnight have behaved afterwards?

– They do seem to deny it on some level, Burt acknowledged.

– The way Melanie acts, I have to suspect that she wishes to deny it even happened, Lisbeth giggled, doing so with a wickedness she didn't even attempt to deny.

– «In the beginning fear created the gods», Freya stated.

– They are scared, Ted said. – Of themselves, of the World, of everything.

– That is sadly true, John said. – There's no lack of praise and excitement, true or false when we talk about the Night itself. It's when the conversation turns to further, future implications, when we talk about repeating the success, they retreat into themselves, back to the safety of their somewhat ordered existence.

– Then, we are truly different from most people, Freya stated.

They looked at her, studying her, studying themselves.

– Everyone gathered here does want to proceed, moving on, right? She persisted.

Yes, echoed a choir of voices.

The other four said «yes», thinking, without thinking.

– More so than anything I've ever wanted, Lisbeth stated with intensity and conviction.

– Everybody said «Yes», right? Abkasha said, – Doing so thinking a bit, not thinking.

They nodded, and nodded again.

Everything seemed to dissolve around them, and they found themselves elsewhere, not knowing whether or not it was day or night, this room or another place, now or later.

Twilight surrounded them on all sides. There were no walls, no ceiling, no floor. When they looked down, they saw dry ground.

– The Shadow is real, Abkasha stated excitedly. – Everything else is illusion.

And wisps of mist danced, and there was no sun, and the light hit them from everywhere, from every possible angle.

They sat in John's living room, drinking wine, having some more, toasting some more, laughing, enjoying each other's company, the chill hardly visible in the depth of their eyes.

A voice sounded in the nothing, in the twilight:

«And the night ended, and the Night began».

That was pretty much how they felt it, the night ended, and began again, doing so more than once.

– And it is said by the Ancients, in their scroll of voice, of rainbow, that when enough Human Beings awaken from their Nightmare, the world will end.

Ted sat in his chair in his office in bright daylight, doing nothing. The phone rang, and he grabbed it, clearly preoccupied.

– Yes?

There was no response at first, then, suddenly, there was.

– Thou shall not SUFFER a Witch to LIVE!

The hoarse, put-on voice cast a trickle down his spine. It seemed to expand from the phone and into the room, invading his very flesh.

Connection was broken immediately afterwards. He sat there, staring at the receiver for a moment, before putting it back on, shrugging, shivering, once more unable to tell if it was day or night, whether or not the walls were closing in on him, and beyond the shadow of doubt… he questioned the nature of his reality.

Chapter Four

The wind was blowing, and the streets stank of garbage, of exhaust and the sickening scent of perfume.

Lisbeth touched his forehead, stroking it tenderly.

– Has anyone actually threatened you?

– No! Ted replied with a haunted look. – The «incidents» are escalating, though. Just a few phone calls at first, then letters and messages through the Internet.

– I've received them as well, she stated.

He looked stunned at her.

– You have?

– Why does that surprise you? She wondered. – You don't think you have some special place in their hearts, do you?

He shook his head.

– Sorry!

– You don't have anything to be sorry about, she said softly.

They stood there for a while, enjoying standing close to each other, hearing each other's beating heart.

Something… shook her, ever so little, making her frown and turn her head, and she spotted Melanie on the other side of the street. She was evidently in a hurry, rushing down the sidewalk at an elevated speed, looking neither left nor right.

Lisbeth waved. There was no reaction.

– HEY, MELANIE! She shouted. – OVER HERE!

There was still no reaction. Lisbeth caught a glimpse of piercing eyes and a sweaty face before Melanie increased her speed further and vanished around the nearest corner.

– That was Melanie, right?

Just the fact that she asked made him look closer at her. He replied with a confirming nod.

– Unless it was her long-lost twin or something, he said.

– I've actually wondered, seriously wondered about that lately, she joked.

She turned solemn in his arms.

– She looked at me, Lisbeth insisted. – I swear, she looked straight at me.

She imagined she saw those piercing, wicked eyes again and wondered if she had imagined them the first time as well.

– She wouldn't be the first that has walked in circles around us lately, he said lightly, striving not to joke, or joke too much, sensing her distress.

– She did seem… upset when I moved out of her apartment, but nothing warranting this.

– Maybe she received one of those phone calls, too, he said cautiously. – Perhaps they got to her in a way they didn't with us?

– You're sweet making up excuses for her, she said, – but I'm afraid that is unlikely, or at least only part of the cause, of her reasoning.

She looked at him with shivering lips, with wet eyes. He looked stunned at her once again.

– I haven't been totally upfront with you guys about her, she choked. – She has been hostile to you all the time and even want me to break contact with you altogether. It isn't totally unfeasible that *she* is behind the crank calls or at least is one of several parties there. I'm sorry!

She sought close to him, and he willingly held her.

– You don't have anything to be sorry about, he stressed, echoing her words earlier.

They smiled to each other again, found each other in the depth of their misty eyes.

– It is frustrating, she admitted. – We have no idea who is hassling us. They could be standing just a few steps away from us, and we wouldn't know.

And as if on cue, they glanced around them, making a closer study of people in their close proximity, making them anxious in the bargain.

– It's impossible to tell. He shook his head. – We may never know the reason either, whether or not there is one at all.

– Then why…

– Bullies tend to bully. He shrugged. – That's practically a law of nature.

She knew he wasn't done and just looked calmly at him.

– We know this is probably only the beginning, and we know at least one more thing: *They* won't stop because we won't stop. We will never give in to them or anyone, whether or not they care about what we do at all.

Lisbeth turned away a moment, before turning back.

– We won't, will we?

She smiled, a smile slowly widening to insane proportions.

One woman, in particular drew attention to herself, at least drew their attention. She was visibly anxious, upset. She walked back and forth on one small area of the sidewalk, taking a good look everywhere she turned.

– Have you seen this man? She showed a photo to people passing by. – He disappeared in a hole in the ground. I've been looking for him everywhere, but he's nowhere to be found.

She didn't look good, didn't look good at all. Her sore, swollen eyes were visible from far away. She was pale, unnaturally pale. Ted imagined she would grow fangs and attack people at any moment. He noticed how tense he was, and that Lisbeth was, too.

– Perhaps the wall fell on him, the woman cried. – The north wall of our house just crumbled and left a heap of brittle bricks. It seemed like decades had passed in a moment or something. Perhaps Phillip aged hundred years in a second, and there's nothing but dust left of him.

She ran off, howling like the lost soul she had become.

The two of them, studying people noticed that very few were actually unmoved by the general temperament in the streets, in the city as a whole. Everyone they cast a second glance looked at the world with flickering eyes.

It was summer and hot, very hot. Lisbeth rubbed her own neck absentmindedly. The added excitement made sweat soak her skin even more. The palm got wet immediately. She unbuttoned two buttons at the top of her blouse.

– The witch reveals her attributes. Let the strict pietist despair.

She saw how added interest darkened his eyes.

– It was more than a little crazy... wasn't it?

She whispered seductively.

He kissed her fiercely.

– I loved, love every fucking minute of it. Witchnight, yesterday, today, tomorrow…

He started touching her. She smiled some more, touching him, kissing him. He touched her breasts, pinching her nipples. Her eyes widened as she suddenly moaned in need, a shockingly loud sound attracting the attention of everyone nearby. He stopped, suddenly uncertain. They looked around them, at the people hurrying by on their way. She went for his groin then, touching his cock, and it turned hard, hard, hard in her hand. They looked around again, not at the people, but just looking.

There was a lamppost close to them, placed on a corner between two busy streets. She leaned her back against it, beckoning him to join her. He did so. They started fumbling with each other's belt. And suddenly, shockingly so, they stood there, half nude, exposed in the middle of the street. He grabbed her hips, turning her around, pushing her hard against the lamppost. She grabbed it with both her shaking hands and held on for dear life. He placed himself behind her, tight to her body. And then…

And then they *did* it, did it in the middle of the street, leaning towards a lamppost. One push, two, and they were rocking up and down, back and forth. Their faces lit up like fire, like shadow.

They weren't interrupted, but they could hear the background noises of snarls and condemnation from the passing crowd.

The surroundings seemed to blink out, dissolve for moments at the time, like a picture on TV without sufficient signal to keep broadcasting. The ground shook under their feet.

Lisbeth tried speaking several times, until she finally succeeded, shockingly loud.

– I can feel the earth move. *I can!* I CAN FEEL THE EARTH MOVE

Her head fell forward, hitting the post. His head fell on hers. They leaned on the lamppost, rocking up and down, as shakes of lust made reason fade in their eyes, as the surroundings dissolved around them into mist and Shadow.

They eventually ended up in the big bed in Ted's house. The bed was all they could see, their entire experience. Ted was on his back. Lisbeth rode him, and her movements were a wave going up and down, up and down.

And then there were the shadows, on the edge of their view, of the bed, before everything turned dark. They, on the bed, were the fire. They could see, could glimpse, in their fever, a few short lengths on either side, then there were the shadows, then there was nothing.

– I can feel them, she mumbled and gasped, – *feel* them here, with us.

The shadows rocked and danced around them, distinct one moment, indistinct the next, constantly shifting and burning, as their attention span waxed and waned. They became the shadows, shifting and burning like them, joining and whispering in the approaching twilight.

And it was day again. Lisbeth stood nude before the mirror, pushing her back against the wall. Eyes were wild, hair in complete disorder.

Ted stood nude in the hall. They looked at each other without hiding their interests, hiding anything. Her sex remained soaking wet, his still half rigid.

– I don't really feel naked, Lisbeth said. – In fact, I feel less naked then I've felt in my entire life.

– Me, too.

– I could feel it, you know, she said, – the ground moving under our feet…

They looked out the window, looked at John, Freya and Burt heading down the road, towards the house, towards them. Kissing and touching Lisbeth and Ted stumbled out in the hall, opening the door to greet them. Lisbeth greeted Burt with the kiss on the lips and undressed him there on the spot. John and Freya started undressing themselves, after just a short hesitation.

– Sex and Magick, Freya mumbled and shouted, mumbled and shouted.

The short day once more gave way to Night. The five of them moved on the bed, in tight, fiery embraces.

The five of them ran nude through the forest. The summer night never turned completely dark.

Abkasha stayed on all fours on the bed. She took John's cock in her mouth as Ted fucked her from behind. Burt and Lisbeth moved under her, as she moved on top of them.

They swam in the twilight, the summer twilight, illuminated by the rays of the full moon. Shouts and loud cries of delight filled the night air.

They floated on their back in the middle of the water, with as much distance as possible to all the four stretches of land far away.

– Am I imagining things, Burt said anxiously, – or is the house, the land around us… disappearing?

They turned a full circle, and it certainly looked that way. Fog and nothingness seemed to close off their vision to the different options of shore.

Burt made a few, hesitant strokes towards land, but was halted by Freya's soft, insistent touch.

– B-but we might have to stay out here forever.

– Relax. Enjoy it.

She pulled him with her, as she floated on her back to Ted's waiting embrace. He held her up while Burt entered her with his waistline below water and fucked her with sudden, hard thrusts.

– We *are* Forever, she said in a hollow, throaty voice.

The water turned agitated, started boiling as the excitement grew and they orgasmed in violent, explosive movement.

She smiled to him, caressing his cheek, giving him soft kisses, as they keep floating out there on the black water, drifting, not drifting through the pervasive summer twilight surrounding them.

2

Lisbeth stretched in bed with lazy, sensual moves, slowly sliding out of it, as the others woke up, happy and content. The men's spent cocks dangled between their thighs. She stretched, as they sunbathed in the garden, as they swam nude in broad daylight, as they walked around nude with impunity for all to see. Even if there was a considerable distance to the nearest neighbor, they could easily be seen… by those who would want to.

Freya danced a few steps away. The drowsy, sensual look still prevalent in her eyes. She seemed fresh, different, transformed.

– The wind blows all the time, now, she said with a wistful voice. – Can you sense it, how it's slowly, seemingly gaining strength, building momentum?

– Your words sound so pale compared to the vivid reality, madam, Lisbeth chuckled.

They had a shower together, all five of them, and it felt so pleasant, so beyond enjoyable. There were no walls, no boundaries between them anymore. Smiles kept painting their faces. They dried each other with slow, lazy movements. It didn't bring more arousal, as they had half expected.

– We aren't becoming a tribe, Abkasha said. – We already are!

Echoes of agreement met her statement. Happy laughter filled the room.

The phone rang. Lisbeth frowned as she glanced at it, as she saw the words UNKNOWN NUMBER and wondered if she should just ignore it.

After some more hesitation she grabbed it and answered.

– WHAT HAVE YOU DONE TO ME?

A voice loud enough to close out all other sounds shouted into Lisbeth's ear. She felt a deep chill run down her spine. There was only that single sentence. The connection broke immediately afterwards.

Lisbeth allowed the arm holding the phone to fall, until it hung useless by her hip.

Everyone had heard it. It had shaken their ears as well.

– Melanie called me… and hung up, she said slowly, unnecessary. – At least I believe that was Melanie. If so, it is definitely one more step in the progression of her erratic behavior lately. It both sounded and didn't sound like her. She sounded… totally out of it.

She welcomed their hugs. The touch of their skin felt warm enough to freeze in the suddenly so cold air.

They spent the day in and around the house, sunbathing, taking repeated strolls through the wild garden, swimming some more, floating in the warm, warm, practically steaming lake.

WHAT HAVE YOU DONE TO ME?

The distorted voice seemed to scream straight into Lisbeth's ears. She shook in shock.

The others couldn't avoid noticing. Ted was there in a whiff, as if he had already been there, right by her side.

– You didn't hear that? She whimpered. – You didn't hear shit?

He shook his head, unable to speak, or risk speaking. The others stayed silent as well.

– It was her again, she confirmed. – The voice was just as clear as on the phone, or if she was right here, as if her mouth was close, close to b-both my ears.

They watched as her mouth grew to a thin line and determination darkened her features.

– They won't stop because we won't stop, she said, gritting her teeth. – So be it!

She started swimming hard and fast. They had trouble keeping up with her at first, but they still kept swimming, far beyond exhaustion. During the afternoon, with the sun quickly boiling bodies chilled by their long presence in the water, they danced to hammering rhythms, until everyone had been soaked in sweat… and they returned to the water. Their appetite, already stoked by weeks of exercise on land and in water grew another notch. Food just faded away on the plate, and they added yet another helping.

Their bodies, mean and lean after those weeks of practically continuous exercise moved as easy as breath.

The day faded, so slowly that they hardly noticed.

They sat by the bonfire, chilling, enjoying the peace. The outside world didn't exist. It was just the five of them, and the dancing fire.

– It's so silent, Burt remarked, – that one can be tempted to believe there's nothing out there.

He sounded unusually pleased, even content.

– There's nothing beyond the fire, Lisbeth stated. – There's no one in the whole world but us.

They turned, turned their heads and attention in all directions, and except for the fire illuminating them and the ground in shades of orange and red, there was only the darkness.

– The house is probably there, where we think it is, about fifty… steps north, but we can't be truly certain, can we?

A howl penetrated the night then. Burt jumped in his tracks.

– What the HELL was that?

– It's the fucking cat, making her markers known to some unlucky bastard wandering too close,

The loud, hellish wail suddenly stopped, as if somehow someone cut it off.

– Seems like she met another really tough bastard this time…

Burt said.

They sat in silence, for a while, without speaking.

– The world is truly stranger than we can imagine, Freya said. – I always… suspected that, but now we know, don't we.

It wasn't a question, even though there was a distinct touch of doubt in her voice, one she couldn't hide.

– Scientists theorize that there is something in the Universe called dense or dark matter, something far more... energized than ordinary matter, John said eagerly, – A substantial, major, dominant part of the universe that can't be measured except by the effect it has on the visible and the measurable.

– I wish they would be honest just for once and call it Unknown Matter...

– But the point is, if there is something to it, John kept going, – that if they, for once, have stumbled on a «greater truth», one well known to the ancients... What if what we perceive as the shadow, a mere pale casting on the ground, an inferior image of our body, is the real world, the real us, and... this is the pale shadow in the moonlight?

Lisbeth giggled.

– I've heard about it. Some scientists are joking about it, and say that since we really know so little about existence, it might be completely different from what we imagine and currently perceive it to be. That it just as well could be comprised of giants moving among the tiny stars and stardust, as oblivious to it, as we would be to dust we're breathing in and out.

Freya nodded eagerly.

– There is a Storm coming, one born of Spirit, making that born of wind seem like nothing.

And now they heard no doubt in her voice.

– Oh, I doubt there's anything profound really, Burt said, returning to his cynical self. – The world is too big for something to truly affect it or affect it like that.

– But haven't you noticed? Ted said passionately. – There aren't just the storms, not merely the unseemly weather, but sudden, unlit fires, testy animals and… and…

– Holes in the very fabric of reality, Freya completed his reasoning, as if the two of them had never done anything but speaking in synch. – Can't you see it, staring at empty air, how it's empty no more?

Burt stared sullenly at them.

– Have we eaten today? Lisbeth asked abruptly. – Can any of you remember actually having eaten?

– We fed like Rhinos, actually, John grinned. – We had to, in order to compensate for our insane amount of exercise.

– Of course, we have eaten…

Burt commented with audible irritation in his voice.

Contradicting himself almost instantly.

– Haven't we?

– It was like we could just pour on with energy, Lisbeth whispered. – I've never felt this strong, this… powerful, as if there was an infinite amount of energy to draw upon.

– No matter how much we've devoured, Ted said quite relaxed. – There's still plenty where that came from. I do happen to have filled up the fridge before all this. Call it instinct or whatever you want. The fact remains. We have a wide selection of food and drinks at our disposal, and don't need to forage for days.

There was soft, almost silent applause, as he stood up, as they joined him. He caught glimpses of shiny faces, exalted expressions as they were all leaving the fire, to move within the confines of the house. They brought torches and were on their way.

Burt glanced around him, casting his stare everywhere.

– Do you guys feel like we're being watched?

– There is something out there, waiting for us, Abkasha noted.

– I feel it, you know, Burt remarked. – I feel it all the time. It's staring at us and it's making my skin *crawl.*

– It? Lisbeth said warily.

John put a hand on the other man's shoulder.

– There's only one way we may deal with it, my man…

He paused just a bit.

– Only one way we may deal with it… and that is to stare back.

– What did we do on Witchnight? Burt said anxiously. – What the fuck happened? What happened *really*?

– You won't get any detailed account from me, John replied. – I remember some of it, but so much happened. It's impossible to recall everything.

– I don't know, Lisbeth shook her head. – None of us do. I don't know what I did and how I did it, either. But the force present is obvious and growing, and we will inevitably gain better control, a better understanding… of it.

She hesitated.

Ted grabbed her hand softly, comfortingly.

– Lisbeth…

– I remember feeling a bit down because it was all more or less parlor tricks, ways for us to create the mood, the setting. The smoke, the speakers placed around among the trees and all. But…then I saw John, and I realized that none of us was operating the controls. I saw the shadow in the mist, and I looked closer at it, and it had my face, and that the garden, the very place had changed. No one had moved the lights. And certainly no one had planted new trees. It was the same place, but at the same time we were also another place, similar, but different. And now I feel it all the time. Something is… moving inside of me, undeniably. Am I making any sense?

Determination and anxiety mixed within her, making war, and there was no winner.

They listened to her words, and she was, too, and they saw, re-experienced Witchnight once more, in flashes and prolonged moments, seconds. Hooded figures walked out of the shadows, towards them, joining with them, as they danced, as they smiled. And there were pain and screams. And then the dance continued, that much more potent, more powerful, a slow, slow movement of low-keyed happiness.

A soft wind, hardly noticeable, not even a breeze began chipping away at the corner of the buildings in an unknown street. It was hardly visible at first. And then… then the wind grew to a storm. They pictured it in their mind, and didn't grow worried. The smile stayed on their lips. The joy lingered within.

And they returned to the quiet moment by the campfire they left only seconds earlier.

– What is it, John? Freya wondered.

John was clearly straining, searching for words, for meaning and confidence.

– Can't you feel it? We touched something. We did it… whatever we did. *We did it!*

And slowly, painfully, they started smiling.

They stayed in high spirits as they walked the short distance through the garden, the wild, wild garden they knew and experienced in an undeniable manner. It was evident in everyone's eyes and on everyone's faces, and body language, as they once more truly *looked* at each other.

Faces shifted and burned in shadow and mist. Ghostly flames danced on constantly moving skin. Dark eyes lit like stars, like the darkest, darkest fire.

Lisbeth called out with her loud voice, a voice penetrating the deep darkness in front of them.

– TAMMY, TAMMY, WHERE ARE YOU GIRL? COME FORTH AND GET YOUR JUST REWARD.

She held out a piece of cake. Nothing happened. No Tammy appeared.

– She hardly ever does that, Lisbeth mumbled, shaking her head in a sudden, deep uneasiness. – She stays with her human pride.

The house slowly grew visible to their straining eyes, there one moment, gone the next. They walked up the stone stairs emerging through their eyes, their aching feet, to the main entrance. Ted frowned, his lips visibly shivering. Everyone stopped, frozen in amber.

The black cat was nailed to the door. One nail for each paw. One punctuating its heart. It was dead, dead as the doornails penetrating its flesh. Its tongue hung out of its open mouth.

And on the wall the obvious perpetrators had left a written message.

Bright red paint on the green house-paint underneath, covering most of the wall:

Thou shall not suffer a Witch to live

They stood there, frozen on the spot, for a long time.

Someone was screaming somewhere. They heard it, but couldn't see the person doing it. It echoed through the forest, and the many gray buildings of the city. The prolonged moment of terror and pain twisting their insides and outsides lasted an eternity.

Ted spoke on the phone. That dawned slowly on the others. Their surroundings remained unreal to them.

– Yes, detective, I want you to see this. In fact, I insist on it.

All of them snapped pictures, with both cell phones and with Ted's SLR-camera.

They sat on the stairs, the cold concrete stairs, not speaking much. It took two hours until the cops arrived and during that time the five had only exchanged a few muted words.

They heard no sound of a car, nothing even sounding remotely like one. There was the sound of steps on the shingle growing louder. Two people dressed in trench coats appeared at the top of the slope, by the parking lot. They walked down to the house, clearly not in a hurry.

– They don't even bother to hide that they've been here the whole time, Lisbeth snarled.

The two stopped in front of them, looking at them with cruel eyes.

– I'm Lieutenant Edgar Gallagher, the male said brusquely. – This is my partner Sarah Knowles. What seems to be the trouble here?

Ted looked at Knowles. She looked at him, too, clearly puzzled. He shook

his head in confusion, in further confusion.
They showed them. The cat hung where someone had left it the moment that someone had killed it, butchered it. No one had touched the dead body.
– I'm a practicing Witch, Lieutenant, we all are. You know that, of course, but I wanted to make it clear, anyway, in order to avoid any possibility for misunderstandings.
– Speak for yourself, Burt barfed, still close to hysteria, even after all the time that had passed.
– I presume this constitutes a valid threat…
Ted said to the cops with a very audible ironic voice.
– That depends, Gallagher snorted. – We do have other things to do then chasing people pissed off at people flying around on broomsticks.
– What's that supposed to mean? John cried unusually agitated. – What constitutes a genuine threat in your eyes, Lieutenant? Would you rather have helped the perpetrators this time around? Perhaps you did!
They photographed the two and made no qualms or secret of it. Gallagher stared at them with his small sticky eyes, but made no threatening moves.
– Do we… know you? Freya wondered, unmoving and uncertain.
Gallagher didn't bother with replying to any of them. He photographed the stuff, then nodded to them and the two cops left. The brief, insane encounter ended.
– We've done our own photographing, Ted called after them.
Knowles had, when the car parked at the gate started and drove off, not uttered a single word.

3

Ted and Lisbeth had a very frustrating conversation with the desk sergeant at the police headquarters. He looked completely indifferent to their plight. Even though they had expected a brushoff, the level of it surprised them and the sense of incredulity lingered.
– I'm telling you. We had a visit from two detectives last night, Lieutenants Gallagher and Knowles.
– Nothing has been filed, the desk sergeant remarked, very full of himself.
– They were also part of the crew you sent to us prior to the festivities, Lisbeth pointed out with badly concealed sarcasm.
Ted glanced at her.
– Nothing has been filed…
The desk sergeant repeated, not bothering to hide his glee.
– We get you, Ted spat. – We get you loud and clear!

He left copies of their own photos from yesterday, including those of the detectives, a look of utter disgust clearly conveyed to the desk sergeant.

The look of pain as he glimpsed the representation of Tammy's unkind fate was more than evident. Lisbeth touched his arm and held his hand in an attempt to comfort him.

Frustration, anger and fear evident in their every move, they left the police station.

– Well, we can't really say that was unexpected, Ted said flamboyant, cocky.

– No, that wasn't unexpected at all.

– You didn't tell me about the two of them being present at the… at the posse.

– You had more than enough to deal with and I wasn't certain it was significant… at first.

He turned towards her, noticing the pale skin, covered in cold sweat.

– John is right, she said, speaking with a voice akin to a whisper. – We did touch something. And now we pay the price. I feel it like a ball stuck in my throat, something inside, something malevolent *moving* inside me. Can't you feel it? The world is rejecting us, casting us *out*.

He stared at her with concern in his eyes.

They walked down the street, wandering aimlessly. There was movement all around them, but it didn't seem to touch them. They heard it then, the flapping of wings. For some reason, that added to their anxiety. A shadow covered them. They looked up and could confirm what they already knew: No clouds drifted close to the sun, not even close. There was a vast area on all sides of the glowing disk completely free of clouds. The scenery of the street looked deeply disturbing to them. The nearest building seemed to… seemed to break down before their eyes. One brick fell off, then another. Bricks kept falling off, hitting the sidewalk in clouds of dust. A tree grew in the middle of the road. They could practically see how it grew. The slow breeze whispered like banshees. People walked through the street with bowed heads and anxious eyes.

A man rushed out of an alley with a pained and scared look on his face. He stared at the ground as he walked away with quick steps, but they could still see his eyes. They hesitated a bit, before stepping forward. Their feet moved, as they headed for the alley, and there, just where the long dark street began, they stopped.

There were a lot of dead birds on the ground, a lot of other birds in the air. The live ones were very energetic and hacked away at the dead birds, and blood danced in the air. Feathers danced, kept afloat by the flapping wings. The birds' eyes were all the same, dead like fisheyes, the sight of them enhanced to insane proportions in the humans' eyes. It was a horrible, beyond horrible sight.

The two of them crouched there, supporting each other in order to keep themselves from falling. Vomit flowed from their mouths, and it kept doing so, until they stood there totally empty and drained, and the blood and the tears flowed from their eyes in equal measure.

Chapter Five

Days passed. Perhaps two, perhaps many. They couldn't tell. Clouds rushed across the sky and couldn't be counted.

Lisbeth was visibly straining while climbing the stairs. She was sweating, but there was more than that ailing her. Her tie was loose. Her appearance was far from her usual flawless execution. The shirt had wrinkles and she had black bags under her eyes.

Ted sat at the top of the stairs, waiting for her. He wore something resembling hippy-clothes and the smile was in place at the corner of his mouth, but the black bags under his eyes were as pronounced as her own, and his flaky appearance no better.

– You, too, huh? Lisbeth said cheerfully.

– You, too, huh? Ted said cheerfully.

Ted shrugged.

– It's no big deal. I've wanted to quit on my own for a long while.

Lisbeth laughed loud and strained, completely out of character. He couldn't help but noticing the bitter taint.

– You sound like someone who has quit smoking.

She looked down, not at him, while fumbling for the keys in her purse.

– It really made Reality come crashing down on us, she said subdued.

He didn't comment on her words, except by silence.

She opened the door. The door to her apartment swung open.

In flashes she heard police sirens, saw red and blue lights, even if there were none. Not the other night. Here, in the city, there were many simultaneously. It made her cringe in slow, dull terror.

She heard Ted' voice, reexperienced the prolonged horror.

– We've done our own photographing.

That had sounded so brave then. Now, it just sounded cocky and silly.

A shadow figure levitated high above the ground. The city below was disintegrating, bathing in the figure's terrible energies. There was no hesitation, no mercy, as it destroyed the city below, as it moved on to the next and the next… as civilization itself died beneath its heel.

An echo, gaining strength and reality.

Lisbeth headed directly for the bathroom and threw up almost immediately. She didn't reach the toilet quite in time and a lot of the half-digested food landed on the floor. A look of panic in her eyes, she reached for the pregnancy test bottle.

Ted stood in the doorway. She froze, looking at him in despair.

– I've thrown up several times today, he told her dully. – The others have, too. I called you all day, but didn't get any reply from you.

She recalled the shrill ringing tone of her phone. It had looked like a monster to her. She had kept her distance.

Her boss had entered her office, taken one look at her sitting there, with saliva flowing from her slack mouth and told her she was fired.

– I want you gone in an hour, he grinned wickedly. – Don't you dare expect any recommendation letter.

She had offered no protest whatsoever, just accepted it with the same indifference she was unable to shake off.

– Don't you see what's happened? She said enraged, frightened. – We've been cast out of the world. Something has e-entered us. First it took Freya, and then through her, the rest of us. We've sought too hard and too far.

He didn't voice any reply. His expression spoke volumes.

She rushed into the bathroom. Her hands moved by themselves, removing the clothes clinging to the sweaty skin. She showered, pouring water on the body, scrubbing it, scrubbing it, scrubbing it.

Afterwards, she was very particular in her choosing of clothes. She took her time. And when through, she was like transformed.

– You look like a Gypsy, he marveled.

And she was ecstatic to hear happiness in his voice, one strained but there.

She rotated her body one single time before him.

– Thank you, good sir.

She walked to him, turning hesitant the last few steps. They embraced and held on to the other, visibly shaking.

– Poor Tammy. She was so… so loving, so… defiant.

He nodded absentmindedly, his eyes like open wounds.

– Do you think that was why they t-took her? They didn't like her independence, her spirited approach to life?

Ted rubbed her head.

– The stuff with the cat was bad, but we'll get through it. We will not give the bastards the satisfaction of it getting to us.

She turned rigid in his arms.

– It isn't the cat, you *know* that.

He turned rigid, too.

She looked up at him, as he looked away.

– You did dream, didn't you?

– I don't think dream, dreams are the… the correct word for it…

He spoke with a beyond strained voice.

Reality faded around them.

There was mist, there was ground, and more.

The voice from elsewhere shouted in the wilderness.

– VISIONS! Prophetic, invasive visions of carnage and destruction, one single, powerful image of a shadow figure floating above the ground, of cities, civilization utterly vanquished.

He stood before the mirror, shaking. Eyes were swollen. He turned towards the toilet. It was full of half-digested food. He threw up again, again and again, until there was nothing more to throw up. He stayed there on his knees, with his head into the bowl.

He kissed her, drowning in her, drowning of desperate need.

She shook him off, despair visible in her expression.

– No, Ted. No.

Ted looked at her with eyes like open wounds.

– But why…

His outstretched hand fell, fell down.

– Don't you get it? I've been violated, we all have. Damn it, Ted, I feel like I've been r-raped.

That stopped him and he left her, there, on the spot. She was alone. She sat down then, right on the spot, on the floor. Despairing, heart-wrenching sobs rose from the broken figure.

She wandered aimlessly through the city. Her face stayed dry. The makeup was meticulously done, a bit overdone perhaps. She meticulously walked on green light, staying still, absolutely still on red light, even when there were no cars, when other people rushed across the street, she stayed, waiting for the green light.

She didn't have any destination in mind. She sat on a bench in the park for a while, before moving on, wandering aimlessly through the city.

In a display window for a television store, there were lots of displayed TV-monitors. Picture and sound were on. She could easily hear what it said.

– Bad weather and other natural disasters continue to worsen on a planetary scale, the calm, not so calm TV-lady reported. – Reports are pouring in worldwide about floods, storms, earthquakes and volcanic eruptions said to be the worst in recorded human history. Scientists are baffled over why this is happening now, but says that natural variations can account for a lot of…

Lisbeth returned to the park, sat down on the same bench. She looked at her watch. It showed her nothing, except fog and… nothing.

Freya joined her, quietly. Her eyes were swollen, too. She was also sweating, sweating hard. Neither one of them spoke for a while.

– The visions are like sparks behind the eyes. Closing the eyes is completely *useless*. They're not coming all the time, but they can come at any time, unbidden, unavoidable.

– I've had it like that for weeks, Freya noted. – I've had it since early childhood, but it's growing, intensifying. The queasiness, the sickness, that's new, though.

Lisbeth turned towards her, then.

– You… you've had it since early childhood? Why haven't you ever said anything?

Freya shifted uncomfortably on the bench.

Lisbeth rubbed the palm back and forth on her forehead.

– *I* have had it since early childhood, too. I remember that I did want to talk about it. But mother got so strange then. And during the following night, I dreamed horrible dreams, of myself being burned as a w-witch during the middle ages. Hell, I can even remember Ted telling me something similar. He was at least attempting to do so, but I cut him off, as others did to me. How could I… forget this? Now, it's like a floodgate being opened, being opened wide.

– I can see The Abyss, Abkasha said with her distant expression. – I realize now that I've always been able to see it, but never so clearly, never such a detailed texture.

Lisbeth was frozen in place, there on the bench.

– There isn't only one life. Jesus, I can see them, like strings on an eternal chain. It's so crazy, so beyond insane.

– You know… Freya said hesitantly. – If we *are* being… violated, it isn't just us, but the boys, too, in equal measure.

She took Lisbeth's hand.

– But I can't…

Lisbeth said.

Then, she brightened, brightened like the sun.

– I *can* feel them, she cried exalted. – I can even… see them, see where they are. Ted is where I left him. He stands by the window, looking out. Burt has closed himself off in his apartment. He's low on food. He needs to forage, go and buy some dinner or food, any food, but he's putting it off. He has been putting it off for days and his fridge is empty. And John, being John, is at a disco. He doesn't think much, doesn't do much, except dancing.

Burt walked towards the door. He stopped and turned back, returning to the living room, like he had done numerous times the last few days.

– Very good, Freya applauded, – you might become a decent witch, yet…

Lisbeth's response was agitated, almost enraged.

– So, you don't think that's what's happening then? How can it not be?

How is it *possible* to feel like… this, without it being bad?

– I don't know, okay… Freya replied in despair. – I don't know. I do think there's someone… something… s-stalking us, but that's just one side of it. I'm… I'm convinced we're… Changing, changing within, and Change will always bring pain.

They were both naked in their sore eyes as they looked subdued at the other.

Silence ruled them. They couldn't shake it off, shake off the wet paper clinging to them, keeping them from breathing.

A police van stopped right by them, by way of screaming brakes. Two cops rushed out. They recognized the cop they had met frequently the last few weeks… and impossibly enough, the forest ranger.

– Please come with us, the man spat.

They grabbed the two women on the bench unceremoniously, dragging them off, without further explanation.

– What is this? Lisbeth protested. – What are you *doing?*

– You don't speak, the forest ranger turned cop snarled. – You come with us, without protest… or you'll be *sorry.*

Whimpering they relented, and didn't protest the rough treatment, as they were being led away, being pushed into the back of the exhaust-breathing monster of a van. Lisbeth puked the instant the cop pushed the gas pedal making the car move, sullying herself and most of the seat.

– You're seriously messed up, aren't ya? You poor thing.

Lisbeth started crying then. Huge, heartbreaking sobs. And the world faded to nothing around her.

Lisbeth sat alone in the interrogation room, in one of two chairs. The other one stood at the other side of the simple table. There were sounds outside, muted, distant. The room wasn't really that hot, but she was sweating, to the point of her hair being wet and sticky. She blinked and the detectives Gallagher and Knowles were in the room with her. Knowles sat, Gallagher stood. He leaned over her, leering like a clown in a circus, like a skull devoid of flesh. She could see it, shrinking from him in horror.

Knowles put a glass of water in front of her. She grabbed it with both hands, lifting it to her lips and drank greedily.

– You get to clean up okay? The woman said, somewhat sympathetic.

Lisbeth nodded once, sniffing.

– Very good.

The policewoman didn't take her eyes off her.

– You don't look okay, though, she said after a distinctive break. – In fact, you look downright sick.

– I'm okay, Lisbeth sniffed. – It's just a bit of nausea, that's all. Look, what's this about? Do I need a lawyer or what?

Gallagher kept leering at her.

– Why do you think you do? You don't happen to have anything to hide, now, do you?

Knowles held up a hand, stopping Gallagher from continuing, stopping Lisbeth from replying, softening her angry stare.

Knowles nodded to Gallagher. He nodded, too. He opened a briefcase, pulling a pile of papers from it, giving it to Knowles. She selected a few photos from the pile, and put one in front of Lisbeth. Lisbeth stared at it blindly for a long time, before looking at Knowles again.

– I know, Knowles said. – Makes cold run down your spine, doesn't it?

It was a photograph of a man nailed to a wall. His entire midsection was cut open.

– P-paul? Lisbeth cried incredulous, fearful.

In another room Freya sat shaking, under the two policemen's scrutinizing glare.

– So, what are you doing here, anyway? She said casually to the forest ranger.

– I've changed jobs, the man replied. – Nothing to it. I felt my… services were more needed at the metropolitan police. These are troubling times, young lady, and you better watch yourself.

He looked honest, sincere on the surface, but beneath that veneer of benevolent anger, the two girls glimpsed a creature with twisted features making them cringe in discomfort and a terror they could hardly conceal.

Lisbeth's eyes stayed glued to the photograph. The man was dead, dead and white, bled empty. On the wall behind him was drawn a pentacle.

– I see you know this man, Knowles noted. – We suspected as much.

Lisbeth nodded numb and dull.

– He was in fact present at your «party» on the thirtieth the previous month, wasn't he?

Lisbeth nodded again, mute and pale, seeing him around the fire, seeing her friend gutted like a fish, nothing remaining but skin and bones, an empty shell.

– We found the cat's hair on all of you, Gallagher informed her with a cruel grin. – On your clothes and in your hair. Everywhere on you.

– Of course. you did, Lisbeth responded. – We've all been petting her regularly for years.

– You suffer from memory lapses, don't you, Lisbeth? Knowles said softly.

– No, I'm not. Absolutely not.

Lisbeth and Ted were in bed, snuggling relaxed, and in an over the top good mood.

– Last night was *wild*, she said. – I can't even remember half of what happened…

– First you did the tryout on the cat, Gallagher accused her. – Then, you graduated to heavier stuff.

Lisbeth looked at him like she didn't see him at all.

– That's… preposterous, and absolutely wrong. You hear me. Wrong! And cruel. Cruel beyond imagining. Where do you people *get off?*

They scrutinized her in silence. She glared back at them, even if her lower lip was shaking.

– That will be all for now, Miss Rowan, Gallagher said formally. – We will keep in touch.

Freya waited for her outside, patiently sitting in Lotus position on a bench, slowly opening her eyes, standing up with a strained look in her eyes.

– They're just attempting to soften us up. I've experienced such shit for years. Don't worry about it.

– But *why?*

Freya smiled softly.

– I've told you before, honey. There doesn't have to be a reason. They get their kicks doing it.

The two of them removed themselves from the area. They walked up and down streets for a while.

– It seems so… unreal, all of this, Lisbeth said.

– What does? Freya wondered, somewhat good humored.

– These streets, everything we've experienced lately, all of the above. I don't know.

They ended up in the park again. It didn't seem that much darker than during their visit earlier in the day. There was still twilight.

They sat there, shaking, shaking hard.

– I want to get a grip, Lisbeth said passionately, desperately. – *I want to!*

– We've all had our moments of doubt and pain, Freya stated. – It's time to embrace them, not run away.

Lisbeth nodded. She was nodding slowly, determined, concentration written in her face, as she slowly stopped shaking.

She lifted her hand, her hand turning to mist and shadow.

Two pair of eyes widened, in amazement, in fear.

– Do it again, Freya besieged her. – *Please.*

And Lisbeth the Witch did. It took hardly any effort at all. It was as if her entire hand disappeared into the air, but still remained visible.

They rose, slowly smiling as they stretched their bodies, stretching their arms. Their hands panned the air. And in the air, there were wisps of smoke, of shadow.

They embraced each other, shaking violently in their tracks.

Eventually they headed back to her apartment. Not a word was spoken, but they were still communicating, with hands and movements, and facial expressions.

Melanie walked towards them. The smile was in place, as she approached them, as they had almost reached the apartment. She embraced Lisbeth. Lisbeth stiffened in her arms. She pulled free. Melanie's smile faded.

– I heard, she said softly.

– You… heard? Lisbeth said incredulous, baffled and spooked, everything simultaneously.

– I most certainly did, and thought I should offer my sympathies and humble help. I want you to move back in, return to the Coven.

Lisbeth looked at Melanie as if she wasn't quite right in the head.

– Surely, you won't hold that one phone call the other day against me? Melanie added hastily.

– Hold it against you? Lisbeth practically echoed.

She turned to Freya.

– C'mon, let's leave.

– That seems like a great idea, Freya agreed.

Lisbeth turned to a foaming Melanie.

– I will have to pass on your kind offer, she said, grinning wide. – We can do without the added drama you bring to the table.

– What about a visit then? Melanie said quickly. – Come and say hello to the guys and all?

Lisbeth looked up at her apartment. She couldn't see Ted in the window, but she could still see him moving around inside.

– Thank you, she relented, wondering if she made a grave mistake, – we would love to come home with you for a visit.

– We would, thank you, Freya said with something that looked very much like a sincere smile.

Melanie looked hesitantly at Freya.

– … okay.

So, the two of them started walking and Melanie tripped in their tracks.

The three of them walked in silence, not exchanging more than a few syllables on their trip back to Melanie's «institute».

Lisbeth and Freya noticed the moment they reached the building how quiet the place had become. The lack of activity was striking. An effect only growing in potency when they stepped inside.

They walked through the door in the large hall, passing by the bedrooms and proceeded to walk up the stairs. Melanie's apartment was big. It covered an entire floor of an old office building, rebuilt to fit her needs. Members of her coven waited for them there. There were only seven of them, five girls and two boys.

– Hi, everyone, Lisbeth waved, sounding and appearing more than a little over the top cheerful.

One girl and one boy came forward to greet her. The others held back.

– Greetings, Sister, are you here to stay?

Lisbeth shook her head.

– No, I can't stay. I've moved so much forward lately and we stood still so long here.

The mood darkened visibly, in all the faces before her.

– Why don't you tell us about it? The boy asked pleasantly.

– Yes, why don't you, Melanie said pointedly.

A voice sounded in Freya's head.

– *She's a piece of art, isn't she…*

Freya stared at Lisbeth, wide-eyed.

Lisbeth danced to one table, the one by the huge window. They could see the city stretch on forever through that window. She jumped up on the table, pausing a bit, looking at them all, before sitting down in the Lotus position, her legs crossed, her knees pointing ninety degrees to each side.

She looked at the floor below her, at four, no five small balls of different color. Suddenly she giggled like a little girl, before her face calmed once more, reaching an almost impassive state.

– I can see so much, you know… I can still not see everything and don't think I ever will, but everything is so much clearer now. It's true that being born hurts. I can attest to that. The last few days haven't exactly been pleasant, but the struggle brings great rewards.

She rocked back and forth on the table, while humming to a song.

– I can see us all. I can see us among the stars, sleeping by a fire. We look very much like us, but aren't quite like us. We're us, but different. I can see us all. Me, Abkasha, Edward, Bertram and John. And there are others.
There is an existence beyond this one, and it is vast beyond imagining.

There was a wind, coming from no window, no open door (all the doors and windows were closed tight).

– I can see Ted leaving my apartment. I can see Bertram leaving his apartment. His steps are very astute, very determined. John is at a disco. I think the electricity is gone, but there is still light. That bothers the others in that creepy semidarkness, but doesn't bother him at all.

She looked at them all with huge, luminous eyes.

One of the girls, not the same as earlier giggled and spoke up.

– Do you know the name of the disco?

Someone hushed her up.

– No, for some reason that is hidden for me.

– You shouldn't expect miracles, Rachel, Lisbeth, the other Lisbeth said.

– How do you know my name? We've never met before.

– I know *everything*…

The boy spoke to Rachel with contempt in his voice.

– Stupid cow. Can't you see through such an obvious ruse?

Melanie took a step forward. She was suddenly pale, with black shadows crossing her face, the pretense of benevolence gone in a whiff.

– So why is it that you are chosen to this honor? Are ya really such a special girl, are ya?

Lisbeth froze in shock, then, but only for a moment.

– I don't know. Perhaps it's because I'm *open.* Nobody has chosen me, though, I've chosen myself. This much I know. I've opened up, not so much to outside forces as to the forces within myself. That is what a Witch does; bringing what's on the inside to the outside.

Freya turned her head to the door. It was open. She turned her attention to the windows. They were open. Every door, all the way out, every window in the entire building, all the floodgates there were, were open. Her face changed from one painted with dull features to one glowing with excitement and ecstasy.

– Red ball, Lisbeth began.

– What? Melanie said perplexed.

The red ball on the floor started rolling, back and forth, back and forth.

– Green ball. Lisbeth called.

The green ball on the floor suddenly moved by itself, seemingly playing, interacting with the red.

Lisbeth panned her open hands in the air, closing them into fists, then choosing a third option and a fourth and a fifth and a sixth… She brought them together… and they started glowing. The air itself, in their immediate vicinity shimmered in a weird glow. The five balls on the floor, the red, green, yellow, blue and black were vanishing… into thin air. And into thin air they reappeared, between the hands of the Witch, hands with fingers stretched like claws.

And then it was as if the entire creature that was Lisbeth changed, as if she turned to Shadow. The effect was quite pronounced and phenomenal, indisputable. There was a collective gasp, as the dark figure started speaking, as its hollow voice thundered in their ears.

– «Human beings are deep wells of energy, immense reservoirs of force, the force of Life determined to subdue matter».

The balls disappeared. The shimmer in the air died. The balls reappeared on the floor on the spot they had previously occupied.

It was over. For now.

Lisbeth (the other Lisbeth with the hollow voice) spoke.

– What you just saw was just something comparable to a parlor trick, a minor outward manifestation of a much greater force.

The room stayed silent.

– There will be another Witchnight in the Wild Garden tomorrow night, Freya said cheerfully. – There will be Magick and there will be Life. Everybody present is cordially invited.

Most of them gathered around the two of them and especially around Lisbeth, and when the two of them left shortly afterwards, Melanie stood there with her fists closed, everybody filing by her, until she was alone in the room and she sank to the floor, staying there without moving.

2

Freya sat on the couch in Lisbeth's apartment with Lisbeth and the others. In flashes of fire she saw Ted, John and Burt. They all brought guests. They did, too.

She watched Burt approaching two girls with an insane grin on his lower face.

– Hi, girls…

They should have been scared or at least worried, but they were not.

– I would just like to tell you that you're cordially invited to an occult evening tomorrow night.

They looked at him with excitement in their wide eyes.

There was knocking on the door. Lisbeth and Freya went to it, opening it. Outside stood Ted, John and Burt, accompanied by giggling boys and girls, of startling dancing shadows.

Lisbeth looked at Ted, at his pale and drawn, but happy face. Slowly she started smiling herself, going to him, kissing him on the lips, embracing him.

She found herself outside at night, walking the familiar streets, walking alone. It dawned on her yet again that her friends and coven-members didn't accompany her. She frowned, but kept moving forward, driven, pulled by notions she didn't understand. There were no people outside tonight. But she could hear steps, the sound of shoes against the tarmac. She could hear it clearly. Her feet started moving faster. She saw it as she looked down for a moment, before turning her head, and looking back towards the dark alley she just exited. And as she started running, started fleeing she saw it, saw the creature stalking her. It resembled a human being, strangely disjointed, puss and rot seemingly flowing freely from the body, the features unrecognizable.

She ran. The city shook around her. She ran as she had never run before, but the pursuer was gaining on her, slowly but surely. In flashes she saw herself and her friends out by the Gate of Madness at dawn. They all looked different, even though they stayed the same. But everybody looked so wild, dressed in skin, waving weapons like savages on a hunt, like she did, like she did herself. She took a wrong turn into a dark alley, realizing startled that it was the same dark alley she had left earlier, and there was nowhere left to run. There were only smooth walls everywhere. The stalker attacked her with a nail in one hand and a huge butcher knife in another, leering and with a tongue hanging from the mouth like a panting dog. She pushed herself against the wall, exhausted and frozen in fear. She could feel her own heart beating, beating, feel the blood boiling in her veins. And as the monster charged her, she raised a hand in front of her, and it was as if a giant, invisible hand grabbed the monster and pulled it into the air, shaking it apart, until nothing but rags and bones remained. It had shrunk, dissolved and she had grown and solidified and she felt power beyond power surging through her. She was able to look at herself from the outside, look at the giant, human-like Shadow she had become. One towering over the buildings, towering over the city itself, exalting and terrifying. Pale lighting and mist emanated from her, dissolving the buildings in front of her to nothing.

And then she woke up screaming.

The scream itself started that, but once the process had begun the very air continued changing. The room vanished around her, becoming a forest, a huge, fabulous forest, one making her chuckle in wild, euphoric joy and the scream only lingered within like an unimportant froth on a wave on the infinite mighty ocean.

Lisbeth and Ted sat on a green bench in the park. There were sounds from the city around them, but muted, distant.

They held hands, both cheerful and apprehensive. Both felt appropriate, reasonable, felt right.

From their position on the green, green bench, they could look out of the park and at the street. What they saw, sensed there filled them with apprehension, an expectation that couldn't be measured. The sounds of the city turned to the usual noise, imposing itself on them with its imagery and sensations.

The queue of cars had stopped moving forward, stopped moving completely. This wasn't the rush hour. They didn't see that many cars, but those they saw had stopped moving. Engines coughed and struggled and died as they watched. A spoiler fell off the chassis, hitting the street with a dull sound.

Several of the drivers left the cars and started wandering aimlessly back and forth in the street, confusion riddling them like the worst possible anguish. Ted recognized Frank as one of them.

– What's happening? Frank asked the closest man, asked everyone present in the street. – What's HAPPENING?

He didn't quite look like himself, but like a facsimile, a twisted mirror image of the man he had once been.

The others shouted in a despair equal to his, and had no answers for him.

One of the cars collapsed altogether, crumbling to a heap of spare parts in mere seconds, or something very close to that effect. Everybody stopped and stared, and couldn't tear their attention off the ruined vehicle. They kept staring with dull, wet eyes.

– People are losing it, Ted said. – They can't deal with a world coming apart at the seams.

– But we can, she said excited. – Even though we struggled a bit initially, we have recovered from that, now, and are ready to take on the world on our own terms.

He looked stunned at her as he realized the truth of her words, of the passion she breathed and moved. He watched as Frank lost it completely and howled like a beast and ran off without direction and any destination in mind.

The two of them moved on. The next street the chaos and disorder weren't that bad, but more than pronounced enough to create the same anxiety and near-panic in people's eyes. There were small signs of discord everywhere they walked. A flower growing by the wayside seemed to be laughing. Ted was pretty much convinced that the insane, twisted sound originated with that tiny biomass seemingly drowning in the concrete.

They stopped at the beginning of another street, frowning, not certain why.

– Look at the museum, she said.

She pointed at a large, square building ahead. He saw what she saw the moment he focused on it. Something distinct separated it from the rest of the structures in the street, a glow that had nothing to do with the light of the sun or anything. They walked there without exchanging glances or voice any agreement, filled with urgency. The walls glowed stronger the closer they came.

They headed up the marble stairs to the museum. It was quite the stretch, quite the number of stairs and steep climb, but they didn't breathe any faster at the top. They couldn't remember actually entering the building, but the walk through it appeared fairly clear in their feverish minds. Something, a specific place within the museum called to them with what was first a muddled, then increasingly distinct voice. They stopped by an entrance reaching all the way to the tall ceiling. A sign, an exhibition glared at them.

THE MARCH OF CIVILIZATION

They fervently looked around, in order to see if more people noticed the river of blood flowing from the sign, bathing the wall, the floor and splashing shoes, but everybody walked around and enjoyed themselves, seemingly enjoyed themselves.

The various exhibitions kept howling at them in silence, loud and clear.

– I can hear it, hear the march, the pain, the blood, the horror, she said with the strange, ghostly voice of the other Lisbeth.

He cocked his head, and he could hear it, too.

They passed the Greek exhibition, the Roman, the German, The American. A man stood on a plain somewhere, with a scalp in his hands, a tiny dark-haired scalp, that of a child.

– It's the egg that becomes lice, he shouted in triumph. – ONLY A DEAD INDIAN IS A GOOD INDIAN.

– I can hear the choir, Lisbeth whimpered, – the cries from the marching soldiers as they're subduing everything in their path, subduing the land itself. And the closer to the present we come, the louder the cry grows, until it is all we can hear. I can see myself poisoned beyond recovery, more dead than alive, stumbling through a landscape of ruins and garbage. I've walked for days but there's no green in sight, only this gray, toxic wasteland without end.

Ted had, at some point started moving his lips, synchronized them with hers, and during the last few sentences he spoke as much, if not more than she did.

A chill, an even stronger chill passed through them.

Knowles stood there, right in front of them, suddenly, shockingly.

– You don't *know* what's going on, do you? You don't have the faintest idea.

– What the fuck are you talking about? Ted responded, unable to hide his irritation.

– Come with me, and I'll show you.

Ted and Lisbeth exchanged glances. They both shrugged, unable to stay the uncertainty they felt, the one gnawing at their bones and tails.

As if in a daze they followed the detective to the library section. A slight, almost unseen wave of her hand, and they followed her.

They sat there, writhing on the unpleasant stools. She placed drawings on the table in front of them, images turning their blood cold.

– These are the police drawings made from dreams. Dreams related by members of the Cult of the Phoenix… A cult of witches, mass-murderers exposed five years ago. Their modus operandi was the nailing of people to the wall, gutting them like pigs are gutted, exactly the way your friend Paul was killed. They were all executed, roasted in the chair for their horrible crimes. But now… now someone seems to have picked up on their cue… whatever that is.

The two of them looked in horror at the images, black and white drawings that seemed to come to life, gain color, texture and life, like a movie. What they saw was the creature from their dreams, the destroyer, the destroyer of worlds.

– Know that I've been investigating psychic phenomena for decades. I know more about it then you've forgotten, know what disasters may come out of a bit of dabbling.

They looked at her with new eyes and a shame they couldn't stop feeling.

– Then, why didn't you *say* something? Lisbeth said with a weak voice.

– You know as well as I do that you don't speak openly about such things, Knowles said pleasantly. – Not without being burned. The important thing is that I can help you, help you to free yourself from the demonic forces ravaging you.

Doubt riddled the youths, visibly. Knowles smiled encouragingly, taking Ted's arm. His entire body turned rigid then. Lisbeth saw something then. She saw a tiny worm crawl from Knowles' ear.

– Get AWAY from me, Ted shouted in panic and disgust.

He was shaking, and the entire museum seemed to shake, too. He pulled his arm free. Knowles staggered backwards, as if being pushed.

The Lieutenant kept smiling. Lisbeth shuddered, as she spotted the hiss beneath the pleasant exterior.

– Be reasonable, Knowles urged them, as if speaking to children.

– That's what people like you always say to people like us, isn't it? Lisbeth spat at her. – Is slavery, is willful destruction reasonable? I don't think so. You don't have any power over us. Not anymore.

– But our power, on the other hand is growing, so you beware, Ted said. – We *are* Power.

– You'll burn in Hell, the detective hissed. – You'll all burn in Hell.

And she turned and left. And it was as if she was turning transparent as she walked away, as if she was becoming one with the building itself.

Ted clutched his numb arm, as pain ravaged his face, as he could slowly move it again.

– I know her, he mumbled. – I *know* her. She has been in my dreams forever. I knew her the very first moment we met.

They stumbled towards the exit. The short walk seemed to last an eternity. Lisbeth looked up at the ceiling with a glaring, haunted look in her face.

– This place makes me sick.

They couldn't recall leaving the museum, but recalled with clarity the streets outside, the sight of the marble stairs leading down to the sidewalk, how the shiny material seemed to crumble and become sullied with dirt from one prolonged moment to the next.

The Café on the corner was quiet. There was music or a facsimile thereof, but it didn't touch them. They were alone in the room. There had been people there. Now, they were gone.

– She is… trustworthy when you first meet her. She reminds me of you, you know...

– Thank you, he responded with a distinct ironic taint.

Indignant, she gave him a jolt in the ribs, so hard it made him gasp.

– You want to… to obey her, she said, – obey her slightest whim… Then… suddenly it was as if a fog was lifted from my mind, and I could see her for what she is… whatever that is. I have a picture in my mind, of us being led away with a silly grin dominating our faces, and we believe everything she sells us, and she's destroying us bit by bit, until there is nothing left.

– It is as if a vast, new reality of an Abyss has opened up below us, he marveled.

– Things are happening so fast, so furious, she said, clearly excited. – It is as if the world may change from one second to the next…

– I know what you mean…

They looked at each other. Every doubt they ever had was visible in their features.

– And it's *great.*

She kissed Ted hungrily on the lips.

And he relaxed, looking at her with a somewhat peaceful look in his eyes.

– We are more now, he stated, – more than we've ever been.

– And this is just the beginning.

Bricks began falling from the museum. It was as if the very building was crumbling before their eyes. Another nearby had already fallen. Only ruins remained. It caused remarkably small ripples in their thoughts. They looked at each other, searching themselves for shock, dismay or anything similar, but found none and turned away, leaving it all behind.

And they walked into the emerging night, fading into shadows. And the streets gave way to wilderness. They spotted no houses, no houses anywhere. Trees grew around them, not exactly fast, but still with a speed making them gasp impressed. It felt real, true, in spite of its obvious unreality. They had seen a lot of that recently, and it didn't impress them, didn't scare them, at least not enough to make them turn back.

Two people reached the glen, the beginning of a forest they couldn't see the end of. And then they stopped. The stench of growth ripped their nostrils. The sound of birds echoed in their ears. Sight, sound and smell made them smile in anticipation. They were There.

Chapter Six

Lisbeth and Ted stepped into the forest.

They five of them sat around the round table in Ted's house.

– What did we do on Witchnight? Burt cried. – What happened?

– I don't know, Burt, my boy, John said, shaking his head. – I remember some of it, but so much happened. It's impossible to recall everything.

– I don't know, Lisbeth mused. – None of us do. I don't know what I did and how I did it, either. But the force, the Power is growing, and we will inevitably gain better control, a better understanding… of it.

A forest path led to two straight trees, growing a meter apart. Beyond the road and the trees, there wasn't really much to see. In addition to the darkness, only dots of white and gray.

– I can see it, a voice breathed, – the Gate of Madness.

Things changed. The room changed. It was hardly there anymore. It had become little more than the table, the chairs and five people.

And an indistinct, deep brown darkness.

He pictured himself in his bedroom in the bright morning.

– I don't know how to explain it, Ted said. – I'm in bed, on my back, with my eyes half closed, observing more than participating. Room seems to disappear... no, *dissolve* around me. I stand straight, rigid before a thin veil. I can't tell its size, its fabric, nothing more, in fact, than that it's *there!* My hands, or not, something that's me, are fumbling at it. A part of it is cast aside and I can see beyond it. But there's nothing there. I try to walk, but no matter how much I struggle I can't go any further.

He returned to the non-existent room with table and chairs and people.

– Maybe something… more is needed. Maybe walking isn't sufficient. We might need to move… without moving?

– That was the same dream I had tonight, John said excited. – Or… whenever.

There were flashes of fire, deep, hissing fire… and the dreams began.

The fireplace was sparking. It was sparking in the fireplace.

There were shadows, dancing, shimmering shapes moving through the darkness. They saw themselves in mirrors (of sorts) and there were shadows.

– I'm in a dark room. It's… difficult, but I can see myself stand before a hidden light. I stand turned, I can only see my back. In a room four people sit around a table formed as a pentagram. Or… is that five? I'm not among them. It isn't clear to me where I am. There and then I'm certain of one thing and one thing only: That I'm There.

The fireplace gave them heat, a shelter from the Storm outside. Rain thundered at the window. Otherwise the room was empty. The light from the fireplace seemed to come from everywhere at once.

– I can feel the surrealism and unreality surrounding me, Freya said in joy and despair, – thoughts of Doom and destruction and Renewal.

She was breathing, breathing, breathing, as sweat poured down her forehead.

– We all dreamed the same dream, Lisbeth stated.

Freya and John nodded eagerly, Burt mumbling and withdrawn.

Freya looked at them all, urgently, worried.

– We all have come here to *try,* right?

Everybody nodded, eagerly, hesitatingly.

Ted put the cups, goblets on the table, one by one. He put a knife before each.

They opened bottles of wine in a frenzy of movement. The loud pop when the corks were removed thundered pleasantly in their ears. Ted placed one bottle at the center of the pentagram and smiled diabolically.

Everybody stood up. For a moment it seemed like John wasn't there, but then he was.

– There's something I'm really wondering about, he said. – I can't actually recall who first told about the dream. Some say it's me. Others say it's Ted. Others again claim Freya did it. Who was it really?

– Wasn't it…

Burt wondered, clearly hesitant.

He shook his head.

– Something's going on here, he chuckled, – knock on wood.

They all took a closer look at the table. Nothing happened. Slowly they started smiling.

– Good, Ted said.

He filled the cups. A white, sparkling wine appeared before their eyes. He picked up the blade before him. The others did the same. They held one hand over the cup. A slight hesitation, one decisive, fast incision on the meat-packed side of the hand, an insignificant pain. One, two, three seconds and drops of blood fell into the wine.

Everybody was given a band-aid. They put it on. The red was sinking slowly to the bottom of the cup. It didn't mix with the present fluid, not until they put their fingers in it and started stirring the fluid.

– Stirring the waters, Ted said.

His words echoed in the Void.

One moment it seemed like Freya wasn't there. Then she was, eagerly grabbing the goblets.

– The Blood of the Gods, she cried in solemn cheerfulness.

Her words echoed in the Void.

They lifted their cup to match the level of their faces.

– Dreams belong to the night, Ted declared.

– DREAMS BELONG TO THE NIGHT, everyone shouted.

The cups met at the center. Eager hands brought them to hot lips and emptied them, emptied them to the last drop.

– You know, it's funny, Lisbeth pondered, with cheeks exposing a pleasant warmth, – I'm certain we've done this before.

– You've probably done something similar, Burt said with a red nose, – or you're imagining you've done it, like with a false memory. They say déjà vu is merely a delay between the left and the right half of the brain.

– No, Burt, Lisbeth insisted, – you don't *understand.* Done *this.* Here and now.

The ghostly voice of Lisbeth (the other Lisbeth) echoed through the room.

– *Yes, knock your heads against the wall not a wall, till you get it right.*

– Yes, I *understand,* Ted beamed.

A deep thunder sounded from a drum, from the Earth itself below, the soft grass and the hard-stamped soil. Walls, floor and ceiling dissolved around them. The table, in a burst of fire, transformed into a giant campfire, strands of Shadow, Night and Fire seeking them. They saw it. They sensed the heat in the face.

A burst of wind, a flash of fire, and they found themselves on the field by the ruin, dancing. Wild dance, boiling blood.

There were more people there, both seen and unseen, and straining their eyes, they could also see the ghosts and the spirits, and it didn't seem strange at all.

As the music at the end calmed them down and they were swaying to it, waving their hands in the ember air, reality, too, once more slowly solidified.

They heard the voice of Abkasha.

– We've come here, a host of Strangers, this night, where the division between the known and hidden world is paper thin, come to break through the veil.

Lisbeth touched Freya's shoulder.

– That sounded great.

– I don't know if I really said that, Freya grinned happily, – but I know that I could have.

They all gathered around the bonfire, the five of them, the additional ten from the city. Dilated pupils, vibrating noses, open mouths took it all in, everything offered to them.

Ted raised a fist to his face.

– One thing becomes increasingly clear, a conviction deeper than rain: This world is *Wrong*. We can all feel that, in our bones. It's about time we do this… do everything.

The night was quiet. They had turned off the music, but they could yet hear it.

– So many lives, Lisbeth mused, – and I can remember ever more.

– There is ever, ever more, Ted stated.

He stood in front of her, dipping the thumb and index finger in a bowl, in a red fluid.

– I'm drawing the symbol of Eternity on your brow and above your… buffet.

She started undressing then, laughing encouragingly to him, and the others, too, around her. He painted one Ankh, the ancient symbol of immortality on her brow and one around her navel. Then he tore off his own rags in fierce, impatient moves. They were all painting each other in rushed, flashing moments.

There was a ghostly voice of thunder from the nothingness, from the vast Void of existence. It wasn't scary to them, not anymore.

– WE DANCE THE DANCE OF LIFE. WE'RE HUNTERS, WE'RE NOMADS. WE SEEK THE FRESH AND UNKNOWN. WHAT ELSE IS THERE TO SEEK?

They gathered by the pentacle, a five-point star inside a circle, prepared earlier in the evening.

Ted spoke with a rough voice giving voice to the air.

– I am the Beast. I give myself Power to rise from the sea, the molten sea. I give myself Power: not just for a thousand days, not merely one thousand years… But Forever.

– Sex-Magick, sex-magick, Lisbeth hummed, – I'm so horny, so horny, I can't wait, I'll wait patiently for the fast and fury.

Laughter, feeling so good, being so good, written in their faces, the movement of the bodies.

Abkasha, the priestess, the Witch, was the first to step into the pentacle.

– I can see us as giants, sleeping by a campfire among the stars. I can see the Gate of Madness and I can see the small mountain above. It isn't us and yet it *is*.

Anubis the Ritemaster, the Witch was the first to step inside the pentacle.

– Dream a Dream deep enough, Ted said, – and it becomes real.

And Freya appeared by his side.

Ted, Freya, John, Lisbeth and Burt placed themselves inside the pentacle, sitting down in each of the five points.

Outside the circle sat the others, holding hands, sending the cup from hand to hand, mouth to mouth, swaying in the shadow twilight. The torches tied to poles well above the ground burned on all sides, but they seemed so far away.

– Time is shooting crooked, Anubis (the other Ted with a beard said. – The only reason we see it as straight, is that we're currently in the habit of preferring it that way. Listen, listen now, to the edge of the Night, to the beating of your own hearts. Picture yourself walking on a path through the forest. It goes deeper and deeper, as you go deeper. As you finally feel the pain, the joy ravaging you.

The ones outside the circle swayed, swayed back and forth, back and forth, as they sang, as their singing grew louder. Words, symbols were drawn in the air, the very fabric of reality. Anubis' hands started glowing then, shockingly, the glow quickly spreading to the rest of his body.

Many of the words spoken were unintelligible, a humming in the background, insistently, threatening, enticing. There were screams of desperation, of fear and delight, and triumph.

– A pattern, initially meaningless is making us see the big picture, Burt declared wild-eyed. – Our *Hunger* gives meaningless to the meaning that isn't there. *He he!*

They were all yawning, growing tired, growing tired in body, astute in Mind. Their astute eyes were visible confirmations to each other.

Humming, there was Humming. There was no sound and no one was moving their lips. Humming was rising from the ground where mist filled the air.

– I am your Guide tonight, Lisbeth explained, – leading you to the foreign beaches, the vast unknown. As I count down from five to Zero, the Journey begins. The body grows heavier and so much lighter. It becomes yours once more.

– I can see it all, just before my eyes, Rachel marveled.

Ted was on the ground tonight, seeing everything from a different perspective.

– FIVE… FOUR… THREE… TWO… ONE…

And then she struck the match, and the last word drowned in the roar of fire, as the pentacle was lit. Flames stretched to the heavens, engulfing the five inside the circle. Someone screamed. Mist rose from the ground, white and gray and shadow.

Sweat poured from wide-open pores. The five sat there with fire on all sides. They breathed in and out, out and in, breathing hard. They stretched their arms. The ones outside stretched bodies, twisting and turning there on the ground.

Ted laid still and suddenly his body started twisting in cramps. It kept going, uncontrollable, and he started gasping. He *screamed* in pain. The ground shook.

He found himself in a room. There were others around him, other strangers, sitting in a circle. Ravens flapped their wings, and their squeak echoed throughout the place. And then he flew through Space, between the planets, between the stars, between the galaxies, and even they turned tiny below him.

A man pushed his palms at his ears in abject desperation.

– It's to no *avail.* The Earth itself is shaking. I can't take it.

And he ran away.

Ted's knuckles turned white as he twisted his hands. His body was still once more. A gasp rose from the assembly, as he turned… transparent, and started disappearing. The others did, too. The Fire kept burning.

They heard Ted's voice.

– *There is something there ahead. Not a door, but a gate.*

They found themselves in daylight, bright, bright daylight.

– I've never before seen a landscape so detailed, a texture so rich, Abkasha related.

John stood on a road. They spotted no visible gate. The road continued into the mist.

They heard a female voice.

– We wander through the mists of time and existence.

– Is that you, Freya? John cried.

Freya entered the mist. She turned and looked back, a short eternity. She was smiling.

Freya stood on a road. They saw no gate anywhere. The road continued into the mists. A man appeared before her. She saw him, as she last saw him; as a nailed, slain sacrifice.

– Is that you Paul?

– Don't worry, Paul replied, – I'm fine. I'm going and all will be good, good, good.

And he rose in the fog, the dark fog. And his legs started burning. In seconds the fire engulfed his body. And he was Gone.

Tears flowed from the girl's eyes, turning into mist, turning into fire.

The forest was empty, but there was movement, there was Life.

They heard Ted's voice.

– I can hear the sounds of the Night. I can feel the trembling of the Earth. Like ghosts we're approaching it, to be ghosts no more.

The Ritemaster rose, rose inside the burning Pentacle, the Wretched Palace by the ruin. He crossed the burning boundaries, to its center. The other four followed him. The flames were still flames, but they didn't burn. Ethereal, they stretched and fondled the human specters.

Outside the ring awaited an unknown number of Strangers. Unknown until the Litany had been completed.

Both the people inside and outside the ring appeared like shadows. The flames didn't illuminate them. It was as if the fire wasn't there at all.

Look at the sky
The moon is in the east
The sun is in the west
Pinpricks of light called stars
Are visible to the naked eye
Sky is dark around the sun
Blue around the moon
Minute differences disappear
Enhanced inside a ring of fire
Day and night are One

– Time may repeat itself, Abkasha cried. – like a loop never ending.

The ritemaster turned towards something that might be west.

I turn to the horizon in the west
I turn unafraid towards
What's different, what's unknown
Shrouded in mists of time and Shadow
The Season of The Witch is here
Let the wind blow

Rachel stepped forward, an eager smile on her face.

Ted and Lisbeth greeted her, choired her welcome with voices fading in and out:

Enter the circle with respect, but unafraid
If you want to turn away, now is the time
Walk through the Gate of Fire
And it's forever closed, you're forever free

The prospective Witch entered the circle. A wave of a hand, a silent cry... And the fire and smoke enveloped her. She was not burned, she was not harmed.

Rachel answered the summing.

I enter the circle with respect, but unafraid

I don't turn away, this is the time
I walk through the Gate of Fire
It's forever closed, I'm forever free

The ritemaster turned and turned. For each new verse another person entered the Circle, until they were all there.

The fire embraced them all, and they were burning, and fading. And suddenly nothing remained, not even embers on the ground. The field was visible, but dark.

A hysteric voice sounded somewhere, crying out for release. There was unrest, real unrest, as people ran from spot to spot, in the Chaos surrounding them.

Frank knelt on the ground, frantic with despair.

– The world is about to END!

Ted looked down on him with a smile, a grin, a poised look.

– You say that as if it is a bad thing!

He/she/they levitated above the ground, in mists, in ruins. They saw forests of broken trees, rotten, dead trees in a city street.

– I… understand, Burt said.

– We jestingly call ourselves witches, John said, appearing to them in a way they had never experienced before, – because we seek our inner spirit, humanity's ancient contact with nature.

The five of them awoke by a forest path at night. Wet, oozing torches, five of them burned bright around them. They woke up with their eyes open.

They arrived.

– All times are now. 200 years ago... 10 000, the voice in the wilderness said, – it's just a way of saying we don't *want* timelessness, we don't want Freedom.

The five of them sat around the campfire. They had thrown up some more, their skin pale and wet, but the good feeling visible in their faces didn't disappear. They could see the ring of light created by the moving flames. Beyond that, there was only a wall of darkness. They partook in a conversation wild and free.

– A fox walked to me and sniffed me out, Lisbeth said with dreamy eyes. – It wasn't afraid. I wasn't afraid.

– I was the wolf hunting in a deep forest, Freya said. – For the first time in my life I know myself.

– Isn't that weird? Burt asked.

They looked at him, looked closer. The open expression in his face, his entire body language, was… *transforming* him. They saw him as he was before and the way he was *now*.

– For all we know we may be the only humans in the entire, fucking world.

At this moment the rest of the world does indeed seem like a dream to me. This is reality, all the other crap the illusion.

The owl hooted in agreement. And then they heard the wolf, its wild elegy making a chill run down their spine.

– I thought all the wolves were gone from this area, Ted pondered.

– They were, Lisbeth said in delight.

– We should move on, Freya said anxiously.

Exchanging glances, they nodded and after just a few moments of gathering their belongings they were on their way again.

– Not much left, is there. John remarked.

– No, Ted acknowledged, – but we don't have that far left to go either.

– Are we really having this conversation? John said incredulous.

– It's great, isn't it? Abkasha said.

They smiled and nodded.

They moved closer to each other then, in gathering joy, but were interrupted, as they were about to touch, to embrace.

Freya froze solid where she stood, then. They, too, looked at the forest. They could hear movement, could hear branches break.

– Something is coming. *Something* is blocking our path…

– Some… thing…? Burt said.

Four… creatures emerged into their view, blocking their path. Creatures both easily and hardly recognizable. It was the forest ranger, the city cop, Melanie and… Clay. They shimmered and oozed, as if they were burning, but there was no fire. Their skin was a dark, unhealthy blue. And they looked menacing beyond words.

– They're demons, Freya stated.

– That description isn't quite fitting, Lisbeth said, shaking her head, – but it will do.

Clay laughed, a shrieking, insane sound.

– You're a part of this, Clay? Ted wondered. – You… killed the cat, didn't you?

The insane glee was a more than sufficient answer.

– For Gaia's sake, man, *why?*

– You showed me another world… showed me how life could be. You fucked me up.

He was pale, unnaturally pale. His eyes and face were more swollen, more bloated than anything they had ever seen, certainly far worse than theirs ever had been.

– Whatever you're doing, you must stop it, Burt urged them. – Don't you know you're destroying the world?

The city cop laughed wickedly.
– *We*... are destroying the world?
– They don't know, do they? The forest ranger said, clearly amused as well.
Melanie added her voice to theirs.
– How delightful...
Clay dropped to his knees.
– It's wrong, it's ALL... wrong.
And then he faded from their eyes, reduced to puss and bones and nothing, as if he had never existed at all. Shock froze all the five wanderers.
Lisbeth stood rigid, fear written in her face, with moving hands, moving lips.
– Red ball... Red twig, she mumbled with determination engraved on her features.
And the twig by her right foot began glowing, burning.
Suddenly Melanie stood right in front of her, giving her a stinging slap in her face. Lisbeth fell backwards. Her hands oozed and twisted before her eyes and she screamed in horror.
Melanie grabbed her throat, lifting her up with one hand, in one incredible show of strength.
– You'll just fade into nothingness, as if you've never existed, Melanie the demon said softly. – Beg for mercy and I may grant it.
– P-please, Lisbeth sobbed.
And she started disintegrating before their eyes, while Melanie seemed to be... *growing*, gaining strength and texture.
Freya threw herself at her, with all the fierceness she possessed, clawing desperately at Melanie's essence, to no avail. Melanie shrugged her off, like she was nothing. Melanie was in uniform, an amalgam of all the uniforms that ever were. An American flag, a German Nazi flag and countless others. And they heard the voices, the many voices of the uniform.
– Scnhell, schnell, Melanie the demon snarled.
It held on to Lisbeth, clearly sucking the life out of her.
– Soon now, very soon, Melanie said pleased.
She looked at the others, her eyes filled with wicked triumph.
She didn't look at Lisbeth.
Lisbeth's hands started glowing and the fingers turned to claws, and with a shriek of anger, a lifetime of Rage, she charged, attacked the other, and like knives her claws tore through the creature in front of her. There was no blood, no flesh, no bowels, merely a cry of united rage, a look of utter disbelief from the other, and then nothing. Melanie had vanished, as if she never was. Lisbeth remained, shaking; her eyes wide and hard like glass,

burning like glass never could.

Freya confronted the forest ranger.

– I know who you are, she told him.

And he vanished in the night air.

John looked at the cop.

And the cop faded away.

Ted gathered his stuff, even some of their stuff.

– What the HELL was that? Burt gasped. – What is HAPPENING?

– We must make haste, Ted told them anxiously.

They followed him, started running, swinging their torches as they ran. The torches burned brighter. They didn't seem to be in danger of being put out. The dark fire burned the night and the five anxious people rushing through it.

The five climbed, climbed through the night with their torch in one hand. Shaking hands kept searching for handles, for cracks in the rock, as they slowly ascended the mountain, slowly found their way up.

They reached the plateau and the strange formation of trees. There was a small rock there, hovering over them. Beyond that was the deep, deep forest. They gathered all the twigs and dry branches they could find. As they gasped for breath, gulping in fresh air, they lit the fire. Dark and bright flames illuminated the surroundings.

All five of them sat down, straight there on the ground, exhausted, spent.

– We must all be going mad.

Burt shook his head repeatedly, laughing his heart out.

– I don't know what happened, Freya half whispered, half cried out, – but I can feel so much more, now. Everything is changing, turning fluid around us.

– Who was he, Freya? Who was the forest ranger? The two of you have just recently met, but you seemed to have… have a connection.

She sat there, caught in a strange mix of shakes and relaxation.

– I… don't know, Freya frowned, – but he seems so very familiar. I see him… every time I look at myself in the *mirror*.

And they were all frozen, as if her very words hurt them.

Lieutenant Edgar Gallagher and his partner Sarah Knowles walked out of the forest, the deep forest. There was something almost profoundly normal about the scene. The two were not sweaty. They were impeccably dressed and groomed. Hair was done, and didn't seem to have been damaged by what must have been a long and strenuous journey through the wilderness.

– What has transpired here? Gallagher snapped, his voice almost cracking at the higher levels.

– *Has* anything transpired here? Ted asked him instantly, deliberately patronizing.

– We heard someone was murdered, Gallagher said.

– From whom did you hear that, Lieutenant? Abkasha countered. – We have heard no such thing.

There was no birdlife anymore, no singing, something abundant before the two latest arrivals.

– Man, I'm chilled to the bone, John shivered.

– You see behind the illusion, Freya told him, – we all are, truly, for the very first time in our lives.

They, all five of them, like one person, looked at the approaching detectives. The Lieutenants stopped, just outside the circle of light of shadow.

– We see the destruction, we see its servants, Ted shouted.

– Gallagher stared at them with his tiny, tiny eyes.

– You're all nutty as fruit loops. I'm gonna take you in and see that you're put away for life.

Fowles put a hand on his shoulder. She gave them her best smile, as John and Burt heard her speak for the first time.

– There's no need to be hasty here, is there? These young men and women have just misunderstood a bit, have they not?

– I wouldn't bet on it, lady, Burt said.

She said nothing, only looked at him, making him sweat and heave.

– What the hell are you talking about, anyway? He wondered, his seemingly confident tone reduced to the brittle uncertainty it was.

– I'm talking about the experience I've gained after fifteen years of investigating paranormal crimes, Knowles replied, very confident. – I'm talking about you upsetting the natural order, endangering everybody.

They stared at her, thunderstruck.

– Yes, you, she nodded. – You know about the approaching disaster. Yes, I know you do.

She gave them another confident smile, an intense, comforting smile, before continuing.

– What you've failed to realize, however, is your crucial participation in that disaster… Don't you see? You've put in motion forces far beyond your comprehension and it must stop, stop *now*, before it's too late.

They looked, stared at each other

– We're doing it? Ted said incredulous. – But… how is that possible?

– I don't know, John shuddered, – but we've all felt *something*, haven't we; felt the power raging inside?

Freya twisted her hands like a nervous old lady.

– What can we do about it?

They looked at Knowles again.

– Something can be done, Knowles assured them. – If you'll accept my aid, there's still time to turn the tide.

They looked at each other, with the first signs of devastation in their eyes.

– I suppose we…

Ted said with the pain very evident in his voice.

The others didn't nod, but they were looking at the ground.

– That's right, you're coming with us, Gallagher boasted and drew his gun.

John drew patterns in the air.

– What…

The very air seemed to condense, to change under his breath.

Gallagher gasped in fear and fired his gun. The bullets never reached John, but disintegrated in flames.

Or quite simply disintegrated in the air in front of John. He didn't move his hands. His eyes glowed in a terrible ruby light.

– TED, remember the museum, Lisbeth shouted. – Never forget.

And during the next seconds, one moment of eternity, they saw history unfold, saw history march, louder and louder, and then suddenly fading, until there was nothing there, nothing but the scowling woman in front of them.

– I… remember, Ted choked. – How could I ever have forgotten?

Knowles screamed in frustration and rage at Gallagher.

– You… IDIOT!

She touched him and he went up in flames before their eyes, the horrible scream echoing endlessly through the forest.

Freya trampled the ground in triumph. The very Earth shook beneath their feet.

– The veil is thrown *aside.*

– A wall NO MORE, Ted cried out.

– I'm still not sure what I did, John shook his head in amazement. – It was instinct more than anything else… but I can *feel* the power coursing through me.

And when they looked at Knowles once more, there was anger and determination in their eyes.

A Knowles foaming and frowning spat at them.

– You're *demons,* set on destroying our world.

– I *know* her, Ted marveled, shaking with emotion. – I've seen her on the edge of my vision and in the mirror, seen her glaring at me from my nightmares.

They saw her filled with pollution, flesh rotting from exposure to chemicals, eyes exposing a spirit disintegrating. They saw her exposed as she truly was.

– We're destroying the illusion, Ted snarled, – nothing more.

– It's been so long, so very long, Knowles said.

She was *growing* as she looked at him with hatred in her eyes.

– Centuries, millennia, what does it matter? Ted shrugged. – It's great.

He was growing, too, as the light was suddenly, shockingly retracting, as there was nothing keeping her away anymore.

– NO! She screamed, throwing herself at him.

He met her with equal force. Hands clutched each other. Bodies pushed themselves beyond endurance. He glowed in fire, in shadow, one short second, pushing her backwards.

She fell two, three steps backwards. He stayed put. She bled from her mouth. She didn't fade.

– Damn you, she glared at him, – you think you've won, do you… but you'll never win.

Ted smiled ironically.

– Win?

She dried blood from her lips.

– There's one thing you haven't counted on…

Her features started *changing* then, flowing like water. The others gasped. Ted took one step back. Knowles grew more muscled and her face was that of a man. Ted looked at his own face, looked at himself, shock and horror exposing itself in his eyes.

– I've stared into the Abyss, Knowles cried.

Ted stumbled a bit. Knowles smiled. Ted shook his head in denial, forming «no, no no» with his lips. But he was slowly straightening himself. Knowles' smile faltered.

– I stare back at you.

Knowles's smile remained confident.

– I accept you, Ted continued.

Knowles froze on the spot.

– *What?*

Ted stretched out his arms to the sides.

– I accept you. You're a part of me. We are One.

– Come on, you can't mean that, the man/woman practically besieged him. – Nobody can be that foolish…

– One…

Ted repeated firmly.

– I'll gut you like a piiig.

Cartland/Knowles squealed.

– ONE! Anubis spoke with a mighty roar shaking the Earth.

And the Earth did shake. The ground was dissolving itself around them.

Knowles stumbled. He/she looked down at herself, himself. The legs weren't there anymore. They were just not there.

NOOOOOOOOOOO

Knowles screamed then, in a terrible rage, before disappearing like dew before the sun. Ted started screaming in that same instant, shrinking to normal size and sinking to his knees on the forest bed.

He had already stood up as the others rushed to help him.

– I'm okay, he assured them. – In fact, I'm more okay now, than I've been in a long, long time. I can feel her, feel him inside. I'm Whole.

And his hands scratched the air, and he made huge holes in it. They stared as if transfixed at the pattern revealing itself. The fire started growing, consuming the very ground they stood on. Freya floated effortlessly twenty centimeters above the rock.

They saw it, and it did shock them, but just for a second, one tiny moment of their eternal existence.

They stared at each other, still incredulous, but filled with a peace and harmony undreamt of.

– We faced ourselves, Lisbeth said. – Clay was…

– My counterpart, Burt interjected. – I know!

– We can stay here as gods, Freya called out to them from her elevated position, – or we can live the Life we're been born to Live, lift the heavy, light lids covering our eyes, our perception.

Images formed in the air before them, of castles and luxurious throne-rooms and dungeons.

They caught a glimpse of themselves as kings and queens, as Masters, and shuddered at the very thought. She lowered herself to the ground.

And they grabbed her hands.

– C'mon let's do it, Lisbeth chuckled. – We're free. We can do whatever we desire.

And they Danced, hand in hand, body against body, inside the ring of fire revealing itself. And they sang. And their song, first merely humming, transformed into words and purpose.

– «The Human being is like an iceberg, we see only a tiny part of it».

Strings of Night and Fire started growing out of them, from their bodies and minds, tight as weed. They expanded and changed, and suddenly five giants stood there looking down at the small forest, the small bush.

They were back inside the pentacle, standing close to the others. And there were more people, standing in the shadows outside the circle.

Factories spewing poison fell, collapsed. Prison walls dissolved around the inmates and they looked up startled. Buildings, cities crumbled to dust. Even nature itself crumbled.

– We're emerging from the chrysalis, Anubis shouted with a mighty voice, – insects no more.

And the world disintegrated around them. A shredded curtain hung from a branch, blowing in the wind. Nothing more remained of the colossal wreck.

The five of them walked into the mist, five shadows, joined by many others.

And then everything dissolved itself into nothing, even the world of mist and shadow.

Another flash of fire and everything disappeared.

2

The color of rust and blood surrounded them. They breathed, long, deep gasps of pleasure. He saw the burned sticks used for the torches the night before, saw them left on the ground. His eyes cleared.

He looked up at Abkasha, her being seemingly distant and regal, closer than ever, she returning his look with a glowing sensuality smothering him.

Distant, almost subconsciously he touched, noticed his own beard. So much was different, so much remained the same.

– Abkasha?

– Yes, Edward, yes, Anubis, you want to ask me something?

– Were they... real, all the other people on the other world?

She smiled, self-consciously, slightly sarcastic. *Alive!*

– Real?

– Come on, he said with good humored irritation, – you know what I mean.

Abkasha looked solemnly at him.

– Reality does not fit into our narrow perception of it. We should never allow ourselves to forget that.

The others woke up, too, not merely being awake. All of the remaining five, and also others.

– A tribe from many tribes, until the end of Time, Rachel stated, her grin wide enough to catch rivers.

There were differences in clothing and jewelry signifying that. The tribe was once more uniting, knitting itself. They embraced, locking eyes. Some of them were crying. Burt *(Bertram)* didn't look so good, but most were crying in joy and relief, watching each other, taking «stock» of themselves with wonder in their eyes.

– We didn't sleep, he said amazed, – but dreamed still.

– I'd say we woke up… still dreaming, John pondered.

– No more picking up food in a store, Bertram said with a sad face. – From now on we have to work our butts off for it, for it all.

– How can you say that, Bertram? Lisbeth cried out to him, slightly agitated. – How can you use that *tone?* Life is not easy, and it never will be, but now we have our self-respect, our dignity, ourselves as Human Beings.

Abkasha faced them, faced them all, hands on her hips, the naked skin just above the loincloth.

– *Ready,* people? Thou art shaken. Thou hast visited The Abyss and returned to tell the tale. Ready to feel the boiling blood in thy veins, the strength in thy limbs, the smell of the Hunt?

– Yes, by the spirits, John said content and excited, – more now than I ever was.

Edward turned to Abkasha, a bit curious, a scratch on a place he couldn't reach vexing him.

– Abkasha, tell me this: Why do we talk like we do, I mean, we speak pretty fluent English, don't we?

Abkasha shrugged totally unconcerned, making no fuzz about it.

– That's not you talking, but «you» as you were this short night. You're a bit stuck, or rather unstuck, it happens sometimes. You've left a bit of yourself back there. It happens. There's an ancient saying: «Even in a second there's an eternity».

She smiled, a dangerous grin.

– We've always talked like this...

They fetched their weapons, picking them up with awe painted on their faces.

– An odd collection of what we have *dreamed*, isn't it? John shook his head in wonder, in more wonder. – But not a single really... complex one. Now, *that* would've been weird indeed...

They were going on their way.

– My whole body is... tingling, a girl said.

– It's the fresh air, baby, John said joyfully, playfully. – And Life. Dreamtime may be okay, but it can't compare to this.

– It's time to face the day, Abkasha told them. – Doing so unafraid. Dreams belong to the night.

They nodded eagerly and mumbled, repeated the last sentence with wide and excited eyes.

The Endless Path, a Nature virtually untouched by Human Beings revealed, re-revealed itself to them. Just around the corner was the wilderness. They left the Gate of Madness without looking back. Ever. The place already forgotten, like a half-remembered dream.

Edward saw a branch in one tree ahead, saw a shredded curtain hanging from it, blowing in the wind. He looked at the others. They didn't look in the direction he did, not even Bertram. Edward took another look at the branch, at the shredded curtain. As he watched it, it faded away.

Edward shuddered a bit thinking about Bertram, looking at him with a bit of fear, of worry, but not that much. Not enough to spoil the beauty of the day, the Life they Lived, visible in their very demeanor, their every movement, as they moved into the broad valley below.

«Are we and everything we see
a dream within a dream»?

Edgar Allan Poe

Author's word

This started life as a movie script, and that is fairly easy to discern. I haven't really rewritten it much, only expanded upon it a bit here and there.

Aside from that, it is, like Red Shadow a story too short to be a novel, but unlike Red Shadow, it was never meant to be a short story.

I guess I could have made this into a novel, but not without completely rewriting it, expanding it in all its small and bigger parts. The story as it is now is just about right, a kind of continuous lightning illuminating the scenes and stages, glimpses of the reality described. The form is completely different from a novel, also different from how I would have and have written one.

I wrote the script as a kind of minimalistic exercise, a low-budget movie because I knew I couldn't afford to make one with a big or even bigger budget, and that has translated into the longer short story or shorter novel. I would usually do some kind of buildup, but here the story is well underway from the first line. The characters are dropped into a maw or something, and it works itself up from there. There's little or no rest and the unrest is pervasive and unrelenting.

Is it possible to glimpse truth, even profound truth in a world filled with distractions and horrors? Can a human being grasp pieces of true value, and go with that, and thereby find greatness in spite of the giant stinking garbage heap dominating our existence?

Absolutely! Exposing the illusion most people call reality today is fairly easy. All it may take is one blink of an eye, one panning of a hand, brushing away the thin veil keeping us from spotting the obvious…

And you're there, right at the start of the path where the true world of the human being begins.

DEATH AND THE MAIDEN

Jointed, disparate images come to me.

I can see paintings on a wall (I've never painted anything. I've tried, but never gotten the hang of it).

I walked on the road past the old house. I walked in darkness, under the streetlights on the main road. Streetlights of the old type. Not those with the great orange glow, but the ones satisfied with glowing in blue and pale light. I turned off the main road where there are rarely any cars at all at night, to the smaller road. I walked across the bridge over the roaring river (there was no river). On my right where I walked on the tarmac-covered private road, a small yacht stood on a pedestal for all to look at and admire. It had been there virtually forever, fit for pedestals no longer. For some reason this particular, (older) pedestal, keeps reminding me of the way the American Indians supposedly were «burying» their dead.

That's when I see her. She has been walking some distance ahead of me for some time, but I haven't really seen her before now, before Now. I study her back. She doesn't turn around. The sleek, black hair covers her back. She dresses in black. Black jacket, black pants. I walk only ten meters behind her. I want to cry out to her. She would then turn around and I would see the face I do not see now.

She turned off onto another road. I do know these parts well, having wandered through them since childhood. I walked merely ten steps behind the lovely snake body, when I turned abruptly around and hurried back the same way I had come. Over the bridge, over the main road again, towards home.

The red gate, the green gate. Some minutes later. A hundred thousand years. I walk by the old white house, empty, ethereal. I'm always looking at the dark windows to see if anybody is standing inside. There was no one this night either. But as always, I'm hearing noises. Creaking of the old, decaying floor, rustling behind green bushes, the howl of poltergeists in the treetops. I run the last stretch to my home one hundred steps away. It's a wise habit of mine, that I'll leave the lights on, when leaving the house for my nocturnal walks.

I stood like frozen on the concrete stairs fumbling with my keys, and watched my shadow casting long shadows in the light from the kitchen. My shadow, I told myself. I had never felt so shaken before and I had walked long trips in the night for many years now. What had changed? What?

I closed the door shut behind me and feverishly turned the key in the lock. The door was closed. I imagined that all kinds of hellhounds butted the green gate to the property. Creatures of fog searched for the keyhole. They might have found it already and were just waiting for the key to be pulled out. I had to pull it out, I had to. If not, they could have used it to enter through the door.

Nothing happened. I stopped breathing for a while to listen for any sound, anything suspicious. I was breathing easier just a few seconds later. There were lots of small sounds in the house, but that was normal, wasn't it? I drew breaths of relief in the warm, cozy hall. Cozy, safe. I downed a glass of juice without being conscious of finding the glass or opening the fridge or pouring anything. The taste felt better than it ever had, like life or death.

The refrigerator door shook when I opened it. I spilled juice over the table, on the floor and I raised an eyebrow. It was supposed to be juice, but the fluid was red. It couldn't be. Not orange juice at all. Certainly not... The color had been... right when I had opened it a... a... long time ago.

It was at this time I heard a noise from the living room. Unmistakably the sound when someone is standing up from a deep chair. Who could it be? A supple creature dressed in snakeskin...?

A shadow stretching her snake body on the dining table. Light is flowing from the two bulbs above, in vain. The Shadow grew. I could hear the steps now, light, demonic. I couldn't move. Everything, also my own house, had become alien to me. Blood flowed from the glass filled with orange juice. The wall clock had been transformed into a face grinning its vicious smile, greeting me with it. And whoever awaited me in the living room would come walking around the corner at any time now. I didn't dare move, staring blindly at the growing shadow. I had an infernal need to turn around and expose whoever was sneaking up on me from behind, but... I didn't dare. I heard steps behind me, I heard steps in front of me and the kitchen wall closed off the path to the right. To my left was the kitchen window. I ran to it, moving with swiftness completely unusual in this type of dreams. Hands shaking like any type of leaves pushed the window and opened it wide. And there she was, the girl from the Night. I saw her face. Death stared at me without its mask and she smiled at me.

I looked outside, and she wasn't to be seen anymore. Not there. One blink of an eye and she was gone (not gone). I had closed all doors, every window, and I had not invited her, but still she had entered my house. I heard her voice and her steps everywhere. She... She was coming for me. I know she is and I can feel the shadow of her cold embrace, the touch of her ghostly limbs.

==========

His office in daylight. Big windows. Much light, filtered through gray windows. Light, pale colored furniture and walls. Modern architecture. Little or no visible dust. The sounds of the city outside muffled, distant. The buzzing voices from the hall.

There were still forty-five minutes to go before the nine o'clock meeting. He didn't have much time left to prepare really. A few phone calls, perhaps.

He made them. It took only a few minutes. The secretaries had pulled all the important files from his personal hard drive before he arrived and had done quite an adequate job of research.

He shrugged. Inactivity always got to him. He used it, used this... imbalance, to refine his approach to going through the meeting in advance, imagining the pointers and possible adversaries. This morning, though, he feared his timing was... off. He couldn't concentrate properly.

Mary Anne entered the room. Shoulder length blond hair combed back from her temples, serious, fast, efficient.

– They're ready for you, now, sir, she said.

He had already stood up and straightened his jacket. He walked behind her out in the hall, and enjoyed staring at her big butt, her swinging hips.

– The changes will be made one day before schedule, according to your exact specifications, she offered, noticing his eyes wandering up and down the walls, at the incomplete work.

He nodded absentmindedly. It didn't matter if she saw him do it. She was used to his indifference when dealing with underlings and didn't notice anything different.

But he did, and it irritated him to no end.

– There is something you may want to know, she said hesitatingly.

– Yes?

– Workers have... there have been some *complaints* about working conditions, working hours and tight schedules.

He pulled breath in through compressed teeth. She noticed and virtually shrank, even before he started to speak.

– It is you who have the overall job and responsibility with the reconstruction and completion of the office, correct?

– Yes, sir, she said hastily.

– Then I'll suggest, for future reference, you solve problems, not create new ones, for both yourself and us.

– Yes, sir, of course, sir. Please rest assured that it will not happen again.

He congratulated himself with this move, this small show of force, through the rest of the day. By crushing her small show of defiance in its infancy, he had both prevented it from growing into a future problem and made her more valuable during the meeting. She was working, striving very hard to compensate for her earlier tactless remark and to regain her loss, to remain in his favor.

– But the risk, sir... a younger up and coming suit protested politely, when there were merely minutes left of the board meeting. – Surely...

– Risk is a part of the game, boy. He raised the voice an octave and then, uncharacteristically slammed his fist on the table before him. – We may obtain the same results if we go the slow and careful way, but it isn't very *likely*, now, isn't it?

– No, sir, the younger man replied sullenly.

He had relied on his older, more experienced «sponsors» to come to his aid, but they had, of course, failed him. They had learned the game long ago. And relied on upstarts such as him, to blunder and generally make an ass of himself, to prod and prowl their opponents.

Robert Coleman knew this tactic well, as he often practiced it himself.

But this time that specific tactic had failed miserably. As his opponents now realized, they had lost the battle before the board meeting started.

He gathered his papers, nodded to them, rewarded his team by acknowledging their existence. Such a gesture, he had discovered early in his career was often sufficient to make them work that harder, «go that extra mile». Fear and intimidation and rewarding gestures. All business ran on such fuel.

He drove home early, rather pleased with himself, the appetite for blood whetted even more.

His home was no more than a thirty minutes' drive from the business area, the center of the city. When traffic wasn't bad, like now, he could even manage the trip in twenty. He had bought the rather estate-like property five years ago, and lived in that rural environment since.

After taking off from the main road, there was a mile or so to drive on a more... rural path. There was pavement, he had made sure of that, but it was still considerably narrower than he would have liked. He saw the girl on the bridge and waved to her. She waved back. His good mood grew even more.

One long slope down, from the main road and he could just as well be in another world, a world where time had stood still. At least for five years, probably longer.

The red gate first. There were a number of other houses beyond this point, belonging to his neighbors.

The green gate. Beyond it there were only two houses, both belonging to him. The white, that he rarely used, except for the occasional bashes and parties. He lived in the green, by the end of the road - alone.

He parked the car in one of the two available spots in the garage and walked the last twenty steps to the house. He opened the door, went inside and closed and locked the door. Dinner was ready in the oven. His combined cook and housekeeper had, as usual, done an impeccable job. And disappeared afterwards without leaving unwanted tracks.

While he sat down by the table and ate, he did as he always did. He went through the day in his mind.

His opponents, adversaries had thought the fist hitting the table had been a deliberate, theatrical act, to throw them off balance, but in truth it hadn't been. He had been a bit out of... whack lately and was at a loss to understand why.

In his more despairing moments, he had considered going to see a shrink. Everyone else did it, so why shouldn't he?

But no, there were some things he just wasn't prepared to do, other than in a last-ditch effort. Everything was fine, he was fine. This was no more than a challenge to be won, like it usually was in business.

Night came early this day, earlier than he would have thought, even if fall was fast approaching.

He selected CNN news on the Internet, then some business channels. Everything told in vivid colors.

He retired early and fell asleep almost immediately. Not so strange, since he had slept rather poorly lately. Outside the window was the rustling of leaves, the howling of wind and he slept.

====================

I went outside, didn't turn around, but could swear I couldn't hear the door slam shut behind me.

Autumn brought darker nights. The chill in the air was not summer. This late in the night, though, one was able to scout the first signs of morning in the east. A twilight light, seemingly stretching on forever.

I passed the garage on my right side. A bit further in the garden, the old house on my left. There was no sound, no wind, but I could hear wind howl through the building when walking by. The green gate was closed. I had closed it the evening before. While I opened it I used the opportunity to take a quick glance back at the house, at the garden full of bushes and trees, almost a forest.

Then the open field, the farm. The road seemed so narrow in between the tall, weedy grass. In the northeast, the barn, a dark shape against the promise of morning.

The road stretches on, making strange turns left and right, up and down, until it reaches the main road. One long slope up, and I can, looking left see the endless road to the north. Looking right I see the endless road to the south. There is a construct bridging the main road, making it safe for everybody to cross. I took a stroll on the bridge and I felt the wind grabbing me.

A car came from the south, driving under the bridge, as all cars had to do. It was an open car, a convertible. I could see her long, black hair blow in the wind. The male driver stopped the car a bit further to the north, by the gas station, and let her off. She kissed him on the cheek. He drove further north, disappearing around a turn far to the north. She was alone.

I studied her as she walked by the gardener's house. She disappeared behind it, appeared on the other side, the other side of the bridge. I crossed it fully, following her.

Fog rose slightly off the ground. There was no fog. The road was broad and gray in front of me, but I saw her glimmering in red and color. The road was visible. There was no fog, the air (and road) dry and windy. The wind whistled in the trees, the boughs and branches moved. I couldn't see them move, but I could hear them, as I couldn't hear myself. And she didn't walk forward, but floated like a ghost in the night. She was dressed in a cloak, a hood and carried her scythe. The cloak hid her legs, hid her arms, her head. Only branches, boughs of her impossible long hair floated in the air. I saw her clearly from behind, as she swung her scythe, and the grass she cut screamed silent and bled its red blood.

I stopped, stood still, while she disappeared around the next turn. Up a slight slope in the road, the road turned ever so slightly behind a row of trees... and she was gone. I started walking, I started running, reached the turn almost instantly, or so it felt like. I couldn't see her. I ran further as my heart beat in my chest, to the next turn. She was nowhere to be been, she was gone.

Sweat poured into my eyes, blurring my vision and suddenly, from one moment till the next, I was scared shitless of closing my eyes. And the sweat stung like hell and I had to close my eyes... the slightest moment. And my breathing stopped, and I turned abruptly around. And there was no one there. I turned again. Again

There was no one there!

There was no one there!

There was no one there!

I started walking fast, back to the main road, to the bright lights. I started to realize she could be anywhere. And it was quite... unsettling. The road back to the house was lit by darkness. Not more than a few minutes walk, but it had always felt like an eternity.

A car drove by and with a start I saw her face reflected in the window.

And for that to happen, she had to be close, very close.

But I couldn't see her.

She could be anywhere. She was everywhere. She was whispering to me through the air, through my feet each time they touched the ground. As I started the dark crossing between the main road and my home, I felt the stench of my sweat, I felt it pour down my face and neck, cold, cold droplets of fear. The temptation to start running was almost overwhelming. It wouldn't do. Not at all! Control - slow, careful steps, that was the ticket.

I do not remember how many times I turned around and looked behind me, during the next minute or so. I ran the last, few steps to the house, unlocked the door, stormed in and slammed the door behind me, turned the key and moved hastily away from the door.

To avoid her bony arm stretching through the door. I could almost see it, between the shadows and light, between the warm and cold air. There was nothing there.

I had assumed she couldn't walk through the door. She might be able to push her hand or arm through, but not her entire body. I realized that I've never really believed that to be accurate. The entrance, the living room, the kitchen, the bathroom, all rooms were lit, but I could sense her in the shadows. I kept telling myself that this was merely paranoid, creative delusions working overtime. Never quite convincing.

She's hiding in the mirrors, you know... Not just the visible mirrors, but that of our mind and soul. I can see glimpses of her, here and there, in the outskirts of the vision, the edge of consciousness.

On these nights I don't turn off the lights. I can't allow the shadows in the corners to spread all over the house. I check under the bed, inside the closet, all the closets. I can't see her. I know she's there!

Why don't you leave me alone? I've done nothing to you. Go away!

And I hear her steps. And I can see dust float in her footsteps above the floor. Hell, the depth of her feet is visible in the carpet. I turn to defend myself, but she's not there. And then I feel her bony fingers touch my shoulders from behind and I'm SCREAMING

=====================

And then he woke up. He sat in his bed, shaking, his body, the bed, the sheets soaked with sweat.

Reality shifted around him, in constantly changing patterns. Changed - and shifted again. The bed was there, the walls were there. The next moment nothing was, not even him. And She was there. He could hear her silent laughter. And cold sweat froze his vision.

He sat there for minutes, sat still, frozen, wide awake. Fell back in the bed, attempting to sleep. He couldn't close his eyes. There was fear, but the fear subsided, as the nightmare faded. More than that, there was no... he wasn't tired. At least not in a way that allowed him to sleep. He closed his eyes. There wasn't the slightest hint of sleep. He rose from the bed with an irritated move of his head.

Insomnia had been another of his perils lately. After awakening from the nightmare, he was unable to get back to sleep, even after the hammering of the heart had stopped and he had dried his sweat-soaked body with a towel.

He dutifully completed the useless ritual this night, too. Then he proceeded to dress. No food, he went straight outside. Slammed the door shut behind him. Didn't lock it. For some reason he never locked the door on these nocturnal trips. They could last for hours, but he left the door unlocked.

It was a bright late summer night. A full moon pale against the light blue sky. It never got very dark this far north in the summer. He could see the road quite clear ahead. Freeheld cameras might have trouble catching enough light during these nights, the human eye didn't.

There was no wind, no sound coming from the old house. It was just a house. Even the barn between the green and red gate, the barn that had frightened him so as a kid was just a barn. It was a dark silhouette towards the northern sky, it always was. The sun would rise behind it a couple of hours from now.

(But not as dark as when passing it on a dark autumn night).

The temperature was pleasant, a typical summer night. Skin on nude arms didn't feel exposed, except for the permanent rush of fresh air to open pores. The chill he felt was entirely in his mind.

The dream still felt ridiculous, as it did even as he dreamed it, even as he was tossing and turning in his bed, running endless fields in fear of what didn't exist. He couldn't deny it any longer, he was slipping. It didn't interfere with his daytime performance yet, but would soon. Just a matter of time and the first cracks would start to show, as he had seen happen with so many of his former colleagues. He admitted that he was at a loss what to do, how to proceed. A shrink was definitely out. He knew it had helped some and they were discreet. They had to be, to attract his kind of demographic group. But things could still be revealed. They usually were, in the end. A revelation that would be just as damaging to a man such as himself, one depending on his hardball reputation.

These nightly trips had always benefited him, helped relieve the pressure. The wind against his face (there was no wind), the soft, ephemeral light (everything was clear as day). It had helped him, even to the point where he didn't need much sleep (and could work more).

No longer!

He had adapted a light, unconcerned walk. This was beneficial both in boardroom meetings and long nightly ventures. Usually he didn't get tired at all. No wonder really, since he paid a man to keep him in top shape.

Now the walk was rather erratic and awkward, revealing in full his rising stress level.

He had to admit to himself that he had felt skittish for months. It was about time he did something, anything about it.

The bridge was there, as it was every time, every dream. He saw the girl, coming from the east. He didn't see her every night, but usually their migration pattern was amazingly similar. She was northbound, he followed her some lengths behind. He saw her back. In the dream he had only seen her back. He saw her butt and swinging hips. Glimpses of her face haunted him. He had seen it in daylight, but it wasn't really the same. It looked the same, but wasn't.

Hello

Hello!

– Hello,

he called after her.

He managed to catch up with her, by the old gas station.

– Hello. She turned and smiled to him, a bit reserved, – another nightwalker? Nice to meet you.

According to statistics he had read, every man (and woman) thought the opposite sex was reserved and even hostile during initial contact, but he knew that wasn't necessarily the truth.

– Nice to finally meet, he said. – I've seen you walk these parts for quite some time now.

– And I've seen you...

– I do not doubt it, he said.

An awkward silence settled between them.

– Uh, where are you headed? He asked straightforward.

– North. Her reply was equally so. – And you?

– North... he smiled then.

The road went straight forward for quite some time, a long, long stretch of gray.

They talked about the weather for some time, or similar issues, talking about nothing. Before they finally, after not so long a walk, started talking.

– You like walking here, don't you, in the dark? You like the Night?

– Sometimes I can't sleep, he said almost apologetically. – And it helps clear my head.

She laughed, a happy satisfied laughter.

– I love *everything* about it, she cried out enthusiastically and turned and turned, made a pirouette, in front of him. – Not only what is accepted as «beneficial», but also what may be considered... dangerous, what is usually hidden, what present day people keep secret from themselves.

He refrained from comment on it. They walked on. They crossed a bridge, reached a stretch where there were no streetlights, they kept walking. Sometimes there was a car passing them, leaving them coughing and dead and blind, for a few seconds.

But most of the time, there was silence. Their voices didn't really disturb the peace, but somehow added to it.

The dark was closer now, here, without a close electric light. He felt it creeping towards him, as a living entity.

She speeded up a little, gaining on him, stopped in front of him, looked

into his eyes, he was drowning in hers.
– I would like to confess something, now, she said, – if you would allow me...

He looked incredulous at her. What strange wording she used, what a strange request. Certainly one quite different from what his secretaries and aides might do.

– I'm afraid of the dark, she confessed. – Or at least I was, that's why I started going out at Night.

– It is difficult to comprehend, he admitted.

She laughed throatily.

– First during summer nights only, then the walks stretched into autumn and winter... And I Changed!

They entered into an area heavy with mist, gray, wet and hard to see through mist. There was the actual road, and the other person, but hardly anything else. Shapes, indistinct extension of the surroundings, that was all.

– So quiet, he said. – No sounds anywhere.

– No people, she said, a bit haunted in her expression, in her voice. – You could just about imagine everything here, that everything is possible, everything.

Everything, everything, everything, he kept thinking.

– Let's have dinner tomorrow, he said, in his mind, stopping and holding her tight. – Lunch? Late dinner?

– I really can't, she laughed softly, regrettably. – I'm going away for a time, but I'll love to take you up on it sometime.

They walked back, took the longer, scenic route, not saying much.

– Let me walk you home, he insisted, when they were close to the bridge, where he would turn left and she right, turn west, turn east.

– There's no need. She shook her head. – I live just beyond the turn of the road.

She stopped and smiled.

– It was nice meeting you. Strange, isn't it? We've both been walking here for ages, and we've never bumped into each other before.

She walked away, leaving him alone in the night. He stood unmoving, as she disappeared beyond the turn in the east... dissolving into mist and shadow.

=====================

He walked the route, the path twice, the next night, without encountering her. There were no distinctive dreams, no nightmare beyond the frantic pace

of his feet.
No fog but the long, endless stretch of cruel clarity.
The days, the weeks, went by, and he slept like the dead.
No dreams, no dreams about her, except in endless waking hours.
He could see the fog drift by his feet, light bending in the corner of his eyes. He had managed somehow by sleeping two hours each night for the last month. Now he slept like a baby every night and he felt like he might be slipping.
Control was a finetuned tool. He had always known that. He knew his «associates», his underlings didn't notice anything obvious in his demeanor, but he was just as certain that they did notice that something was amiss or not quite right. And sooner or later they would make their attempt at taking advantage of the crack in the armor. They always did, of course, they always looked for openings, for cracks, so it wouldn't be anything new really. But sensing blood, they would be that much more dangerous, and they would probably make it a coordinated effort. A good opportunity to rid himself of opposition and excess baggage, for sure... if he was up to the task.
Doubt... had always been a foreign concept to him. Now, he felt it creeping towards him, creeping inside like a cancer, eating away at the bone.
The bone dancing on his calluses like rubber. He was presenting a project to an assembly of sharks. Minutes, hours later, he was alone in his office, looking out of the window, on the streets far below, wondering what was wrong.
What went wrong, damn it!
They hadn't bought it, hadn't accepted his «proposal». A bunch of losers he had been able to easily wrap around his fingers merely a few weeks ago.
Mary Ann entered the room. She didn't walk close to him, but stood by his desk, facing him.
– Rough day? She said sympathetically.
He looked at her with his usual icy stare, the look she didn't dare meet.
– Not really. People may be rough, not days. But don't fret about it! I've waited for some time, now, for them to make their move. It could just as well happen today as any other day. I think they'll really see this as a hard-won victory, patting each other on each other's back, congratulating one another. They might think themselves a match for me. So much sweeter, that much more devastating, the day I take them out completely.
She looked at him with a lot of the old admiration returned, her confidence in him restored. He read trust in her eyes. She didn't notice any of the doubt in his.
The day ended. Finally! He had imagined it would be a thousand years

long. He went home a couple of minutes later than usual. Walking through the office floor, taking the elevator down, he could sense the whispering, the staring, the rumor mill, buzzing even more energetic than usual. They couldn't see anything in his demeanor, of course, he made sure of that, but it was impossible to put a lid on the events earlier this day. News always traveled fast in places like this, and never faster than after a Shakedown.

He had time, he knew that. Dethroning, in the business world, like elsewhere, didn't happen over night. At least it didn't seem that way. It was over a month until next important board meeting, though his enemies might use the interim meeting a fortnight before that to strike the final blow. Yes, he had to assume that they would.

He was slightly speeding when driving home. That was unlike him, he knew that, but just now he didn't care. He had the roof off and the wind was blowing through his hair. It certainly felt good.

It was her, wasn't it, on the bridge? He saw her just a short while, and she was gone. There were always just glimpses, during the light of day.

He went out early that night. The sun hadn't set, as he walked east. And then, as the sun's last rays made everything red, he saw her, standing on the bridge, awaiting him. Her face colored by the fire of the sun, her black hair burning, as the wind was playing with it.

– Hello, she greeted him. – I just got back. It's lovely to be back.

She smiled and kept staring at him, undeniably posing where she stood, her hips slightly bent, speaking with pouting lips. As he reached her, he took her by the hand and pulled her close to him. A shadow crossed her face. His shadow, he realized. The red and yellow shadows mixed like fire.

– It's lovely to have you back, he said, his smile tight and bold.

And he kissed her on the lips, the full, full lips. She stiffened just a moment before melting, forming her body to his, her mouth opening to him, like blossom fire.

The sun had set now, far below the horizon. Her face was clearly visible in the twilight. It was midnight. There was no one out tonight. The two of them walked west, to his house. The red gate, the green gate, he hardly noticed. Through the green gate, and he could smell the garden.

Truth to tell, he had smelled the garden from far away.

– Do you want to come inside? He said. They stopped a second before the door.

– Yes, she said.

He held open the door for her, and she was dancing inside, dancing in front of him, into the living room, enticing him with her moves. She took a look around the room, looking at him cheerfully.

. Hmmm, not bad...

She took the sword down from the wall and started swinging it back and forth.

– Balance is good, and it has a *name*. You paid blood and tears for this, didn't you?

– It did cost me some hours of wages, he said admittedly.

She laughed throatily, as she started swinging it more boldly, and he was amazed by her skill. Around the head, above the head, from hand to hand.

– I won't argue with you, since you seem to be an expert and all...

– I am! She stated as a matter of fact. – I've been in training since I was a little girl. Swords, knives, all kind of martial arts, I'm a veritable one girl army.

She put the sword back in the sheath with an elegant swing of the arm.

– Such a nice and tidy place, not at all your typical bachelor home...

– What can I say, he admitted, – I like to know where things are.

– But you don't know where you have me, she said teasingly, – and you're enjoying that, too...

The shadow and the rainbow were dancing constantly around her, blinding him, binding him.

They were dining, with red wine and candles. There were hot stares over the table, toasts of liberation and mist.

– An excellent cook, too, but I would have been surprised if you weren't...

She revealed clearly that she was teasing by winking to him. Just a tiny wink, but her face was so... expressive that every change spoke... volumes.

He had opened all windows, all doors. The fireplace burned with a low, pleasant flame, not really turning up the heat anymore than it already was.

She was reading his diary. She had found it in one of the shelves and picked it up, before he had been able to stop her.

There was silence a while, before she finally spoke.

– Have you written this?

– My pastime pastime, he grinned.

– This is *good,* she said pleased. – I knew you were not the hopeless bore you seemed to be...

Winking again.

– The world may seem both ordered and chaotic, but isn't really any of it, but is rather filled with chaotic and ordered strife... expressions of mind and Shadow.

They were dancing, two shadows, on the edge of the Night.

– You know, she was pondering, looking up at him from his shoulder.
– Death, in occult symbolic tradition is seen as Change, or the need for

change. In some Tarot decks, for instance, it's not necessarily a negative card. Without change something falls asleep inside us. We need it perhaps even more than our bodies need water.

– Most people are afraid of it, she said, almost as an afterthought.

– There seems to be something missing from my life, he said, admitted eloquently.

She laughed softly.

– You should *embrace* this aspect of yourself, she insisted. – Many people go through their entire existence without expressing themselves. What happens to such people, to a person denying the Self, to one denying it so thoroughly that it seems to belong to a different person?

He took the initiative, kissing her so hard that her lips started bleeding. Her eyes grew big and her body supple.

And she melted into his cold embrace.

==============================

She was levitating above the highway. She was smiling. It was the most frightening sight he had ever seen.

– You didn't accept the gifts I bestowed upon you, she said. – Know that you are forever damned.

And then she was gone.

Later that night. He was driving north (again). A boy and a girl were sitting along the highway, kissing. Suddenly the boy fell to the ground, merely a skeleton left. The girl was turning towards him, the man in the car, and she was smiling. And the car was gone. He was standing still in the middle of the road, while she started walking towards him.

– I'm inside you now, she said. – I'll never let you go.

And then she was gone, as suddenly as she had appeared. But he could feel her everywhere, in the air around him.

He woke up screaming.

The bed was wet with sweat. The air was so damp that the sweat kept flowing from his shaking body. He stumbled to the window. It was wide open. He had been thoroughly convinced that it had been closed, closed, closed.

He half dresses himself in shorts and T - shirt and running shoes, hurrying out the door, closing it behind him.

It's autumn. It should be much colder, he thinks. It is as if summer is staying with him. Breathing easier, having left the house, he starts on his usual route, walking east.

It's summer twilight, light darkness. He can easily see everything, everywhere, light as day. He glances behind him one second, casting hurried glances to the side the next, hardly ever casting more than a glance ahead. He's attempting to look in all directions at once, like when he was a kid, often stumbling, almost falling more than once.

The single streetlight ahead is blinding him, preventing him from seeing properly. She's hiding in the shadows, he knows that, just outside the blinding light.

The road to the highway has always been dark, a long stretch of charcoal, where dark corners are everywhere. Reaching the highway, with all its streetlights had always been a relief, a salve on wretched nerves. Not so anymore. Not inside his well-lit house, not here, in the middle of the road. Even in the middle of the road there wasn't sufficient distance between him and the whistling bushes, the ground darker than the gray pavement. There are cars and he had to move a bit to the side. He feels compelled to look at the cars as they're passing, look at the blinding lights obscuring his vision, blinding him to the threats from the edge.

No cars anymore. There were no more cars. He continued to look around him. His neck started to hurt, he hardly noticed.

He looked left, he looked right, he turned his head and looked behind his back. And with a sudden start, forward again. There was no one anywhere.

And then he looked up.

And there she was, floating horizontally above him, her smiling face close to his own.

And he is SCREAMING from the top of his lungs. And without looking back he flees back to the house, to the fragile sanctity of his home. While all the time imagining how her fangs are growing, how her claws are reaching for him, sinking into his back.

He ran all the way to the door, doing the three steps in one stride. Stopping, looking around. Looking up. Looking down. Sideways. All ways. One more time, all the time. There is no one there. Fumbling in his pocket for the keys, finding them, dragging them into sight, loosing them on the porch. Bending down, picking them up, unlocking the door, storming inside. Closing the door behind him, locking it tight.

He was breathing hard, crouching one or two times, before standing straight. Sweat poured down his cheeks, his forehead, into his eyes, obscuring his vision. He grabbed a towel, rubbing his face hard, hysterically keeping his hair from obscuring his vision.

The house was silent. Even while listening he could hear no sound. He could feel himself calming down. Opening the fridge, grabbing himself something to eat, something to drink, drinking juice from the bottle, he sat down by the kitchen table, staring at hands still shaking.

It was almost dawn when he walked to his bedroom, to his bed. He opened the door, walking inside, seeing her as she was turning on the bed, looking at him with gleaming, inviting eyes...

==========================

He couldn't tell if he was dreaming or not. He grabbed the desk in front of him, the desk in his office, in broad daylight, a warm, sultry summer afternoon. It felt solid, it felt as if he was actually touching it... but he wasn't certain, he could never be certain, could he?

There was the sound of the city traffic, the fans on the shelves cooling the room. He started breathing and life-giving air burned in his lungs. Everything felt as it usually did, but he couldn't really tell how it usually felt anymore. For all he knew, all he feared, this was the dream.

Perhaps a man strolling through the night wasn't really unusual? It could be common as grass (if grass was common). There was just *no way* to be absolutely, objectively certain.

Rachel entered the room. Or perhaps she had been here all the time, was here, all the time. Her gypsy look only moderately devaluated by her smart, modern business dress.

She walked up behind him and started scratching him softly in the neck.

– Trouble sleeping?

He nodded.

– You poor boy. She touched him lightly on the cheek.

He looked at his hand. It was bleeding. A part of the desk had broken in his grip, and penetrated the skin. She took his hand, lifted it to her mouth and started licking off the blood.

– It tastes good, she whispered, the rays of the sun entering the room, illuminating her pale skin. – So good...

He could feel her tongue, feel it inside his veins, inside himself. And the blood was like water to it. And it grew, in size and eagerness. The blood was nourishment, soaked up by the forest floor like a dry sponge. The eyes, all three of them, were like points, sinking deep into the head. And he sank with them.

Kissing her he took a small bite of her lips, drawing blood. Startled she took a step back, looking at him with big, deep eyes. Before reentering his space, snuggling her body tightly to his.

Mary Anne entered the room.

– Everything is in order, I gather? He exclaimed.

– Yes, sir, the secretary replied respectfully, eagerly. – You have seven meetings today. I've taken the liberty to sort them, by time and by importance.

She put a neat pile of paper on his desk and left it there.

– That would be all, Mary Anne, he told her.

She nodded and left quickly and efficiently.

– What a nice girl. Rachel smiled to him.

– She is, isn't she?

– And quite indispensable…

He nodded, didn't trust his voice.

Later that day deliverymen entered the office, carrying a new desk, an exact copy of the one damaged. They carried the old one away, leaving the new on the old spot. Mary Anne had placed all essentials in neat piles on the floor. He looked at his watch. It was time to leave. He knew everything would be in order by the time he returned here tomorrow.

He strolled to the elevator, took it down, down, down, up, up, up. The door opened, and he entered the garage. His car was on the left, just a few steps away. He passed it and walked further off, all the way to the exit. Out through the exit and immediately he found himself in the swirling images of the city. He started coughing almost immediately. The exhaust from the long, long line of homebound cars surrounded him like a wet blanket. He took off from the business district, finally reaching its boundaries a few minutes later, to a street of restaurants, bars and stores a bit quieter, with quite a bit better air quality. He wasn't coughing anymore, he just wanted to.

It was late Friday afternoon. Friday Night was emerging from its cocoon. Excitement was in the air. Dull, feigned excitement, but excitement nevertheless. Most people had changed clothes already, changed before leaving the office, throwing themselves into the fake-colored streets.

He sat by the desk in a noisy bar. Half of the people had wedding rings on their fingers, the other half did not.

– This existence is really quite insane, he said to the girl beside him. – We're working our butts off the entire week, and for what? For some extra commodities in our home, a few hours of desperate partying by the week's end. I don't want to be a put down here, but sometimes a body has to wonder, that's all.

– And last Friday we, my friend, and me, were at a party on the Westside, you know. It was one of the wildest gigs we've ever been to. Quite remarkable, I tell you.

The girl's voice was modulated and soft. She looked at him with misty, pondering eyes.

– I take strolls in the night, he said. – I don't really know why. There are no other people out then, so it's really quiet and peaceful. And I get a change of perspective, I guess. But I really don't now why.

– We got to know a lot of new people and received an invitation to other parties, the girl said, – so it was a great move for us, going there.

– I mean, I don't know why I'm here either, I thought I needed a change of pace, you know.

The girl rose from her chair.

– I'm going to the bathroom, she said. – I should do it now, before they become too crowded. Crowded bathrooms are one of the major obstacles in these places. For the sake of me I can't understand why they don't make them bigger.

She left. Or did she? He didn't think she ever returned, but he couldn't say for sure. For all he knew, the girl who sat down on the chair a few seconds later was the same girl. Perhaps she didn't look the same, but he couldn't really tell. Not by her looks, not by her voice, not by her choice of conversation.

He rose steadily. Strange, he would've thought he would've become drunk by now. There was a buzz in his ear or in his brain. Probably the loud music, the screaming into each other's ears, but he couldn't say for certain. It seemed… different, somehow, in a way he was unable to quantify.

The bathroom was crowded. He didn't seem to have any problems getting through, though, to relieve his pent-up bladder. It could, of course, just be his imagination, pure wishful thinking. For all he knew he could be standing by the bar, pissing on the expensive, filthy carpet. The laughter was hard and wild at the same time. It both disturbed and excited him.

The room was red, shattered by red. Chairs, tables carpet, walls. The designer was obsessed by shades of red. Red light gave the mahogany bar, the shining mirrors and tools and glasses and bottles a rainbow shade of gray.

The… Buzz was calling his name. The Rose was calling his name, showing her thorns. He froze, looking up, squinting his eyes, looking at the other side of the smoke and haze filled room… and there she was.

There she walked, sliding between the other, transparent ghosts. Her feet touched the floor with her every step, but still it seemed as if she was floating above it. The wings protruding from her shoulder blades were black, shattered in red and fire. And her face was a marble white. The yellow mix shining like tears flowing down her cheeks. The buzz filling his ears silent, like thunder. In her hand she had a knife. An ebony shaft, an ivory blade, pointing to the floor, the red carpet, tearing it up like paper.

And he had a hard time breathing. And he felt the blade cut into his skin. And he had a hard time breathing.

And then he woke up, and he was home in his bed, and his bed was a pool of sweat and body waste. Her dark eyes shone in the air in the bright, bright-lit room and he SCREEEEEEEEAMED.

He looked around. There was no one here, no one there. As he jumped out of bed, standing on the cold floor shaking. Autumn winds howled outside. He fought his way to the bathroom, on shaky feet, opened doors with shaky hands. He placed himself straight in the way of the foaming-like air from the wall heater. There was no heat. He could just as well be standing on a pile of ice.

Suddenly there was light outside. It had been dark a minute ago, hadn't it?

It was hot, a hot summer morning. He whimpered as he looked at himself in the mirror, the wild wide eyes, and the unhealthy complexion. How silly of him. Of course, it was light outside. It was summer. The sun was about to rise, goddammit. HOW FUCKING SILLY OF HIM.

And he could smell her scent in the very air.

=================================

I'm walking up the stairs. There is someone following me. I'm somewhere in the office building. The stairs are running along the wall up and down. I'm standing by the banister, looking up, looking down the center, infinitely far up, infinitely far down. There is the sound of the elevator, approaching no closer, the buzz of talk among the employees, the sound of the many computers.

Jointed, disparate images come to me, jagged hard-edged flashes of reality.

The hose of the fire hose, sticking out of the wall outlet. The elevator moving up and down, occasionally passing my floor, but never stopping there. Its passing leaves a brief light, then nothing. There is light on my floor, but it isn't illuminating anything. There is this big meeting coming up. I should come up with something. Anything. It has never been any problem for me before. Now my enemies are moving in for the kill, and I'm frozen on the spot, awaiting their move with passive indifference. My defenses clumsy, ineffective, unequal to the task.

I see the woman. She's moving down the stairs now, away from me, but her way of moving, her floating, unnerving steps continue to haunt me. She's holding one hand on the banister, floating down, down, down. I can see her feet well above the stairs. I can't see her face. Her body is usually visible to me, though, as it is gliding in and out of the shadows, and as it is hidden by the stairs presently above her. The movements are like clockwork. Now I see her, now I don't, as she's gliding towards the ground far below.

I can hear her voice, a whisper in the wind, a thunder in my ears.

«I dreamt that I was falling. Not through space, but through time».

Or is the voice really my own?

See her, don't see her, see her, don't see her, see her, don't see her, don't see her, don't see her…

Suddenly I don't see her. Not until moving my attention several floors above. She couldn't have gotten there without me having discovered her. But she has.

She's moving upwards, towards me. And I can see her face. She's smiling at me. I can see the skeleton, the framework of her features, and she smiles sweetly, enticing me to be calm, to be accepting of her gifts. A bony hand is emerging from her cloak. Its claws are clutching the blood red dagger. I can see Henderson, cheering her on, a passing ghost, vanishing in the shadows. But she isn't disappearing. She's turning more solid, ever more so, as she's closing in on me. Just one floor more now. And then she's walking the last few stairs. And as she's emerging from the stairway, she's smiling sweetly to me, and is raising her knife, her sharp scythe above her head.

And then…

And then the lights

And then the lights are out.

And I can't see anything, but I can hear, hear the whispers of her cloak as she's moving, moving closer, hear my own, ragged breathing, as I'm standing still, frozen on my spot.

==========================

The fog is lifting. The velvet curtains are torn, shattered on the floor.

It's Time, Time for everything to finally be explained and understood. No doubt will remain, no stone be unturned.

The air stinks of exhaust fumes, of bad breath and rot. I don't think I've ever beheld a better dressed, better smelling bunch of rats in my life.

I can see Henderson clearly. He sits on the opposite end of the long conference table. He's very smug and cocky and confident, even if he's quite good at hiding it. This is just a minor meeting, a preparation. We're gathered, symbolically, in his office.

The mood is tense… and full of anticipation. A smell of blood is more than lingering in the air.

The windows are open, doing nothing to improve upon the foul air.

– We're a modern company. Henderson stands rigid as he's making his case. – But we're still stuck in the older, geriatric structure. To further improve our profit, we must ever strive to improve ourselves. There's no time for rest in this business, nothing to gain for those who want to rest on old laurels…

The room is empty. I've taken a stroll back in, to look at the battlefield. It's unnecessary, really. You don't need a crystal ball to realize the obvious. It went badly. Henderson acted very efficient, very modern, very clever. He did say enough, without saying too much. There were times when one could be tempted to suspect he was inspired by a higher power. That piece of stinking garbage.

Something on his extensive bookshelves is attracting my attention, a glimmer, a…

It's a blade, a knife, with a hand-cut pattern he claims he bought on his trip to Africa last year. He's talking incessantly about that trip, as if immortal truths appeared to him while he was living in a village hut for nine months.

I pocket the knife. It slides comfortably in place hidden behind my wallet. Let him wonder who took it, let him suspect all the people walking out and in here today, including the cleaning crew.

Let him sweat.

The cold breeze on the roof is refreshing to me. There's no sense of vertigo, as I look down on the street far below, as I turn and she's standing just a few feet away, looking at me with her auburn eyes flashing in red.

– You know what you have to do, she says. – There's no other choice, you know that.

As I stare at her, as I learn the true meaning of the old expression and reality of «a cold trickle down the spine», she turns and walks away, and is fading to nothing as I watch.

Rachel is curled in the chair, lightly dressed, her drowsy, auburn eyes are flashing in red. I'm stretched out on the floor below her.

– I *loved* that, she says huskily.

I can see her dripping wet cunt, her stiff nipples under the thin fabric of the t-shirt. I can feel my sticky wet, drowned dick between my legs.

The heat from the fireplace is heating up the room in ever-stronger waves of air. I can see them as veins, as blood running through the body. I can hear the blowing of the wind outside. It's a sharp, howling sound, cutting deep.

– You must do something, she says in a lovely, persuasive voice. – You must make a decisive choice, take control of your life.

– I'm so glad I met you, I tell her, kissing her foot. – You've made me see life in completely new and different and interesting ways.

She chuckles softly.

– It's mutual, she says pleased, with a momentarily glimpse of fear, soon forgotten. – I dream at night, I dream at day. I… I dream that I'm *falling*… not through space, but through time. I can't seem to remember why, but the images are so vivid, so powerful that they're keeping be awake all night. I paint, I strive, and I can't escape it, as if I'm its slave, the slave of Time.

And I can hear the curtains falling, and the curtains are sharp knives, cutting every vein in the body.

– You know, I've never been able to paint, I say. – I've done a lot of other stuff occasionally, even if that, too, never turned out to be much, much of anything. But drawing and painting and sculpturing, that has ever been off my province.

– Come, she says, jumping out of the chair, grabbing my hand.

We walk through her home galleria, back and forth, back and forth. Her images have a form of extreme realism that is very… very…

There's one image of an elevator, painted in shadow red. A shadowy figure is walking up the stairs on its right side, seen from some obscure point, and far below, one can glimpse another shadowy figure, walking down the stairs.

There's a woman falling. Another painting, the same scene, painted from above. On a road, a twilight night, a car is driving by. A woman is floating in the air. Her face is a mix of extremes, radiant skin and a dry husk where the skeleton is clearly visible.

– Disturbing, aren't they? She whispers half aloud. – Some mystics claim that death is a metaphor for change and change can indeed be frightening.

– Yes, I say in a voice seemingly reaching me from far away.

– Why don't we go away somewhere? She kisses me hungrily, longingly. – Tell no one where we're going, so no one will ever disturb us? I've always wanted to do that, sailing away… into nothing…

– I know about such a place, I tell her. – No one will ever reach us there.

And her face is fading from view, as dew before the morning sun.

She's not there as I make my night walk. She's not there as I go to bed or when I awake the next morning.

Her house is empty. There's only the row of paintings. I'm fully clothed and the bed is made, as if I've never slept there at all. In one of the paintings I see myself standing before the row of paintings, looking quite unresolved.

I hear the rattling of keys, and the sound of someone opening the door, and there she is, fully clothed, with two full plastic bags of food in her hands. And here I am, cobwebs in my eyes, standing naked in front of her. It doesn't really bother me though, not when drowning in the deep of her smile.

– I bought some tasty morning food, she says brightly. – We should fatten you up a bit. You've been looking more and more skinny lately.

Fast and effectively she puts some of the food inside the fridge and leaving some on the counter.

A light, a flash is lit in her eyes. She walks around me, appraisingly, standing by the window a minute

– Yes, this has distinct possibilities… Hold that pose. Don't you dare move, not even an inch.

She made food then, made big, juicy sandwiches that made him feel upright, made him feel alive. He was allowed to eat while she sat down with a canvas and a brush and started on the painting. He could see it before his inner eye, his slightly lost expression, standing there looking at the paintings. She drew him with his clothes on, even if her teasing smile told him that she rather wouldn't. He stood still all the time. Except for moving his arm and chewing his food (his delicious sandwiches) he stood there most of the day.

He heard the church bells ring. He saw the sun move across the sky. And in the layers of her art he could sense it all.

– You can take a pee now, she said mercifully. – When I think of it, you may dress. I've got you burned into my memory…

He did pee, and he stood on the john a long time as the hot fluid flowed from his loins.

She met him in the outer hall, as he had dressed and was ready to leave.

– Are you ready? He asked.

She took a look at herself, at them in the mirror, the costume of Death and The Maiden. They hadn't put on the masks yet, but they could sense them, as if they had already become a part of their faces.

She turned slowly towards him, with her arms lifted above the head.

– What do you think? She asked.

He swallowed hard. She laughed her thrilling laughter.

– I love costume parties, she exclaimed. – Everybody gets a chance to be exactly who they are.

She turned and embraced him.

– You may keep your key, she said, kissing him on the lips. – I've got a spare.

They took a cab to the festivities, to obscure their identities and put on the masks, as the car turned around the last corner before the intended stop, the main entrance of the rather large building ahead.

Everybody gathered here tonight, everybody being something. Both worried and expectant they smelled rust and blood. As ever there was a considerable number of onlookers and hopeful groupies outside, forming an honor guard to those allowed inside.

He looked at her, his companion, as everybody looked at her, at her face of light and shadow, half hidden by the mask, through the slits in the ivory covering his own face.

Lights blinked, camera flashes and other flares, and most of those present excelled in the attention. He saw Henderson almost immediately. The man moved around with a new confidence, almost bloated on it, in fact. He acted as if his future mark already was hit. Introduction was fast, formal. Rachel smiled sweetly to him, as they shook hands. Henderson smiled a bit insecure in return.

He danced with Mary Anne, but kept his eyes on Rachel dancing with Henderson. She said something to him, said more to him, and he lost his confident demeanor. It was palpable, almost visible in the very air surrounding him.

Mary Anne and Rachel were dressed exactly alike. They behaved alike, and

Henderson grew a deep furrow in his forehead as the evening progressed, as he could no longer tell which was which, as he lost his footing and no longer stood on solid ground.

He kissed Rachel as Mary Anne was dancing with Henderson… Or was that the other way around? He enjoyed himself as the evening progressed, as the solid walls crumbled, and he crumbled, and he put himself back together.

The next day they drove to the cabin by the coast. He sat behind the wheel. She sketched, did simple sketches on her pad.

– It's so beautiful. She stepped out of the car, embracing the place with her arms. – No one will find us here.

There was no sound of machines, only of the wind and wild, wild nature. It whispered to him. All of it whispered to him. Jointed, disparate impressions of sound and fury came to him. He could see the row of paintings clearer than ever.

Her sketches were about the road, the cabin. He wondered if she had drawn the cabin before she had seen it.

They walked inside.

– You're using gloves in this heat, she said teasingly.

– Sorry, it's my eczema acting up again, he said apologetically.

– I can't believe you, she said exasperated. – You're apologizing on behalf of your eczema…

She kissed him on the lips, sultry, hungrily.

The cabin was huge, even excessively so. Her eyes widened. The furniture wasn't cheap, far from it.

– I'm not so sure this is you, she told him. – How many times have you been here?

– Counting this? One…

He slapped her on her butt.

– I'm sure we can re-arrange something…

He told her, kissing her in the neck. Her stiffened body softened in his grip. She leaned on him, warm and eager.

She moved away from him, walked to a chair, pausing a bit, raising an eyebrow, before kicking the chair hard straight across the room.

– Not much to work with here… but we'll manage, won't we darlin'?

– We will indeed, he said, swallowing hard.

They started moving furniture around in earnest.

This chair, she said conspiratorially. – I gotta tell ya… it just plain hopeless. – Straight on the fire it goes.

He took it from her. The fireplace had already burned for several minutes, making the cabin even hotter, making them even hotter. Her eyes really widened this time. He smashed the chair on the floor, smashing it to pieces and threw them in the fire.

The night, the darkness came abruptly, unexpected. They discontinued their rearranging of furniture without really having started it. She turned on one light, the one above the bed, illuminating it, illuminating herself. He saw shadow and he saw fire and he saw the wall behind her. She sat down on the bed displaying herself for him. He turned off the single light. There was shadow, there was fire. Sweat penetrated his clothes, making him queasy. The sun rose, the sun set. He touched her body, the dry and warm skin. She penetrated him, the deeper he incursed her. And afterwards the dreams wouldn't stop. He had almost got used to them by now, like memories of friends and enemies from a distant past.

– I love your leather hands on my body, she whispered in his ears.

The deep and glowing red floated off and on her body. Her grin was hardly a grin, since he could only glimpse the skin. The light in her eyes was truly fire and not a figment of his imagination.

The fireplace didn't burn anymore. He could no longer be certain that it ever had. Absolute darkness surrounded them, as if it wasn't summer at all, but the blackest winter night. He could sense her in the darkness, but not see her. The smell of smoke lingered in his nostrils, but even if his imagination didn't play tricks on him, it might just as well be smoke from the neighbor cabin several hundred meters away. Smoke could linger in the air for a very long time. He knew that.

Her head was resting on his chest.

– «I dreamt that I was falling», he heard her mumble, heard her hum her song.

He heard the silent rain outside, in the dry summer night.

He sensed her close, even if his eyes saw nothing but soft unidentifiable shapes. Her face, as she smiled, showed nothing but blackened, charcoal features and hardly that, shifting swiftly in impenetrable night.

– This was only a test anyway, he said aloud to the empty air.

– Oh, how so? She inquired sheepishly.

– You know the white, old house by the garage? She nodded. He imagined she did anyway. – I've wanted to do something about it for years.

– So, you do own it, she (probably) nodded. – I've been wondering about that.

– It's almost like a revenant in itself, he shuddered, grinning, – but the furniture and most of the interior is still in pretty good shape.

– So, you used your cabin as a proverbial spontaneous try-out arena then?

Effective perhaps, but potentially very costly…

– I have a confession to make, he told her, truly grinning now.

– I love confessions, she whispered. – It's good for the soul. Do go on.

– This isn't my cabin, he admitted willingly.

– Not your cabin…

– Both the cabin and the car belong to Henderson.

He heard her breathing in the dark, sensed her expectation, as it dawned on her.

– And he didn't mind you borrowing it…

– I think he definitely would have… if he had known about it.

She burst out in laughter. He imagined he heard the echo of her laughter long gone. She crawled up on him, as she started touching and kissing him.

– I love you, she mumbled. – I will do anything for you.

– I know that, he said.

– The rubber. She rose, sat with her ass on his chest. – Let's take it off.

– I would rather not, he said, kissing her hard, kissing her softly. – Not yet.

Not yet. He heard her whisper in the shadows.

Dawn, the color of rust and blood.

He awoke from the dream, drenched in sweat. He felt it grow worse every night, until he certainly would wake up screaming. As he sat down by the kitchen table, enjoying breakfast, he hummed a melody, with words he knew too well. And the morning sun didn't penetrate the big windows. He heard the echo of her song. Every shadow grew from the corners, to encompass the room. And it was night again. He passed the old derelict house, opened the gate and looked back.

Mary Anne entered his office, leaving a pile of papers, a pile of ashes. He sat there in the dark, unmoving like a statue, as the sun moved across the sky.

Finally moving he combed his fingers through the hair. The trees outside… they were dark. He could sense the wind, but the trees didn't move. Nothing moved around him, not even he. The still world refused to move on. He walked through the building, the cheap set pieces of modern human life. He didn't really walk, but sort of floated through it all, affecting nothing. Henderson walked around with a widening grin these days, one that threatened to break his face in two. He waved cheerfully to Henderson, seeing how the grin seemed to shrink a bit, before the man's face thankfully disappeared from view.

He met Rachel outside. She greeted him with a sultry kiss and they went on their way. A café, just a few blocks away, was filled with people.

– I've always felt… strange in my creative mood, she said hesitatingly. –

When painting there's both elation… and fear.

– You're going to your depths, meeting yourself, he said lightly, grinning to her. – It's only natural to feel some discomfort.

She gave him a grateful smile.

– You know what I've heard? She smiled wickedly. – That it was the Storytellers, the Artists who originally created the world, and that, to this day, some of that Power remains. All creative people can sometimes make real what they create.

He looked teasingly at her.

– I feel it, you know, she insisted. – It's like I'm drawing something from another world, giving it form and substance.

And he actually felt a chill, a gnawing at his bones. He laughed.

He kissed her.

The food finally arrived. He looked at his watch. Just a few minutes. It seemed like they had been sitting here forever. His sense of time had really gone whacko lately.

They drank coffee. They ate their sandwiches. The sandwiches tasted like paper. Perhaps…. it was… paper?

– Yes, I know, she said, noticing his slight headshake. – Paper, right?

– Right, he nodded.

They sat there in relative silence for a few minutes. They did speak, but they talked more with the body and their eyes then with words.

– What if it is paper? He said good humored. – Such a venture would certainly save them a fortune in expenses. I mean, it looks like meat, it smells like meat. One can say it even tastes like meat, to a certain degree, anyway, but who can really tell these days…

– I love your sense of humor, she giggled.

Fog lingered low in the street outside. For once it didn't matter. He had no problem breathing.

– You're smiling, she said.

– I've always loved the city, he said. – The countryside has always been… spooky to me.

– I love the countryside, she said. – I would want to stay there forever. We met there, in the twilight, remember? Not a bad win for the countryside, huh?

– I remember, he said. – Believe me, I do.

Everything was close, so close now. He could almost reach out and touch it.

– Let's go home, she said.

– Yes, let us, he said, nodding.

They walked to the car. The huge, multilevel garage facility felt gray and cold. He observed her as she walked by his side, as she shifted and faded, faded in and out, saw her face… turning bony and back. Sometimes as he looked down he couldn't see his own feet. He could feel himself walk, but there was nothing there. Sweat broke through his skin in waves and he nearly panicked until he was once more visible to his own eye.

They seated themselves. He turned the key and the car started with a roar. Wheels turned, and he drove slowly and carefully out of the garage complex, the car engine humming and growling.

Could an engine hum or growl? Could a construct feel pain, sense life move within itself? He frowned a bit, before shaking his head, dismissing the thought.

The road, the car itself dissolved, giving way to forest, to trees. They walked on the trail until darkness descended around them. They sat by the fire, grilling hot dogs. It was all so prosaic that it made sweat break out all over his body.

It was peaceful here, it truly was, but he yet felt wasps and ants roaming his stomach and innards. The fire was a beast reaching for him, clawing at his soft belly skin.

– This is such a thrill, isn't it? She said.

– Yes, he replied.

– We must do this far more often. She bent forward, leaning her tight, muscular body into his. – I want to come and visit you every night.

– I want that, too, he said.

– Oh, you're such a sweetie… She tempted him, letting him see, as she stretched her body, the arms high above her head. – You know exactly what to say to please a girl.

– Well, be that as it may. He looked at his watch. – It is time to head back. As you well know, it's a big day tomorrow.

She was disappointed, even though she hid it well. She was hurt. He knew that.

And he couldn't say he felt bad about it.

They left the woods well before the sky started brightening in the northeast. It was actually a few minutes left until the night was at its darkest, too. It didn't get very dark in summer, but on a cloudy night like this, it wasn't so bad. They had some trouble walking the narrow forest trail back. She stumbled, and he had to catch her and she laughed softly. They met no one, they saw no one. The night was silent, the wind itself was still. They crossed the highway at a spot where they needed to actually walk on it as little as possible. But it was still a surprise that no cars were passing them.

Cars used to pass him all the time during the nightly walks, irritating him to no end. Now there were none.

Awfully convenient, he'd say. So convenient, in fact, that he turned seriously scared.

They walked through the red gate, walked upwards for a while after that. Around a turn and the barn appeared on their right. Everything was turned around. Left was right. In was out. And he didn't feel too comfortable. They walked through the green gate and behind it was the old, white house.

– You should really do something about it, she said, shaking her head.

– I have had plans for quite a while now, he said. – But I have been busy.

– Busy, my ass, she grinned.

She ran up the stairs, past the small, but growing tree (growing in the middle of the stairs), and into the house. He followed her inside. The air looked misty to him, as if unreal. Figures started forming in the mist. The walls reflecting the non-existing light could just as well be numerous dots of fog floating around in the humid darkness. He caught up with her in the living room. Everything caught up. She stood there, looking around, shaking her head.

– Christ, she exclaimed. – This is even worse than I thought. What's with the plastic on the floor?

– I recently made one, desperate attempt to keep the water from spreading to the entire place, he explained. – It didn't work.

– No shit, she whistled.

He walked closer to her, kept walking until he stood close by her.

The room seemed to… shift. The room stayed the same, but different. Everything shifted and turned calm and centered.

– So, what did you want me to see here, she smiled teasingly to him, – beside a lot of water-stained furniture?

– I had no interest in you coming here, he said. – You came here of your own free will.

She had just started to shake her head when he stabbed her with the knife. It penetrated her skin just below the ribs. Pain riddled her face and she looked incredulous and shocked at him. He twisted the blade, tore her up inside. She attempted to grab the blade, grab him, but her strength was already waning. With strength he wouldn't have believed possible he held her up after the hair, as he pulled out the knife and stabbed her again and again. There was a strange sound every time the sharp metal slid in and out of the mangled flesh. He pulled out the blade a final time and let go. She fell and hit the floor with a thud, like a dead sack of sand. There was still life in her eyes, but it died fast. Blood flowed from her open mouth and if she attempted to say anything it got lost in a waterfall of bubbles and thick fluid. She lay still. Empty eyes stared at the roof. Round, polished glass, nothing more.

He wrapped the body, the body of dead meat in the plastic. After it was completely wrapped up he undressed completely and wrapped his clothes up in another roll of plastic. He investigated his own body. There were a few stains here and there, but nothing a good shower wouldn't take care of. He wrapped the body one more time. Then he lifted it up and carried it to the car, both the heaps of plastic. He opened the trunk and threw the big sack of plastic in there. The house, the new house was quiet. There were no sounds he couldn't identify. The shower was done in ten minutes. He rubbed the skin a bit more than usual and that was all.

Lighting the fireplace was a true pleasure. He burned the smaller heap of plastic first. As the flames rose he sensed the heat return to his body. The heated, steamy shower had made him cold. He threw the diary on the fire, tore it apart and burned it page by page. Then he walked the walk, talked the silent talk through the night to her house, where he broke the paintings, tore them apart, burned them piece-by-piece. Everything happened so fast, so efficient. He had every reason to be proud.

Morning rose fast. The city surrounded him. His building surrounded him, in its comforting embrace.

There was a tense mood around the boardroom table. It shouldn't be, really. Everything was over and done, as far as Henderson and his cohorts were concerned.

– Before we begin today's meeting, I would like to change the order a bit.

He opened his map while looking at Henderson. A nervous excitement and fear rose in the room.

– Isn't that a bit late? Henderson spoke up instantly.

– Relax, he said. – I just want to add a bit, to slightly broaden the perspective. Will those in favor say «aye»?

– «Aye», most of them said without really thinking it through.

And that was it, easy as pie.

Henderson looked shattered already. He knew he had lost. And he crumbled to dust before everybody's eyes.

– Will someone tell me how much we're earning with the planned lay-offs?

There were no takers.

– Well, will someone tell me how much we're earning by *not* implementing the layoffs?

– I can, sir. Mary Anne rose from her chair. – I have the numbers right here.

There wasn't really any contest after that. The bloated balloon had blown.

He kissed Mary Anne hungrily on the lips afterwards, as they were alone in the quiet room. The city outside was close, was below his feet. Balance had been restored.

He notices the details. He has never noticed the details before.

Down there, on the garden hedge, as he is closing the door behind him and starts on his nightly walk, he is able to see a fly dancing on the leaves.

There is the garage on his right, up the slight slope. The old run-down house is on the left, the green gate just slightly beyond that. He passes the old house, closing in on the green gate. The old barn is to his north, on the way east. There is a slight chill in the air. He ignores it, moving on.

He opens the gate, walking through, closing it behind him. Reassuring thoughts float through the upper levels of his brain. A stray thought, and he images that the well-known figure in the living room window in the old house stares at him with a direct, burning look. He's confident, as he walks further east, that there is no one there.

But he doesn't turn his head and look.

Author's word

I wrote Death and the Maiden twenty years ago in an effort to cure myself from my fear of the dark. It worked great. Two days after having completed the story, I walked into the forest and stayed there for several nights. I didn't have a campfire or any light. It was late fall and completely dark. I remember thinking that someone quiet could stand or sit or hover a step away from me, or above me, and I couldn't possibly know if he/she/It did…

But in a strange way, it didn't really matter anymore.

I scared myself completely shitless writing the story, but when I was done, I could write other scary stories (among them Alarums of Reality) without scaring myself shitless. I recommend such a catharsis for everyone.

I could also walk long walks in the night on roads with no streetlights without constantly turning my head and tying my neck in knots.

My fear was never crippling or anything like that, but it did bother me to the point that I decided to do something about it, to confront my fears, in all areas, really.

To everyone scared shitless after having read the story; my insincere apologies.

FIRE BURNING IN THE WIND

Heat became hot. Sea rose. The Wind increased in strength. Heat became visible in the very air. With the heat came the sneaking, violent Death. Land turned to seabed. The whisper of the wind turned to the roar of the Storm. Stone deserts of the world, once called cities were crushed to dust. It was said that many did not leave their habitats in time. This, I know, is difficult to comprehend, but know that this came to pass in a time when humanity was as countless as ants in the ground. They, each and every one of them, it seemed ruled their one private hill and convinced themselves it was the whole world.

The stone desert not swallowed by the sea was devoured by time. Everything disappeared in green and brown, in mud and dirt, and blood and vomit and decaying corpses. Disease and corruption ruled so terrible, so brutal that no one could resist. Those not taken by the water and the wind were drowned by another kind of flood. They were torn asunder from without, from within. Humanity didn't feel like kings of their hill anymore. Fire burned in the wind anew.

$$

The young girl stumbled down the slight slope in a cloud of dust, dry dirt whirling in the air. She fell and rolled down to the bottom where the terrain righted itself. The maimed body stayed still on the ground, between mounds of dried, yellow grass.

It lasted a while, her relative absence of life, before she managed to raise her head a little. Then she managed a little more. She smelled a scent in the air. Something attracted her, something in the very air, hot, arid and quelling. A scent attracted her, undefined, as good as forgotten.

She dragged herself forward, dragged herself away. There was hardly any recognition, any at all when long weeds of green grass seemed to rise around her, infinitely juicy and green. She had smelled it and heard the sound of it, the water, long before she actually saw it. She hardly had the strength to crawl the last few stretches, to the small pond and the crystalclear water. A sharp, fast movement or two she didn't remember doing and she looked down, into the water mirror, at a broken, bloodied face. She bowed down carefully. Sore, swollen hands splashed water in her face. It did hurt, but made her feel better, fresher. She washed herself on the side of the head with fast, instinctive moves and fresh blood flowed into the clear water, making it filthy.

After a while, she had no idea how much time had passed, she managed to stand on two legs. She stayed there on the spot, looking down in the water.

It was clear once again. There was no sign of the blood and the dirt.

She pulled back, without any idea of how to count the passing time. She turned around and began retracing her own tracks, following them up the hill, across the plains. Then... she didn't do more than blink, that was how it felt, and even more time had gone by without her remembering anything. The grass started to turn greener and juicier the higher in the terrain she climbed. It felt like climbing, an ever-steeper uphill stumble towards some unknown, unreachable place.

Her head started to hurt again. Blink... *Flash!* The ground seemed to sway, the green grass to blacken, before her eyes. *Blink*. She lay flat on the ground. The night embraced her on all sides. She shivered. A short flash of it was all she got. *Morning*. She couldn't tell if it was the first or second morning. Or the third or fourth. She remembered a surface, a water, a face, but not when, not where. Sometimes she didn't recall anything of the step before this, this moment now. She struggled to hold on to the thoughts, one single thought. They always seemed to be evading her. The only thing she did remember, it dawned on her was that she didn't remember.

She suspected that she hadn't been walking in these parts before. That she never before had been remotely close to this place. It felt unknown, foreign. The grass stretching so high above her, around her. After a while it dawned on her that she remembered what she didn't remember. The realization was somehow comforting. Everything, the surroundings, her *aloneness* didn't impact so hard on her after that.

Lines stretched unreal out beyond her vision. She didn't really see them. Not with the two eyes. Just inside the head, her head. Tracks. Ruts someone had called them. Tracks left by a wagon. By wheels that allowed wagons to be pulled. Pulled by snorting, suffering bulls. She realized she had to follow tracks. She needed to.

Thirsty. Skin dehydrating the second the thought crossed her mind. Tongue swollen in the mouth, her mouth. The sore throat. Sun stretching down, touching her, consuming her. What wasn't already consumed. The self disappeared, only the self remained. Shehadwalked far, so far when the forest grew around her fragile form, embracing her. The sun didn't, couldn't reach her anymore. It reached for her, stretched its tentacles, its shining rays down between the treetops, but to no avail.

Downwards, she moved downwards, along a dried-out river. Good! She found herself digging fervently and reached humidity and half set mud. Smeared it over dry, cracking skin, couldn't persuade herself to drink it. Not yet. Didn't know how long she could afford to wait. Drove herself on. Rivers, even dried-out rivers led to water. She had heard this often enough...

wherever she had heard it.

Good, good, it tasted so good. She found water and had to blink, blink. The vision did not disappear. Water, water flooded her beyond thirsty mind. The river came flowing from the opposite side of the little more than a big pond, twinkling in the twilight sunshine. She threw herself into the small pond. The abrupt chill refreshed her. She slurped life-giving liquid, drank huge swallows. An instinct, a memory, made her cautious. She halted the drinking orgy a good while before she had too much. She felt incredible. Hungry. So hungry. She dried herself on and around the lips with a dirty hand, dried the hand on the worn, pale-colored pants. This had to be her only pair. She couldn't remember another and absolutely not a third or a fourth. Tears made long lines on dust-covered cheeks. She looked at herself, looked at herself in the water mirror again, the way she (might have) had done once, not so long ago. Tracks. Wheeltracks. She remembered that in flashes, virtually nothing else. Round things rolling away. Carrying little houses over even and uneven ground, bumpy forest treks and overgrown roads. Quivering fingers carefully touched skin by the hot wound by the temple. Immediately dizzy she sank to the ground by the pond. Water. Thirsty. She drank. Slept.

Day again. She crawled inch by inch an awfully long stretch to some thick branches of bush and sought out ripe berries. Ate them with a greed and a hunger that didn't come close to shocking her. Hid from the sharp light of day. Crawled back to the pond and water. Cleaned the wound again. Drank. Slept.

Next morning, she stood on her two feet, stood steady and with just a slight dizziness. Her view was clear (like the water), and she knew this was really the morning after the last. She remembered the night. It was a crystal-clear image in her mind. The overwhelming impact of the forest made her stand rigid for a long time, but it wasn't in any way such that she felt fear. She knew what fear was and this wasn't it. Just the memory of it provoked a reaction in her. A memory, as distant as all the others. Why couldn't she (remember)?

This was far from fear, what she felt, standing rigid in the deep forest. This was something else altogether.

Hunger gnawed in her and drove her on. She needed food. A vague emotion that didn't disappear gave her a notion that this wasn't anything new to her. She had starved before, also in the forest, the huge strange forest, when she had followed those who... hunted. Only followed. Sucking up impressions from a world seemingly so scary, hearing the adults talk about it.

She remembered! They had left her with other women and told her in a strange voice that it was nothing to fear in this place. The huge man hadn't been able to keep his eyes from flickering anxiously. Nothing had happened. But... according to them it didn't matter. They were there, the forest people, the creatures haunting the human sleep. It wasn't this forest, she knew that. Absolutely not. There were spirits in the forest, they had told her, and vengeful, restless ghouls seeking young human souls...

A resolute glow ignited the eyes, the insecure, flickering pools of fluids and flesh. She sniffed in the air. It felt completely natural, like the right thing to do. Without her ever thinking about whether it was right or not.

She climbed the nearest tall tree and started on her eager scouting. Her heart hadn't beaten many times before life in the forest started to come alive to her inner and outer view. She saw rabbit and she saw fox, chasing the poor rabbit. Hints, flashes of game. Food! Deer, big and proud. Gracious Roe. And they all had in common that they kept far away from her. Heart sank in her chest. Yes, the kind of disheartening she felt just then fit that description. Someone had taught her to read and write. This she knew, because she realized immediately how wasted, completely useless it was in her predicament.

She threw herself from the tree and started chasing the rabbit with everything she got. Leaves and branches hit her face and body when she was compelled to leave the forest trail and enter the wilderness. Leaves and branches stung her. The rabbit disappeared almost immediately. She continued to circle long after she had given up on the chase. She saw nothing, nothing at all. On the forest floor there was nothing to see, nothing to gauge. The animals had long since taught themselves to keep their distance from humans.

After a while she fell exhausted to the ground, exhausted in spirit as well as body. She more crawled than walked from the spot, both angry and discouraged. She had to enjoy berries and berries only this dark, too. But the day after and day by day after that even they became hard to find and she had to widen her search to ever-wider circles. And in her need she started to dig for roots, to sample them and carefully taste everything she did run into. Some samples made her ill, others did not. She tried new ones evening by evening, morning by morning, meal by meal. After some time, she couldn't measure, it subsided her hunger, even if it didn't still it. She fed morning and evening, on these two times only. Fed. Rested. Learned. Or moved around. Or sat still. She sat still for many hours each day. At night she gathered strength. The long days she spent studying the movement of the rabbit, how it trekked and paused inside the quivering forest. She didn't hunt it. Not once did she give in to overwhelming temptation. She learned, taught herself slowly, surely its habits, how it moved and moved as one with its environment, the ground, the trees, the bushes, the air. She studied the predator's dance, its song, the way it moved in on its prey, and she shuddered, shuddered in eerie anticipation. Night brought impatience and troubled sleep. She heard prolonged howls and didn't know whether they were real or not.

She could never really be certain that any of this really happened. In a way she experienced as real, it seemed to her that everything happened for the first time.

One day she stood by a pond she remembered from several former recent visits «later», «after» the pond where she had washed the blood from her face. Everything became clearer, *focused,* to her from then on. She studied the young girl in the water surface mirror. She was *skinny.* The clothes hardly fit her anymore. It didn't matter, she felt, as they had become more rags than clothes. She fit them better, by tying, sewing the rags together. Also in this effort, she improved after a while of trying and failing. And thought they fitted her better now. She enjoyed the fact that she felt so much lighter, how easy the air reached the body, how the skin itself seemed to be able to breathe better.

In twilight, one twilight gray and heavy she managed to close in on a rabbit. She attacked it, but just as she was about to grab the damn thing, it jumped fluently out of her reach. It disappeared like smoke and she was left in despair and frenzy, with fists hammering the ground.

Sounds from the forest first made her listen with all her senses, and then made her rise with a wary, wondering look. She stood like that for some time, like bewitched, listening to a ruckus nearby. The Hunger won over the fear and she sought the place of the snarls and hysterical screams. She sniffed and sought, but found nothing. No blood, no bone, no signs of remains or struggle. No rabbit. She had to go to sleep hungry this dark, too.

She awoke with a start sometime during the night and lifted her head, where she slept in her nest up in the tree. She heard wolves or near-wolves howlhowl and she froze in the night heat. She didn't sleep much after that. After a while she gave up trying and started breaking branches into sticks and practiced sharpening them with flat rocks.

She sat up with a start. She remembered this much from one moment to the other, before instinct took over. Listening, she heard only her own rapid breathing. She looked up, staring, beyond the trees and the surroundings. The moon climbed swollen and stumbling over the forest, its walk across the sky like that of a drunken man. This sight created a strange resonance in her. Its rays reached her through thick treetops, thin, silver like, like needles of ice and fire. She was convinced she heard all the sounds of the forest, but continued listening, without being conscious why. Why it felt so important.

Then... she heard it. Consciousness, what she somehow had... lost finally fractured the last bit, and the echoes, the pieces, collected themselves, the tide washed over her, and the wave was stronger than what had left her. She heard it. She heard the howl of the owl, a hoot resembling the howl of a wolf. Bits of... yes, she remembered what it was... ice gathered in her stomach. She fumbled her spear, tightened her fingers around it. Slowly she felt the burden of it, the lack of burden, and a smile cracked the young face.

It was a marvelous thing, what a person saw, when looking beyond what was right in front of oneself. One saw what was right in front of oneself so much clearer. She knew she needed meat. She wished to live. The rest of the night she used for concentration, preparation, building her anger, evoking, awakening what might remain of the forest gods. She painted her body with juice from berries, smeared dirt and mud all over herself, filled the night with screams from her inner self. And the echo returned as the mighty howl of the owl.

Very early the next morning, before the first light, she followed rabbit tracks. Quite often the quick view of all the small animals in the forest threatened to interrupt her search. She wouldn't allow herself to be distracted, where she walked and ran and tripped. Her eyes moved restlessly back and forth, up and down, attempting to register every single movement. Feet drummed against the forest bed, while the sun moved like a drunken sailor across the sky. She saw without seeing the glowing disk, while she closed in on one single rabbit in the uneven terrain.

She was nearly frozen, but not paralyzed. So simple it was, to move, so... natural. Her face was rigid in her concentration, but not the smile, the one from inside. She flowed forward, seemingly without straining herself. Each step was a light, effortless, natural succession of the last. Her fatigue rested, faded away, until it no longer mattered.

The rabbit began circling. Finally! It closed in on its spawn. She realized this, without really thinking about it. And something was... wrong! The behavior of the she-rabbit became wrong. Not wrong. Right. What happened became wrong, in this... context. So many words whirled through her mind, her still fractured mind. She wondered if she had really learned all this, or was she merely remembering, remembering from a distant memory. Thoughts. They became fleeting, pointless.

The young human female rushed forward. She understood in a flash of raw knowledge. She had no problem understanding. The sight came to her in a vision before she actually saw it, the near-wolf bitch that impatient and hungry pushed a paw into the whole in the ground.

NO! A fundamental *rage* rose from the deep, from the human being. *No,* the game belonged to *her!* It was hers. She threw herself forward. The near-wolf backed off a little, unused as it was with aggression in the two-legged predators. Not far, not long. It attacked with a paralyzing snarl. The two-legged one drove her spear through its heart, pushed the four-legged bitch backwards with volatile, irresistible force. A steaming mouth bit around her arm and she felt teeth scraping the skin. They hit the ground, rolled over each other over and over. She fought herself to her knees and stabbed her lethal enemy time and time again. The once so human face consorted in black rage. But the bitch was already dead. Her last movements had been merely cramps. Even in death, far beyond death, the four-legged beast had fought to kill. The young girl, the two-legged beast slowly relaxed and her facial features softened. She picked one of the sharp stones she carried with her, used it to slice open the chest of the beast. Then she pushed a hand inside it... and pulled out the still beating heart. Her mouth opened wide and she took a big bite, tearing the big muscle apart. Blood flowed down her throat, within and without. The meat tasted delicious, the blood even better. She couldn't have imagined how delicious it was, how it made her feel. Her blood, it boiled and flowed through the veins. She caught the lame, frozen rabbit mother with her stare, through the red fog, snarled triumphantly at the lamb facing the wolf. The small animal fled and left its young at the predator's mercy. The female howled in triumph. She was alive, and she would continue to live, live long. The howl of the human beast resounded like fire through the wild, through the forest, the earth and the air.

She had passed another body of water on her way further down, into the valley. The remaining humid heat made her move faster and more during the evening, the twilight. She still covered quite a distance during the day. Two days earlier she had discovered smoke on the horizon and knew now that it came from this valley. She flowed through the forest, ran across the plains, bathed with great pleasure when the opportunity and her need warranted it. Without hurry, she got closer to her goal, the far valley. Smoke, other people.

Late one day, shockingly sudden, she stood rigid in the forest glen and stared at a wall of raised timber pushed into the ground. Pushed far down, they had to be, to stand so firm and secure. Someone had placed them tight together, so tight that it was impossible to look through the space between them. They formed a huge circle at the center of the plain. People lived there inside the circle. How could they stand it? The Sun. Even now, late in the day, it shone mercilessly down into the circle. Every sunny day (and now these days, there were mostly sunny days). She remembered. She knew of such villages, such buildings, houses upon houses, remembered how they looked inside. People built a whole lot of cramped homes inside such walls of dead trees.

An old, burned out war machine rested peaceful just inside the open gate. It was pretty much blocking the gate and she wondered why it hadn't been moved. Away from the open closed gate.

Her eyes moved, to those who worked on the field outside the tall wall. Men and women, humans like herself, caring for the growing things they had put into the ground and cut in the soil to plant more. Damaged it. She had a certain idea that this was something she somehow had seen before. She was filled with both happy wonder and dark curiosity. Her expression didn't change from the obviously eager look and she hardly missed anything of what was going on. As the forest had taught her to teach herself. Big-eyed she studied these members of her own species staying, at least temporarily in the open landscape, staying there voluntarily. She shuddered without knowing why. Gooseflesh ran all over her naked skin. Shrank with misery, she did, when she without any problem what so ever sensed their misery. As they strained themselves. Also, here among the trees, inside cooler shadows of the forest the heat rose violently in the middle of the day and the following hours. Still it continued to rise. But out there in the field, in the full exposure of the sun the heat had to be unbearable. She kept her silent stare on them, saw how they strained and how much they suffered.

And her eyes touched the many scattered remains of the old world. The junk was not in any use, but was visible above the grass and plants all over the field, obstructing the movement of those working there. That, too, seemed odd to her curious mind.

Her eyes came to rest on a young male, a boy working pretty far away from her modest hiding place. She lost the doubting, concentrated look and her face lightened up yet again. Thought and action were virtually instantaneous. She moved carefully closer to the boy, filled with careless, excited eagerness. She had her entire attention focused on him. Studied all of him, both the body and what was hidden. She wondered, in the back of her head what might lead her to such carelessness. A worried, but not very insistent voice kept speaking incessantly, but she didn't heed it. He was... different than the rest. The dark skin, the smooth, black hair marked him. He was different because of his outward appearance, but also... in other ways.

Her thorough, intense study revealed why he had attracted her attention, from the very first look. To her it was easily understood that he did not thrive digging the earth. She read it in the way his body spoke to her.

Couldn't the others see it? How he disliked every movement?

She heard someone cry out and twitched, saw them all discover her one by one. There were more shouting and more people turning their eyes on her. A huge man walked towards her. He had almost covered the entire distance between them before she was conscious of how close he truly was. She took one step back. He halted too, with an uncertain look in his eyes. He started to talk to her, in a kind, soothing voice. She understood his words. Some she had some problems with, but their immediate significance she quickly understood. Where did she come from, what was her name? She didn't really know how to answer those questions. They seemed important to him. She didn't remember, she told him so. How was it possible that she had survived in the wilderness? By hunting, she replied flat out. He asked her about the scrape on the arm and nodded when she told him the sharp teeth of the near-wolf had caused it. Many dogs had become wild in the time after the breakdown. He wondered how she had gotten away, though, stupid man. She replied with a proud stance that the near-wolf bitch had not escaped, that she herself had personally killed her and eaten her warm flesh. Her words didn't cause the expected reaction from the big man. He looked rather worried. The meaning of all the strange questions and their strangely cautious way of approach slowly dawned on her. She remembered and understood, in a way.

A woman came forward and asked if she was hungry, if she wouldn't come with her inside the palisade and take a bath. The words were expressed with a certain kindness, but it wasn't prominent. The girl looked hard at the woman. Hadn't she just told them of her prowess as a hunter? That she could manage outside the palisade and didn't need their smothering comfort? And she had been bathing. The smell she scented from these people was far worse than she had ever smelled. Here, out in the open, it drifted in the wind, not so distinctive, but was still like a sharp pain in the nose. The smell of boredom, imprisonment assaulted her.

She didn't want to stay at this place a moment longer and moved carefully the size of a heel backwards. Everybody got seemingly restless then.

She declared quietly her desire to leave their company, to walk away. She didn't really see the purpose of telling them this. The action in itself should be sufficient. But she recalled something then, that it had been seen as important to the people she had stayed with. She turned and with light, springy steps headed for the woods. The huge man started chasing her then. Her walk turned immediately to running. It happened so fast, from one moment to the next. Like the *wind,* it was later claimed. *We saw nothing but the wind!* The young face brightened when she saw that the male halted by the forest glen and advanced no further. He breathed hard already. But her deeper senses told her it wasn't his sole reason for stopping his chase prematurely. She stopped running, but continued deeper into the forest, keeping watchful eyes on him. Relief and a kind of euphoria flooded her mind. Seconds passed and then he cried out to her from far behind, furious, enraged, at a loss of what to do, with a slight touch of anxiety, that she gathered his fellow tribe members didn't notice, or wished to notice.

– What's WRONG with you? Don't you want shelter and safety?

His words didn't really register in her mind, her inner self. She suspected that they would have, once, but she had changed now, beyond what once would have been her wildest imagination.

She kept running on the outskirts of the woods a few hundred steps, long enough for her to have the opportunity to wave to the special boy. Did she imagine it, hope in vain, or did his hand really move in a slight, almost invisible wave? The thought, hope alone made her blood boil a little extra, when she once again moved deep into the forest, far away from those who wanted to imprison her.

After sleep, after hunt, she forgot them all, also the boy with the dark skin. Only the moment existed to her.

The next days and nights she used to familiarize herself with the new land. She killed two rabbits early the first day and therefore she could use a lot of time to explore and to satisfy her undying curiosity. It got dark early this time of the year, the cycle, one more than clear indication, in spite of the heat that it was not Summer. It didn't discourage her in any way. She saw it as a challenge to learn to move in the dark.

Feet drummed on paths, tight-grown forest floor, through the silent, noisy night. Hours melted away. It was like time itself disappeared. Some time during the silent run, she made a quick glance up, at the treetops, at leaves woven tight. Clouds dark and heavy, in a night truly dark covered the stars. She could have stopped and made a fire, but decided, without contemplation not to do that. She ran on.

After a while, she stopped, without knowing why. Uncertain and hesitant, she sniffed for danger. There was none. There was no prey close enough either. Usually she stopped without needing a reason. This time she felt there was one. She stayed under the tree where she had stopped her wild run, hesitantly, unmoving, attempting to understand.

Something hit her left hand. She looked down, at small droplets of water jumping on and off her skin. It made her upset at first, since she couldn't determine from where it came. She touched the corner of an eye with the fingers on her right hand. Wet? Were these droplets tears? She looked up. There was no water from the sky. She was certain of this. It could, she supposed, have been gathered moist on the leaves during the twilight, enough to form water, turned into droplets, hitting her.

Next morning, she packed her supplies of food and weapons and went on her way, with the purpose of putting the biggest possible distance between her and the village.

Far, far away was her goal. Further west, to what she imagined would await her, the big water. Daystar on her back felt good. She put on extra speed, traveling without thinking.

It was not so far, so long, afterwards, it couldn't be, that she noticed that daystar didn't warm her behind anymore. It blinded her in its brilliance. She realized with a start, that she had turned and circled back, and had done so for quite a while now, towards the loathed place. There was no mistake. This was familiar territory to her. She had prowled these parts only yesterday. She stopped fighting against what was fast becoming a compulsion almost immediately, taught herself as she had, to trust her instincts.

Daystar warmed her behind anew, but now it was setting behind the lone mountain in the west. She reached the settlement well within twilight and kept herself hidden while awaiting patiently the darkness.

Clouds gathered with the darkness. This night, too. Distant thunder rolled in from the mountains in the east. The top, the points of the palisade was drawn sharp in the bleak glow of the fires inside. She wanted to take a trip, a brief peek inside. A quick smile crossed her lips. It could be fun. Action followed thought virtually immediately. She covered the final distance to the wall half-crouched, and on all fours. Without hesitation she jumped and climbed the wall, quiet and easy. She swung herself over and landed with a soft noise in the grass on the other side. As she had gathered there was nobody close to her. None of the guards had moved as much as an inch. Their smells had not changed. There was no way they had discovered her. They could just as well be made of stone, as far as she was concerned. She could not fathom why they were there. Both why they guarded and why such useless dorks had been assigned guard duty.

The wilderness already cried out for her return. Comprehension dawned slowly, why this place was so heavily guarded, why the guards behaved more like stone than actual guards. This place... she wanted to huddle up on the ground merely by being here. She remembered. She had stayed, even lived, in such places before. It wasn't long ago either, it just felt that way, until this moment, when fractured and unpleasant memories flooded back to the surface of her mind.

The war machine was placed by the entrance, as if on a pedestal, a representation of a god. The very sight of it made her shiver in disgust, a disgust enhanced rather than lessened.

The houses, they had built them no more than a few lengths apart, like small cages placed tight together, in one single big entrapment. The rancid smell struck her hard. To build shelter from the rain was one thing... but this... How could they stand it? She suspected strongly that they did not. Of the people she smelled, sensed close, no one seemed any happier than the people she had observed on the field. They all paid dearly for their attempt to close off Nature, close themselves off from it. They had to be both deaf and blind to not realize that themselves.

No one discovered her on her journey between the shadows. In a moment of weakness, she was tempted to make a loud, unmistakable sound, to see if they discovered *that.*

Common sense and a damp fear she did not manage to embrace kept her from such a stupid act.

She moved fast and silent between the houses, went in and out of every single one of them. Some people slept in, others were empty. It did not matter to her. She was not discovered or even detected. Nobody noticed the changes between the shadow and light or sensed movement in the air where she moved. They did not smell her alien smell. Every single one of them had to be deaf and blind and lacking the use of their senses.

She saw it in the center of it all, the big hut. As she had gathered, the biggest and most important house could be seen from virtually every other in the settlement. There were no guards, but the closed entrance, the door, attracted her interest. The girl remembered seeing some of these in her life. Not many, but some. They closed people out and the people inside, in. She tried the handle. The door was not locked. She opened it further and before she had really thought about it, she was inside.

There was so much interesting stuff, so much catching her eye. Utterly useless, but interesting. Only a few items of any practical use to her. She brightened when she discovered a whole collection of steel blades on the wall by the dining table. It was as she had gathered. These people had such abundance of them that they wouldn't miss a couple. Fresh meat, on the other hand seemed to some extent to be lacking. Old words mixed with her new, more natural ways of expression brought a quick smile to the young face. She loosened the rabbit meat she had brought from her belt and put it on the table. Then she meticulously studied the steel blades and after a while, chose two of them. She fastened them to her belt and was immediately fast on her way.

She had just opened the door when she heard steps, and a slight change in the breathing of one of the people sleeping by the opposite wall. A woman screamed. *Behind her.* The steps, the heavy steps, thundered in front of her. It was a close call, but she managed to avoid the grip of the fast approaching bear of a man. After that, she threw all caution to the wind. She ran in a straight line. All of her became occasionally visible in the light of the many fires. Suddenly it seemed that everyone who was not asleep, and then some more were chasing her. In desperation and exhilaration mixed together to something more then, she felt in truth, as one with the wind, the one they wanted to ban her from she raced towards the palisade - and Freedom. Some of the people chasing her, stopped in their tracks, frozen like stone. To them it seemed like she flew. Flew, flew, flew. Flew away on eagle wings. One flash, one twinkle, and she reached the wall of dead trees. Another flash, another twinkle, and she reached the top of it. And then - she was gone, vanished into the menacing darkness.

Later. She heard them all around her, seemingly everywhere in the woods, the vast forest. Torches glowed in the boiling hot night. They didn't, wouldn't stop, the jerks. No way! They seemed determined to stay in here indefinitely until they had found and captured her. There wasn't any great danger of that happening, she assured herself. Their persistence irritated her, that's all. The way she saw it they totally exposed their clumsiness and ineptitude, and should not, in any way cause or even contribute to her misfortune.

But they were many. And she was alone, so alone.

She still felt... dirty, after her visit inside the dead, dead trees, as if something of the disease there had tainted her somehow. She did feel tainted... and f-frightened. It had, to a certain degree been luck, when she had avoided capture. She didn't know for certain what would have happened if she had been caught. She didn't want to know. Perhaps it wouldn't have been so bad... on the surface, where it didn't count.

– RED HAIR! A woman shrieked. – A witch, I wager. May the Almighty give her the deserved punishment!

– We must find her, a pious voice spoke up, – do so for her own sake, save the wee child from eternal damnation.

The girl had grown herself big and strong in the time since arriving in this forest, and also gained speed and agility. She did not doubt her ability to defend herself, to survive in a hard, ruthless world. But she felt as if she froze now, and that the frost sank to her deep and stayed there. One horrible moment she thought she wanted to crawl into the closest hole. And stay there. Insane images flickered for her inner eye. She realized they stemmed from the time Before, before what kept her from remembering. The images meant nothing to her, gave her no release, but filled her with a horror she just barely could imagine.

She kept in constant motion, forced it on herself occasionally, but it worked. Human instincts worked no matter what horrors filled the conscious mind.

Kept herself nearby, close to their oozing fires. It would have been the easiest task in the world for her to pull back, far into the deep forest, disappear from the close proximity of this people forever and ever. She didn't want that. Not yet! The fear lurked close to her all the time, chasing her. Only something within she hardly understood kept her from giving in to it. She pulled herself together, raised herself to full height. In a sudden, almost painful insight she realized what the villagers never would realize, that without risk life would never be worth living.

They didn't leave the forest fast, as she had believed they would, but made more fires not far away from where her sleeping place had been. She imagined it was not the first time they had spent nights here. Still, there was no hiding their nervousness to her, coating them like infested dirt as it was. They tended to avoid the forest. Looked upon it as a place they reluctantly visited, rather than as a pleasant home.

She circled around them several times, counting them carefully, making sure no one was hiding anywhere, waiting to ambush her. She felt more secure, bolder. They were in her kingdom now...

There was a huge trunk of a tree close to one of the circles of tall fires. She climbed it silently, effortlessly. One of the inner, thick branches stretched so far out from the tree, into the night air, that it reached almost inside the circle of fires. She straightened her body to its full length, stood there for a while, enjoying the moment.

I can see you, she thought with a wolfish grin.

She studied them, in vain. There was no discernible difference between them. There was nothing *there,* except a single, homogenous mass.

Shaking her head in sudden anger, she stretched her arms straight out from the body. The sound started deep down in her throat, a low, growling-like sound, rising to a noisy, dark laughter of a *snarl.* In that exact moment the owl howled, hooted from the deep of the night. Each and every one of them almost jumped out of their pale, thin skin. The laughter and the owl howl echoed through the forest and seemed to come from everywhere at once. They spotted her, floating in the air above them. Maybe they, for a tiny moment took their eyes off the demon, the abysmal sight in the tree, maybe not. They had seen her. Now, they didn't.

They stood there for a long time, frozen in their tracks. Many sat straight down on the ground without softening their descent in any way. If the leader, the big man from the big hut hadn't screamed to them, commanded them to rise and bring their weapons, they probably wouldn't have moved at all until morning.

No one got any sleep that night, not the forest spirit, nor the people who in fear and hatred and deep, fundamental confusion chased and hunted her like a trophy.

By dawn she sat wide-awake on a hill and stared at the people below and what they had built. They had returned to their dwellings during twilight, grateful because they had survived the night. Furious that they had let themselves be terrorized by the small, helpless girl and had let her get away with it.

She sat by an anthill, studying it intensely, with a wondering, despairing look. These people, by the way they lived their life sought to imprison themselves. She nodded sadly. They admired and honored the ant. She didn't really find anything wrong with that. But... they didn't need to live like it, did they? They were human beings, were they not, and not ants?

The human-made anthill awoke slowly, painfully. And late, very late. She lightened up. Was it arrogance on her part, assuming she could claim credit for this? Partying late often caused late awakening the following morning. And they had partied a lot. She giggled. It sounded strange, like an echo from an early dream one night, right after awakening in the morning.

Quite a few of those digging in the dirt this morning exposed a restless, nervous attitude, to each other, to the surrounding area and to themselves. It so happened that they looked in all directions with shifty-eyed stares. She didn't feel any pity for them whatsoever. The fact that they seemed scared to death by her presence told her everything she needed to know about them.

The wolfish grin came to her easily and effortlessly.

The daystar shone and did so mercilessly. The day grew so hot that she routinely needed to brush sweat from her forehead. And she hardly moved, hardly felt like moving, even there inside the forest shade. Finally, she tore off a strip of her already torn sleeve and tied it around her head. It worked somehow. She didn't constantly get sweat in her eyes anymore.

Contrary to yesterday and the days before yesterday, this day the very air grew dry, dry as paper. And that was how her tongue felt, too. Humidity was virtually non-existent, seemingly a distant memory. There was no wind, to dry anything, but everything was still dried. And drying. Her gaze changed between the ground and the distant mountains. Didn't they get it, the ant people? Didn't they hear the silent sound of the distant thunder?

She closed in on the boy, silently moving to a position where she was as close to the dark-skinned boy as she possible could, without being seen by the other villagers. She couldn't really stomach using her talent for stealth in such a fashion, but there was not a choice was there, if she wanted to speak to him in private. If they captured her, they would probably burn her at the stake or what she felt was even worse; *force* her to conform to their ways. Images of ropes tied around her ankles and wrists, and a lifted beating stick arose in her mind. And the image that filled her with dread to her very core: her kneeling and submitting before them, erasing her own self.

This close she could see the nuances in his face. Fear dissolved and was substituted with a boundless curiosity akin to blindness.

He stood by himself a bit away from the others, as he always did. It was funny. As far as the eye could see, physically speaking, he wasn't far away. Still, he was always apart from them.

She stood up and waved to him, totally reckless. He froze and looked warily around. But he didn't cry out. She rewarded him with her best, sweet smile and wanted to jump up and down in boundless joy. Reluctantly, she held back, and didn't do more than sign to him that she wanted him to meet with her inside the forest. He hesitated a bit, said something to the man on this right, and then started walking. She had already disappeared between the bushes.

A flash there, a waving hand there. She allowed him to see glimpses of her, enticing him, luring him ever further into the deep of the forest, until she decided they would be fairly safe from being... distracted.

She sat down on a thick rotting fallen tree in the middle of nowhere. He approached her hesitantly, with a sullen skeptic look in his eyes. This approach felt perfectly normal to him. It was, after all, the way he was brought up. He had been taught to fear strangers.

He accused her immediately for having stolen the two knives, bursting with righteous anger. She did return his angry stare with her unconcerned, shameless look. The two knives in her belt were a telltale sign. His outburst didn't seem to carry much punch, though, and sounded, in spite of the apparent harshness pretty weak. She stretched her legs with a satisfied smile. She hadn't been the slightest bit wrong about him.

With an obviously innocent demeanor, she reminded him about the rabbit she had left in place of the knives. He revealed that he was aware of that fact, but didn't feel it would amount to much... to the others. The young female's smile widened ever more. When she implied that she wanted them to bathe together, however, her tone of voice quickly become less brazen. There was a body of water, she told him, not far from here, deep enough to be both cool and refreshing. After a short hesitation, he replied with a sulky

No (and wavering eyes). He had to return, return to the work, he insisted. They would miss him, if he was too long gone. She became sad then. The game was done. She carefully hinted at the fact that he didn't need to return to them. He could go with her, live as she did, in freedom, unfettered by walls, in forests and wilderness. He attempted to make her return with him. And kept assuring her that he would easily be able to make them forget her minor *pranks,* assuming she would agree to submit to their ways. She shook her head. She wanted to go with him, be with him, but shook her head in dismay and sadness. She was alone, but didn't want to move in there, to be trapped inside the dead trees.

They said goodbye. She told him about the signs of the approaching Thunder. He gave her a strange look, but did thank her. And then left her. He disappeared in the forest. Usually, she would have smelled him, even if she didn't see him. Now, no senses came to her, none what so ever. A throbbing head sank down between the knees. She had had such a nice feeling inside, outside... all over herself, while he was close. Now, there was only the feeling of deep loss washing over her, a hollowness, a Hunger that made her sit still much longer than was supposedly safe. She sat still and dead and hardly moved.

(for a long, long time)

In the end there was hunger, survival instinct making her stand up on her feet, making her move, away from there, into the frenzy of the Hunt. She hunted for a while, but even if she did manage to kill game, it was a clumsy and sad kill. Not soon afterwards, she found herself back on her spot at the edge of the forest, keeping virtually her complete attention on the dark-skinned boy. She stayed careful, though. No sound came from her. Light did not reflect from her surface. A person glimpsing her shape would be wondering if she existed at all. She smiled with longing in her eyes and drew to her the young male's every move and gesture. She sat still without moving, and time just went away.

Then... something abruptly changed. Bewildered she felt moisture when touching herself and couldn't stop a moan from being released from her suddenly paper dry throat, between lips she could no more keep pressed together. She looked down between her wet thighs, looked at him - and understood. The girl remembered, without that being necessary for her to understand. He needed her, too. Male and female needed each other.

By the third Dark in a row, the fifth she recalled since her arrival, dark clouds covered the night sky. Twilight had not brought humidity, as it usually did. The ground stayed dry and the very air seemed to quiver. The girl moaned. She knew beyond doubt that she should leave this place. Go far away. Every time she drew breath she felt the smell the very air gave away. Her consciousness, the real one, half hidden, half hiding, cried RUN, but it also spoke of staying, in many fever-pitch voices. Such was the entire her. Filled with contradictory emotions. She stayed.

The animals in the forest, they ran. They had no reason to balance their instinct, no instinct to balance their reason. She could feel them, feeling the Storm. She felt the Storm.

The animals «who do not run away», those tied to posts and imprisoned by their human masters, they were worried. They stretched their rope, paced endlessly in their cages. But in a strangely calm way. As if something, something indescribably precious had been bred out of them long ago.

The girl shivered some more.

The villagers had pulled back into their cage-like homes, to the safety within dead trees, within the unnatural wall where nothing of importance was happening. It should. The people inside should long since have left the place then, or at least been on their way out. No one, at this time could avoid seeing the violent approaching storm. Searing lightning grew from the mountaintops, to the heavy clouds. Roaring thunder superseded the lightning. Lightning superseded the roaring thunder. An endless row of sound and fury. And everything seemed to be happening simultaneously. Death came rolling on its plowing wheel and all the ants hid their head in their hill.

What were they *doing* in there, the idiots? Were they singing? Were they preying to their deaf gods about mercy... instead of listening to their own, inner voice? The nausea, coming on to her since her arrival, turned overwhelming. Partly digested food decorated the ground in a circular pattern. Pale and shaking she stayed put and kept observing the unfolding drama.

She had never seen anything remotely like it, she knew that. It dawned on her that she had heard stories, but they had seemed very much akin to the ones about Old Nick and such, stories designed to scare children into being nice and quiet. Also later, though, during her awakening, her own rediscovery, she had learned about wild and brutal Nature. Nothing compared to this brutal reality.

Somebody had thrown her off a wagon. The memory came to her in a flash of revelation.

The flashes of lightning... there seemed to be an army of them... looked like they were moving down the mountain sides, towards the valley. There wasn't any rain. Not a sign of it anywhere. The first lightning, the first in an endless line, hit the clouds from the cornfield and a veritable firestorm came in its stead. The lone female sat tight with tightly closed eyes, but she still *saw.*

She sensed it all, as she couldn't close her senses. Through narrow chinks, like shadows she saw one of the watchtowers be blown to pieces and the pieces being spread throughout the field. The dead wood caught fire. First the remains of the destroyed watchtower, then the rest of the palisade, when the next lightning struck the sky from the center of the village. Merely seconds later, the entire field became an inferno of fire and ashes and smoke. There was no safe place anywhere, but small pockets in the open field, where the lightning had already made deep holes, long, broad wounds in the ground, became a haven of sorts. The deeper the hole, the better the safety. People ran in panic from their homes, finally using their instincts. Many were burned to cinder because they attempted to bring their things. The inferno of flames and sparks inside the village devoured them in an instant.

Suddenly... it was silent, violently silent, a tiny hope of redemption. The suction from the inferno-like fires melding into one, drowned in the roar of silence. The girl in the forest glen looked up. She saw small, insignificant shadows run from the river with buckets filled to the rim with water, the steaming river, the steaming water, so totally inadequate against the raging fire. The fire swallowed every drop of water, like countless pees in the ocean.

And it all turned even more insignificant when she lifted her head a bit further, further up the valley, where another wave of lightning seemingly competed in a hundred meters run. A long, long line. Even longer, even more powerful than the former. The girl felt both repulsed and attracted by the incredible spectacle. Had she experienced anything remotely like this when living with her parents as a little girl? Her thoughts were distracted a moment, she was distracted. A moment too long. She forgot where she was. The army of lightning swooped the trees just a small stretch from her. The entire forest seemed to catch fire simultaneously and she was forced to join the other refugees, out there on the naked field. She was not distracted for long, unable as she was to keep her thoughts from the fabulous, horrifying experience the last few minutes. She kept moving, realizing with a start, what she already knew, that this was her best hope of surviving the next minutes.

A new, horrible thunder filled the air, deafening, all consuming. And then, finally, the rain came. Without warning or transition the rain supplanted the air. Suddenly it poured, and it became difficult to breathe. The lightning continued to flash in a seemingly endless row. The fires stopped in seconds. The violent lightning continued to fry the ground. A huge part of the nearest forest was reduced to ashes. The villagers had stopped doing anything. They ran in mindless panic in all directions. It was no use. Wherever they ran, the sky hammer hit the anvil of Earth, sparks that could easily devour a human being. The girl threw herself into a pit with several others. Nobody cared about it the least. At this time, she was, both to herself and them, just another ant hiding in the ground. They stayed there for a while, until they once more had to flee. And again and again. She got away from them, they disappeared for her. The Storm didn't stop, didn't quit, no matter how desperate or numb one became. Nature didn't acknowledge some poor ants crawling in the wreckage of their lives, without direction, without purpose. Time became meaningless. Measuring anything an impossibility. There was no Hunger. Not even the understanding, the realization of it. Everything was wrecked, flattened in the eternal Storm. She lay still in the end, quiet and without voice. Nightmare images haunted her. In flashes she saw others, unmoving, nonbreathing. Quiet.

Quiet, stillness. A club against the head, persistently claiming its existence. Reluctantly, eagerly, half dead, half dreaming she dragged herself on her feet. The silence whistled and flowed afterwards. She didn't hear the falling rain, just whistling in her ears and - she imagined - water flowing over burnt soil. A male running by screamed insane. She didn't hear any of it. Slowly she got steady on her feet and pulled towards the fortress, a heap of black burnt trees. She found the main gate easy enough. It was crushed, but still there. Whether or not it was on the same spot it had been, she couldn't say. As the war machine was nowhere to be seen, it could mean that the gate had been *moved,* but she didn't care. She stopped where she supposed the opening had been, and decided, with a distant look in her eyes to remain there for a while.

Slowly, the heat and the blood, returned to her bruised and battered body. She stood to her ankles in mud. Water flowed around her legs. She had injured her hand. Her clothes (and her) were soaked by water and shit. Huge parts of the red hair were burnt away. It seemed dirty brown now. She stood still and breathed, while whistling increased in her ears. Adrenaline gushed into the blood flowing through the veins. She had survived, she lived. Many bodies were stiff and cold on the ground, but she wasn't. She felt fresh and alive.

The Night darkened around her as the last embers of woodwork and field faded. The Night brightened around her as her eyes once again adapted to the darkness. She stood still, quiet. There was movement in the terrain and the ruin. She paid it no heed. The people she glimpsed, and she hardly even glimpsed them, looked like ghosts to her. And she didn't exist to them. At least they didn't speak to her, didn't look at her or acknowledge her presence in any way. Perhaps they would, after reaching out of the mud they had placed themselves, when they needed somebody to point at, somebody to blame.

It had happened to her Before. She remembered. Strangely enough the painful, crystal clear memory encouraged her to once again keep herself going.

He materialized in front of her, a long time after she had stopped hoping he would, a long time after she should have moved on. To safety, to solitude. She stared at him with an intense, burning look. Compared to the ghosts he vibrated of rainbow and embers. She gave away a cry of joy. The flash, the *Life* in his eyes mirrored her own.

They talked for a long time, while hesitatingly touching each other. Physical touch, looks, small glimpses of Hunger, in the edges of their view, nuances of longing, very few spoken words. The choice of the crossroads was there in front of her. A major division, a change. She had a choice. So did he.

They left the place together, side by side. He turned and looked back one single time. A few of the survivors had started to clean up the mess. He noticed that they did so slowly, reluctantly.

– There will always be those who want to repeat the mistakes of the past, she said softly. She heard her own voice again, for the first time in days and nights. And it sounded markedly different, as if belonging to another person.
– Fire is Nature's way of cleansing itself. After its ravaging, everything may sprout anew. Those entombing themselves will ever be vulnerable in the Storm.

By daybreak the sky was once more clear and blue. When the sun rose beyond the mountains, and warmed and dried them, they were already far above the field. They took a bath and relaxed at the first water they reached. A few hundred steps later they felt as dry as ever, but significantly more vigorous. The grass grew greener, the air fresher, the higher they came into the mountains. They kept walking. They didn't need words to know they both wanted to walk a considerable distance higher up, before even consider stopping.

He pulled in air, breathed deeply, because he felt a bit out of breath, but most of all because he enjoyed himself. The forest seemed endless up here. Everything felt, was felt more powerful. He enjoyed himself, as he watched her rear and felt no shame. And marveled at how easy she moved through even the thickest forest. Every tree, every obstacle felt like a fortress to him. Everything seemed to just... move aside for her, instead of the other way around. He forced himself to sit on high ground while she went looking for game, went hunting. It even came to be a source of joy for him, that he felt no considerable envy because of her skill. Instead he enjoyed her... hunt. He saw glimpses and flashes of the man-beast now and then, a mix of deer and panther, as the female ducked in and out of brushes and bushes. The firehair was blowing in the wind.

And slowly, unnoticeable at first, even on the first day, he suspected more than noticed the changes in himself. Tiny reflections, really, on the edge of consciousness. It felt like that at first, the first nights with trial and error, journeys and dreams. The extreme awareness came later, rose slowly, inevitable. Already the coming night, he had never before experienced one without walls, walls within, without, he more than suspected he would never be able to return, to the walls, to the person he had been. He wouldn't have survived. The body might have been able to breathe and walk, but he doubted if the heart would have beaten and the blood flowed through his veins.

He learned through her, through himself, to not stumble on the numerous roots, from trees, from bushes, sticking up everywhere on the forest bed. Stumbling walk and run became as transformed. He transformed, rediscovered himself. And he knew he would never be able to describe this, express it in words. Even if an integral part of this consti... constituted of walking days and nights with the pain of hunger in stomach and body and mind. He realized that it would ever be thus, that lack of safety from now on would be a part of daily, mundane life, never again mundane. He laughed. Funny how his ability to express himself had grown, rather than shrunk since the departure from the village. He had heard so many horror stories about the «savages» roaming the wilderness, all of it lies and hearsay.

She laughed, too, sharing his laughter, not knowing what caused his laughter specifically, sharing his joy. She was also laughing every time he beat his knotted fists in wild anger against the ground, recognizing his marring frustration and desperation when he failed to catch his hunted game. He knew she laughed with him, not at him. Well, there was a partly certain viscous tendency there somewhere, a mocking, a challenge, in her voice, in the stance of her body. It didn't faze him, not as it had done when the villagers had mocked and demoralized him.

Just before, during the few, hectic hours before he killed his first game the shock rattled him. As a tiny pond in the road squashed by the foot, a flood not even feet as countless as trees in the forest could stop. He heard... the howl of the owl. Only as an echo of what he had heard the night before, but infinitely more powerful. His breath, so light, so much in tandem with the rhythm he more than sensed in his immediate and distant surroundings.

He realized with a jolt that his rhythm, his very breath, only marginally differentiated from that of the forest, the wilderness. Where did this originate, where had it hidden itself? Such a question, so useless and wasted, was easily and eagerly put to rest. He knew the answer, knew it from the first time he opened his eyes.

He missed the rabbit on his first attempt. The knife sank into hard and wiry forest bed just as the animal jumped away. The weapon was stuck. A stray thought in the mind of the hunter, discarded as yesterday's shit. His forward movement never stopped, not in the slightest, smallest way. He got hold of the animal's left hind foot, squeezed, and just by an afterthought did compassion caused by the scream of the little beast threaten to halt his goal. The hunter squeezed even harder. Bones broke under the relentless pull of the hand. He held it until he got hold of the neck and snapped it like a twig. He kept squeezing, holding the game inside whitened knuckles, while he gasped and breathed in silence, noisier than the night.

Thirsty, so thirsty. He tried to remember where he was compared to the nearest pond. Thirst overwhelmed him as everything did right now. Suddenly she was there before him. He looked at her. She sat on her heels. In a cup made of huge, green leaves water glimmered and sparkled. In the cup, in her deep eyes. She offered the life-giving fluid to his open, hungry mouth and he drank it all in big slurps and even then, it seemed to him it would never be empty. It wasn't. Perhaps Nature's hospitality did have a limit, as it had been for the humans living before the Disaster, but if it did, they were far away from reaching it.

With a look he couldn't quite comprehend, she relieved the dead animal from his weak grip. She started smearing its blood all over his body, drawing and painting his body, already leaner and stronger than just a few nights ago. Her eyes sparked even more. He wanted her. As usual discovery, knowledge, certainty came as it always did out here, suddenly, violently. She kissed his hand. Bit his flesh hard. While her enticing look never left him. They had been bathing together several times, fully conscious of the nudity, but to go any further hadn't felt right, then. It did now. It would never be more right than in this exact moment.

They held hands while walking back to the camp, touching each other with their many free hands. They held the rabbit between them, the lifeless animal hanging from its bloodstained ears. It was important. Food was important. But not now.

Skin, indeed all senses felt extremely sensitive. Soft forest floor pinched hypersensitive sole skin. It didn't feel strange, but part of it all. They didn't ask questions, didn't bother to answer any. Later they could seek all the questions and find all the answers the world had to offer. Not now. All senses, all impressions, were enormously enhanced. They really were, they didn't just experience it that way. The body, simply put felt completely different, as everything within awoke, came alive outside.

I'm alive!

They knelt on the ground, chest against chest, touching, kissing, gasping, both wild and relaxed. Some time or another he would certainly tell her his name and she would tell him hers. Not important now. She knew what she was, what they were. *Human Beings!* As they were born to live. Their fierceness, their «humanity»... there were no contradictions to it. There were no contradictions. The even bolder touching progressed naturally from the more enticing. It started now. *Now!* Everything. Rough, merciless, savage. Breathing mouth to mouth, sharing breath. Pushing against each other, pulling and tearing, feeling the first signs of Awakening, of gathering pain and boundless joy. Death and Life. Ice and Fire.

They knew who they were.

Author's word

I considered making Fire Burning in the Wind into a novel, but I was already writing a post-civilization novel, Thunder Road - Ice and Fire.

It's a slightly different focus anyway.

The way I considered expanding it didn't sit well with me either. It mostly involved the girl being captured by the villagers and forced to stay with them, to adopt to their ways. The entire premise was that she was a tabula rasa, an empty vessel, and I wanted her to stay that way, wanted her to stay innocent throughout the story.

I wanted her to stay primitive. She saved him. Staying with them and him in the village would have doomed her. They were ruined by a civilization gone long ago. She never would be.

It didn't matter what she had been before, only what she had become.

Her being beaten and raped by the villagers would have changed the story completely.

Her more or less voluntarily staying with the villagers would have been against her very nature.

Tall and big red blonde girl

Tall and big red blonde girl joined the queue outside the disco. There was quite the long line, but it evaporated quickly. A fairly long line of sentries made sure everything proceeded smoothly.

Inside was smoke and sweat and perfume and other fumes playing pleasantly and unruly in her nostrils. It was Friday night, and everybody went out to blow the steam stored through the week.

Hers was a daring deep-green dress, one revealing already daring curves and attributes. She felt naked, exposed, felt vulnerable and excited. A boy she knew greeted her in the dark tunnel leading to the dance hall. He took her in his strong arms and kissed her. She found herself responding. They parted company, exchanging quick smiles.

She went straight for the dance floor, like many others not bothering to find a place to sit. The music had already begun, the DJ sweating and grunting in his booth, behind the dark glass. The dancers quickly adapted to the rhythm, and began swaying to the music, began humming it in their mind, and she did, too, joined the sea of human flesh there, between the blinking lights.

There was a face in the whirling mass, a woman with pale skin and flowing dark hair and eyes huge as windows. One moment she was there. The next she was gone.

The dance ended. The row of dances ended. Tall and big red blonde girl didn't know exactly what made her take a break. She was fit and could have danced forever, but she left the floor and headed for the bar after four, six, ten dances.

The bar was different, darker, without all the flashing lights. The choir of voices buzzing in her ears seemed almost silent compared to the noise of the dance hall. There was something in her ears, an irritation, a whistle or something like it. She shook her head and it was gone.

The bar was as crowded as the rest of the place. She had to maneuver between people on all sides. Bodies pushed at her and hands governed by lewd thoughts touched her, making her queasy and angry and queasy again. She finally reached the desk and paid for and was handed her drink.

As usual, as she made her way deeper into the shadows of the vast mansion she saw that, as expected every table was taken. She scoured them all and their people patiently, her eyes wandering between the various candidates. Most of the unfortunates without a seat walked back and forth several times. Girls had a bigger change of being offered a seat than boys, but everybody struggled.

She walked straight to a table where there were two girls and four boys.

– May a needy girl sit here with you guys? She asked sweetly, cockily.

One of the boys studied her with unflinching eyes. She performed for him unashamed without overdoing it.

– A needy girl may sit in my lap, he said, not the least concerned with her possible anguish.

She took her time, performing a bit more for him before slipping into his lap, putting her arms around his neck.

– What do I call you, red? He asked casually.

– Red is fine, she replied huskily.

He leaned a bit forward, his lips moving closer to hers.

– It might be fine, might indeed be a suitable name, but I still find it slightly lacking, actually. I think I'll call you… Bloody Mary…

She looked down at her drink, then met his eyes and reddened.

– That is acceptable, she whispered, a dizzy spell briefly overwhelming her.

– Loud cheers to Bloody Mary.

He raised his glass. The others grinned and did as well.

– LOUD CHEERS TO BLOODY MARY

Bloody Mary drank, drank with her new and sudden friends.

– This is…

He said the others' names or their num de guerre. She forgot them instantly. He didn't offer his own name. She didn't ask.

– I'm a big girl, she said pointedly, looking down at his sweet face. – I may be heavy, at least eventually.

That unnerved him a little

– I like big girls, he said. – And I can handle a little weight.

The blush returned unbidden, and she hated it, but then shrugged and relaxed. He noticed and the initial interest in his eyes grew to something more.

She enjoyed sitting there, rocking in his lap, feeling his muscles against her thighs and upper body. He got a hard-on fairly quickly. She noticed and stared at him with a cruel smile.

– So, have you come here, before, Bloody Mary? Petite Blonde Girl asked pleasantly.

– I do consider myself a regular, Bloody Mary replied.

– I love it here, Petite Blonde Girl cried. – The industrial feel, the deep shadows, it's SO attractive, so tens, leaving the zeroes behind. I come here *every* Friday!

– At nights such as these, at least I let the Dance take me where the Dance takes me, Dark Executive Girl said with dreamy eyes.

Her words stirred something in Tall and Big Red Blonde Girl. She let it, let herself be stirred.

– Do you want to dance? The boy asked?

– Love to, Hard-on Paul, she replied.

That also unnerved him a little, but he recovered fast. The others giggled wickedly.

They rose. She let him hold her hand. They returned to the dance floor through the long tunnel. She caught glimpses of his face, as light and shadow crossed it.

– I like it here, too, he said.

– Oh, why is that?

She countered, a bit caustic. It just made him smile.

– Most people here are so immediate, no matter how fake they are…

She wasn't put off either, but kept staring at him.

– I like immediate, he said. – Think about it. Humans are just like blinking lights in eternity. Life's too short to care about the trifles most people, for some weird and horrible reason are so concerned with.

It was different dancing with a partner. Even though they didn't touch they had eye-contact and moved in relation to each other. The girl saw him with her eyes closed and his scent remained a pervasive presence in her nostrils. She imagined they were alone on the floor.

The next dance was slow, and they held hands and moved close together. Lights were turned off or dimmed. They moved close together, through shadows and heat and the steam of the bodies surrounding them.

Then he kissed her. She responded with a lazy smile. Lips met and parted again. Both the boy and the girl began breathing faster.

The dance ended. They pulled off the bright floor, hand in hand and sought the shadows, where they began making out almost before they had reached the partly concealed spot behind a column.

– You will fuck him, a female voice said.

Bloody Mary frowned. He didn't notice, but kept going at her, very energetic and persistent.

She pulled back, smiled at him, and touched his cheek, before leaving him there. He tried to grab her, but his hand just grabbed empty air, and her smiled turned teasing and wicked.

Her fast breath slowed down, as she made her way back to the bar. A chuckle escaped from her throat. She touched her lips and the pleasant memory of his kisses. Music made her rock as she walked. It was darker, moodier here. She found herself humming.

The boy behind the bar handed her her drink, and she found herself smiling to him, too, as she was handing him her money. She remained by the desk, sipping her drink, downing her drink, immediately ordering another.

There was a movement, a glimpse of a pair of eyes in the mirror. When she turned they weren't there. A chill passed through her from nowhere.

A boy grabbed her and pulled her down on his lap. The vocals of the singer turned even a notch darker. She found herself responding to the boy's advances. The sound of the electric guitar played in her ears.

– Isn't it great? The boy said. – Isn't that great music?

– Yes, she mumbled. – Yes!

She kissed him on the lips, kissing him hard, drawing blood. He cried out in pain.

– My Goddess, she gasped. – I didn't mean to do that. Are you all right?

He mumbled something. She slipped off his knee. It happened without conscious thought. The moment had come and gone and could never be recaptured.

– Crazy bitch, she heard him curse her, as she rushed off.

– Poor boy, the female voice snarled. – Poor, weak boy!

Tall and big red blonde girl returned to the table where she had briefly shared a seat with a boy earlier in the evening. Others sat there, now. She didn't recognize any of them. There was no recognition in their eyes either and no attempt from either them or her to make contact.

She walked, aimlessly, through dark hallways and tunnels, not really knowing where she was headed. Sweat poured from her brow, and she realized she had been dancing, was still dancing, following the dark voice singing in her ear. There was a metal staircase at the end of the hall. She knew there was an office of sorts up there, off limits to the guests. Music flowed from the speakers in the large room. She realized startled that she had already ascended the stairs and was dancing with others in the luxurious room, looking through the window at the people down there. Her hair was in disorder, some of it falling down in her face and covering her eyes. Boys and girls danced their wild dance, as the music, as the song filled their mind and entire perception.

– I don't even know how I came here, a girl complained. – How did I come here?

Several others looked confused at each other.

Everything seemed wild and disorganized, and was, at first, but as things progressed Bloody Mary began to glimpse a pattern through her disheveled hair and hazy vision. As she watched the girl who had spoken up and the others that had displayed similar notions began to change, their eyes and expression turning hazy and empty.

Her eyes, all eyes were drawn across the room, towards the woman sitting on the sofa, the face haunting Tall and big red blonde girl the entire evening.

The dance, the swaying, the horny gasps, their every movement was according to her, in relation to her desire. When they listened to the music they listened to her voice. Bloody Mary found herself joining them. When they began singing, choiring the lyrics, she did, too.

Dark is the wind
Hot is the blood
Stark is the draft
From the shadows
From the corners
Of the wild Earth

The woman on the sofa nodded, repeatedly moving her head up and down, following the beat that way, and everybody else in the room did the same.

They began filing past her, displaying themselves before her invasive eyes. Males and females stretched their body, their arms above their head and sent her their best smiles, begging for her mercy and attention. It reminded Bloody Mary of an audition, except it was far more fundamental, primal. One by one they bowed down and bared their neck for her, before she sent them on their way, rejected them.

Tall and big red blonde girl stopped, too, frowning, standing still, and looked in discomfort and distress at the other woman.

The dark woman rose, not quite as tall as the red blonde, but to red blonde it seemed as if she was towering far above her. She shrunk in her presence. A name echoed in her mind, diluted at first, but then slowly distinct, gaining terrifying reality.

– Selene, she whimpered.

Selene smiled, as she reached out and touched the other's jaw, appraising her. Tall and big red blonde girl tried to grab her hand.

Suddenly, in a move fast as lightning Selene grabbed her arm, and twisted it around, forced her down on the floor, made her kneel before her.

– Do you yield?

Tall and big red blonde girl gasped, as her lips parted, but no matter how much she wanted to, she couldn't speak. A shiver passed through her, before her body, her mind, her very self settled into a fugue state. Selene filled her, took her over, made her bow and she bared her neck.

– Yes, you yield. You are ready.

Dark Woman pulled her on her feet, grabbing her again, appraising her some more, kissing her lips, grabbing her hand and leading her out of there, leaving all the others, leaving them to rot.

Tall and big red blonde girl displayed herself to Dark Woman, now, with every little move she made. There was still the occasional frown, but only in passing. She noticed they were outside, in the cold, but it didn't seem to matter. Nothing did, except the need to smile, smile, smile to the Dark Woman, crouching in her divine presence.

Dark Woman waved a hand and a taxi stopped in front of her. They sat down inside. The taxi drove off. There were no words or Tall and big red blonde girl heard none being voiced. She glimpsed the driver's hazy eyes in the mirror, like she glimpsed her own in Dark Woman's opaque and dark ponds.

Everything was muted, and so pleasant. The sound of the engine seemed far away. She wanted to ask about that, to voice her concern, but everything just floated away in the pleasant haze her mind had become.

Selene petted her cheek.

– You're filled with questions, but also know that questions are immaterial. You're a smart girl. You know what's happening. Soon all your questions will be answered.

The voice was so sweet, so powerful and horrible, echoing through the girl's buzzing mind.

The car stopped by a lonely house at the end of a remote road, not that far from the population center. It didn't really stand out or was remarkable in any way, but it still spoke to the girl.

They left the car. The driver left them without mentioning anything about payment, or saying a single word. Selene didn't dismiss him. She just ignored him. Fear and awe coursed through the part of the girl not totally mesmerized by the dark creature before her.

The Dark Woman, the Goddess flowed towards the house and the girl trailed her, submerged in her shadow. The door opened, seemed to open on its own accord. Selene didn't touch it, or didn't seem to, but her moves were so quick, so much like lightning that they seemed invisible through the girl's dull vision.

The door closed behind them. They were inside. The girl hardly more than glimpsed her surroundings, Selene drawing all attention to herself. What seemed like a whirling mass of shadow flowed up the stairs, and Tall and big red blonde girl followed her breathlessly, filled to the brim with anticipation.

Selene entered a bedroom, and the speck in her shadow did as well. Selene turned, and Tall and big red blonde girl rushed forward in her eagerness to comply with the silent command. The kiss exploded on the girl's lips. She released a loud moan of longing and beyond powerful need. Selene flashed her fangs, her long, long fangs in anticipation. For the very first time Tall and big red blonde girl saw the other woman's terrifying visage. Selene began undressing her, taking her time, with a pleased grin making Tall and big red blonde girl feel wanted, feel desired.

– You've kept yourself fit. This is good, very good.

Selene kissed her prey on the neck. The girl shuddered in delight with half closed eyes.

– And your scent is absolutely irresistible.

Then she kissed the other on the lips and the girl responded with a muffled moan.

– Yes, yes, you're so filled with desire and life, and so very, very wanted.

The Dark One took her time, savoring the slow-moving moments, exploring Bloody Mary with invasive, sensuous touches. She bit a nipple, her long, pointed fangs pushing at it from both above and below. Red hair in her mouth muffled another moan rising from the girl's throat.

A hand pushed itself between thighs.

A gasp echoed in the room.

– Wet, Selene whispered excitedly. – So needy. Such a lovely prey! Dance for me, prey; dance for your Selene.

Tall and big red blonde girl stepped a bit back and began turning, turning, swaying, keeping her large, unfocused eyes at the darkness running her. It was no effort. The dance just happened, the most natural thing of the world. She fondled her breasts and rubbed her already inflamed skin, her palms turning wet as she caressed the inside of her thighs.

The predator licked her lips, her tongue playing with her long, long fangs.

– Come to me, sweet one, come to me, Fury, and earn your reward.

Redhead approached Dark One with a dazed but yet hungry look in her eyes.

She kissed the lips, caressed the other tongue and the fangs with her own. Words, commands, emotions boiled and burned in her mind, her entire needy body. Then, after hesitating just a bit she kissed pale skin on the neck. Selene half closed her eyes, too, and pushed her head back. Hands and fingers bathing in both red and dark hair began unbuttoning lavender clothes.

– Yes, that's it! Dark Voice hissed. – You're learning, learning so fast, like I knew you would.

Redhead knelt before Dark Hair, removing the stockings, the final fabric from the other's powerful body.

Selene grabbed her jaw and looked down at her in triumph and dark lust, raising her up and leading her to the bed. Redhead felt the soft fabric as she knelt on it, as the bed rocked beneath them both. They moved against each other, caressing both parts of the single entity they had become.

A long, loud and needy moan erupted from the young one's throat, echoed instantly by the Old One's darker, murkier equivalent.

Selene turned her around, making the young one kneel with her back to her. Then she smacked her on the butt. The young one cried out in pain.

– Yes, feel the pain, the sweet pain.

She smacked her again, and again, and again. Tears jumped from the young one's wide open eyes. By the fifth smack she began gasping and moaning again, looking incredulous and increasingly happy at the shadow behind her.

– Good girl! You're learning the truth we all know deep down: pain and pleasure are the same, the very same.

She spread the muscular thighs and began touching the warm and wet thing in there, grinning, snarling, filling the girl under her thumb with happy, excited thoughts.

Can you feel it, fierce one? The young one, startled heard the Dark One's thoughts. We're closer than we can ever be. It's *happening…*

Selene grabbed both shoulders of the prey in front of her and opened her mouth wide. Ivory fangs twinkled in the moonlight. Then, in one swift, brutal move she bent down and penetrated the skin between the shoulder and the neck, hitting the exact spot of the pulsing and so irresistible vein. Tall and big red blonde girl cried out, stiffening a moment, before turning limp in the other's powerful grip. The sound of the other's feeding sounded so pleasantly in her ears. It wasn't instantaneous, as she had watched it on film, but took time, even as time didn't matter. Her limbs and body turned weak, as the hunter devoured virtually all the blood in her veins. Arms fell down. Selene let go of her and she fell on her back on the bed, watching detached how the blood decorated the pale skin towering above her, making it even more beautiful.

– Do you want to live? The dark, indistinct shape hissed.

The creature held out a hand, held it just out of reach. Tall and big red blonde girl understood.

Her heart beat in her chest, straining, straining, and fading, fading.

Her upper body rose abruptly ninety degrees in the bed. Hands like claws grabbed the outstretched hand, clawing at it, biting it, breaking its skin. Blood gushed from the wound, and the fiery human being, being hungry beyond Hunger began sucking it into her mouth, ingesting, consuming it in huge gulps.

– Good. Selene closed and opened her eyes, biting her lip, licking her lips and her fangs. – It's good.

The mouth in the flow of red drank and kept drinking. It was done in a clumsy way, not very effective at all, and there wasn't that much blood to feed on, but she managed. Slowly, slowly she felt the growing fullness and drowsiness overcome her. Her hands let go, her teeth let go, and she fell back on her back, writhing on the bed, keeping her attention on the lovely, glowing form above.

A hand touched her forehead, tenderly, affectionate.

– Is that it? The girl mumbled happily.

– No. Dark One shook her head. – It hurts. Being born hurts.

The girl gasped, and cried in pain and stared in resentment at the other, at her betrayer.

– You're leaving the dead, old world behind, Selene said softly, – being born into a new, better one, into one of eternal Hunger, of feast and joy.

The young one screamed.

The rigid body began shaking on the bed, as the blood she had ingested began changing it, transforming it into something new and vastly different. Sweat poured from the brow. Selene had a little trouble keeping it down for a while. She held it and whispered into the fevered, fading mind. The blood moved in the veins, invaded the flesh on its path around the body

The screams turned into whimpers, as consciousness slowly faded, as the horrible pain changed into slow-burning ache. Selene let go and rose to her full heights, looking down at the almost unmoving body down there, the last few seconds until it rested completely still in the heap of bloody sheets.

– You'll sleep, Selene hummed, – and be transformed.

Eyes still moved, but fluttering, like tiny wings. Eyes closed. Darkness swept the nascent creature of the night into a world of soft shadows and dark mist, into a slowly enveloping darkness, until all thoughts, even the most basic awareness had gone, and only a tiny ember of life remained.

2

Eyes opened. It happened in one, single movement. There was no blinking, only the wide-open eyes.

She sat up in the bed. Eyes took in the room in one sweep. Selene sat in a chair across the room, so different now, when the girl could perceive her fully. Eyes locked on to her, but only one moment, two later all attention was focused on the nude male body at Dark Woman's feet.

He was conscious, but dazed, paralyzed by Selene's charm.

Eyes moved from the bed. Her mouth opened. Saliva flowed from her fangs, the fangs puncturing her lips. She didn't notice.

– You desire him, don't you? You want him more than anything?
– Yes.
She heard a voice she knew to be her own.
– You may have him. It's a gift from me to you.
Selene kicked him out on the floor. He crouched there. Eyes noticed how the light of intelligence and reason returned to him. She stepped forward. His attention was instantly locked on her.
– Hello, she said, smiling to him.
– H-hello.
– Don't be afraid, she soothed him. – There is nothing to be afraid of.
Eyes became neck, became torso, arms and feet.
– Come here, she grinned. – Come and please me.
Eyes grew to mind, to desire.
His expression turned blank again, before looking at her with lust and need and hardly anything but. She found the sense of power and triumph rising within her so pleasing, so beyond exhilarating, and this, she knew, positively was nothing compared to the delights in store.
His cock rose as he approached her. She chuckled throatily, as she welcomed him into her embrace.
He whimpered, as the pale face, the huge opaque eyes filled his sky. She kissed him, and the pain below rose to full force. He wanted to grab her, to take her in his strong arms, but he couldn't. She knew he couldn't. His powerful muscles didn't work. She admired them and caressed them, rubbed her bloodstained body at them.
It was a small matter for her to grab him and put him down on the bed. He rested on his back and looked at her with dog-like eyes. She crawled on top of him and sat on his cock, pushing it deep within her. He pushed, pushed, pushed, like the eager dog he was. She felt him all over, like every piece of her was on fire, not just the tiny piece his cock touched, and they had hardly begun.
– My boy, she mewed. – My sweet boy.
She rode him, softly, pleasantly at first, then *harder*. Nails scratched him, making long deep gashes on his skin, his broad chest. He filled her, as she filled him. It was such a delight, and it grew, grew, until it seemed to expand even beyond her flesh and fill the room, and touch Selene, there, in the chair, across the floor. The rider began rocking up and down on her prey. Saliva flowed from her fangs, the ebony twinkling in the darkness. They pushed at each other, and then it happened. Their limbs froze. Need and lust transformed into infinite pleasure. He cried out in happiness. She growled in joy.

And then she fell on him. The hungry mouth sought the pulsing vein between his shoulder and neck and bit deep into feverish skin. Blood filled her mouth, and now she was able to swallow it faster, far more effectively. A bit of the clumsiness remained, the first few seconds, before certainty and skill filled her just as boundless satisfaction did. She began scratching, tearing at him, tearing him apart. Almost all his blood had flowed down her throat when she began devouring the rest of him, but not everything. In a total, savage frenzy she began gobbling his flesh, ripping limbs and pieces of meat from the body that was fairly quickly, during a minute or two reduced to a heap of flesh and bones.

The predator stood there, on her knees, snarling in wild satisfaction to the other across the room, acknowledging her inferiority with a lowering of eyes, still glowing in pride.

The blood… the blood and pieces of flesh were distilled and used by the body in a matter of minutes, with a pleasure only slowly, slowly fading, lingering forever.

Strength unimagined surged through her, as she underwent the final stages of the transformation, as she Became.

Selene rose, towering above her spawn, a pleased expression in her dark pool eyes.

– Blood, she said. – Your name is Blood!

Blood growled in gratitude and pride.

– You may call yourself Mary when you venture outside, when you mingle with your prey, if you want.

– I would like that, Dark One. Blood spoke for the first time. – Thank you.

Selene undressed. It was done quickly, elegantly. Blood looked at her with love and devotion in her green eyes. Selene took her hand and led her out of the room, into the hall outside it, a completely new world, one that Blood had never before known. There was a bathroom two doors down the hall, a place with no electric light, but one that twinkled and burned in shadow.

They stepped into the shower. Selene turned the water on. She began soaping in her charge with slow, lingering movements. Blood smiled in anticipation.

Sensation assaulted her anew as Selene began touching her, cleaning off the blood and pieces of flesh and intestines. She noticed, beyond noticing the large holes in the filter on the shower floor, the slight touch of the Dark One's nail as it briefly scratched her side. Everything was enhanced, but yet muted compared to the excesses, the beyond powerful emotions at the Feasting.

– So peaceful and lovely, isn't it?

Blood nodded, with eyes wide open, unprotected by the onslaught of water. It didn't bother her, but enhanced her further.

She began soaping in and rinsing Selene, the newborn getting good at it, as she learned from her Mother, like children learned from any parent during the early stages of life.

They dried each other, flowing from one spot to the other, each stage ripe with a dreamlike but yet wide awake quality. The surroundings of the bathroom shifted to those of another bedroom. They were in bed caressing each other, loving each other.

Selene grabbed her arm, flashed her fangs, bit into the wrist and drank. Blood grabbed Selene's arm, flashed fangs, bit into the wrist and drank. It was just a little taste, but still so good, so very good.

Only a few drops of blood were wasted, the wounds closing fast afterwards.

– We'll do this properly once you are better trained, the Dark One whispered in her ear.

Blood stared at the closed wound in amazement and happiness.

The minor feeding instantly brought her to a higher level of excitement, made her squirm and writhe, as she turned wet and hot between her legs, all of it spreading like wildfire to her entire body.

– So pleasant, she mumbled. – So pleasant.

– It is indeed, the other said, teaching her. – And this is just the start of your life, not its eternal heyday.

Blood's attention was locked on Selene, totally devoted to her overwhelming presence. They touched, and feasted on each other's fever, and it exploded in a million stars and campfires in the night. Blood stretched on the bed later, in Selene's embrace. She noticed, now, finally the room and her surroundings in more details. She didn't really look at the room, its walls, at the lack of windows there, but knew it still. There were no walls, only the night, and the wilderness outside.

Eyes became thought, consideration, almost alien after the eternity of feasting. Selene looked at her, waiting patiently, with a look of fond maternity in her eyes. A look of scorn and suffering touched Blood's features.

– Why choose me? What made you pick me from the hundreds of people present? Was it because I am alone?

– No, no, nothing like that. If you had been my prey that would have been a smart move, though, and that is certainly something to be aware of for you in your Age to come.

A brief pause and consideration touched the ancient face. She moved off

the bed and Blood followed her, the move that was more a flow than a walk.
– Why you, child? That one is easy. You were the only one among those heeding my call that even resisted my charm. You're strong and fierce, and I wanted that, craved that.
– But I didn't ask for this, you did it to me without my permission.
Selene chuckled softly.
– Didn't you? Did I?
Blood sniffed, bowing her head in acknowledgment. Selene stepped close to her.
– Search yourself, know yourself, and you'll know how silly your previous statement was, how much a remnant of your old life it was. You know, beyond those petty concerns that you wanted, desired with the greatest of passion what I offered you.
Blood did as Selene told her to do. One blink, two was all it took, and everything that was new and powerful returned to her. Everything inside… sang to her, and she practically gasped in ecstasy, and that was nothing compared to how the feeding had felt. She watched herself in the mirror, the long fangs, the luminous pale skin and huge eyes. Saliva flowed from the fangs, as the terrifying smile transformed her face further.
Then she took in Selene in one brief glance and fell on her knees, stricken and beyond happiness.
Selene looked at her with fondness in her eyes. Blood knew this, even though she didn't see it.
– This is how it works: You are not a supernatural being, but tied to physical reality, to nature, even human reality. That being said you are far stronger and sturdier than other humans. You are immortal, and if you are skilled, fairly cautious and lucky, you'll live forever. You won't age, not a single second. Nothing can kill you except prolonged exposure to sunlight or fire or beyond grave injuries. Crosses, garlic, «holy water» and stakes through your heart will hardly harm you at all, won't hardly do more than distract you. If you're in a good mood that night, it might make you laugh yourself silly. You have a «charm», an ability to sway the will of other people. There is nothing keeping you from entering any house. You don't have to be invited or anything like that, anything like that bullshit. You must feed, drink the blood of other humans, or you will die. What you were you are no longer. You are a newborn, a baby just popped from my loins. That's all there is to it, my child. You are humanity in its pure form, the fangs and claws of the Earth, a predator without peer. They say the hunters are dying off, but we are not. We are just buried beneath the pile of garbage they call civilization. I will keep you with me until you are able to reject my charm, which will

probably happen sooner or later. Then you may make up your own mind how to spend eternity.

– *Eternity*, Blood exhaled, once more displaying the pleased grin she knew would be so terrifying to her prey.

The word, the notion, the reality echoed in the room, in the vast mind and form she had become.

Selene took her head in her hands and kissed her on the lips, a fire consuming her. Moans of unlimited pleasure already echoed in her room.

Suddenly a loud yawn escaped her. She looked curious at the other, also yawning.

– … sleepy…?

– Yes, it's daybreak, time for us to rest, to sleep like the dead.

– Are we dead? Blood wondered.

– Do you feel dead, my sweet one?

– No. A decisive shaking of the head. – I feel alive, more alive than I could ever imagine being.

– And so you are. You've had your brush with death. Now, Eternity awaits you.

They returned to bed. Blood felt a bit sluggish and had trouble staying on her feet the last few steps.

– You'll learn to master the approaching Sleep like you'll master everything else, Mother taught her. – I felt the approaching dawn come quite some time ago. If I had been out hunting late, I would have had time to return before Sleep caught up with me. You wouldn't have.

– But we're helpless during… Sleep… aren't we?

– As much as we possibly can be, yes, but we're safe here. They would have to use powerful explosives to enter this house, this room. I had it made generations ago. Everybody working on it is dead, our secret lost in time. I have several houses, scattered across the land and world.

– That's good, Blood said, excitement and joy easily supplanting her brief anxiety. – That's so good.

Lethargy overcame her, overcame them both, as they rested on the bed. Blood blinked slowly, and she saw Selene do that as well. Selene was able to move, though, one final gesture of affection touching her daughter's cheek, before they both rested unmoving.

Selene and Blood, her brood slept.

3

Blood opened her eyes, her unblinking stare, instantly aware of her surroundings.

She flowed from the bed, reaching out with her senses. Selene was below, in the dining room, waiting for her. Blood flowed down the stairs, slowly reining herself in a bit, deliberately reducing her speed closer to a normal human level.

Selene sat at the end of the long table. One glass with twinkling red fluid waited for her, the other, at the other end of the table waited for her brood.

Hungry eyes caught the sight of the dress on the chair.

– It's yours. Put it on.

It was a bit more casual compared to last night's gown, but still beautiful. Blood dressed in slow, sensuous moves and displayed herself further for the Dark One.

– It's such a lovely dress, thank you.

– We do make an effort not to stand out too much. Selene continued her teaching. – Fortunately, we don't need to make a production out of it. There will always be those emulating us, longing to be us.

Blood walked to her place at the end of the table.

– Sit.

She obeyed eagerly, without conscious or long-lasting thought. Selene grabbed the glass and raised it, until it rested before her lips. Blood did, too.

– It's just an appetizer, a little snack before the feasting. It gives us better control over our urges, and you need to feed a lot until you settle in your new form.

They drank. The fluid was cold and only a pale reflection of the hot, fresh nourishment from last night. It was a more lingering pleasure, spreading slower through Blood's veins and being. The gasps still rolled from the newborn's open mouth.

She leaned back in her chair with half closed eyes, looking at the world through her incredibly improved perception.

– Dark One…

The young beast said humbly, with lowered eyes.

– Yes?

– You've taught me so much already. Can there possibly be more left to learn?

– There are endless delights of discovery and Hunger left to learn, little bitch.

And little bitch felt it, could imagine it, even as it currently stayed out of her reach.

– Call for an ordinance, will you, Selene said casually.

A car, a taxi, a transport, Blood thought on the superficial surface of her new and vast and vastly improved mind.

– At once, Dark One.

She flowed to the cell phone on the table in front of the creature, the overwhelming presence in her life. Her finger pushed a button activating a pre-recorded number. She spoke, not really registering the words. It all seemed so mundane, so irrelevant. She put the phone in her pocket, something she knew the dark one desired.

They flowed to the hall some time later, when Blood heard the first sounds of an engine in the distance. She opened what she knew was a heavy door and held it open for Mother to pass through. They didn't speak to the driver, or vocalized anything the man could hear. The communication was on a far deeper level, on one she who was now Blood had hardly imagined existed in her previous existence.

The old her would have called the drive uneventful. Blood registered everything happening within and without the tiny compartment. A fly enjoyed the sweat on the driver's neck. Tiny creatures swarmed several spots. And on that deeper level the entire car was filled with life.

Outside howls and squeaks and snarls swarmed the night. The muted, tiny roar of the engine didn't keep her from noticing any of it.

The mechanical, artificial drive was irrelevant in the vast existence her life had become.

– I want you to blend in, but still make your presence known, understand, infant?

– Yes, Mother.

Understanding wasn't hard at all. Mother's thoughts and sensations and presence flooded her, dwarfed her, and were even bigger than the vast world her existence had become.

The building containing the disco appeared completely different to her. She realized startled that it was the same, exactly the same, but that her perception had changed so dramatically that it, and everything else that had ever felt familiar to her looked completely different.

Selene walked past the queue without even acknowledging it and Blood followed her, followed her inside a strange and startling world.

– I've come here since I first started… dating, Blood whispered, – and it looks like a different planet.

– This is your first time here, Selene shrugged.

– Yes, Mother, Blood replied.

The place was filled with people, or so it seemed to Blood. They surrounded her and seemed to embrace her, the scent of rust and dawn assaulting her from all sides. Every single individual felt close, even those standing far away. She felt how her fangs began growing. It was impossible to stop it from happening. Even keeping her mouth closed proved difficult. She started panting, totally immersed in the scape of sound, sight, smell, taste and a sensation beyond anything sensible. Drops of saliva flowed from her exposed fangs. Dizziness almost overcame her. She felt faint and had trouble standing.

With a light touch of the jaw and demanding the newborn's attention Selene closed her off from the overwhelming surroundings, saved her from sensory overload.

– You're an infant, she said, – so hungry that you may forget your own safety. Take it slow. Focus on one prey or two first. Then, when you have learned to do that you may expand your appetites.

The child did as she was told. Her fangs shrunk again, no longer pushing at her lower lip. The pleasant sensation didn't really wane, but she was able to delegate it to a part of herself in a way that didn't overwhelm her.

She remembered outside, when the first stirrings of Hunger had touched her, but it was nothing compared to what it felt like inside, enclosed by walls. Outside she had encountered numerous potential kills for the first time.

– Look around you, my child, the Dark One whispered, – at the smorgasbord offered to you.

Blood did. She zoomed in on one at the time, but moved her attention quickly to the next, moved her eyes back and forth between the prey, but realized it was way too fast, and slowed down and began dwelling more on each. A smile grew slowly on her lips.

– They‘re all here, Selene said, her voice filled with promise. – They're everywhere and don't go anywhere.

Blood turned towards her, inquisitive.

– You shouldn't rush things, Selene shrugged, but enjoy the experience, savor the hunt and the kill.

And Blood's smile widened.

The tunnel leading further inside did no longer look dark to her, but like shimmering shadows in a pale light. A girl crossed her path. She bled from an earlobe. The stench tore at Blood's nostrils.

She headed for the dance floor. This was fairly late in the evening and people had been filling the place for hours. The tall red blonde girl slipped between them in anticipation and Hunger. Shadows danced around her form. Males and females alike looked at her with apprehension and longing in their eyes.

The whirl of dancers surrounded her. There was no whirl to her anymore, but abject clarity. She was able to study them all without distortion. Their blood tugged at her and raised her Need, but she didn't lose control. The smell was a pleasant sensation. She was able to savor the excitement of the hunt.

The hunt… That word echoed so pleasantly within her and she only wondered why in a remote, indifferent part of herself.

She saw herself through their eyes, her enticing body, her breasts and hips, her alluring eyes. One glance and they were lost. She danced, and they surrounded her, helplessly attracted to what she offered them, what they believed she offered them, both, neither.

– Hello, a girl said, a beautiful girl, seduction clothed in flesh said, performing for her, catching her interest.

Blood reached out a hand to her and caught her in her net. That was all it took. She pulled the girl to her, drawing her into her embrace, giving her a lingering kiss, one that would linger long after it was done. The girl gasped, and her eyes turned big and shiny, shiny, shiny.

– … feels so good, she mumbled, her boyfriend just a few steps away turning into a distant memory.

The music rose with the blood, boiling in the air, becoming the air, becoming flesh.

– They're all yours, Selene told her.

– Mine, Blood breathed.

The girl unbuttoned the buttons in her blouse, exposing her swelling breasts, her hard nipples. A boy watching it all moved in on her. Blood easily stopped him and shifted his attention. He was lost before he met her eyes. She touched his jaw with a feather-light hand. He pulled down his pants, revealing his swelling cock. Several other girls and boys exposed themselves. Those not doing it stared at the spectacle, but no one cried out or made any overt sign of watching anything extraordinary. They looked straight ahead with hazy eyes.

– M-mary?

Blood turned and spotted the girl in the crowd. She dimly recognized the blonde. It took just a little shift in her attention to focus on her.

– Hello, Tina, she said sweetly.

– Hello.

Tina's frown of worry quickly faded away and was supplanted with more rapid breathing and hazy eyes.

– Come here, she called the girl.

She didn't have to speak out aloud to call the girl to her any more than the others, but just then it felt natural.

– Where have you *been?*

– Why do you ask? Blood grinned.

– We were supposed to meet… weren't we?

Blood rubbed her cheek.

– You're so beautiful, she breathed in the other's ear.

She kissed the full lips and they responded instantly. Only a faint shock remained in the hazy eyes.

Blood had her attention at her, at the rest simultaneously, a task taking no effort at all.

– I've always wanted you, desired you…

Tina gasped in shock, one followed by quite the different gasp, sounding so sweet. She chuckled startled, incredulous at first. Blood held back, deliberately, allowing her to regain a semblance of independence. She kissed the full lips again. Tina responded with an almost visible Hunger, her blood heating up second by second.

Blood took her hand and led her away. The half-denuded boy and girl trailed them, their gasps of longing and need roaring so pleasantly in Blood's ears and being. Tall and big red blonde girl felt how she began to slip, how the Hunger rose in her, beyond potent and irresistible, but she held on. They reached the restroom. There were only two girls there, one in a stall and one making her face in front of the mirror. Blood licked her lips, and it felt completely natural. The stench of blood in her nostrils excited her.

She locked the door. Neither her three companions nor the girl in front of the mirror seemed noticeably startled by this. Triumph flooded pleasantly Blood's being and her anticipation grew, slowly becoming unbearable and impossible to resist.

– W-what… the girl in front of the mirror managed before her lips and body and mind froze.

– Hush, Blood whispered, suddenly standing right in front of her, a finger on her shivering lips. – Relax, sweet girl. Enjoy it.

The lipstick fell from the girl's weak grip.

Blood cupped one of her breasts, squeezed lightly a nipple. It grew hard and sore. The girl moaned in silence, but Blood heard her, heard her needy cry. She kissed the lips shivering in fear and need. The two others joined them. The girl behind the door rose from the toilet bowl and dragged her feet to the irresistible creature in their midst without pulling up her pants and panties.

Tina kissed Blood on her lips. She panted and stamped her feet at the floor in her eagerness.

– I know, sweet child, Blood acknowledged her. – You want this, you want this so very much, but you will need to be patient, to wait for your moment, fight to be worthy of the honor potentially bestowed upon you.

Blood already felt ancient, compared to the baby that had been her age only nights ago.

She called the boy with the hard on to her. He came with the empty look in his eyes. She received him in her fawn with a smothering passion. He gasped in need and expectation. She brushed aside his collar. His pulsing jugular vein pulled her and attracted her to the point of excluding everything else. She strived to stay aware of her surroundings, to keep the others under her control.

Then there was no more conscious thought, only need and passion and power. The other three gasped as he gasped, as she punctured his skin and drank deep of his nectar, his water of life.

They both fell on their knees. His cock twitched and ejaculated bursts of semen. She felt her hot water break and he slipped from her grip.

He writhed on his back. She knew by a casual glance that he would survive.

– Good boy, she whispered. – Good boy…

She wished for two of the girls, Tina and the other she had brought here to join her on the floor and they eagerly did. They pushed against her with tongue and breasts and hips. She had lost control of them momentarily during her beyond potent orgasm, but had quickly regained it. They were hers to do with as she pleased.

They caressed and coddled and kissed her as the pleasant servants they were. She hugged them without physically touching them and pulled them even closer into her soft embrace.

She bit into Tina's jugular and the child's sweet blood filled her still ravenous veins. Tina stopped resisting completely and looked at her with complete trust in her dazed eyes.

There was very little visible blood. Blood had become quite skilled already, since the short, short time since her birth.

A child knew how to swim, if it wasn't damaged by its upbringing. A predator knew how to use its fangs and claws. Blood rejoiced inside.

She let go of Tina and started on the other girl. The pleasure hammered her less by now, making her able to consciously enjoy it more. She sensed acutely and astutely the moment her body consumed the blood, when its energies passed from her stomach to her veins. It made her giggle and hum, and her three companions eagerly followed her lead.

The muscles, her physique kept hardening and strengthening. Her very bones shifted and grew.

When she drank of the two remaining females the sound of her bones resetting themselves had become loud, like a phantom screech in the night.

There was a hammering on the door. She frowned, until she realized that the hammering hadn't started yet. A woman had pushed down the handle. Unable to open the door, she had lifted the hand to knock.

She never would. Blood watched as she turned and walked away. Taller and even bigger red blond girl left the five there in the bright room. They had bitemarks on their throat. There was blood, but not very much. They might notice the wound eventually, but it would mean little to them and hold even less terror. Friends would perhaps joke about it and they would laugh uneasily.

Mary had blood on her jaw, inevitably. No one would notice, except in dreamy, elusive nightmares. She walked through the crowd of people, her powers and control over them stronger than ever. Mother called her, and they met by the dance floor. They didn't make physical contact, but the minds touched in a way bodies never could.

Selene had fed, too, and fed well. The imagery and emotions rushed like a storm through Blood's mind and being. All of it lingered, hot and potent. They left, just as quiet and seemingly unassuming as they had arrived.

A cab waited for them. It opened its doors and they sat down inside. The cab left. There was a driver behind the wheel, Blood imagined, but she hardly saw him or her, except as mist of flesh slipping in and out of her attention.

She hardly noticed her own shrugging. It didn't really matter. She noticed every little detail, everything happening in her surroundings. Nothing slipped by her.

Her blood, both old and new sang in her veins, igniting her entire body and inflaming her mind.

– So, child, Selene mused, – how was your first hunting night?

– So… thrilling, Mother, Blood breathed. – I loved it, loved every single moment of it.

– It didn't matter to you what your prey thought or felt, then?

– No, not at all, they were just there, like a glass of milk or a piece of meat, even though I am enriched by their terror and joy as well. It's all so… pleasant and satisfying beyond… words. I feel such *power,* Mother.

Blood writhed in her seat, the wetness between her thighs spreading further. She displayed herself to her maker without conscious thought or pretence.

Selene grabbed her and played with her, and loud, high-pitched moans rose from Blood's open mouth.

The cab driver kept staring straight forward, as if he was alone in the car.

They shared blood, an act inflaming the touches and caresses further.

Consciousness faded as Blood submitted completely to the other's advances and control. The moans turned even louder and more intense. The burning wetness and heat below kept spreading, until turning unbearable and finally exploded into rapture all over her body, deep recesses of her already ravaged mind.

Blood fell, the smile on her lips growing wider, wider, wider. The beyond pleasant glow persisted, even as thought slowly returned to her mind.

– You're such a pleasing pet, aren't you?

– Yes, My Lady, Blood mumbled with a dreamy expression on her doll-like face, striving half-heartedly to speak properly with her fangs fully extended.

She licked her lips with her versatile tongue. Even those few drops of blood made her feel the ecstasy like a tiny storm within. She grunted content, wide awake and aware.

The cab stopped, right outside the old house. The two creatures of the night slipped outside. He drove on, with the same, distant stare in his eyes.

They walked, *flowed* inside. Blood felt like the place welcomed her, like a home.

– Will… will every night be like this, this exciting and invigorating?

– Yes and no, the Dark One replied. – There will always be the blood and its rushes, but an eternal being will inevitably need to seek out variety even more than other creatures, find ways to break the cycle of routine and potential boredom. Our prey is too easy to catch. Our superiority becomes a risk. There are times, though rare, where circumstances may work against us, where we may truly be in jeopardy. Do you understand, my child?

– Yes, Mother, Blood breathed.

They showered and spent the last few hours before dawn in each other's company.

– You will learn the wisdom of the grimoires, of course, Selene stated, – to better know the Magick of this and other realms.

– Magick, Dark One? Blood inquired both puzzled and excited. – Realms?

– Yes, existence is so much bigger than you have imagined. Surely you can sense it, every time you reach out with your power?

It wasn't a question. Blood nodded.

– There are forces out there that can make even our lives a bit too exciting. You will learn everything I know about them, and thereby be even better prepared to survive the centuries ahead.

One blink and Blood experienced much of what the Dark One spoke of, even though it didn't quite make sense to her.

Selene put the music on loud.

– Dance for me, young one. Imagine yourself back at the club. Indulge in every fantasy you've ever had.

Blood eagerly obeyed, knowing beyond knowing that she was about to break every single restraint she had ever possessed. She moved, and the air became alive around her.

Her surroundings changed, turning into the tall ceiling, the far walls of the club, but that was just the beginning. The consciousness she had believed only existed within her head spread from there, spread from this house in an expanding, ever expanding circle.

– Life… is within me, she gasped.

Very good, Selene nodded.

Had the tall, dark woman spoken?

A deer stood by a pond far away. It drank, sating its thirst, and Blood's thirst manifested itself again, grew, in spite of her having fed well that night. Everything in her shouted *prey* to her.

She opened her eyes, a fixed, natural stare.

Her maker nodded pleased.

– You know what you are, now, don't you?

– *Yes!*

It was hardly a word at all, hardly even a sound, but an atavistic sensation reaching far beyond her.

– And it was so easy, wasn't it?

Blood nodded with an ecstatic smile on her lips.

– You did it just by shifting your consciousness, not ingesting blood. Very good!

The Dark One rose, and it was as if the entire room, Blood's entire perception changed with her position.

– Our kind is well read, scholars by default, encouraged to study by our long life, but more than anything we are and will always be Wild, be beyond savage creatures and never forget it.

– I won't, Blood breathed.

And in her even more heightened state of awareness she sensed the brightening sky in the east before she otherwise would have.

– You are so talented, the Dark One said cheerfully. – I knew you were, from the very first moment my eyes and power spotted you.

It almost sounded ominous. Blood exhaled in both anxiety and anticipation.

The little death of sleep imposed itself on her and her Master.

Their chamber of eternity appeared to them. The soft bed appeared before them, just as it vanished, transformed into a deep darkness of pleasant nothing.

The creatures of the night were dead to the day.

4

Blood opened her eyes, her unblinking stare, instantly aware of her surroundings.

The Dark One towered above her, her features both soft and a snarl.

– I'm taking a walk, little one, she said casually, the subtext of her voice not casually at all. – You mind the fort, okay?

– Yes, Mother.

– The house is yours in my absence. You do whatever strikes your fancy.

– Yes, Mother.

Blood brightened and frowned simultaneously.

A flash of movement and Selene was gone, still very much present.

Blood felt her, no matter where she turned her attention, no matter what wall she faced.

She found a bottle and filled a glass, emptied it in one, single slurp.

– My breakfast, she giggled.

And even her giggle filled the house, the ether, bubbling from something deep within.

She showered and dressed, daring to study herself in the mirror, not even certain that the mirror was there, and not something growing out of the air itself.

Her fangs twinkled in the dark light. She loved studying them. They were so deadly, so beautiful, like two tiny swords cutting flesh, the very air in which they moved.

Her awareness noticed a presence outside, but she didn't really act on it until she heard the knocking on the door. She flowed down the stairs, and as she did so details of the visitor to be revealed themselves to her.

It was a woman. Mary knew her, or knew of her, a detective, a cop, a tall and big and lethal creature. A few steps before the door she knew a lot more about her.

Mary opened the door, her fangs shrinking, pulling back into their sheaths.

– Yes, can I help you?

– Perhaps, the woman said, flashing her shield, – I am Lieutenant Trish McKenzie. May I come in?

– Sure! Mary shrugged, stepping back into the hall.

She moved like a dance in front of the clumsy woman. When she pondered the differences between them, they became even more amazing.

– Can I offer you anything? She asked brightly. – Coffee, tea, stronger

stuff?
– No, thank you, Trish replied.
Mary sat down on a chair. It didn't feel like she was sitting at all, but floating in an endless stream.
– So, detective, what can I help you with?
– Are you the owner? Trish frowned. – I seem to remember you from somewhere.
– No, I am the daughter of the house. Mother isn't here right now, but will be back tonight, I believe.
– Oh, well, the detective said. – We're investigating a string of disappearances and deaths and attacks in this area going back years. The entire department is up in arms. We walk from house to house and ask around, as a matter of routine.
Trish spoke with an even, modulated voice. It sounded like a melody in Mary's ears.
– Where is your partner? The girl asked abruptly. – You do have one, haven't you? All of you have.
Trish frowned again.
– He's at the hospital right now, being treated for a slight infection. It's nothing serious.
– I'm afraid I can't help you with the disappearances, attacks and deaths, Mary said, even more brightly. – I haven't seen anything and have in fact hardly heard about them at all.
– Are you sure?
– Pretty sure, the girl replied. – Midterms are coming up at school, I'm afraid and contrary to common opinion students are quite immersed in studying.
– You haven't heard anything?
The detective studied her, Mary knew she did and smiled, flashing her fangs. Trish frowned, but didn't catch the flash in her conscious mind.
Mary rose, making sure she didn't move at what had now become her normal speed, but excruciatingly slow to her enhanced senses and abilities.
– I have actually heard something, she said, shrugging. – I heard that your partner isn't really treated for an infection, but that he is really sick and is believed to be one of the victims of the malady you described so eloquently.
– What? Trish said, repeating it in a daze. – What?
She jumped on her feet and drew her gun, suddenly sweating profusely.
– Don't move! She said weakly.
Mary smiled, looking unconcerned at her.
– Put that silly thing away, she said. – It is useless anyway. Okay?

– Okay? Trish echoed and obeyed the mesmerizing voice. – You're right. I don't need it anyway, do I?

– I am absolutely right.

Mary moved fast and suddenly stood right before the big woman, assessing her, probing and controlling her. She touched the woman's jaw, pulling away her collar, exposing her skin and the pulsing, pulsing jugular vein.

– You haven't really told anyone you're here, have you?

– I have not.

– There is no official investigation, is there? You're alone in this and do it in your spare time?

– Yes.

– That's a good, honest girl…

Mary rubbed the big woman's neck in slow, deliberate and relaxed movements.

Trish stared straight ahead, seeing nothing, except perhaps the flashing fangs filling her consciousness. She moaned in hardly revealed anguish.

– Come with me, pretty Trish, Mary commanded, and Trish, in her dreamlike state of mind obeyed.

Mary sensed no resistance in her, none whatsoever and giggled darkly in triumph, savoring her expectation like cold spring water in summer.

– You're so strong, she whispered, – such a powerful mind, and yet you are like nothing to me, nothing but a pleasant breeze and tasty snack of my existence.

The stench of the woman's sweat, but most of all the smell of the sweet blood in her veins threatened to sweep Mary down in a river of ecstasy.

She felt like she was flowing up the stairs, to the bedroom, and even greater: her prey was floating with her.

And then, in the room with no windows, as she buried her fangs in the delicious jugular vein the ecstasy did sweep her away, down the delicious river.

She didn't stop. When the point came when the body in her grip had been drained almost to the point of being unable to handle the loss of more blood she kept going. Trish gasped, gasped, shook and stopped breathing. Her death bathed Mary in its heat. She lowered the body to the floor.

Everything around her turned into such a pleasant haze. She was aware, aware beyond anything and dazed at the same time. When Selene approached, she was very much conscious of it. The brazing trail the Dark One made wherever she walked would always be impossible to avoid noticing.

Bloody Mary sensed pleasure, sensed… approval, and joy kept pulsing within.

The blood cleansed her and strengthened her, and prepared her for all the trials and delights to come, as the last remnants of her old existence faded to nothing in her memory.

THE HITCHHIKER IN THE WOODS

A girl is sticking out her thumb on a desolate road late at night. You're driving on your way to your friend's house. It's late and you're tired. You're going to sleep over at your friends' home. It's the first time you've visited, you'll see your friend since he moved out of his old home. In fact, you have been looking forward to it for some time, now. It's been too long since you saw your friend.

This area is almost famous for drivers getting lost, and you've thoroughly confirmed that for yourself tonight. Several times the last hour you've taken the wrong turn, driven back to familiar territory, and started all over again. You'll retire early tonight and sleep soundly. And it's late. And the whole scene looks a little... odd to you. But you want to help the girl, and she's not likely to encounter other cars this evening. It is late, after all.

So you stop and she gets in, in the passenger seat beside you. The fog and the cold seem to enter with her.

– Thank god, you drove by, she says aloud, grinning insanely happy. – You're the first car I've seen for ages.

– It almost seems like fate, doesn't it? You counter lightly.

She's pushing herself at you and you're wondering if she's gonna kiss you in her gratitude, but she doesn't and pulls away quite fast, probably a bit taken back with her own exuberance.

She pulls her legs into the car and closes the door. The whisper of the wind between the trees is muted, but you can yet hear it, hear it all, as the huge forest continues to surround the narrow stretch of road.

The car engine is muted. The sounds coming from it, coming from it through the entire drive have caused you to suspect there are some irregularities somewhere, but the car's performance hasn't really shown signs of abating, so you keep driving.

The whispers from the forest keep echoing in your ears.

– It has turned quite cold, hasn't it? You say, shaking slightly.

– Yes, she agrees. – I've never felt so cold in my entire life.

You're turning on the heater. Even if it's summer outside. And almost immediately you have to check it, to see if you really turned it on. You did, and you can feel the warm air touching the skin of your fingers. But this is close to the vent. Ten, fifteen centimeters away, and the heat seems to dissolve into a hole in the very air.

– So, how did you happen to end up out here? You ask lightly. – There can't be a house for miles in these parts.

– There... was a cab, she says. – It… disappeared.
What an odd phrase. You're wrinkling your brow in sudden deep thought. Wouldn't the correct be «drove off», or something?
Shrugging, you stop thinking about it. Or try to.
– I was out here with friends, she suddenly bursts out, – but they disappeared, too. I was Alone.
– Listen, you say casually, – I can't imagine what has happened here tonight, but it must have been pretty awful for you. Can I interest you in a cup of tea or something? I'm on my way to a friend of mine, he lives nearby, and I can drive you home afterwards?
– I live with my father, she said slowly. – Driving me home sounds fine, tea... sounds fine. Thank you!
She looks at you with a grateful look in her eyes, those great almond eyes.
There is a hill on the left hand, as you can see the first signs of civilization. The first signs of life, beyond the forest, beyond the road. There is a house on that hill. The moon is just about visible among the storm clouds, just above the roof.
– That's my house, the girl says happily.
You drive into town. You finally reach your destination. As you suspected no pub or inn is open at this time and hour and you set course to your friends' house. You notice that the lights are on, are still on, and draw deep breaths of relief. Your friend has been very patient. You hope you can make it up to him someday.
The courtyard is lit. Even so, you still almost miss it. The fog is both in the air and your eyes. You're tired. It's been a long drive.
Your friend meets you in the yard. He's not wearing a jacket, a fact you find strange. It's after all not the hottest of summer nights. Oh, well, he's not planning on spending any extended time out here tonight, and neither are you.
– Nice drive, eh... He's grinning at you.
– An excellent drive, you're returning the grin. – I want to do it every night.
– Well, I'm just glad I can invite you in, finally.
You shake hands.
– I met a girl tonight; I've invited her to tea. I hope it's all right.
Your friend is nodding. It's okay. Of course it is.
He leads the way inside. You stop a bit, to allow the girl to enter before you. The house' warmth is embracing you all. Inside the living room the fire is burning in the hearth, fog is floating in the dry air.
– You're gonna love this, you say loud. – I brought a mobile phone with me. Since I haven't been able to contact you the last day or so, I feared all

your lines are acting up.
– Nothing wrong with our phones, but there has been a problem calling outside the village.
The tea is boiling hot. You sit in a deep chair, taking the first sip. Even if you can hear the distinct sound of both the wind and the rain outside the warmth of the house is starting to sink in.
– It sure is wet and windy outside, isn't it?
– It's been like that for some time now, your friend shrugs.
– The house sure is quite solidly built, you say impressed. – Trees are bending outside and it's hardly affecting it at all.
– I'm glad you came, your friend says. – You're the first from the old bunch to visit me.
– I'm the first? You cry out excitedly. – I thought I was fourth or fifth or something.
– You're the first to visit me here, he says with a strange look on his face.
The fireplace casts its glow all over the living room. You still feel the dreaded fog from the car and outside, but now it's mixed with the heat torching your limbs. Your friend smiles.
– So you finally bought a cell phone, huh?
– I told you, you scowl at him. – It was a matter of circumstance. I had to make sure I could call out of here.
The girl sits in her chair, smiling at you. She's not saying much. Not so strange really. After spending most of a chilly, wet evening walking a long walk along the road, it's not so strange that she's somewhat content to just enjoy the heat of the fire, of other people's company.
– We hardly ever get visitors anymore, she says.
– But you're not really backward these days, are you?
– Backward? Your friend is shaking his head. – No, not at all! This is a modern village, but we do not get many visitors here anymore.
– It is kinda modern, the girl says in a husky voice. – We've got computers, the latest communication technology, the works, but it's still not fully the 20th century.
– You mean the 21st century, of course, you're chiding.
– Of course, the girl replies.
– Of course, your friend replies, a bit stiff.
You lean a bit back in your chair, enjoying the conversation.
– It's all about appearances anyway, isn't it? The human brain is an amazing instrument. It can create any reality we would want, and help us avoid the more unpleasant aspects of it.
– I don't think instrument is quite the right word, the girl smiles to you, –

but I basically agree with the sentiment.
Your friend says nothing.
– You know how it is, right? You continue eagerly. – We're inventing our own reality all the time. We're pretending we're not strangers to the world, pretending we're not stumbling on, in a semblance of walk.
– Says the man, pouring on his version of reality, your friend says mockingly mocking.
And you manage a sitting bow.
– Don't we all? the girl says.
There is much, much laughter.
– And the roads around here stink, the girl says.
– The roads stink, you agree vehemently. – They give new meaning to the word «bumpy».
– It's just a temporary thing, your friend insists. – The Storm turned some stones, that's all.
And the storm continues to pick up outside. But good food, good wine and the safety of the thick walls, the joy of good company, are leading you to enjoy the evening regardless.
And the evening moves on.
There's music. Your friend has this incredible elaborate system built into the walls, something he had always wanted, but couldn't afford.
– Music, a fine new house and all. Your arms are indicating your pleasant surroundings. – Did you win in the lottery or something?
– I wanted to get away from all that, you know that, your friend replies. – Sometimes everything is better with less, that's all. Focus... is turned inwards, towards what really matters.
A draft rubs your back... Or is that down your spine? You're having another sip of wine. This is just your second glass and you're not planning on having more. This is nothing of the usual drinking contest party, but a pleasant evening with friends. The wine is burning pleasantly in your belly, that's all.
– Time sure is flying, you say. – I thought about driving down here last year, or even the year before that. I sensed an urgency in your voice this time around, though, an urgency I also felt in myself. Funny, huh?
– It is urgent, your friend says.
– Does everyone get so weird after living here just a few years, you're jokingly asking the girl.
– This is nothing. You should see the rest of the people here. They're truly nuts.
Did the girl say that, or your friend?
– The Storm is really shaking things up tonight, she says. – Moving the

Earth, Changing Reality itself.

– I've never really thought about it that way, you state in a reflecting manner.

– What have you never thought about? your friend asks in a strange manner.

– About storms as a metaphor for disturbances in our concept of Reality, you're saying to your evidently absentminded friend. – I mean, nothing really changes during a storm, does it? Trees and houses are roughed up a bit, but then everything returns to normal. Normality is obviously the stable course of events.

Your friend looks at you with a twinkle in his eyes.

– Didn't some scientist... Heisenberg, wasn't it, state, with his uncertainty principle, that it was the other way around, that reality is really quite unstable, that it's an accident waiting to happen?

Your friend looks downright weird then.

– Didn't he... also state that «God isn't playing dice with the universe»?

– Nope. The girl is shaking her head. – That was Einstein. I believe Heisenberg was more realistic...

– That was Einstein, your friend confirms quite unnecessary.

The tea tastes good. It's a different kind of tea, one you can't remember having tasted before. You want to ask your host, your friend, what brand it is, but you don't. The opportunity never seems to present itself. You're quite engaged in the conversation, in your company, the friend and the girl. Engaged in ways you could hardly imagine until tonight.

It isn't just a matter of enjoying the curve of the girl's breasts, the feral sensuality of her being.

It goes far beyond that.

You're forced to excuse yourself and go to the bathroom.

– Too much tea, you joke.

There's not much of an ongoing conversation while you're away. You're looking out from the bathroom while peeing, and your friend and the girl just sit there, enjoying their tea. Well, perhaps they do not know each other, after all. The village isn't that small and your friend hasn't stayed here that long, and they're of an entirely different age group. You, yourself, are probably the glue tying them to each other, keeping the conversation, the party going.

You wash your hands afterwards, cleaning the clean fluid from your skin. There is a mirror above the sink. Looking into it, at your own mirror image, is giving you a strange feeling inside. It's as if... you can't see yourself in the mirror. You're shaking your head, returning to the party in the living room.

The Storm shakes the house then, making it screech and howl. The Storm or the house? you're asking yourself.

– Ouch! you exclaim. The two others are not forthcoming in their comments.

Sometimes you feel right at home here, more at home than anywhere else, ever before. And then there are moments like this, with quite an awkward silence.

– I'd like to go home, now, please. You're drowning in the layer upon layer of her eyes, her presence.

– Of course, you nod.

– Of course, what? the man in the sofa ask.

A strange girl, a strange place. Layers upon layers of complexity. You kinda like it.

– I have to take a drive, you tell your friend. – I'll be back shortly.

Your friend nods.

– That's quite okay. What about a late dinner when you return?

– A splendid suggestion, you exclaim. – Let's burn the midnight oil, shall we?

There's laughter. There's an echo, but there's still laughter.

Outside you're surprised by the fact that there is hardly any wind. Not at all the calamity you were expecting after spending a considerable amount of time between shaking walls and hearing the howling of something very much resembling a Storm. You look at the girl. She doesn't look surprised, but is merely giving you her sweet expectant smile.

Even the hood of your car is dry. You study the ground, and realize that there is no sign of rain. There is no sign that it has been raining the last few hours. The dust rises easily from the ground. It isn't wet.

– Nice weather, isn't it? She reveals her pearly white, flawless teeth.

– I've seen worse. You give her your best smile in return, in an attempt to mask your unease.

The seat in the car is dry and pleasant, very pleasant. Even compared to the deep sofa and chairs in your friend's house. The steering wheel is also almost awkwardly solid. The roar from the engine seemingly deafening. You drive through the gate, entering the main street. That's when you notice it...

The moisture in the air. The cold breath from somewhere, chilling you to the bone.

– It's the car, the fucking car. It's been acting up for some time now. At least since...

– Perhaps you should consider buying a new one.

– It's a rental. Do you know a place where I may rent another in this town?

She looks hurt. You want to apologize, but your throat feels constricted and not a word escapes the confines of your mind.

The town is quite small, just a few blocks really, a typical village. But the drive seems to take some time anyway. The girl's home is on the other side of town, a few hundred meters from the «tighter» cluster of houses, but still... You shake your head and drive it from your mind.

It's a nice little «town», a village hidden away in the countryside and in the woods. The trees are quite close to most of the houses, like the houses are close to any road, as the trees, the forest itself seem to close in on you. It feels quite unnerving really, to one born and bred in a big city.

– The trees are nice, are they not?

The girl speaks up with a bright, energetic voice. Almost sensual in its deep, singing tone.

Now, that is an odd phrase, if you have ever heard one. A sight of a forest... or the sight of a tree, may be deemed nice, not the trees themselves. Trees weren't «nice» or anything, they didn't have a *personality*... did they?

– You have quite a liking for this place, haven't you? you're pondering.

– What are you saying? She smiles at you.

– I mean, one thing is to move to a place like this, like my friend did, being fed up with life in the fast lane. But a... a younger person like yourself will usually want to leave it behind, at least for a number of years. You must really be attached to the place since you're evidently not even considering it.

– Sure, she says unfazed, – it's nice here.

She doesn't seem to mind the chill either. Talk about indomitable spirit of youth.

You reflect, bringing one hand tight to the other, attempting to rub the stiffness and the cold out of them both.

Steering with one hand is easy enough. By habit you keep looking behind you, to see if there are impatient drivers there, who want you to increase your speed, making their point with the horn and a lot of obscene gestures. But there isn't likely to be any crowd of them in these parts.

Is there?

As you stop the car, there seem to be something akin to an aurora borealis, a northern light, hanging over the house on the hill. But once you actually look at it, there is nothing, except the night and the trees and the house. You realize you've been here before, a few hours ago, asking the old man in the house for directions.

– You know, I was here a couple of hours ago, you laugh, – asking your father for directions. Talk about driving in circles...

You want to go outside and open the door for the girl, but before you've managed to completely stop the car, she has opened the door and left the car. Quiet as a shadow, fast as the wind.

– Thank you, thank you, she says with her bright smile. – You're a true lifesaver. I'll see you around, okay?

– Sure, you say, a bit out of breath. – Anytime.

You see her walk safely to the house, before driving off.

You return to your destination, driving the same, horrible, bumpy road. The birds can be heard singing in the trees. And you stop for a moment. Not the car, but your train of thoughts. Did you actually hear the birds sing before? Had the road been bumpy?

It's a nice little town or township this. White walls, one house, one home, not more than two floors. A nice place to settle down, if that is one's desire. And bumpy roads, like most of the more unsavory aspects of village lifestyle, are probably something that will grow on a person.

There aren't any people outside this evening, but that's hardly surprising either, with this weather.

You look out through the windshield. The weather isn't so bad really, almost quiet and dry, compared to the hairy impression one gets while being inside a house. Another village peculiarity, you gather. Villages are very quiet compared to big cities. Though, while nature rears its head, it tends to be experienced (by visitors) as worse than it actually is.

Your new car behaves… strangely tonight. The noise from the engine makes it sound as if it's really struggling. And on flat ground to boot.

You shake your head and keep on driving.

Just a few turns and you're there. Your friend's picturesque and truly nice home is seen in a cold, silver-blue glow in the moonlight. Translucent and strangely inviting.

You leave the car as it is, unlocked. Your friend is waiting in the hallway. The door is open. You walk inside. Your old friend closes the door behind you.

– Oh, it's just you...

– Yes, for now, you reply, looking closer at the other man. Was he expecting other dinner guests as well?

The table is set for three. Glasses, forks, knives, plates in three sets are shining at you. The air seems even more smoke-filled than earlier. There is no discomfort.

The meal starts a bit apprehensive, but the hot food and drinks are loosening tongues fast enough. At least yours. The man you haven't seen for years, is still behaving a bit pulled back, a bit strange, compared to how you remember him.

But that isn't really strange, is it? Absence does that to a friendship. Words are haltingly begun and spoken, as the mind is looking for rusty phrases and forlorn memories.

You give each other a toast. The sound of the two glasses clinking is strangely muted in the smoke-filled room, the hazy air.

– I do believe there's logic in the universe, you state eagerly, after a sip or two. – It's just quite different from the one we usually imagine. Layer upon layer of complexity for the inquisitive mind to peel away.

Your friend looks downright weird then.

– Is something going on in this town? you ask casually.

– What do you mean? Your friend is replying.

– I mean, you laugh, – is something special happening these days?

– Not that I'm aware of, your friend laughs. – I told you nothing ever happens in this town. If you're looking for action, you've come to the wrong place.

You swallow a huge sip…

There's a loud crack outside, as if something is hitting the wall. The house shakes violently. You look at your friend. He isn't looking overly worried. You slightly brace yourself, awaiting a possibly more devastating attack at the house.

– Cheers, your friend says aloud, lifting his glass.

The two glasses meet with a sound of two glasses meeting. You drink some more. You relax.

There isn't really a storm outside. You know that. You've been outside. The wind occasionally gains strength a bit (more than a bit), that's all. One second the wind is there, the other second there isn't any. And the peace and quiet of the village is accentuated… until the next gale of a wind rocks the ground, rocks the village.

Not like any wind you've ever seen, but a wind nonetheless.

And yes, you know that you can't really see the wind, only the results of it. Like you can't hear the rippling in a pond, after a rock has hit its surface. And you might not have been present while the actual stone hit the surface, but you may still observe and be caught in the effects.

Food is hot, mixing with the liquor, causing an explosive mix in your stomach.

And you can sense it. You can sense it all around you.

There is a tingling, suddenly, gone before you're really noticing it. Looking at your skin, you see no gooseflesh, no rising hairs and you're no longer sure what you felt an instant ago.

– Cheers, your friend exclaims cheerfully.

– Cheeeeers, you exclaim at least as cheerfully.

Two glasses meet and part. The sound is lingering in the room, as an echo, a resonance.

– So, what have you been up to, since you moved, you're asking.

– Just living, you know. Life is all in all pretty quiet down here.

– You're right, you agree. – A man could really learn to appreciate it.

That weird look again. You decide it must be a trick of the light. The light is funny in here.

A loud whine from the oven, signifying more food soon to be available on the table. So convenient a timing. You swear you can smell cameras in here…

Your friend comes sliding with the bowl of shrimp in one hand, a new bottle of wine in the other.

– Shrimp, you're saying floored. – And Margeux '69, too. You're evidently recalling all my favorites. Me? I can't recall your memory being that good.

– It's the countryside air, your friend exclaims cheerfully.

He wants me to stay, you think. That must be it. What other explanation can there be?

Calm sets in the house once more. There is the wind outside and the talk and fun shared between two old friends, but there is silence. Quiet perhaps, but no calm. The storm is already raging.

– It can be a bit lonely here, he says suddenly. – The villagers are nice people, but they're not like having a bunch of old friends around.

– Hardly a bunch, you hear yourself saying. – Why didn't you invite the bunch by the way?

– I did, he says, sobering a bit. – The entire bunch. You were the only who replied.

Now, *that* is odd. You want to give voice to your concern, but find that you can't quite find the words.

– That's hard to comprehend. You did get replies, didn't you, their reasons for not attending?

– No. He shakes his head. – Not a word.

It's hot in here. Not so strange that. The fireplace seems to extend its flames ever further out in the room, its tongues stretching, touching the walls, the ceiling, the floor, the furniture. You can feel it close to you, like a living thing. It's at least five steps to the fireplace from where you are sitting… or so it seems.

A loud wail makes you jump in your chair, a whisper in the fog of suffering and torment.

– What was THAT? You exclaim, almost shout.

– The mist creates funny sounds around here, your friend says unfazed.

Or so it seems.
– It sounded human, man. Didn't you *hear* it?
– You'll get used to it.
Your friend says unfazed.
Later. It has calmed down a bit outside. Inside there's a pleasant, tempered atmosphere. The food is good. You taste the fluid in your mouth. The wine is good. In fact, you can't remember having a better meal for some time. If ever. You can't remember your friend being such a good cook either, but you let it slide. It is your friend sitting there. His eyes, his face, his ever so pale complexion. You wonder if there is ever sunshine down here. Perhaps every evening, also during the summer, as the sun sets behind the hills, and the heat of the day dissipates, moisture is created, lots of moisture in the interim between day and night, and the fog is rising from the wet moors. And it might stay during the next day, and the next, until summer is done, and autumn and darkness envelope the land and the village.
There are the moors, the wet moors, where fog rises and creates strange shapes, like reality itself is forming there in the afternoon air. You saw them earlier today, from the road. For each opening in the forest, where trees were scarce, there was a moor.
– Devon has got nothing on this place, you mumble.
– I didn't quite catch that, your friend says.
You raise your head, speaking up a bit.
– I'm willing to bet that Sir Arthur Canon Doyle's inspiration for «The Hound of Baskerville» didn't come from him traveling in Devonshire, you say, a bit pointedly. – But from this place. He just changed the setting or the names, for one reason or another. Writers do that.
– Or perhaps the story came to him in a dream. Your friend shrugs. – It was a damn good story, anyway, wasn't it?
– You know… you lean forward a bit, suddenly quite eager. – Want to know what I think? I think he really met a demon dog, but was too afraid, too shaken after the experience, to write the truth about it.
– Or he was afraid they wouldn't believe him or worse, that he would be the laughing stock of everybody.
Your old friend says, seemingly quite sober.
– You know, you say, squinting your eye slightly. – For just a moment there, you seemed quite sober. But that, as they say…
– IS QUITE IMPOSSIBLE TO CONTEMPLATE, they complete in unison.
The sofa. It's like you're floating on it. But you get that sometimes, during your most wild drinking evenings. You've often reflected upon the fact that

during many such an evening, your feet seem to stay higher than your head most of the time. Your head points at the floor, your feet at the ceiling.

– The value of contemplative moments like this, you're staring at your glass, – should never be underestimated.

– I understand what you mean, the man on the other side of the table says. – I understand it very well. Don't think I don't.

– I'm not, you say, looking serious and serene. – I don't doubt that at all.

Do I?

Your friend looks at his watch again. Who is he waiting for, this late?

Something keeps gnawing at your subconscious, but you can't for the life of you call it forth and remember. It can't be anything important, can it? This is a strange village, true, but didn't you expect that? There is a question you won't ask, and just the thought of it is making you afraid. You can hear the giants knocking at the door and the walls are crumbling.

– Cheers, you salute again, raising your glass.

– Cheers. The man on the sofa clinks his glass against yours, and again you hear the echo resonate through the room.

You sit on the sofa, looking at the man on the chair across the table. There is frequent movement as you and your friend trade off the duty of going to the reserve and picking up new bottles.

– There are considerations I use to reflect over at times like these, you say a bit mumbled. – While ingesting alcohol the body turns numb and also certain areas of the brain are more or less paralyzed... But there are areas of the brain hardly affected at all... or that even work better.

– It's said about alcohol, as about many narcotics, that it's a portal to the subconscious, your friend says, speaking with evident difficulty.

You keep nodding in solemn agreement, even if you're not quite certain what you're in agreement about. During the evening you've developed quite a need for looking over your shoulder. You do that again at this time. As with the hundredth times you've done so earlier, there is nothing there.

At least you don't see anything. The cold trickle down your spine, however, isn't imaginary.

– Something isn't right here, you're mumbling

– Well... it isn't *perfect* if that's what you're insinuating, your friend laughs, – but compared to other places... it's a rather nice resort.

– Last resort. You're laughing, too. – But except for that it's quite excellent.

You're looking under your chair. There's nothing there.

The road to the toilet is a rather strenuous one. You get there in time, though. You miss at your first attempt at hitting the bowl, but then you hear the clear sound of the waterfall striking the water below. There's a lot of humidity in here. You can hardly see yourself in the mirror because of all the steam. One attempt to clean the glass with your hand is a failure. Repeated attempts are all failures. You clean your hands with cold water, drying them with the soft, pleasant towel. The towel does the job. You can finally see your mirror image, take a good look at your bloated face, a look distorted through a more than shaky vision.

– Your bathroom has at least one ruptured pipe somewhere, you inform your friend upon your return to the living room.

– Yeah, believe me, I've noticed. Your friend shakes his head. – I've been chasing the plumber for days, but so far he has managed to avoid me.

– It wasn't like this earlier tonight, though…

– It is behaving rather unpredictable. Sometimes during the last few days I've got the feeling that it's sentient and just playing tricks on me.

You fall back onto your chair and grabbing, raising your glass.

– Here is to sentient bathrooms.

– Cheers.

Two glasses are once more connected over the table. The sound is as muted as ever.

The two men drink, emptying their glasses.

– Christ, you exclaim. – That one hit several spots. In fact, I'll bet it hit an entire field of spots…

They have another laughter riot.

Room starts spinning. Your head falls back, and you're half sitting, half leaning back, staring at the ceiling. There's a lamp hanging from the ceiling. It seems to be very, very high up. You're wrinkling the skin of your forehead. There are circles around the lamp, black concentric circles, spinning round and round and round…

You're stretched out on the sofa. Your friend still sits upright in the chair.

– I find your endurance pretty darn impressive, you're virtually shouting across the room, to your far away friend. – I mean… I find it annoying, but still darn impressive.

Your friend sits close to you. You can easily see the wrinkles on his forehead as he's concentrating, concentrating about looking at his glass and holding it steady.

– Alcohol, you know, is strange stuff, he says.

He holds his glass a bit unbalanced. No fluid decorates the table yet.

– Hi! you exclaim and point somewhere with your finger. – Didn't you have a full glass?

– One can drink a lot and not really get drunk. He leans further over the table. – Did you, by any chance, read about the double-blind laboratory sessions, where one half got served alcohol and the remaining half lemonade or something?

– Sure. By now you're wrinkling the skin of your forehead, too. – Both groups were told that they were served drinks with alcohol, but the group that wasn't, the control group, got more drunk than the group who was.

– Life is strange, your friend nods.

You sit on the chair, studying your hands, mumbling.

– Was... wasn't... was... he he

You look down in your glass. There's nothing there.

– Something is not RIGHT here, you shout exasperated, hitting the table with your fist. – I've felt it in my gut since I got here... early this evening.

No whiskey is spilled. Not a drop decorates the table.

– Your gut isn't feeling much of anything at this moment, the man across the table grins.

The man sitting either on the couch or on the chair.

– He he, you grin.

– There's something wrong here, you whimper. – I can feel it in my gut.

And the wind is laughing its heart out outside.

You rise from the chair (or from the couch), standing on your two feet. Or so it seems. A man stands by the window, looking out. You can see the porch and the lawn outside. The man might be you.

But you're not sure.

– I hate to be the one pointing it out, your friend says, – but it's getting late.

– Late? you say.

– You spoke of a girl. She's late, isn't she?

You turn towards your friend. Suddenly you feel damn sober and all the alcohol you may have ingested is pushed in painful ways out through your skin.

– What are you talking about? The girl was with me when I arrived and left after a while. There isn't more than one.

The fog is drifting into the room; condensing from the smoke and humidity inside, drifting in from the outside, through keyholes and windows not open.

This is it. Whatever it is.

You realize you've been waiting for something all evening. The shock hits you unexpectedly and cruel.

You're sweating. You're not hot anymore, but you're sweating.

– How... did she look like? Your friend finally speaks, but what is he *saying?*

– She's young, blonde, quite pale, tall, full lips, full everything... Why are you even asking me this? You saw her well enough yourself, didn't you? She even knew you, for god's sake.

– Jesus, your friend cries. – You've seen the Ghost.

You keep staring at him. He's dead serious.

– It's a prank, right? Tell me it's a prank.

You've always suspected that people in the countryside were half crazy, but this is a bit too much.

– I didn't see her, he tells you somberly.

– B-but… you were *talking*.

But had they really been talking? You attempt to reach back, through the fog of time. You recall now, how they both replied to you, how they both spoke as if the other wasn't there.

You rush to the bathroom, you rush outside, starting the car. You stare at yourself in the mirror.

And in your mind, you're revisiting the house on the hill. You see what your mind didn't or couldn't acknowledge before: The girl walking up to the house and entering it. But she doesn't open the door... she's just walks straight through it.

You run up the slope to the door. A man, her father comes out.

The whispers from the forest echo in your mind.

You almost drive off the road several times as you race back to the house on the hill. The sunken old man stands on his porch, and starts talking the moment you jump out of your car.

– I've been waiting for you, he says. – A runaway driver ran down my daughter last fall. She's been following drivers back here ever since.

You're backing off, backing off rapidly, without really seeing where you're heading.

There's fog everywhere, and you can hardly find your way, find your car.

You experience the drive back as even more unreal. Did that drive ever take place?

The bathroom doesn't feel even remotely comforting now. Water keeps flooding your face, as your hands move up and down, up and down, from the sink. The water turns into mist the moment it's released to air.

You look at yourself in the mirror, the sweaty face, the dilated pupils, the shaking lips. And you know, you know, beyond words, that this is not the end. And all the lights, all the bright spots in the small room can't keep the darkness away.

Santa on the prowl

Santa has had a bad hair day. He has quarreled with his wife, quarreled with his wife yet again. Actually, this is practically an ongoing thing, and the missus is quite pissed off at him. One of his reindeers has a bad toe and is on sick leave, and must stay at home. His sleight gets fewer reindeer powers. But the sleight is still no slouch. Santa stamps on the gas. The missus has left home without him tonight, and left him with the stinking reindeers, and Santa is in a very bad mood.

He has moved around aimlessly for a while when he realizes that the house the missus is visiting is right up the alley. The reindeer howls as he cut the next corner, to the big, bright lit house at the end of the road. He stops the sleight so abruptly that the animals grunt and shit hot shit. The sound of christmas carols reaches his ears, and a happy smile brightens his face. He twists a bit in his seat and grabs his flamethrower and the two semiautomatic guns. The final preparations don't take long. He has already loaded the guns. The flamethrower is also ready for action. He throws his tools across the shoulders and sets off towards the house at the top of the hill. Slightly out of breath he can finally stop in front of the door and ring the bell. An older gentleman opens the door.

– Santa lends a hand, Santa Clause cries.

– You are early, the old gentleman says happily. – Come in, come in.

– Oh, yes, Santa says, also in a very good mood, – I was done with the last job a lot sooner than expected, so I…

But the older gentleman has already walked back inside and left the door open. Santa chuckles wickedly and jumps inside. He produces both weapons. A little girl comes running.

– Santa, she cries. – SANTA IS HERE

He pulls the trigger and hits her right in the middle of her happy grin. The thunderous crack makes the walls shake. An older girl turns to run, and he shoots her in the back. The missus stands there, before him with a silly expression of extreme surprise on her face. Santa cackles and shoots her right in the open mouth. He fires his weapons in an even flow, hitting someone virtually every time. They go down like felled trees. Howling and whining those still able flee the premises. One of the weapons runs out of ammo. He grabs the flamethrower and begins spraying walls and roasting flesh. In less than a minute the flames are licking the walls everywhere, and one may safely assume that the christmas party is a bust. Santa slips in the blood and guts on the floor. He loses his balance, and while falling, his weapon is jammed between himself and the floor. The final load goes off and he blows off his own head. The eerie, silly grin on his face remains to the last possible moment. The bullet holes make the mask-like smile look very inspired, almost like a work of art.

Author's word: This story is completely true, even though the author admittedly took some creative liberties upon bringing the tale to life.

Dried blood

I wake up in the morning with the familiar sweet stench itching in my nose. It's a hot, dark summer's day where no birds are singing, and everything is quiet. I rise from the bed and cross the floor nude. Semen is dropping from my half-erected cock. I look out the window, at the yard, and see a lot of bloody bodies hanging from thick ropes, swinging back and forth in an endless movement. They hang in a long row. Birds with bloody beaks are happily feeding off the set and tasty table. I glance back at the table. The cunt still sleeps and dreams her sweet dreams. She's a cold bitch. Nothing can rouse her from her sleep. I stumble out in the hallway. There is lot of dirt on the floor, dried blood and a lot of other stuff generally ruining any chance of a decent walk, forcing me to navigate instead of walking, really. Feet are constantly bumping into something. Several cut-off heads have been left in a corner. I ignore their reproachful, dull eyes.

The kitchen is, generally speaking very dirty and unclean. Yes, it can certainly be said that it is downright *filthy*. There is a lot of hair and pieces of skin everywhere. I finally find a somewhat clean table. The kettle is still there, and the food is still hot. It was hot yesterday and is still hot now. I sit down and start wolfing it down heartily. It tastes great. The eggs, the sandwiches and ham are all marvelous. The warm juice drenches my thirst in a way I didn't believe was possible. The hotel is silent. I can't hear a single sound anywhere. Both the guests and employees seem to have left the place. Or they might still be sleeping. Some people sleep way too much.

I return to my room and fetch my jacket and things in the tiny suitcase, and resume my wanderings. Blood is still flowing from the bodies hanging upside down from branches on trees on both sides of the alley, swinging back and forth in an endless cycle. The branches move slightly up and down, making the blood jump a little further than it usually would. The birds stare at me with their cold eyes, and I get delightful trickles down my spine. I pull my SLR-camera from my jacket and start documenting my art, snapping many pictures. There are fabulous possibilities for great composition here, and I exploit each and every one. I imagine how everything will look after a turn or two in the electronic darkroom, in Photoshop and other programs, and almost get an orgasm on the spot. I have used a pirated copy of Photoshop for ten years, by now, and am very pleased with it.

The photos are practically snapping themselves, like they did during my first excursion last night. I have many Terabytes of storage capacity available, and use a lot of it, but all good things come to an end, and I put the camera away, and take a final look at the many works of art surrounding me, before resuming my eternal walk.

The sun is rising in the sky. It will be yet another fine day.

Horny women for sale

The man stands outside the public marriage office and holds up a poster. A text is inscribed on it with large, black letters:

HORNY WOMEN FOR SALE

People glare at him as they pass by, as they walk into the judge's office in their wedding dress and suit. They stare at him with condemning eyes, but he ignores them and stares indifferent straight ahead.

– What is your PROBLEM? A man in a suit shouts.

The man holding the poster doesn't react in any visible way. The bride grabs her husband to be and whisper calming words in his ears. They both move on. Most people hurry on with flickering eyes.

The following Sunday there is another wedding in the local church. The man in question stands outside with the same revealing poster in his hands. The letters and the poster itself have obviously been through a somewhat rough treatment. The man's face isn't exactly untouched either.

The church bells toll. The man waves his poster. One of the late wedding guests, a gusset of a man goes for the man fond of posters and hammers him brutally. Blood and teeth jump everywhere as the poor man is struck repeatedly and also kicked after he falls to the ground. The poster is smashed to pieces.

The wedding ceremony is done. People depart the church in a good mood. The man stands there on shaky legs, holding the repaired poster in shaking hands. The big, black letters are still very much visible. The bride stares at him with haunted eyes. She throws away the flowers in her hands before she hurries into the waiting car. She and the groom drive away in a dust cloud and accompanied by the clatter of empty soup cans.

The next wedding starts half an hour later. The man with the poster is still there. He has a large bandage around his head. There is blood on it. People glare at him with murder on their mind. He stands there smiling and laughing, as if he's having a conversation with someone. Two men glance at each other, nod and approach the man with a very decisive expression painted on their faces. They grab him, lift him up and carry him off, all the way to the gate down the road. They throw him on the ground, brushing themselves and rejoin the happy event.

Everybody goes inside and lock the door behind them. The wedding commences, and the wedding march is played. Everyone smiles and laughs. The mood visibly improves.

The music stops. The bride and groom stand before the priest and he's about to begin his deed.

A loud applause from the gallery interrupts the proceedings. Everybody stares incredulous at the man with the poster. He shouts with his loud, forceful voice.

HORNY WOMEN FOR SALE

The gathering moves like one being. With the priest spearheading the assault they charge upstairs and attack the unruly visitor. They drag him back down and out in the yard.

– Find a rope, a woman shouts. – FIND A SOLID ROPE!

They drag the man to an old tree, throw the rope over a thick branch and tighten a loop, a hangman's noose around the man's neck.

– God have mercy with you, the priest says unctuously. – I can't.

The man's face is so bruised that it's just a singular mass, without distinct features. The priest nods and everybody present pulls the rope. The man is strung up. His legs wiggle, wiggle a lot and for a long time. There doesn't seem to be an end to wiggling. People eventually glance anxiously at the priest.

– Stay the course, he admonishes his flock. – Have faith.

People have trouble breathing and turn blue in the face, but hold on to the rope.

Something snaps, and the legs finally stop moving. The stubborn unwelcome visitor hangs still. Cheers rise from the church choir.

– We have a wedding to complete, the priest grins wickedly. – Let neither God nor Satan keep us from our sacred duty.

They return to the church. The ceremony continues. The wedding march is repeated, and the priest declares that the man and the woman are joined in holy matrimony, in the name of the Father, the Son and the Holy Ghost.

– You may kiss the bride, he tells the hesitant groom.

The man and the woman embrace and kiss wild and uninhibited. He tears off her dress and when she stands nude before him he throws her on the altar and fucks her mind out. She howls in joy and mindless lust.

After having fucked her at least five times he carries her to the car and they drive off on whining tires, accompanied by the clatter of empty soup cans.

The next wedding is at the peace officer office the next day. There is a relieved mood all over town. People smile and laugh. The good mood has returned after a hard time. The wedding procession moves up the stairs in a light haze, laughing and smiling.

The sound of the accordion makes them frown. Several of those present at yesterday's happy wedding frown deeper.

There, waiting at the top of the stairs is the man with the poster, a new and shiny poster. He's singing and laughing with a wide and sick grin, and a loud and clear voice.

HORNY WOMEN FOR SALE

The members of the assembly glance at each other with weary eyes and deep, deep despair. The future looks very bleak indeed.

She who Dances in the Forest

She Who Dances in the forest pauses for a moment in her dance and looks at a bunch of old, worn photographs and newspaper clippings. There's one of a man with a gun in a dank room, one of many taking her breath away, making the catching in her throat grow.

One single drop falls from the corner of her eye and hits the images like a waterfall, making them all fade away like tears in the rain.

3 minutes+

Three years in a bind, three minutes in a rush. She glanced at her watch again and once more feared it had stopped working. Her pacing picked up speed. She stood still in the silence of the quiet rain. A shadow moved away from the window at the top of the tall building in front of her.

She pushed a button. Her watch showed 03.00, and then not long afterwards 02.59, 02.58 and counting backwards. She pushed her dark glasses back up her nose and unbuttoned her coat with slow, deliberate moves.

A man and a girl walked down the sidewalk on the other side of the street. The man pulled the girl with him, ignoring the girl's simpering protest. The bloody face of the girl glared at her.

The woman ignored them, not allowing herself to be distracted, but they never truly left the edge of her eye, of her attention.

Her watch showed 02.00 and for a long, long time the numbers didn't change, didn't change at all, and when they did, they were just a blur, and she was unable to actually read them.

A man walked past her. She more than sensed the draft when he did. The rain hit his umbrella in an even stream. The drops weren't drops but a waterfall of ice-cold fluid. The man walking past her wore dark, round John Lennon glasses, a funny hat and a gray coat with a missing button. The edge of the coat was soaked in water and the fabric there looked more black than gray.

Her watch showed 01.00, 00.59, 00.58, picking up speed as her heart slowed to a crawl.

The man and the girl had disappeared. She recalled that the girl had a ponytail, a red shirt and a green skirt. The woman also saw a pair of pink shoes before her inner eye, but wrote that off as a part of her overactive imagination. The square glasses and the pale skin seemed spot on to her, though. The girl wore a deep red, red coat. The bloody visage of the pale face stared at her with its dead eyes. All their dead eyes did.

The man, for some reason had a number of faces and she couldn't decide which one was the right one. She made the exercise in her head, calming down, and his face, a detailed painting, appeared slowly in her mind.

Her watch showed 00.10, 00.09, 00.05 and she stopped watching it and her inner clock counted down the last few seconds on her own.

A taxi stopped in front of the main entrance. A man walked through the sliding door, tensing, preparing to cross the broad sidewalk in a rush to avoid most of the pouring rain.

The woman wearing glasses and a trenchcoat drew the gun with the silencer from its hiding place in the exact moment the car door opened, and the man charged the taxi. She shot him twice in the chest. He yelped, but didn't scream. He fell and hit the ground. She stepped close to him and shot him twice in the head. He rested unmoving on the wet sidewalk.

She walked away with fast, measured steps. The taxi door remained open. In a few seconds the driver would realize something was amiss and he would turn his attention from the front of the car to the open door and after a few uncertain glances discover the still body bathing in the gray and red pool.

But by then she would be far gone.

To get away with murder - a fictional story

The two police officers walk down the street a warm afternoon. People walk up and down the street, passing them on both sidewalks. Several individuals cast wary glances at them.

One of the uniformed men stops. The other stops right afterwards.

– HEY, YOU SON OF BITCH, he shouts across the street. – STOP STARING AT ME!

More people stare at them.

– STOP, the enraged cop shouts.

Many people across the street stop. Others keep walking.

Both officers draw their gun. They fire it once, twice and keep firing. One of the black men across the street is hit, is hit several times. He falls and hits the ground. They keep filling him with lead. People scream in hysteria and run away. Two of them are also hit. They keep running.

The man on the ground groans and dies.

Both cops grin viciously to the bystanders as they cross the street.

– You people hope this time will be different, the cop grinning the widest states calmly, – but it won't be. Cops can do almost anything without being punished for it. The exceptions are only when we truly piss off our superiors or break a given important rule of conduct those in charge have ordained. If you want to get away with murder become a cop.

He chuckles darkly and pleased, so very pleased, looking at them with glee and spite in his eyes.

No one says anything. They know the man's words to be true. Experience has shown them that long ago and nothing has changed.

The priest and his congregation

The priest looked sternly at the few people gathered in the church. They huddled pretty much in a cluster below him. He towered above them. They had to raise their eyes and look up on him.

– Sin is everywhere today, he began, using his most impressive voice.

They didn't really react or anything, but just sat there, doing their duty as good Christians, listening half-heartedly at the voice of authority in their midst.

– Like God the Lord tells us in Galatians five, nineteen to twenty-one: «When you follow the desires of your sinful nature, the results are very clear: sexual immorality, impurity, lustful pleasures, idolatry, sorcery, hostility, quarreling, jealousy, outbursts of anger, selfish ambition, dissension, division, envy, drunkenness, wild parties, and other sins like these. Let me tell you again, as I have before, that anyone living that sort of life will not inherit the Kingdom of God»…

He paused, studying the congregation with triumph in his eyes.

– We are gathered here today to say NO to all that, to everything removing us from God. Hallelujah!

– Hallelujah! The weak choir from the small number of people echoed his shout.

The priest slowly turned red, as his performance picked up. Spittle flowed from his mouth.

– We, the good humans will restore humanity in God's holy service.

– IN GOD'S HOLY SERVICE.

He had them now. He felt it in every nerve-ending and neuron. It was almost a tangible thing, a certainty many years as God's servant had granted him. He imagined that his next words resembled a roar and shook the church to its foundations.

– So, go now and sin NO MORE

It was late in the afternoon. The church had fallen silent, or so most people would claim. But he sensed the words from the sermon repeat themselves, felt them light his bones.

Night had fallen. Very few people were out at this hour. He easily avoided the few that were. There was a road through the forest, no more than a trail, really that was hardly used at all, except by him.

He approached a certain building with caution, glancing around him several times before crossing its small backyard. There was a staircase leading up to the second floor. There was no dust on these stairs, he knew that, even without looking. They were well used.

But not tonight. Most working men slept at this hour, preparing themselves for tomorrow's hard work, and most other customers chose the front door. This was a discreet enterprise, after all.

He knocked on the door and didn't have long to wait before a light–clad woman opened it.

– Good evening, Reverend, she greeted him softly.

– Good evening, Lisa, he said briskly.

– Ready to sin, Reverend, she wondered seductively, – ready for a lot to be regretted and repented?

– Yes, by God, he replied hoarsely.

– Little me is shivering in anticipation, she whispered her sweet words in both his ears.

He walked inside, and she closed the door behind them. The evening's carnal delights were about to begin.

Afraid (I)

– Don't be afraid, Sasha soothed her.

But Lily was afraid, as Sasha put her hands on her shoulders. The heart hammered in her chest, like in a rabbit fleeing from a predator. She visualized how the girl standing behind her grew long, pointed fangs and her sweet features turned into a demonic visage.

Then Sasha fell on her, held her in her paralyzing grip and bit into her jugular vein with her fangs, and all of it turned all too real, and then Lily found out how it was like when her heart truly hammered in her chest.

The sound of Sasha slurping her blood as she sucked the life out of her became Lily's entire world. The room faded around her and a terrible weakness overwhelmed the tiny rabbit as it breathed for the last time. She stopped struggling and turned limp in the predator's iron grip.

Sasha let go of the empty husk and it fell dead to the floor. Ecstasy, building forever in her mind rose to a fever pitch, and Sasha laughed loud and triumphant as she beheld the vanquished piece of meat at her feet.

Afraid (II)

– Don't be afraid, Sasha soothed her.

But Lily was afraid, as Sasha put her hands on her shoulders. The heart hammered in her chest, like in a rabbit fleeing from a predator. She visualized how the girl standing behind her grew long, pointed fangs and her sweet features turned into a demonic visage.

Then Sasha fell on her, held her in her paralyzing grip and bit into her jugular vein with her fangs, and all of it turned all too real, and then Lily found out how it was like when her heart truly hammered in her chest.

She struggled, she did, or imagined she did, unable to tell if it was real, but if she fought physically against the assault, it was to no avail. The sound of Sasha slurping her blood as she sucked the life out of her became Lily's entire world. The room faded around her and a terrible weakness overwhelmed the tiny rabbit as it breathed for the last time. She stopped struggling and turned limp in the predator's iron grip.

Sasha turned her around.

– Drink from me the nectar of life and enjoy the pleasures of the hunt forever, she said softly. – *Hurry,* before it's too late.

They stood there, face to face, as Lilly's eyes slid half closed and her vision turned weak and hazy.

Sasha scratched her wrist and put it in Lily's open mouth. One more heartbeat, two and Lily closed her mouth, biting hard down on Sasha's wrist. Blood flowed into her mouth and down her throat. A strength and sensation beyond anything she had ever experienced charged through her, as the alien blood flooded her system.

– Good girl, Sasha whispered. – Good girl!

Lilly twisted and shook in the other's arms. Her mouth let go of the wrist. She stopped moving, practically froze in slow, slow moment and collapsed in the other's arms. Sasha picked her up and carried her without effort out of the living room. Lily was aware to some degree, even as her eyes slid close and everything stopped within her. Sasha carried her down the stairs to the basement. The door closed and everything turned dark, but Lily still saw details in her surroundings. She sensed them in slow, slow flashes slowly fading. Lily was fading. Everything vanished around her, except the creature taking her into her lap.

Sasha put her to bed. Its white sheets turned black. Even Sasha faded. Everything turned black. All sensations faded. Everything turned to nothing. Her dreamless sleep began.

The figure on the bed opened its eyes. The pattern on the ceiling slowly revealed itself. It moved its eyes. Two sweeps, three and it spotted the creature standing slightly to the right of the bed's front. It sat up and directed its entire attention on the other.

– There you are. Welcome to the world.

It recognized the woman somehow, even as confusion kept confounding it. It tried to speak. There were sounds, but she couldn't form words.

– It's mostly the fangs. They keep you from speaking properly. It, like everything else will take time and effort. You're an infant. You must learn everything from scratch.

It rose, doing so effortlessly, as part of an ongoing, flowing movement.

– Walk to the mirror, infant.

It did, obeying the compelling voice, stopping in front of the luminous, smooth surface. The mirror did seem to glow in the infant's wide-open vision. The female looked at her face in the mirror, at the long, pointed fangs dripping with saliva. She mumbled something inarticulate.

– Don't worry, child, I know what you need. Come with me!

The woman turned and opened the door. A bright light flooded the dark room and made the child cover her eyes. Tears jumped from the eyes and flooded her cheeks. She kept following the woman up the stairs, into the hall and out the door. Fresh air ripped into sniffing nostrils. Then something else, a beyond powerful, overwhelming sweet stench took its place, making the girl frantic and making her release a loud moan of longing.

She speeded up, catching up to the woman in a moment, about to overtake her the next. The woman grabbed her and held her back effortlessly. The girl turned limp in her grip and lowered her eyes with a whimper, submitting without a struggle to the dominant force in her presence.

– Relax, little one, you will get everything you yearn for. You just need to be patient a little longer, take a few more cautious baby steps before you can stride through the night as the great hunter you are.

They entered a forest, a wilderness almost well within the city limits. The woman followed a trail and the girl followed her. The wet cheeks dried fast as the air pushed at her skin. The many scents overwhelmed her. They surrounded her on all sides, confusing her. She could hardly hear or see because of the overwhelming scents.

But one in particular, the dominant that had drawn her to the forest pulled her and kept pulling her, making her move without thought and sense of direction. She approached a woman walking in her direction on the trail.

– Lily? The woman facing her cried out, making her ears hurt. – What happened to you, girl? You've been gone for days.

The girl frowned. The sounds, the syllables, the name sounded vaguely familiar.

Then it didn't matter anymore. The near, sweet scent brought by the wind brought her close to the anxious woman. The beating of the jugular vein on the woman's neck narrowed her vision to nothing.

The prey turned limp in her grip before she had grabbed her. Huge, vacant eyes stared at nothing. The girl pushed her fangs at the jugular vein and bit through it. Blood, the sweet, tasty blood filled her mouth, flowing down her throat, filling her flesh, her self.

Ecstasy poured into her. Time lost its meaning again. She swallowed as fast she could, but couldn't keep some of the blood from flowing from her mouth. It didn't matter. Her veins, her limbs and everything began burning in the pleasant flame filling her up. She released happy sounds as she fed on the blood of the other woman.

She felt the prey surrender its life, and it was such a glorious sensation. She swayed a little, the happy smile never leaving her face.

The empty husk drew its final breath. She dropped it to the ground, while standing there completely mesmerized by the feeling of life surging through her. The hands changed before her eyes, the same transformation she couldn't see but only sense in her body at large. She stood there swaying and chuckling as she faced the other.

Speaking proved just as difficult as before. The words, if words they were came out garbled, more like incoherent babble then actual speech.

– I know, Sasha soothed her. – You want to re-experience this feeling again and again and again. Don't worry. You will! You shall!

Sasha stepped close to her. She took some of the blood on the girl's jaw and splashed it on her forehead.

– I baptize you Ali and bid you to live a long life filled with pleasures.

Ali repeated that name, that sound, at least in her mind. Sasha moved, and the youngling moved with her. Their movement felt like the wind itself to Ali, like they had become one with it, and she rejoiced in her beating heart.

During the three years of The Wanderer he ate a lot of people and drank a lot of blood. End #flashfiction

The Nick Cave interview

Yes, this is *the* Nick Cave interview, the important part of it. I copied it during the broadcast. My employers have ordered us to delete all, absolutely all copies in existence, but I felt it's just too juicy to deny posterity.

It was early summer in Sidney Harbor. The two men sat outside, on a stage wearing shorts and shirts.

– Good evening, Nick and thank you for coming here, the interviewer, the tough, investigative reporter said.

– Glad to be here, Cave replied.

– So, Nick, you've stated that this record is different from your previous. In what way?

– I would say it is more reflective, Cave replied. – I have matured as a human being, and that is certainly reflected in the music and texts.

The interview goes on for a while, more or less a typical interview with a musician.

– You played in Israel recently…

– I did, Cave acknowledged.

– You also were pretty hard on those advising you to not do that, and on others boycotting Israel, refusing to perform there. You accused them of censorship and worse.

The mood and the very nature of the conversation changed. Sweat formed on Cave's brow.

– I did. I felt and feel that they deserved it.

– But all they did were voicing their opinion. They didn't really attempt to censor you or force you in any way, did they?

– They did, and deserve every harsh word and worse, Cave said, his voice rising just a little.

– So, you mean them voicing their opinion amounts to censorship?

– I do, their campaign is such blatant censorship.

– But isn't what they are doing pretty much what you, yourself are doing?

Cave blinked.

– In what way?

– Well, you are criticizing those boycotting Israel and states, in no uncertain manner that they should stop doing that.

– They should, Cave cried. – What they do is wrong, horribly wrong!

– Do they deserve some kind of sanction, in your opinion? The interviewer asked casually.

– It would serve them right! Cave cried at the other man.
– A boycott, perhaps?
Cave stared hard at him.
– The BDS-movement certainly feel there are quite a few strong arguments in favor of their actions.
– They are deluded! Cave snapped.
– You don't think the fact that thousands of Palestinian children have been tortured and killed by Israeli soldiers is a worthy argument, then?
– What you're talking about is just one more anti-Semitic plot, Cave mumbled, with bulging eyes.
– The Israeli torturing and killing of thousands of minors is an anti-Semitic plot?
– Stop that! Cave said, gritting his teeth. – Stop doing that *right* away.
– Stop doing what? The interviewer wondered perplexed.
Cave didn't verbally respond. His expression spoke volumes, though.
– Your critics claim that you, by playing in Israel, and your very strong attack on the people criticizing Israel's horrible and numerous crimes are legitimizing them. Won't you concede that they have a point?
– C-concede?
– Won't you also concede that the Palestinians have been patient beyond belief, with its peaceful boycott, divestment and sanctions policy and that that puts Israel's crimes in an even worse light? Shouldn't Israel be isolated from the international community and its leaders and officials be judged in the harshest way possible in public opinion and at the International Criminal Court in Hague?
– Are you out of your fucking mind? Cave raged.
– Are you aware that the BDS-movement and anyone criticizing Israel, really, are victims of censorship and persecution all over the world?
Cave caved and stood abruptly up from his chair.
– I've had enough of this SHIT! The interview is OVER.
He stormed out, frothing around his mouth.
– You should be censored and drawn, he shouted and spat brimstone, as he turned at the edge of the stage. – They should fire you, and you should never get another job, not even in an igloo in Antarctica. I will make Harvey Weinstein sic his Shin Bet GOONS on you. YOU - DAMN - ANTI-SEMITE!!!
– There are no igloos in Antarctica, the interviewer said in a very helpful attempt at enlightening tonight's guest.
But Cave had disappeared, had already dived deep into his cave and saw only the world through the narrow chinks of his cavern.

The wanderers in darkness

My sister walks by my side, in the mirror floating to my left on the trail through the Wasteland. The snake dances on her beautiful skin and coils around her curvy body. My sister is dead. She is rotting in the grave. I sit in front of the fire and stare into its fire-red, dancing surface, and I scream into the dark, throw my Magick at the night.

I see the wolf pace around me. Its howl rises from my throat and into the air with the dancing embers. I hear the raven flap its wings. Its dark, invisible wings are mine. They glow in black and gray and fire. The witch wanders in the forest. I wander and the dead and their remains wander by my side. My Magick is Death Magick, like all Magick is. There are no angels, no creatures of light, but spirits in all forms and of all kinds are all around us, both living and dead. They travel in the dark, like we all do. The mirror not a mirror is an echo of everything that is, everything we are. We are the shadows of the raven, humanity's outcasts and deep thought.

Nothing is hidden to those wandering in the darkness.

Everything is there, in the quivering air, the whispering forest. I walk backwards, and in my own steps I find myself. Three steps to the left, three jumps to the right, and the trail is no more, and only wilderness' claws and fangs remain, and the dull knife is no more.

I make love to my dead sister in the heat of the night, and I fuck her brains out on the bed of fading embers, and I feel an ecstasy greater than I've ever before felt.

In death there is life.

Germs

She stood by the window, looking out.

Looking blindly at the shades of gray and red. The room was lit by many small lights. The window glass was thick, difficult to see through, like meters of liquid, clouding and clearing her vision in quick succession.

There was no sound. All the windows, all the walls were soundproof. She looked down at the people scurrying back and forth far below. Most of them were coughing, she knew. Occasionally she could clearly see them clutch their throat. They fell and hit the tarmac… with a dump sound.

Hands folded behind her back she returned to the center of the room. It was a nice room. Pale colored paint on the walls, pale colored furniture. Scarce furniture, a chair, a table, nothing more. A very clean room. She walked to the dinner table, scratching her arm in a distant manner. Shaking hands grabbed the pills on the platter and the glass of water. She swallowed the pills. Good, clean food, a nutritious dinner. No waste of time. During the time it would take to eat an old-fashioned full meal she could do a lot of work, perform several necessary social services. She was a humanitarian, after all. Perhaps she couldn't help those poor beggars below, but she could do a lot beside that.

A flash of light made her turn. She walked to the window once more, knowing fully well she shouldn't. There could never be any point to it. Down below the cleaning crew drove by, their huge, imposing machines sweeping up all who had died the last hour. People yet not sick desperately attempted to escape, to run into the nearest shelter. Many did not make it in time.

The left arm started shaking, shaking slightly. She didn't scratch it. It would stop by itself. It always did.

She looked out the window, looked at the violent eruptions of red and gray.

It stopped. The arm stopped shaking. And she told herself that it hadn't really shaken at all.

She turned abruptly and returned to the relative calm of the room.

The trenchcoat brigade

The man in the trenchcoat and cap left the women's restroom in the international departure lounge at Stanstead Airport. He walked in a slow, lavish pace. The odor of weeks' old sweat was unmistakable. His face was strangely clean and unshaven, the rest of him of quite the dubious quality. People stared at him. Some people stared hard, and with anger burning in their eyes, but he ignored them.

A sign said, in very large letters.

The airport community charter is here to help you, but we will not tolerate:

- Drunkenness
- Insulting words or behavior
- Threats or actual physical violence
- Abusive language

BAA Stanstead/Essex Police

People had filed into the lounge for quite some time. It was just a few minutes until the gate would open, and the passengers would be let onboard the plane.

The man bumped into a woman with a baby on her arm.

– HEY, watch where you're going, you sow.

He belched, very loud and distinct. The woman quickly removed herself from his immediate vicinity.

– What are you guys STARING at? He shouted. – It isn't nice to stare, you know.

At this time the man had already been observed by the guards through the surveillance cameras, and they began paying attention to him. A couple of them sat course towards the lounge, to calm the situation at an early stage.

– I can smell your cunt, the man said to an overdressed woman.

He sat down by her side, moving his nose over her groin. His sniffing was very pronounced and loud, almost eerily so. She struck him on the head, struck him hard.

– You fucking cocksucker, she screamed, very loud.

He rose and stumbled off. Quite a few of the passengers applauded. The woman took a bow. He stumbled in a foot and fell over an entire row of people. Quite a few of them fell of the chairs. He grabbed the rest and

pulled them with him to the floor.
– Sorry, sorry, he grinned, – all you stinking shits.
The first few guards appeared, striving to keep up their appearance of calm, as they approached the clearly disturbed man.
– Please, sir, one of them said soothingly, – you need to calm down.
– So, I need to calm down, you stinking SHIT! The man sniveled. – How do you people get off, anyway, how do you get laid, for that matter?
The last part of the sentence he added as an afterthought, clearly, seemingly pondering something.
Then he visibly brightened.
– Jesus fucked Maria, he said with absolute certainty and conviction.
– Your behavior is disturbing, deeply disturbing to the other passengers, the officer in charge said with a frown on his brow. – I'm afraid we have to ask you to come with us.
– Am I disturbing? The man turned and asked the passengers. – Am I offensive?
– I don't think so, a young man grinned. – But then I'm biased, I guess.
He and several others chuckled darkly.
– I have no misgivings, the woman with the smelly cunt shrugged.
People stared astonished at her.
The frown deepened, as the officer in charge hesitated a bit, clearly sensing that something was… off, that something wasn't… right.
He was sweating, looking around him with a pained expression in his face. It was clearly visible on the monitors.
One of the other guards grinned. He looked forward to this. That was also visible on the monitors.
– C'mon, sir, he said, – you need to come with us and stop hassling these fine people.
They stepped forward.
The man stepped backwards, scowling at them.
The police officers were, in general quite confident, fairly certain of their place in the world, in the scheme of things. They surrounded the man in a maneuver they had practiced by doing many times.
The disturbing man laughed out aloud, a very patronizing laughter making them stop in their tracks.
– You guys never cease to amaze me, in negative ways.
He shook his head in mock despair.
Suddenly they felt a chill, and they couldn't for the life of them tell why.
The man began removing his clothes, his cap, his coat and his pants, leaving his jacket for some reason.

– That's enough, the officer in charge snarled.

They charged the disturbing man. In an amazing move he grabbed the two in front and pushed them back. The entire group of six was stopped. To the spectators it looked like they hit a wall.

Then, in an even more amazing move, before anyone managed to catch their breath he struck the biggest police officer in the face, felling him with one blow. He was unconscious long before he hit the floor.

The big, very big man threw his jacket away, revealing a large, ugly machinegun hanging from his belt. He drew it, and before the security forces managed to even utter a word of protest he mowed them all down. The screaming began.

Several more guards approached, guns in hand. Some of the perceived passengers, among them the woman with the smelly cunt drew large guns, too, firing totally indiscriminately at anything moving, and everyone was moving, attempting in vain to escape the barrage of hot lead. The woman and the baby in her arms were among the first casualties. Many more followed in the seconds and long minutes to come.

The sign with the big letters were blown to bits.

For a while, a few seconds at least a temporary, eerie silence reigned.

– That was FUCKING invigorating, the woman with the smelly cunt shouted. – WASN'T THAT FUN?

She threw herself into the arms of the big man and kissed him on the lips.

– I love you, Timothy, she cried. – I fucking love you. You know how to keep a girl entertained.

The young man with a dark chuckle threw his head back and howled at the invisible moon, and fired a salvo at the ceiling.

There were wounded people on the floor. The disturbing gang took care of everybody, before they moved on to the next gate. People fled in droves from it. Some got away, but most of them were either hit by a rain of bullets, roasted by flamethrowers or blown to pieces by exploding rocket grenades. The twenty-two people walked in a fast pace, but didn't run. They calmly (with the exception of a few excited cries) eradicated everything in their path. More security guards showed up. They were exterminated with the rest.

– TO FUCKING HELL ON EARTH, Timothy Joyce shouted and cackled insanely, as he walked in front of the lethal procession. – TO THE DESECRATION AND SODOMIZING OF ANGELS!

Everybody, also those far away, fleeing with their hearts stuck in their throat heard his voice, heard it above the thunder of the guns.

They would never forget it. Long after they had stopped having nightmares filled with blood and thunder they would remember the demonic face and voice.

Timothy Joyce and those enthusiastically following him stopped at an intersection and began shooting to pieces all the surveillance cameras. All screens turned black.

No more bullshit - The Trenchcoat Brigade - Author's word

The story above stars Timothy Joyce, one of the main characters in my novel Your Own Fate. It is part of the extensive extra material on the website, offering further understanding and perspective of the story.

It wasn't included in the novel because it's fairly similar to several other scenes there, and because it didn't quite fit. The story in the book is mostly told from Jeremy Zahn's perspective.

This short story about the events on a modern airport would also have to be at least four times longer than the one you have just read. Perhaps I will write the extended version someday.

Timothy Joyce is a man with no more patience for bullshit, as you can plainly observe and certainly appreciate. If you want to find out more about him, go to the website, or read the book. He certainly would appreciate it.

Author's word - Red Shadow and Other Stories

This is an anthology of novellas and short stories and short short stories I've written the last twenty years.

It contains two novellas, four short stories and several short short stories.

There's no central theme in this book, no common denominator. It's quite simply all the stories ready for publishing I had yet to publish, everyone not novels.

They are almost all Transgression Art in one way or another, though. Most of my work are.

I considered publishing Red Shadow as a single story, but decided against it. I had enough material for an anthology, and I had wanted to publish my unpublished work for years, and Red Shadow was a great cover story.

The story Fangs and Claws of the Earth was originally meant to be included as a novella, but I decided to make that a novel instead.

Some of the stories are clearly experimental, even more so than what I usually do. Most of the stories are very different from each other, so much that it might be hard to see that they are written by the same author. I guess they are recognizable as «a Keppler story», though, even though I don't have a clear idea of what that is…

Other titles I considered for the book:
The Ruthless Photographer and other stories
The Drunk Bartender and other stories
The Yawning Waitress and other stories

But since none of those stories is actually written yet, the choice was easy.

Printed version ready 2018-01-31
Final print version done 2018-09-26

Earth and sky, day and Night, first story:

Season of the Witch

Lori is happily married. She and her husband of twenty years have three great children together. They have nice jobs and nice salaries, a nice house in a nice neighborhood. Life is good

Lori wakes up one morning, soaked in sweat after a particularly disturbing dream. Then she takes a good, hard look at herself in the mirror.

The world is no longer the same. She is no longer the same. The happy housewife and mother and company executive no longer exist. Suddenly familiar and pleasant surroundings are neither familiar nor pleasant. Increasingly disturbing events are pulling her ever further away from what she has known, confirming that the world has changed, that she has changed. She meets new people, people further opening her eyes to the world, to the world she has denied for so long. Perhaps her previous life and neighborhood and job and all weren't so great, after all?

Lori is cast brutally out of her world and headlong into the next. The people she encounters, both friend and foe are very much like herself a new breed, seekers in a world where seekers are frowned at, at best, and at worst hounded and hunted. Lori doesn't fit in in the old world anymore, and the new is still not quite there yet, emerging, like its people from the chrysalis, the dark corners and shadows of modern society.

They are the emerging Earth and Sky, Day and Night, and the world will never be the same.

ISBN 978-82-91693-22-4

EARTH AND SKY, DAY AND NIGHT

Existential horror.
(ten stand-alone, interrelated stories
about the beginning, the returned Power,
at the twilight of the modern world)
(novels, TV, Internet, serializing)

Season of the Witch
Resurrection Dreams
Burning in Gray
A Night in Hyde Park
Dead Woman Walking
The Twilight Storm
The Path of Shadows
The Returned Power
Winds of Change
(blowing wild)
The New Barbarians

Other published and upcoming novels by **Amos Keppler** from **Midnight Fire Media**:

The Janus Clan - (ten chapters about the Wild Man in the modern world, a world balancing on a razor's edge):

The Defenseless
The Slaves
Birds Flying in the Dark
At the End of the Rainbow
Lewis of Modern York
The Werewolf of Locus Bradle
The Valley of Kings
Eye in the Sky
The Iron Cage
Phoenix Green Earth

The Defenseless

The two rivers meet and join in the city of Denver, becoming one...

The two dark brothers, growing up with their sister Linda in a mundane, average suburb, a place well entrenched in modern United States and the world, have since their moment of birth been at odds with the world... and with each other.

Mike and Ted Cousin are not who they are. There is a mystery here, one of birth and upbringing, one of fate. Violence and death, blood and fire follow them all the days of their lives. The fire is resting somewhere inside... waiting for the Spark.

Their parents know something, but are not telling it. The policeman Mark Stewart and their aunt Trudy do, too. Everybody knows something, pieces of the whole, but nobody knows the whole truth, nobody telling it.

The ancient power is returning to the world, a world massively suffering from physical and spiritual poison, on the brink of collapse and a collective tailspin suicide run without its like in human history.

Magick is returning from its long exile. Thus begins the story of the wild beasts rising from their ashes.

The Spark is struck, horrible and terrifying.

First book of ten in the Janus Clan series: Ten stories of the wild man in the modern world, forty years of wandering, before the Phoenix is rising from its ashes.

ISBN 978-82-91693-08-8

Shadow Walk

The world is changing. They know this, in their core of cores, where everything moves and shifts. Night and fire have followed them all the days of their lives.

What they carry inside has always scared them, always intrigued them...

They have always felt different, apart from the crowd. And here, now, they get the confirmation they have always wanted, always yearned for, that they are truly different, a breed apart. The metamorphosis begins. Their minds, their bodies are changing in shocking and unpredictable ways, as what's on the inside is brought to the outside. And as they themselves are changing they are also changing the world.

Danger awaits them, Life awaits them, in the small, backward New England town. Magick and Mystery may be found beneath unturned stones.

People, young and old, are descending on the small, insignificant town of Northfield, New England.

Boys and girls, students at the school of Life, Seekers, yearning for what's different, what's hidden.

They're seeking within and without, high and low.

And here, in this dusty, remote place they're finding it, turning the stone, finding the strength within themselves to be themselves, to break out of confines, to the world beyond. And in time, after the initial, tentative steps, pushing down paths new and undreamed of.

And the present-day order sees them for what they are... Agents of Change, a threat to any establishment, any imposed reality. The heatwave, the worst in living memory, is nothing compared to the boiling within the human heart. The Indian Summer heralds the twilight of mankind.

ISBN 978-82-91693-12-5

Your Own Fate

From the Book of Fate:

In the Book of Fate there is everything. Every incident, all times, everything that has been, that is, that will ever be, everything that might be, everything that could have been.

But who is writing it? Who is penning it? Who is turning page by page, too many to be counted, blowing in the wind? Does it perhaps write itself, with a pen moving across the yellow sheets? Or is it a hand moving the pen, one unseen, one stretching back into the past, back to the time before everything was created, creating itself from nothing?

Timothy Joyce is an enigma, a man without a past, appearing from nowhere, to go on a rampage in an astonished world.

Jeremy Zahn is hunting Timothy Joyce. It seems like he has always been hunting him, from old London, from the island of angels, where it is said they met for the first time, to the city of angels, California, the new world.

Here, on this shaky ground, following confrontations spanning the globe, its time and space the two will fight for the last time.

And the world is watching, its people shivering in their frozen hearts.

ISBN 978-82-91693-05-7

Night on Earth

This is said to be the age of enlightenment and reason...
A culmination of thousands of years' development and illumination.

The hunters are dying off, they say. Their day is done, in favor of the new, enlightened time of neon lights, technology and civilization.

But a hunter is stalking the streets of London. A creature without form, eyes and skin. In a city on the brink of chaos, of social and economic collapse, it is stalking cops, killing them in ever more horrible ways. Sheila Watts is a hunter. She's a cop.

Sheila is lost, losing herself further by the second. She's losing herself, finding herself, as she's closing in on the creature of the night, as it is closing in on her.

Sheila Watts can taste the sweet blood in her mouth...

ISBN 978-82-91693-07-1

Dreams Belong to the Night

New, emerging urban rebel guerilla groups, freedom fighters, called terrorists by enraged authorities are overwhelming Europe.

What is, in truth terrorism? Who does it to whom?
How much can a human being take of bondage, injustice, degradation and destruction of spirit... before being fed up?

Present day society is a wound not closing.
In a modern world society destroying everything making life worth living there are those, who, through coincidence and fate, have decided not to take it anymore.
And as they are making that decision, together and as individuals, they are also starting on a journey, a journey back to humanity's roots.
Judith, Sivert, Kim, Willhelm, Anya and many more.
A handful of people against an entire world.

This is their story...

ISBN 978-82-91693-11-8

Experience the defeat of civilization, of tyranny, of anti-life in:

Thunder Road - Book One: Ice and Fire

Damon Terrill is the Storm Child. He is born into the life hostile civilization's last years, as humanity starts on its return to nature, return to Life.

It started with the need for Freedom, the passion of life, and went from there, in new and unforeseen directions, in one, final attempt to get it right.

– It's the human being's path through life, Anya told them. – What challenges, destroys and strengthens it.

The Thunder Road is making a turn. It always is. Burning Ice, Biting Flame...that is how life began. And that's how it will renew itself. No matter where humans are going. And now the blade is laid bare, ready to be tempered once more. Humanity's idiocy, their hubris has finally and fully been visited upon them. The End Time, the final hour, Ragnarok is here. The sea is rising, winds are increasing in strength. A thoroughly rotten society is collapsing under its own weight.

Humans are natural nomads. Now they become nomads anew, pulled together in small tribes once more, pulled into a fellowship of fate in a final, desperate attempt to survive, to live the life humans are born to live. Finally. Damon, Anya, Andrè, Myriam and many others have started on their way Home.

ISBN 978-82-91693-21-7

Alarums of reality

The end is the beginning. The beginning is the end…

The once so great Caine Manor has become a ruin, one only fit for carrion birds and revenants. No one but daring children and crazed souls dare breach its confines.

The proud and shiny Caine Manor is an outstanding example of renovated architecture at the heart of the city.

Looking at the building, the house, resembling a castle, hidden in a strange, illuminated mist, squinting your eyes, it's often hard to tell what's illusion and what's real. Reality shifts and burns around the Caine Manor, either ruin or proud house, reaching out with strands of night and fire to the surrounding areas and to existence at large. It is the center, or at least one center, in an ever-shifting world.

Is Chloe Webster dead or alive? Is Marion Dexter? Is Marlon Caine? Or David Fallon Somby? Are they perhaps both? Or neither? What is the world? Is it a brick, a hard, impenetrable wall or closer to something akin to mist and shadow? Existence might make sense, to us, to them, but only in glimpses, only in passing, beyond a corner somewhere ahead. They may wonder. They may die clueless. Because they don't know, don't know why terror strikes them and makes their heart beat like a sledgehammer in their chest.

From a place unbound by time and space alarums of reality are reaching out to touch and ultimately engulf them all.

ISBN 978-82-91693-13-2

FALLING

She can not rid herself of it, the sense of falling. It is lurking in her dreams, every time she looks at the world from the edge of her vision. The old, cruel oracle at the fair did not tell her anything she did not know.

Janet of the Blue Flame is born a sorcerer, one with powers of the mind and the body far exceeding those of most others, one in a line reaching far back in antiquity.

In this modern age she, like many others is virtually unaware of the potential resting in the murky parts of her being. She may know, deep down, but she is not aware… not until the day Malone the Sorcerer comes for her.

Malone is dark and powerful. His skills and might are unquestionable. His power speaks to her, to her murky depths, roaring in her consciousness like a storm. Janet is only Sweet Sixteen and is overwhelmed in Malone's presence. When he offers to train her, for her to become his apprentice she consents with an eagerness of a mule chasing the carrot. He is everything she is not, everything she has ever dreamed of being. She leaves her friends and family, leaves behind everything she knows and joins the mighty and enigmatic sorcerer on his quest. His harsh teaching takes her far away, into the nine realms and beyond.

He gives her her devoirs, gives her everything he promised and more, wishing her good luck, leaving her to pick up the pieces of her life.

Janet of the Blue Flame is ready for the world.

ISBN 978-82-91693-19-4

AFTERGLOW DUST

She has died a million times…

Someone is stalking her. She knows this, knows it at the edge of her vision, where nothing really is seen, only dreamed. Her nightmares give her no peace. She turns and looks behind her. There is nothing there her eyes can see. But in the wind, she can hear the wailing cry, the cry of Death. Sniffing that wind, she can smell the blood in her nostrils.

There is truth in flesh, they say… and there is truth in that. But there is also substance in what cannot be seen, cannot be touched. Claws and fangs cut ceaselessly through the night, looking for her. A silent cry is heard in the dark.

Someone… or something is stalking her.

She remembers a kind touch and a slap in the face, and hardly anything else.

Kathryn Caldwell is Afterglow, a woman of undetermined age, a strange creature wandering the dark corners of the world. Something happened to her once, something horrible, something she can never forget or put out of her mind. It is haunting her every second of her dark days, every moment of her pitiful sleep. She has become an empty shell, a pale imitation of the human being she once was. Long ago, as she measures time, she lost everything valuable in a human being, saw it fall through a crack, irreversible, never to be found again.

So she is wandering the darkened streets of the modern world, aimlessly, adrift, hardly ever seen, hardly ever there. People cannot see her, but she is there, present in their daily lives, an open wound that will never close.

No one is safe for Afterglow…

ISBN 978-82-91693-16-3

Black Dragon

One unexplainable, beyond mysterious event changed the world. In one moment, lasting an eternity the Earth and all its creatures was cast in shadow. The sun was blocked out in the sky, and people could only glimpse each other as flickering shapes in a seemingly endless night.

They called it the Great Darkness, and spent years and countless hours attempting to explain it, speculating in vain on its origin.

The results of the event weren't instantaneous, weren't obvious, but in the years to come many people transformed, and gained new and startling abilities, powers of the mind and body never before seen on this Earth.

Lady Grace, Flight Captain, Gimmick, Oracle, The Bowman, Raven Bird and many others rose from the sea of mankind, creatures straight from people's imagination, the fantastic writings of the world, crime fighters, vigilantes and master criminals similar to those previously described only in comic books living the life of their dreams.

The world changed, irrevocably, each new big and small dramatic event removing it further from what it had been, its status quo and social relations altered forever.

Unsettling dreams began haunting them, first at night, in their sleep, and then, slowly, spilling over into their days and waken lives. A creature, a terrifying nightmare rose from the primordial consciousness of them all.

They called it the Black Dragon...

ISBN 978-82-91693-18-7

Secrets

These are descriptions of what cannot be described.

These words within deal with the current world as it is, its prevalent and extensive alienation, inequality and injustice, its ongoing destruction of both spirit and flesh, of everything making life worth living.

But most of all it's about the Night, the great darkness, the dark passions ruling us all, what those in charge more than anything want to take away from us.

Words have power...

Contains 140 poems written from August 2003 to July 2013.

ISBN 978-82-91693-15-6

www.ingramcontent.com/pod-product-compliance
Lightning Source LLC
Chambersburg PA
CBHW060605310726
48982CB00008B/1239/J

* 9 7 8 8 2 9 1 6 9 3 2 3 1 *